Gun Ship

OTHER BOOKS BY MWM

G U N
SHIP

Mark Wayne McGinnis

Published by:
Avenstar Productions

ISBN: 978-1-7335143-9-2

To join Mark's mailing list, jump to:
http://eepurl.com/bs7M9r

Visit Mark Wayne McGinnis at:
http://www.markwaynemcginnis.com

Prologue

OB5 Asteroid Belt—Outlying Fringe Space, Demyan Empire Territory

He held his tongue as the pilot ratcheted up the controls—first left, and then right. Loham Babar, although confident of the pilot's keen abilities, straightened his back, doing his best not to appear nervous. With shoulders that were both broad and muscular, Babar emanated raw strength. The top of his head was hairless and his facial features striking—a long, aquiline nose, high cheekbones, a strong jawline, and intelligent eyes that missed absolutely nothing.

"Move it, Puk . . . they're gaining on us . . ." Babar said, in a measured tone.

"Well aware of that," Puk said back, with an edge to his voice. "Sir . . . why don't you sit down. You're making me nervous, hovering over me like that. Or maybe go back and check on your new passengers."

Mintz, the co-pilot, laughed out loud at that.

Babar stood directly behind the pilot's chair. With Puk piloting the point ship, the three Dow Dynasty Defender-Class Stingers were traversing the dense debris field at five times the velocity of what would be considered treacherous. Babar marveled at the pilot's skill as he glanced down at the control board. The autopilot was disengaged. This was all Puk—doing what he did best.

The three Stingers flew in a tight formation—dodging one space boulder after another. Mostly fragmented asteroids, some were small, about the size of a medium sized spacecraft— perhaps as small as a scouting frigate—but a few were as large as a battle cruiser.

Mintz, seated next to Puk, was currently manning the guns. Each Stinger was equipped with an array of weaponry: six 360-degree pivoting plasma cannons—two forward, two mid-ship, two aft—and two big Pounders, projectile-firing rail guns, mounted forward and aft. And if that arsenal wasn't sufficient enough, there was a full complement of longer-range missile ordinances at the ready. For their relatively compact size, *Stingers* were among the most-menacing warships within the Dow Dynasty's vast fleet. Could they hold their own against an Empire battle cruiser, or a dreadnought? No, of course not. These menacing smaller ships were better suited for special operations, like the one they'd just completed. Now, if they could just make it through this debris field in one piece, they could engage the Zyln-strap and jump to faster than lightspeed.

On each side, both port and starboard, bright green plasma

bolts shot past them. The wraparound, boomerang-shaped bow starshield window enabled Babar to watch two vessels, now accelerating forward on the right.

Babar yelled, "Portside!"

"See them!" Mintz said, manning the virt-stick controls.

Babar felt the plasma cannons come alive, a repeated *pap-pap-pap* sound as they fired. First one, then the second Empire Rage-Fighter erupted into fireballs.

"Two down . . . twenty Demyan Rage-Fighters still on our tail," the copilot said.

Babar relaxed a little, realizing he'd been holding his breath. Even twenty Empire Rage Fighters were no match for the three Dow Dynasty Stingers.

"Aft shields down to 72 percent . . ." Mintz said.

"Six hundred thousand meters 'till open space . . . just keep our friends back there occupied for a few more minutes," Puk said.

Babar allowed himself a brief smile. Had they actually done it? He shook his head in disbelief. Their three ships had accomplished—well—the impossible. Each Stinger held a complement of fifteen highly trained Special Ops personnel. They'd infiltrated deep within Empire lines. Stolen Empire craft identification codes had allowed them access into Broudy-Lum itself, the largest of the spacial cities of the Demyan Empire. The starstation was more like a planet than a station, holding one billion inhabitants. The three Dow Dynasty Stingers had only one destination, the *Enclave*; a municipal structure even more protected than the royal palaces down on the planet Demyan.

Today's success was nothing less than historical enormity. The course of events from today's mission would be spoken about for a millennium. Parents would tell this tale to their children, who would later share it with their children, and on and on. Today would be the day that brought back home their own aristocracy—the Dow Dynasty's Magistor and Magistra Pietra, and their two teenage children, Prince Markus and Princess Lena—the royal family having been abducted exactly four years prior.

On that day, Babar—Noble-Fist to the aristocracy and Protector of the Realm—was not aboard that infiltrated ship. Instead, many light years' distance away, he remained in a coma on their home world of Calunoth—recovering from injuries incurred during a vicious, albeit unsuccessful, assassination attempt against the Magistor.

The Empire had become far more aggressive over the last decade, causing strife within the realm through covert proxies, some thought to have been among the most loyal of subjects—even within Cristine Castle itself, the center of the Dow Dynasty. This time, it had been the Magistor's personal tailor, Jod Ringman, who in the process of measuring the Magistor for a new ceremonial garment, had pulled a Gnar-Rasp, a small throwing blade. From across the room, Ringman had put all his significant weight into the throw. The intended target, the Magistor, would surely have been killed if Babar had not dove in front of the lethal weapon, taking the strike himself in his upper chest.

The royal family had subsequently been abducted while

vacationing, and only later was it discovered that they had been placed into *stasis-tubes*—each one asleep, lulled into suspended animation ever since. They'd been kept under heavy guard for many months.

Eventually, the news spread quickly within the Empire—the infamous Pietra family were to be exhibited at the Museum of Calico's Enclave. The Empire took great delight in flouting their superiority over the weakening Dynasty, encouraging their loyal subjects to come to gawk and disparage the royal family, as they languished unaware, on display in their respective hyper-tubes.

For as long as anyone could remember, it had always been Dynasty versus Empire. But after the abduction, the skirmishes that had seemed evenly balanced between the two galactic superpowers began to get ugly and unbalanced. Over the past few years, the Empire had been chipping away at the Dow Dynasty realm. The outer-rim frontier planets were the first to go, though to date, no core worlds had been attacked. As such, officially, war between the two ruling realms still did not exist.

The two realms methods of ruling could not have been more different. While the Empire ruled with an iron fist, the Dow Dynasty was far more benevolent. Newly acquired Empire subjects, such as from those from frontier-space worlds, were taught early on that full compliance would be their only means of survival. Whereas the Dow-Dynasty had little interest in realm-building and had renounced all forms of capital punishment more than a thousand years prior, the Demyan Empire's very foundation was built upon subjugation—brutish power and control over the masses.

In the swerving ship, Loham Babar reflected back on the day's rescue mission—one that he had led himself, and that had gone off almost more perfectly than planned. Approaching Broudy-Lum StarStation, the three Stinger gunships, equipped with sensor-deceiving identification tags (which had cost the Dynasty a small fortune), had disguised themselves as innocuous and pre-approved sub-space moving crafts. Having timed the incursion late at night and during a security shift change, the three vessels had landed within a rarely used, remotely opened delivery bay.

The ten-man, highly practiced special operations team then had then stealthily invaded the Enclave. The patrolling guards, fresh from a shift change, had been killed, one-by-one, mostly from behind with their throats cut from ear to ear. The infiltration team had found the four towering stasis tubes, each eerily glowing green in the dimly lit museum. Babar had been shocked and momentarily paralyzed at seeing the royal family floating there within their individual, glass-like containers. Looking up into each of their faces, he found the sight both disheartening and infuriating. He'd ordered his team to get the stasis tubes configured for transport. Finding several museum hover-carts within a backroom, the royal family had been quickly and quietly transported out through the hushed interior of the Enclave to the awaiting gunships. Although he'd never been held responsible for the loss of the Magistor family, he still felt the weight of that burden just the same. Only now was some of the weight starting to lessen.

The Stinger banked sharply to the right, bringing Babar back to the present, as Puk maneuvered around an approaching jagged asteroid. After all the planning—the success of the mission—being killed here in this asteroid field was unthinkable. Glancing back over his shoulder, into the narrow passageways and bulkheads, he looked upon the ship's primary hold. Within it were two hyper-tubes holding Prince Markus Pietra and Princess Lena Pietra. Their parents' tubes were held within a similar hold, but onboard the trailing Stinger, now positioned on their starboard side. Soon, the Dow-Dynasty aristocracy would return to the throne, perhaps more a symbol of power than of actual power. It was what the realm badly needed right now—essential, too, if the realm was to repel further enemy incursions.

"No! No!" Puk yelled out as he maneuvered around another asteroid.

"I see them!" Mintz yelled back.

"What is it?" Babar asked.

"More . . . a lot more Empire fighters have just joined in the pursuit," Puk said. "Must have been stationed within Quadrant Nine. Complicates things . . ."

"How many are there?" Babar asked.

"Another twenty . . . no, make that close to thirty."

Babar's earlier mood of jubilation evaporated. Fifty total Rage Fighters? They truly were screwed. "Maybe we should turn around? Go deeper into the asteroid field."

Puk yanked the controls, first left then right, narrowly missing a satellite rock the size of a house. "Ultimately, you're the one in charge . . . Noble-Fist. What say you?"

Before Babar could respond, a barrage of incoming plasma fire illuminated both side windows of the bridge.

"They have a targeting lock on us . . ." Mintz said, both hands wrapped around the virt-stick controls while firing off multiple weaponry systems at once.

Babar, hurrying over to one of the console seats behind Mintz, took up an ancillary set of virtual joystick controls. "I've got the *Pounders*!" he yelled. The moment his hands came into contact with the virtual, full-tactile touch joysticks, a 3D model of the localized battle logistics projected above the console before him—one identical to both the pilot and the co-pilot. He realized how desperate their situation had become. The fifty or so Empire Rage fighters were not only pursuing them, but had assumed incoming flanking positions on both their port and starboard sides as well. Babar unleashed both forward and aft *Pounders* rail-gun systems at once.

Babar felt thunderous vibrations rising up through the deck plates as thousands of explosive projectiles blazed toward the enemy fighters and surrounding asteroids alike. While smaller asteroids were quickly eviscerated—turned into mere space dust—the fighters were blasted into fireballs, one after another.

"Not bad for a realm aristocrat," Puk said.

"Shields down to twenty percent!" Mintz yelled out.

A sudden and intense explosion catapulted Babar out of his

seat. Struggling to get back to his controls, he yelled, "Are we hit? Was that us?"

"No! We lost Stinger 3! She's—she's gone . . ." Puk said, his voice filling with dread.

Babar felt the gravity of those words. Along with the fifteen crew members onboard that craft, the Dow-Dynasty's Magistor and Magistra Pietra were also now dead.

The loss was beyond horrific, although it had always been a possibility, perhaps even a probability. As the weight of their new reality took hold, Babar fought the despair that wanted to bring him to his knees. In a single moment, he'd lost his charge, his reason for being—not to mention his best friend— Magistor Pietra.

"Shields are officially down!" Mintz shouted.

Babar again reseated, back at his controls, trying not to think, let loose with a devastating hail of fiery destruction. One Empire fighter after another fell victim to Babar's single-minded rampage of revenge. He would destroy them all—until every vile Empire Demyan was eradicated.

A klaxon wailed from above.

"Damage reports coming in. Five compartments breached portside!" Mintz exclaimed.

"What about the hold?" No one spoke out.

Another brilliant explosion caused Babar to almost lose his seat for a second time. He didn't need to hear Mintz's words to know they'd just lost Stinger 2 on their port side.

"I've lost helm control," Puk said, no longer yelling. Outside, beyond the bay window, the vastness of space spun around and around before their eyes. Any moment now and they would careen, either into an asteroid or into an Empire Fighter, or be blown to smithereens by the heavy incoming fire.

As they spun violently, the motion sickness had all three of them retching, but Babar still managed to rise to his feet. Grabbing ahold of the nearest bulkhead, he headed aft. "Get this ship stabilized, Puk ... whatever you have to do ... do it!"

"Where are you going?" Puk asked, his fingers a blur of flying motion across his control board.

"Primary hold. To be with the Prince and Princess."

At that same moment, one of the smaller bridge-side windows began to splinter, web-like, into thousands of tiny hairline cracks.

"Shit! Get out of here, Babar!" Puk yelled, forgetting his antagonism as the dire situation became clear. "Get into an EnvironSuit! Hurry!"

Loham Babar hesitated, reluctantly taking a step backward across the threshold and off the bridge. In that brief instant, just as the hatchway door slid shut before his eyes, he saw the front window explode outward.

chapter 1

Justin Trip

Bridgeport High School—
Bridgeport, Chicago

Partially obscured behind the screen of his MacBook Air, Justin's eyes momentarily flicked up, taking in the quiet, soft-lit surroundings. It was 7:22 p.m., and the Bridgeport High School library was as deserted and lifeless as a graveyard. Sitting at his favorite table, Justin's eyes scanned his E-trade Pro screen, checking the closing figures of three new stocks he was prospecting for purchase when the stock markets opened in the morning. Justin, who was seventeen, had been buying and selling penny stocks since he was fourteen. Three aspects of playing the stock market set Justin apart from most other traders. First, of course, was his young age. Second, 90 percent of his weekday trading was made from one classroom or another; his iPhone, hidden below his desktop, generally rested on his lap, in constant use. And third, Justin was a millionaire. A millionaire three times over.

To say Justin was circumspect about his life would be an understatement. He loathed being noticed, would rather have jumped in front of a city bus than been caught in the limelight. The number of folks who knew about his monetary exploits could be listed on one hand: his mother, his banker, and his best friend, Kyle Hombly. Actually, Kyle was more a virtual friend—he lived in Manhattan, was in his twenties, and also dabbled in buying and selling so-called penny stocks. Also, oddly enough, the high school's vice principal, Mr. Stanpipe. But their tie was mainly due to the number of times Justin had been sent to the VP's office for "screwing around" with his mobile phone during class-time. The good news there—Stanpipe was keen on getting into day-trading.

Situated now where there was little to no foot-traffic, and a good distance from the other tables, Justin was assured of the one thing he desired most—isolationism. About six feet tall, Justin's slim frame was long and lanky. Having avoided athletics, taking any excuse not to be outdoors more than absolutely necessary, he'd built up little in the way of musculature. He wore his blonde hair short on the sides and longish on top—mod-style. His mother had donned the scissors. For the most part, his facial features blended together well enough, and he'd have been considered handsome by most people's standards. Yet handsome he was not.

In a single, absentminded motion, Justin ran several fingers down the left side of his face, feeling his cheek's now-familiar ragged contours. The skin mask of crisscrossing scar tissue so aptly afforded him an ugly moniker: "Scarface."

As his mobile phone vibrated on the table, he leaned over and saw a text from his mother:

Mom: Garrett picking you up from library?

Justin: Think so—at 7:30

Mom: Early shift in morn so going to bed. There's spaghetti in the fridge. Just nuke it

Justin: Thanks. Leaving here in a min...

Suddenly, distant voices became more audible, emanating from beyond the nearest tall stack of bookshelves.

Damn! Justin, slouching lower in his seat, readjusted his computer screen to be in a more vertical position. Still, he didn't need to peer around his laptop to gain a clearer vision of what was happening. It was a bevy of chattering teenage girls. Chairs clattered and banged together as multiple backpacks thumped down onto the tabletop some ten feet away. Justin closed his eyes, his fingers poised above the keyboard. *Perhaps they won't even notice me sitting here.* Multiple, competing female conversations were audible.

"Mr. Rankin is a tool. Gave me a 'C' ... can you believe that? A 'C', for God's sake!"

"Yeah, I had him last semester. So what's with his teeth? Like ... orthodentistry wasn't invented yet back when he was a kid?"

"Lisa, come here. Check out this text from Shane."

"Hey, anyone have a tampon?"

Justin ventured a one-eyed peek around his computer. *Terrific.* Six girls were sitting there. Of course, he knew who they were—everyone did. All were pretty, essentially the most popular girls in school, and, like Justin, they were seniors.

"You have to sneak out with me Saturday night ... hit that party."

"Can't. Babysitting"

"Huh? Really?"

Then another backpack thumped down loudly onto their tabletop.

"Hey girl ... thought you were blowing us off!"

"Sorry. Had to drop by my locker first."

Justin's heart skipped a beat, recognizing the latest arrival's voice. *Aila.* She was new to Bridgeport High this semester—new to Chicago. He was fairly sure she'd never given him a second thought, even though they'd been paired as lab partners twice in Chemistry. Not only was she quirky and pretty, she was also funny, and smelled amazing. Her chestnut-colored hair, scissored in an abstract arrangement of both short and long sections, somehow worked, looked cool. Not tall, although not short either, she wore brightly colored, mostly 80s-styled rock band T-shirts, skinny jeans, and unlaced boots. Kinda tomboy-ish—yet still all girl.

Justin closed his eyes, then breathed in deeply, hoping to catch a whiff, the scent of her perfume. *Did I really just do that?* he mused, shaking his head, annoyed at himself for what he knew would be thought of as creepy.

He refocused his attention on his laptop screen, studying several market bottom bouncers that intrigued him. Their RSI's, Relative Strength Indexes, weren't too bad . . .

At some point, the nearby table's loud chitchat had become muted. Justin's stomach now tightened up, beginning to twist and knot. Someone giggled. Someone else hushed her, then more giggling erupted. Unable to breathe, Justin felt half his face glow hot with color. The other half, the mask of scar tissue, was impervious to such things. He listened to their rapid-fire whispering, only an occasional word decipherable.

". . . didn't even know he was here . . ."

". . . lurking about . . ."

". . . creeps me . . ."

"Name's Justin . . . yeah, Scarface . . ."

If only he could disappear. Become invisible. He knew he should be used to such comments by now. He'd looked a monster to others as long as he could remember. Justin checked his watch. His ride would be waiting for him in a minute or two, so he forced himself to breathe in deeply to steady his nerves. *I'll do this fast. I won't make eye contact. I'll get up, hurry past them, and then scoot on out of here.*

Justin sat up and closed his laptop. Gathering up his loose

papers, two pencils, and his iPhone, he quickly jammed everything into his backpack. He stood up, then tried to push in his chair. One of the legs had caught on something, so he decided to just leave it. Then he remembered and, turning back, grabbed up his hoodie off the chair. *Fuck!* He strode forward, keeping his facial expression impassive, like someone who couldn't care less—perfectly fine with who and what he was. He ordered himself not to make eye contact with any of the girls. *Don't you dare!* But damn it, he made eye contact. Aila was watching him as he strode past them. The only one at the table not hiding a smirk, or holding back a snicker, which was sure to follow.

By the time he reached the front of the school library and had crashed through the double glass doors, he was cursing himself aloud. "You had to forget your stupid hoodie, bring more attention to yourself, didn't you? Oh! And then what did you do? You looked right at Aila. You *fucking* looked straight at her!"

Walking forward toward the front of the school, then out into the totally empty parking lot, he calmed down some. He checked his watch: 7:38. Digging his phone from his backpack, he dialed Garrett. He listened to it ring four times before going to voicemail.

"Leave your message and I might get back to you."

"Hey, this is Justin. Um … were you going to pick me up tonight? Can you call me back? I'm in front of the school. Oh … and it's almost 7:40."

Garrett, also a senior, lived in the house next door to his mom's. He was everything Justin was not: popular, handsome, and a varsity football star—first-string quarterback, *of course.* Although, strangely, Garret was genuinely cool. He had always watched out for Justin, and saved him from needing to take the bus most days. Well . . . lately, not so much, but that was understandable. He was entitled to have a life of his own, too. Didn't need to cart around the town freak each night and day. Justin looked at his phone and thought about calling his mom, but he knew she'd be in bed by now. She worked the early shift at the hospital. He thought about texting Garrett again, then shook his head. *Jeez, get a grip, snowflake. You're seventeen . . . walking a couple of miles won't kill you.*

Putting on his sweatshirt, Justin pulled the hood up, then swung his backpack over one shoulder. Outside, keeping his head down, he headed off for home.

It wasn't long before he regretted his decision not to call his mother for a ride. Sure, walking home from school in the daytime was not a big deal. But after dark, forced to cross through one of the worst crime-ridden, gang-infested areas in all of eastern Chicago was not a brilliant move. He lived in Brightwood Manor, which sounded a hell of a lot nicer than it actually was. But to arrive there, he'd be crossing through the south section of Harland Park—part industrial wasteland, part slum apartment buildings, and part dilapidated, boarded-up housing ghetto.

Justin walked in silence along Ashland Avenue, willing his pristine white Nikes not to make a sound. His mother would freak out at his shoe selection today. She'd never warmed up to him playing the stock market. Hated it, in fact, until she realized not only was he proficient at it, he was some kind of young virtuoso. Whereas some kids were child prodigy pianists, and could play Mozart or Beethoven while standing on their heads or whatever, Justin's inclinations leaned toward cutting market losses quickly—making low-risk, high-reward trades. She capitulated her strong disapproval of his investment hobby by setting unwavering rules of the house. He couldn't spend his fortune. Whatever money he made each month, beyond his $75,000 investing fund, went into ridiculously low-yield U.S. savings bonds—where it sat, ready for him to use when he turned eighteen. But he was allowed a pittance of spending money, for purchasing a few of his *extravagances*, as she referred to them. One such extravagance included his collection of rare, pricey athletic shoes. He displayed them all within an enclosed, tempered-glass display case that took up one full wall in his small bedroom. And his choice of footwear for today: the Nike Foamposite One—Sole Collector. The price? A mere $6,000 for the pair.

Justin kept his eyes lowered, focusing on the cracked, fragmented sidewalk. Although there were streetlights all around, none of them worked. He ran his hand along the close-by chain-link fence. Beyond, just off to his left, was an immense old factory—probably shuttered down soon after WW II ended. The building's dark silhouette loomed up ten stories high in the moonless night. Every so often, a car passed him by, its headlights illuminating mounds of gutter trash. An empty liquor bottle, its Johnny Walker label reflective in the light. Justin noticed several hypodermic needles, a Hostess DingDong wrapper, and some old car part. Maybe a car's side-mirror? Something like that—built back in the day, when such things were actually made of metal.

Justin breathed a little easier, noting Mankin's Liquor sign a few blocks ahead. *Back to civilization!* That was when he heard many footsteps—the heavy clomping of multiple pairs of shoes, worn by those who cared little about being stealthy. Someone was dragging *something*. What was that? The sound a metal pipe made when dragged along asphalt was meant to be intimidating. Meant to scare him. And it was working. Justin was not a particularly good fighter, although you'd think he ought to be, considering the number of times he'd been forced into altercations. They couldn't really be considered fights though—since only one side threw punches. At nearly six feet tall, Justin had the size, just no fighting skills. He had one motto when it came to self-defense: duck and cover. His grandfather used to say that even the worst of hurricanes eventually lose their ferocity and blow back out to sea.

Distracted by the sounds that followed mere steps behind him, Justin paid no attention to what might lay ahead of him in the darkness.

A loud stomping sound, coinciding with the closest street-lights coming on, stopped him in his tracks. *Cool trick*, he thought, suddenly feeling like a stage performer beneath a bright spotlight. Without raising his head, he peered outward at what lay ahead—seven angry faces stared back at him. They were a mixture of white, black, and a few shades in between, but all with the same expression, and he had little doubt that an equal number of angry faces were stationed behind him, too. He knew these thugs were called the MP140s—as badass a Chicago gang as it got. Their gang name stood for Municipal Police 140, the radio dispatch code for murder. Dressed in baggy jeans, their pants hung low baggy at their asses. And like Justin, they too wore oversized hoodies. Pistol grips peeked out from more than a few waistbands.

Justin contemplated when he should enact his standard duck-and-cover routine. Staring at them, their eyes as dark and lifeless as the night itself, he knew that ploy wouldn't cut it tonight. *No. He was going to die*, right on this shitty ghetto street, next to the guttered hypodermic needles and the faded Ding Dong wrapper.

One of the gang members approached. Not the largest guy, just the meanest-looking one. His face was twisted into an angry snarl.

"You in the wrong place, kid."

Justin thought about agreeing with him. Instead, he lowered his head. His oversized hoodie covered most of his face, hiding it in shadow.

The thug stepped up to him, close enough to shake hands, or play rock-paper-scissors. Justin said, "Sorry. Shouldn't be here. Um ... stupid of me."

"Did I say you could talk? Are we like ... friends here? Compadres? BFFs?"

His peeps snickered.

"I have twenty-three bucks ... maybe I can buy ... um ... passage? Just this one time?"

The gangster wore a surprised expression as he glanced back at his cronies. "You hear that? He wants to buy passage. He must have heard that in a movie, or something."

They all laughed—the ones in front along with the others behind him.

"What the fuck's that on your face, boy?" Taking a step closer, he tilted Justin's head into the light. His eyes narrowed as he examined the facial scars, close enough that Justin could smell the guy's dank breath. Justin figured the guy wasn't that much older than himself. Whatever spirit had once resided behind those now-lifeless eyes appeared long-since gone. The gang leader, raising both hands up, slowly pushed Justin's hoodie back from his head.

The insults then came, some almost funny. Others, more biting than Justin was used to, stung a little.

"What's your name? Or should I just call you Scarface?"

Justin had heard all the jokes, a lifetime of insults, most of them multiple times. "Don't feel sad, don't feel blue, Frankenstein was ugly too, or." "I've seen folks looking just like you, but I had to pay admission." "Did your parents keep the placenta and throw the baby away?" "Your face is so ugly, when you cry the tears run *up* your face." "I heard you went to a haunted house and they offered you a job!"

He finally interrupted the barrage. "Please! Just let me go . . . let me continue on my way."

The punch came so fast Justin didn't have time to flinch, let alone react. His head whipped backward. Lightning bolts erupted in his vision. With his right cheek throbbing, Justin considered it probably would be best to just duck and cover up. Instead, he said, "Justin . . . my name is Justin."

The man's eyes stared back at him. "I won't kill you, Justin. But after tonight, you'll learn . . . to never walk alone at night on one of my streets."

A car, or truck, or something equally big, was fast approaching, its dark shape momentarily blocking the illuminated liquor sign just down the road.

"My name is Lewis. And this here is my twin brother, Harland."

Justin heard the other twin's approach, caught him out his peripheral vision standing next to him at the curb. Like Lewis, Harland had a tangle of long, dyed-blonde dreadlocks falling free beneath his black ballcap.

"And yes," Lewis said, "I know . . . we look identical. Everybody says that shit. Drives me fucking crazy. I don't think we look identical—similar, maybe, but not identical. He's who he is, I'm who I am. But you probably know what it's like hearing people say things you don't want to hear." Lewis, studying Justin's scarred face again, asked, "Fuck, man—how'd that shit happen to you?"

Justin didn't like talking about it, but his cheek really hurt. To avoid another walloping, he said, "Happened when I was a baby. An explosion, of sorts."

This time it was Harland who spoke. "What kind of explosion?"

"Meth lab . . . my mother, my real mother, was cooking meth. I was in a baby carrier, slung across her back. When everything went up in a firebomb, she died. And this scarring happened to me."

He saw a truck coming—almost upon them. Maybe fifty yards away. Justin wondered if he could somehow signal the driver, make some kind of hand gesture? What was the right hand gesture for "Help me, I'm about to be murdered"?

Lewis said, "Shit happens, man, I get that. So yeah, we won't be too rough on you tonight." He looked at his brother. "Smack him around a bit, Harland. Then catch up to us. I got that meet I need to get to. Oh, and grab his fancy kicks. They look expensive."

Harland smiled back, clearly liking this aspect of gangster life.

chapter 2

Loham Babar

Wrigley's Chewing Gum Factory— Bridgeport, Chicago

B abar worked in the darkness, his physiology well equipped for extreme low-light perception. He was on the third floor of the Bridgeport Chicago Wrigley factory, originally built in 1911. Toiling within the long-abandoned 175,000 square feet of space, Babar had learned that the company's signature chewing gum flavors, such as Spearmint and Doublemint, had first been manufactured here.

Working now on the third floor—cutting a length of copper piping nested between two floor joists—he heard someone's soft footfalls on the street below. *Not very smart, walking alone down there at night,* he thought.

Wiping his hands on an oily rag, he moved across to an area open to the elements, one with a bird's eye view down to the street below. He spied a lone hooded figure, wearing bright white athletic shoes, walking along the sidewalk close to the fence. *You are indeed a fool, young human.* Babar knew the gangs around here came in a variety of cultural ethnicities, and some even mixed. There were the Gangster Disciples, the Latin Kings, Surenos 13, the MP140s, the Maniac Latin Disciples, and the Vice Lords. Of course, the bigger-ticketed gangs, like the Crips and the Bloods, could also be found around here. Close to five hundred deaths a year were attributed to gang violence. Parts of the city were largely abandoned to the gangs, which for Babar's purposes, was perfect. Few intruders dared to live around here. Especially since he'd affixed twenty-five "CAUTION—ASBESTOS" signs onto outer walls and signposts, placing them all around the dilapidated old building. The indigent and homeless, rarely particular about where they squatted, were not around. Absolutely none wanted to risk getting cancer. For the past eighteen months, Babar had endured few interruptions as he completed his important repair work far below, within the old factory's subterranean cellar.

Babar watched as two groups converged on the intruder. *Ah . . . the MP140s.* This was, after all, their turf. Counting fourteen in all, he realized he'd seen some of them before, even knew several by name. A sudden kick, and the streetlight illuminated. Yeah, they'd run this same scenario before too. Babar, standing more erect now, flexed his jaw muscles. He knew the young human below with the facial scars—had seen him often walking along the corridors at the high school, or waiting for a ride in the parking lot.

Working as a janitor at the high school during the day, Babar recognized most of the students. *What better way to hide from the world than to be in plain sight?* He was well aware that within this vast universe, alien life was uniquely diverse. From the spider-like beings on Storg-world, a neighboring planet to his own Calunoth, to the more lizard-like people of PR99GWYN, here within frontier space, Babar had never encountered such a similar, dare he say identical-looking bipedal vertebrate. Knowledge of this backwater world, these humans, interstellar genetic cousins to his Parian race, had been a contributing factor to him coming here in the first place.

He watched now as the boy's hood was pushed back from his head. Taunts and insults followed. *Whack!* The sound echoed into the nighttime air. The solid punch to his scarred face came fast and hard, but to the boy's credit he didn't crumble, didn't whimper like a wounded animal. Just the same, Babar clasped onto a protruding section of rusted rebar as poisonous anger coursed through him. His muscles tensed and his breathing slowed into what his people called *Shajla*, a mental and phys-iological state when one was preparing for battle. His voice, little more than a whisper, said, "Best you not harm that boy any further . . ."

The boy was now face to face with the MP140s' gang leader. *Ah yes, one of the twins—both heartless punks.* Babar stepped closer to the precipice. Even though his third-story perch was close to forty feet above the ground, he was certain he could make the leap down without injury. He'd been trained for such maneuvers.

The two groups merging together were now heading off. Only one twin remained behind: *Harland.* He raised an object, perhaps a metal pipe, so the boy could see it, and be adequately intimidated. Before Babar could move, the first strike came. The boy, doubled over, clutched his midsection. With no further thought, Babar leaped.

Even before hitting the ground and rolling, his eyes locked on to the developing mayhem ahead. Bolting to his feet, Babar sprinted some forty yards farther on, then leaped high, easily clearing the seven-foot-high chain-link fence. Crouch-landing onto the sidewalk, his heart rate was constant and his breathing slow and steady. All Parians had the ability to track the lapse of time far more accurately than humans, and Babar knew it had taken him thirteen seconds to arrive at the scene. Even in that short amount of time, Harland had inflicted another three strikes with the metal pipe—two on the boy's back and one to the side of his head. Babar suspected that even one more strike from the metal pipe might end the boy's life.

Babar sprang forward, landing between Harland and the boy, now lying prone and looking semi-conscious on the sidewalk. Again, Harland raised the metal pipe high over his head, its downward thrust gaining momentum. It was a blow Babar easily caught in his outstretched hand. A loud clap echoed in the night as the curved metal slapped hard into his palm's flesh. Babar tossed the pipe away—it clanged onto the sidewalk and rolled into the gutter.

Harland assessed Babar, and his lips drew back into an angry snarl. "Big mistake, man . . . should have minded your own fucking business." Harland pulled back his arm, the muscular bicep billowing and stretching the upper sleeve of his sweatshirt. A white-knuckled fist came up, in preparation for what Babar surmised would be the throwing of a haymaker punch. Babar immediately stepped in with lightning speed while planting a hard jab into Harland's chin, which staggered him backward.

Babar hesitated. He didn't want this to escalate out of control—he certainly didn't want to seriously injure the big man, no matter how vicious his intentions clearly had been. But Harland didn't go down. His eyes watery, full of hate and fury, both his fists came back up, and Harland charged. Babar side-stepped him, his movements now going from reserved and calculated to automatic, a natural response derived from decades of training. Babar spun to his right, taking hold of his own right fist, then delivering a pile-driver of a right elbow into the bridge of Harland's nose.

He heard an audible crack as cartilage snapped and crumbled from the powerful blow. Now Harland teetered, his eyes losing focus. Copious amounts of blood were pouring down the lower half of his face. Finally, Harland dropped down to the sidewalk, and stayed there on all fours, swaying unsteady back and forth.

But then, unfathomably, impossibly, he reached for the gutter—reached for the metal pipe lying there in the shadows, where Babar had discarded it. He sprang up with the raw power of an out-of-control freight train. The pipe, with its jagged and sharp end, was coming at Babar—poised to spear him through the abdomen. Babar had just enough time to grab the thing before being skewered. In one fluid motion, he twisted the pipe upwards and out of Harland's grip.

No longer thinking, only reacting, Babar spun the freed pipe over his head, readjusted his grip upon the cool metal shaft, and drove it deep into Harland's midsection. Impaled, but still standing, Harland took a step backward, and then another. He cried out in agony, but the sound was obscured by another: the squeal of a 1981 GMC 7000 Tanker Truck. As the big 6.0L V8 engine roared closer, Babar held on to the metal pipe in a one-handed grip, easily twisting it free of Harland's grasp. Taking sole possession of the pipe, with no hesitation, he thrust the metal pipe's sharp ragged end into the gangster's abdomen.

Again, shoving it even harder, he drove the pipe all the way through the middle of Harland's back. The gangster stared back at Babar. His eyes conveyed both shock and dismay at what had happened to him—what was still happening. Releasing his hold on the pipe, Babar shoved Harland backward and into the street. With a few thousand gallons of diesel fuel sloshing around within its attached oil tank, the oncoming truck was running both full and heavy. Even if the driver could have braked in time, the vehicle's forward momentum would have made stopping fast enough well outside the laws of physics—at least as humans understood them.

Harland's harpooned-body was struck by the forty

mile-per-hour tanker truck's grill—out of view of the vehicle's bug-splattered windshield. Babar took in the driver's frantic expression, his look of impending dread as his brakes screamed and his tires skidded. The driver didn't know the young hoodlum had already been dead. Smoke from burning rubber filled the air.

chapter 3

Justin Trip

Bridgeport, Chicago

Justin awoke within the confines of a fast-moving ambulance. He heard a siren whine outside and the vehicle's roaring engine. He tried to look about him but was unable to move his head—only then realizing he was strapped atop a backboard, secured in place. He was aware that the others nearby were attending him. A drip line dangled from a saline pouch above, and a plastic oxygen mask covered his nose and mouth. When he tried to speak, pain shot through his cheek and lower jaw.

A woman's voice by his ear, said, "Don't try to talk. You're going to be okay . . . I know this must be scary for you."

You think? Justin tried to remember what had happened, how he got here. He last recalled being at school, doing his homework in the library. He heard someone relaying information into a radio—the driver? "10-4 dispatch . . . transport in progress; patient is stable and semi-conscious; possible internal injuries. Confirmed . . . we are en route to University of Chicago Medical Center, over."

Perhaps he'd been in a car wreck? Justin tried to sit up. Did Garrett pick him up at school and then crash? *Oh God . . . or was it my mother who picked me up? Is she okay?* He tried to look around, see if anyone was lying next to him.

"Try to relax . . . it won't be long now," the female EMT said.

"My mom . . ." His words underneath the oxygen mask came out distorted—he had to speak through clenched teeth.

"Yes . . . she'll be there waiting." She gave Justin a pat on the shoulder. Relieved, he relaxed some.

"Is Garrett okay?"

The EMT's face came into view above him. "Don't talk. I don't know him, who you are referring to . . . the truck driver? He's shook up some, but otherwise he's fine."

Truck driver? Justin tried to remember, but any events pertaining to the crash kept coming up blank. He closed his eyes, the jostling ambulance coaxing him to sleep.

He awoke when the vehicle's rear doors flew open. He heard new voices—a male doctor, or was it a nurse, barking off orders. Once again, Justin lost consciousness.

The next time he awoke, he found himself lying flat on his back on a hospital bed, a ceiling-to-floor curtain drawn so he couldn't really see anything. Still, he knew it was the ER—just listening confirmed that. A baby was crying somewhere nearby. And a trauma team was trying to resuscitate someone—he heard a heart monitor alarm droning on, not an encouraging sign.

Justin, moving his head around some, found that even though it hurt like hell, it was possible. He tried to move his jaw, and tentatively opened his mouth. That hurt too, but it seemed to operate as nature intended. At some point, he'd been garbed into a hospital gown. He wondered if he'd done it, or if someone else had had to perform that job. Two pouches hung from the IV stand: saline and morphine drips. That explained why he wasn't feeling all that bad.

Suddenly, something strange popped into his head. Not a memory—more like . . . *what do they call them?* Oh yeah—a *false* memory. He couldn't smile, his jaw hurt too much for that, but just thinking about the high school janitor . . . what was his name? Mr. Jabar? No, Mr. Babar! *Yeah, like the story-book elephant.* The man was deep into Kung Fu fighting—had jumped in to help him from God knows where—*oh shit.* Justin then remembered. At least he now could recall some of what occurred—why he had decided to walk home from school, his trek along the dark street, the streetlights suddenly coming on, then being surrounded by a shitload of gangbangers. Justin placed a hand upon his cheek, recalling the punch. Bandaged, he could feel sutures beneath it. *Great. As if I'm not hideous enough already.*

He remembered being left alone with Harland, then soon

after that, the gangster swinging a metal pipe at him. *That explains the sutures.*

Loud voices could be heard just beyond the drawn curtain. "Where is he? He killed him! He killed my brother! Where is that motherfucker?"

"Security! Get him out of my ER!" a doctor yelled out.

A scuffle ensued. Justin could see some of what was going on through the gap underneath the curtain. Someone lay on the ground, thrashing about. Multiple pairs of legs wearing scrubs and hospital shoes encircled him.

"Hold him down!" a man yelled out.

"Let me go! He killed Harland!" the desperate voice screamed out between labored sobs.

Justin let that sink in, thinking about the heart monitor's endless-droning death-tone, then about Harland's final seconds alive, lying on that darkened street—and the look in his eyes.

Blubbering, soft murmurs were coming from the other side of the curtain. "I'm gonna' kill that son of a bitch . . . that freak . . . I swear . . . I'll find him . . . I'll kill him . . ."

Justin wanted to yell through the folds of plastic curtain that he wasn't the one who'd killed his brother. He wasn't the one who drove that metal pipe into his brother's abdomen. And he wasn't the one who shoved Harland into the path of that oncoming tanker truck either. No! He was sure of it now—It was the janitor, Babar, or whatever his *fucking* name was.

Properly subdued, Justin listened as security took Lewis away. No more yelling, spewing out promises of revenge. But he was certain that wasn't the last of it.

The curtain suddenly flew open. An older nurse with an ample bosom, wearing blue scrubs, bustled into the confined space. "Sorry, hon, that you had to hear that. Don't pay any heed to what he was saying." Removing his oxygen mask, she checked Justin's IVs first, then the heart monitor. "My name is Gladys." Placing a few fingers on Justin's chin, she moved his head a couple degrees leftward and then toward the right. "Hurts, huh?"

"Yeah. Like I got hit with a steel pipe."

"You want some water?"

As Justin nodded in assent, Gladys placed a plastic straw in his mouth. Sucking in, he gratefully swallowed the container's cool water.

"Is the doctor going to see me?" he asked.

"Been there, done that already, sweetie," Gladys affirmed. "You've been x-rayed and cat-scanned, poked and prodded. Dr. Mullin says you're lucky to be alive. You have a mild concussion, two cracked ribs, and assorted abrasions and lacerations, but you'll live."

Justin nodded. "My mom?"

"Yes, Kilian was called as soon as they pulled your school I.D. from your wallet. Honey, she and I go way back . . . at least ten years. Work different shifts these days, though."

"That heart monitor . . . before. Is he—"

"Let's not worry about that right now, okay? You have a visitor. You up to seeing somebody?

Visitor? Maybe Garrett? he thought. "Uh, sure," Justin said.

Gladys left his bedside just as quickly as she'd arrived,

leaving him alone again. He tried not to think about Harland. The curtain opened wide again—it wasn't Gladys..

"Hi . . . Justin,"

"Um . . . Hi."

Aila looking about the small space, spotting a stool with wheels. Sitting on it, she rolled a tad closer to his bed while nervously smiling.

Justin's mind raced, trying to resolve her presence here.

"I was in the car. The first one on the, ah, accident scene." She held up her smartphone. "I called 911."

He stared at her, probably a moment too long. *God, she's beautiful.* "You were in the library," he said.

"Yeah . . . wasn't sure you noticed me."

Are you kidding? "Thanks for checking on me. You didn't have to . . .".

"No, I wanted to. That was pretty intense. *Fucking* intense!" she added with a laugh.

Justin laughed too and regretted doing so—feeling a sharp pain in his jaw. "So, did you see . . . what actually happened?"

"Oh yeah, the whole thing played out right in front of us. The dude with the metal pipe sticking out his back getting run over by that big truck . . . un-fricking believable."

"How 'bout right before that?"

Aila stared at him quizzically, then gestured outward beyond the curtain. "Some of it . . . I just finished telling the police all about it." Placing a hand on his knee, she added, "I was emphatic—you didn't push that guy. You were splayed out on the ground."

"So, you saw him? The one who jumped in . . . and saved me?"

"We really didn't get a good look at him. But, boy, did he move fast . . . like a ninja! You do know he saved your life, Justin. Right?"

He nodded, loving that she knew his name. "Wait, you said *we*."

Her expression turned more serious. "Oh, yeah. I'd gotten a ride from . . . a friend. Someone you know!"

"Knock knock," came a deep voice. Garrett, smiling, stood by the now-opened curtain. Justin wondered how anyone could possess such perfect posture. His smile was warm. He looked as if he could audition for the next Superman movie, whenever they next rebooted it.

"Hey man . . . this is all my fault. I got your voicemail. Already told your mother, bro, that I was supposed to pick you up. I'm so sorry, I got my wires crossed." Garrett and Aila's exchanged look explained everything: the two were an *item*. Of course they were. The two most perfect people on the planet— it made total sense.

"Your mom's talking to the police right now. I guess they'll want to talk to you too."

"Okay, that's fine," Justin heard himself reply, realizing Aila had removed her hand from his knee. Strange, he could almost feel it there still.

"Did you hear me, dude?" Garrett asked.

"Sorry. What?"

Again, longish eye contact exchanged between Aila and

Garrett. "There's some kind of gang contract out on you. The police are assigning you your own protective special detail, like the president has."

Terrific. As if I don't feel pathetic enough. Now the whole world is going to know how big a pussy I am. Justin let out a tired breath.

Aila, as if reading his thoughts, shook her head and said, "Justin, that gang is one of the largest in all of Chicago. You'll need the protection."

"I've got your back, little buddy. I promise you that," Garrett said, just as Justin thought he couldn't feel any worse.

chapter 4

Harrage Zeab

Demyan Empire Museum of Calico, Broudy-Lum StarStation

Harrage Zeab stood alone within the stark grey walls of the Encore municipal facility. Tall and slender, impeccably dressed in a long-coat and matching trousers—made from the finest threads of Tholgian silkworm larvae—he was a most severe-appearing individual. Zeab's hair, as black as obsidian, was worn long and pulled back into a ponytail. His dark eyes, always inky-wet within their sockets, betrayed his bleak, often hateful, mindset. He pursed his moist, worm-like lips.

The floor was strewn with litter—packing materials and part of a shipping crate, and an intentionally left behind rolling furniture dolly. All, of course, were props. With today's gravpallets, no one needed a rickety old rolling dolly. No, the items had been placed in here during the heist in order to mislead the inevitable investigation that would follow. The caper had certainly been bold. Zeab had to admit that. Placing a foot upon the dolly, he rolled it back and forth for a while as he considered the impact of this brazen act. The loss of the four stasis-tubes was beyond devastating. Thousands came here daily to view the Empire's prized trophies. So many visited, in fact, that it was the reason the captives were to be transported to the Museum of Calico, where the Dom-Dynasty's reigning aristocracy—the Magistor and Magistra Pietra, along with their two wretched teen offspring, Prince Markus Pietra and Princess Lena Pietra—could be more adequately viewed. Millions of *dalshacks* had been spent on that intended display—*a multimedia extravaganza.*

Zeab, hands on his narrow hips, surveyed the scene. He'd spent many an afternoon standing just where he was standing now—gloating. For it had been Zeab himself who had masterminded that family's deep space abduction, four years prior. Granted favor with the Emperor, Zeab had been promoted to Chancellor of Broudy-Lum StarStation with its billion inhabitants—the largest spatial structure within the Demyan Empire.

Zeab spotted Constable Gilmie, along with his team of inspectors, lurking in the shadows. "Come . . . do your crime scene analysis," he urged.

As the investigative team began their work in earnest, Zeab moved away from the crime scene. Deep in thought, he had zero doubt about who had orchestrated the heist: Loham

Babar, Noble-Fist to the aristocracy and Protector of the Realm. Reflectively, Zeab touched his left earlobe, or what was left of it. No one had ever bested him before with an arcblade until that day. And now this . . .

"Sire . . . there is news."

Zeab spun around to find the team's young assistant behind him. Little more than a boy. "Danly, isn't it?"

"Yes, sire . . . Shorban Danly. I have news of the chase, the pursuit. Three Dynasty Stingers. They tried to lose us within the belt."

Zeab, nodding, put on an interested, contemplative, facial expression. *An act*. He was well aware of the harrowing chase, now transpiring this very moment within the OB5 asteroid belt. Like other elite personage, Zeab was outfitted with the latest technology—such as the comms-membrane display, fused to the inside of his left forearm. Although he hadn't known they were Stingers, he knew two of the craft had been destroyed. The third, heavily damaged, had been sent tumbling off into the most treacherous depths of the asteroid belt, where further pursuit was impossible.

The fifty Demyan Rage Fighters engaged in the battle had been reduced in number to ten. Zeab would ensure that each surviving pilot, and crew member, was publicly executed. The fatal destruction of those stasis-tubes, the Dom-Dynasty's reigning aristocracy, was unforgivable. Those escaping space vessels were to be damaged only—stopped, but not destroyed. Still, there was a slim chance that one or more family member's tubes had survived the ordeal on the lone remaining Stinger.

The emperor had already sent for Zeab and was to meet with him later today. That could be bad, Chancellor Zeab thought. He would be ready—would suggest that his Eminence dispatch the Empire's Fifth Fleet, consisting of six hundred warships. That all local star systems, and perhaps even frontier worlds be scoured—no primitive, backwater world left unchecked. A residual energy-wake would be detectable, along with other means of tracking the surviving Stinger's passage. Zeab would find that cursed little ship if it was his last living act. And then, his life's sole ambition and purpose would be to find, then kill, Loham Babar.

Harrage Zeab, realizing the young apprentice was staring up at him, said, "I apologize . . . lost in my own cluttered mind. How would you like to ride along with me in my personal shuttle? It must be midday . . . we can lunch together." Zeab's dark eyes leveled on the handsome young apprentice like a venomous snake watching a small rodent. "You can tell me all about yourself. I can see you are built like an athlete. You must be into sports, am I correct on that? Let me guess, you're on a tournament Gonchi team . . . how I love watching combative-wrestling."

chapter 5

Kilian Trip

Bridgeport, Chicago

It had been a long day, and after having to cover an extra half-shift for Cassandra, who was having surgery on her bunions, well—Killian was both tired and cranky. Four days had passed since Justin's ordeal, and she just wanted to be home with him. Not here, irrigating that mail carrier's infected thumbnail, or bandaging that bitchy cross-trainer's ankle.

"Half-day today, Killian?" Doctor Branch asked, approaching the Campus B Parking structure.

Killian looked up after rummaging in her purse for her car keys. "Funny . . . yeah. Well, some of us don't have cushy doctor's hours." Having fingered her keys, she swiped at an errant strand of hair and tucked it behind her ear. Doctor Branch, about fifty-five, was a few years older than herself.

Good-looking and single, he typically dated twenty- or thirty-year-olds. Killian always secretly hoped he'd get tired of chasing young tail; realize there were benefits to dating someone closer to his own age. Hell, she was in relatively good shape, even could squeeze into the same jeans she'd worn as a freshman in college. And she actually could carry on an intelligent conversation, on a myriad of subjects.

He stopped an arm's length before her. "How's your boy? Any more trouble from . . . ?"

"No. He's managing the pain with ibuprofen—"

"I meant emotionally. What he went through was traumatic. Is he talking about it?"

Killian thought about that. *Does Justin ever talk about his feelings? Not really.* "Yeah, well, you know how teenagers are. Moody and introspective. I figure he'll come to me when he wants to talk."

"Well, if you think talking to an old dude like me would help, I'd be willing to—"

"Oh, I'm sure you're far too busy to get caught up in our family drama, Dr. Branch."

"Dave . . . for the umpteenth time, just call me Dave. And no, I'm not too busy to help a friend. I'd love to."

Killian swiped at the same errant strand of hair again, even though it was still tucked firmly in place behind her ear. "Okay . . . yeah, thanks. I'll keep that in mind." She didn't allow herself to read anything personal into it. The good doctor was simply being kind. Supportive. Nothing more.

"Guess I should get myself into the zoo," he said, still not moving.

"Good luck in there. You may want to get a tetanus booster shot one of these days."

He laughed and hesitantly strode away, and Killian began to walk as well.

She was two strides away when she heard him call after her. "Killian?"

"Yeah?"

"Maybe . . . when our shifts align, we can grab dinner?"

Looking back over her shoulder at him while still walking ahead, she said, "Um, sure. Why not?" She then hurried off, nervously pressing the unlock button on her key fob. With her heart pounding in her chest like a drum, she wondered, *Wow, did that just happen?*

Lost in her thoughts, she heard the beep of her Civic, near the far side of the parking garage. Her footsteps echoed within the enclosed concrete surroundings. It suddenly occurred to Killian just how alone she was. How vulnerable. An abrupt noise startled her—something in the shadows off to her left, hidden behind a white panel van. Right where the overhead florescent lights were out. *Terrific—as if that's not the least bit creepy,* she mused. Ten yards to go and she'd be safe within her car. She picked up her pace.

But it wasn't from the dark, creepy, shadows on her left that the gangbanger stepped out. It was from her right. "Ahh!" she yelped.

The obvious leader stood a full stride in front of the rest

of his intimidating crew. The three others, similarly dressed in oversized black hoodies and dark ball caps, took up positions in front of her car. "Mrs. Trip . . . you've been keeping us waiting. *Fuck*, lady, you bitches work some long hours, huh?"

"What do you want? This garage is patrolled every ten minutes. Security is tight here—"

"I just told you. Been here for hours. I know exactly when that small, fat, roving troll comes snooping around. But we still got some time . . . to talk. And such."

Killian said, "Please . . . just leave us, leave me, alone." Pulling her purse up higher, she crossed her arms—a shield against what might be coming.

The leader, strangely, appeared to be the youngest of the four. She noticed it was a mixed-race bunch of hoodlums. The man in front of her was black, but two others were Hispanic, and there was a young Asian man as well. What they all had in common, though, was the same dead-set eyes—eyes numb to egregious acts of violence, eyes that seemed to view life with hatred and malevolence.

He came closer to her—close enough that she could smell his musky cologne mixed with a sour body odor. "You're a pretty lady . . . got that MILF thing going on. Yeah, I could *do* you." He looked back to his boys. "Any of you want my sloppy seconds?"

"She's doable," one said enthusiastically. Killian wasn't sure which, since her eyes were tightly squeezed shut.

"Now, now, Mrs. T . . . don't get all defensive-like. We just want to chat with you some. Talk to you about your boy, hidden away in that little house of yours. We've been, um, checking you all out. Getting the lay of the land, so to speak."

Killian was well aware of that fact. She'd seen them loitering around during the day. Even more so at night, huddled together on the sidewalk. Sometimes they'd make taunting sounds, cat calls.

When the open-handed slap came, she wasn't prepared for it. Staggering, Killian dropped her purse, then crumpled to her knees. She wanted to scream. Wanted to use her keys as a weapon—punch out—poke the leader in the eye with them. But she was too scared for any of that. Too scared to do anything but kneel trembling on the cold concrete floor.

His face drew close—came within an inch of hers. "Tell that boy of yours he won't get away with what he's done. And this ain't no eye-for-an-eye bullshit either. Before I cut him, slice his throat from ear to ear, he's going to learn what scorched earth means. That everyone he cares about . . . will die. I just might let him watch, when your turn comes. What do you think about that, Mrs. T?"

She could hear a car's engine driving up the second-level ramp. *God . . . please let it be security,* Killian prayed.

"We're going to be leaving you, for now. But we'll be around." He traced a forefinger down her already bruised cheek and jaw, then onto her neck and left breast. "Maybe you and I will have a little fun first. Yeah, I'm still open to that."

Abruptly, the gang leader stood upright. Within seconds, they were gone. Killian remained where she was, still too scared to move, and only vaguely aware of the SUV idling nearby her.

"You okay there, Ma'am? You need assistance?"

She glanced up, seeing it was the hospital security vehicle. The squat little man behind the wheel stared down at her.

"I'm fine, just dropped my purse . . . keep on going."

"You sure. Maybe best if I give you—"

"I said I'm fine!" Killian yelled. Gathering up the items of her purse, she stood, car keys still tightly clenched within her fist. Opening her driver-side door, she climbed in, wanting to swipe at the tears on her wet cheeks. But she knew the frog-faced man driving the little SUV would notice, so she smiled back instead. *Everything's just fine here . . . so move along now, you useless man.* She started the engine and put the Civic into reverse after the SUV pulled away. She sat there a moment, watching it patrol slowly through the structure.

chapter 6

Justin Trip

Bridgeport, Chicago

Justin pushed the front curtains aside, just enough to peer out onto the street beyond. It was the third time that morning he'd checked to see if the Chicago PD cruiser was at the curb. It was not. The detective, who'd questioned him at the hospital, had promised him there'd be an increase in patrols—especially at night. But after a week's time, their presence nearby had become less and less frequent. Justin hated being afraid—he wanted his life to return to normal.

"Your sack lunch is in the fridge. Tuna, banana, bag of Doritos," his mother said, hurrying down the staircase. She was wearing her light pink scrubs and white hospital shoes. His mind flashed back to the ER—to Lewis sprawled out on the linoleum floor, flailing and sobbing at the loss of his twin brother, Harland.

"You sure you're ready to go back to school? Maybe take a few more days off, hon?"

"No, Mom. I'm going crazy cooped up in here."

"A week is probably not enough time. Not for the kind of injuries you incurred."

"Mom, I'm fine. Really, can you just hurry? I don't want to be late today."

Grabbing the sack lunch off the top shelf of the refrigerator, Killian handed it to Justin. "Put it in your pack—you'll be hungry later."

Justin waited for her to snatch up both her car keys and purse before heading out the front door, then walked over to the passenger side of his mother's Honda Civic. Waiting for her to unlock the car door, he scanned the nearby street and the adjacent sidewalk. On four separate occasions over the past week he'd seen them loitering around: gang members from the MP140s. They all wore the same, now-familiar uniform—oversized blue jeans, black hoodies, and black ball caps flipped backward. They came in groups of either four or five, messed around for a while there across the street from his mom's house, making no real pretense for being here. They were there for one reason only—intimidation. To let Justin know his time was coming. That Lewis would claim revenge.

They drove in silence for a few minutes before his mother said, "Can't drive you to school tomorrow. I've missed too much work this past week already . . . can't lose this job, sweetie."

Justin, who had his EarPods in and blaring, shrugged non-committally. Only then did he notice her bruised cheek. She had tried to hide it under a ton of makeup, but it still showed through. "What happened to you?" he asked, gesturing to his own cheek.

"Oh, um, patient . . . out-of-control junkie. Don't change the subject. Maybe Garrett? He can drive you, I'm sure. I'll call him later . . ."

Justin continued to stare at her cheek. His mother was a terrible liar. Although he'd been adopted, he'd somehow inherited that same aspect. "No! Don't do that . . . I'll take the bus."

Killian glanced his way, concerned. "What happened between you two? You loved getting rides from him in the mornings?"

Justin acted as if he didn't hear her over the loud rap track blaring in his ears. Truth was, Justin didn't know why he was avoiding Garrett. He felt betrayed, somehow, although he knew that was bullshit. His personal crush on Aila was beyond stupid. She deserved someone like Garrett. Still, that didn't mean he had to like it. "Just drop me off at the corner, Mom."

"Oh, I know the routine . . . God forbid a teenager is caught driving around with their mom." Pulling close to the corner, she placed a hand on his arm. "No walking home after school. Call me if you need anything. I love you."

Justin, nodding back, climbed out. Shutting the car door, he gave his mother a halfhearted wave goodbye. After first readjusting his backpack, he pulled his hood back over his head, hiding the new, smaller bandage on his cheek. He had to walk more hunched-over than usual due to his sore ribs. He'd wondered how much of what had happened to him had gotten around, and now he knew—it seemed like everyone was gawking at him. Conversations were interrupted as they watched him pass. *Fuck!* He craved to again be seated in his back-row seat in homeroom. Although tempted to bypass a trip to his locker, he knew he'd need his trigonometry textbook later. Deep in thought, he walked right into the school custodian's large, rolling, fifty-gallon trashcan.

"Shit . . . sorry," Justin said, startled. He looked up to see Mr. Babar near him, dressed in his usual green overalls, and wearing workman's gloves. The two stared at one another. Justin's mind raced as he tried to speak, wanting to thank the big man for saving his life. He hadn't mentioned anything about the janitor to the police, given them no explanation as how Harland had become impaled on that metal pipe. But just the same, he wanted to let the guy know he hadn't taken it lightly—that beyond all doubt his life had been saved that night.

But studying the man now, his striking bald head and large muscular form, strangely hunched over, he noticed the janitor walked with a definite limp. Justin wondered how this could possibly be the same person. The one who'd come to his rescue, who had moved like some kind of Parkour athlete, and fought like a Ninja.

The corners of Mr. Babar's lips pulled up. "You . . . feeling better?" He spoke with an Indian, or maybe Pakistani accent.

Justin nodded. Keeping his voice low, he asked, "It was you . . . wasn't it?"

"Me?"

"Who was there . . . that night. The one who—"

"No. You are mistaken," Mr. Babar said, maneuvering the oversized trashcan around him.

Justin, placing a hand on the trashcan's rubber rim, held on. "Wait. Can I just ask you something?"

The custodian looked annoyed, as if he couldn't get away from Justin fast enough. "What is it, young man? I have much to do this morning."

"Can you show me how you did that?"

Mr. Babar assessed Justin with suspicion in his eyes.

"They're going to get me. Maybe my mom . . . you saw them. Saw what happened."

What came back was almost a whisper. "I cannot get involved. I have my own . . . issues, boy."

"Please! There's no one else that—"

"No. Leave me be." Angrily, he shoved past Justin, metallic caster wheels clattering.

Justin ran after him. "Help me or I'll tell them—the police. What you did. The metal pipe."

"Why me?" Babar asked, still pushing his trash bin ahead.

"I don't know . . . I just know things have to change for me. And I know you can help me. I saw"

The man sighed. "I'll think about it. Go about your day, boy." Powering the trashcan forward, he turned left at the next corner.

Justin's first period class went by in a blur; the same with the second. He ignored the other students, the overly sympathetic glances from his teachers. Sitting low in his seat, he thought, *Something's got to change.* He mused about the nightmares he'd been experiencing nightly, ever since he'd returned home from the hospital. Mused about his life, once perfectly on track, now becoming dismal, a shit-show, and only getting worse. *Something's got to change.* He'd gone from simply being the resident school monstrosity to becoming a true liability, to his mother and anyone around him. Fear was suffocating him—and he realized it had been even before the MP140s' calamitous attack. Justin thought about his life going forward. Sure, he had good grades—great grades! A scholarship was in the bag from more than one university. Terrific. He could go from being the high school freak to a university freak. Timid and afraid, he'd spend the next four years shuttered within his dorm room. *Something's got to change . . . I don't want to live like this anymore.*

"Hey there . . . found you."

Justin glanced up, then around him. The room was empty. The class, at some point, had ended. But sitting in front of him, turned around backward in a seat facing him, was Aila, who wore a bemused smile—as if she was privy to some secret goings-on. She looked around playfully. "Are we hiding out in here?"

"Um, no. Just got lost in thought."

"I see," she said, conveying back that she didn't really believe his excuse. "Why haven't you returned any of my phone calls?"

Justin stared at her. The truth, he'd thought about doing little else. But the last thing his fragile ego needed right then was pity. The truth was, he didn't really know this girl. She owed him nothing. He didn't want to play a role—one where he'd inevitably be made the fool.

"Hello? Are you lost in thought again?"

"No. I'm . . . reevaluating."

"Reevaluating what?" she asked, looking genuinely interested. She leaned forward, studying his face, his features. Her breasts, now squeezed together, emphasized her cleavage. Justin forced himself to look away. "I'm reevaluating my life as a whole . . . if you must know."

"What will you do with that evaluation? You're not going to jump off some bridge, or in front of a city bus, are you?" Aila cringed. "Eek, too soon for run-over jokes?"

Justin laughed, not wanting to. "Yeah, probably. And no, I'm not suicidal, just . . . fed up."

"Fed up. Not going to take it anymore!" she said back.

He looked at her, recalling the ancient movie he'd watched with his mom—Albert

Finny bellowing out a window, "I'm fed up . . . not going to take it anymore!"

"Network," he said in response.

"Yup. I love old movies. I have that one on a DVD."

"You watch DVDs still?" Justin asked.

"I do . . . have a library of 397 of them. I can bring some over, if you want. Popcorn, movies, what could be better?"

Again, Justin simply stared at her. She didn't need to do this, the whole *adopt a wounded freak* thing. "Uh, I don't have a DVD player . . . not sure anyone does anymore." He gave her a crooked smile.

"What was that?" she asked, turning serious and pointing at his face. Instinctively, he placed a palm over his scars.

"No, not that—that thing you just did with your mouth. Was that a smile?"

He gave a short, sarcastic laugh. The last thing now he wanted to do was leave this perfect, funny, wonderful, person— but he had to. Every moment he spent with her, he was falling further and further under her spell. "I have to go."

"Me too. Do you want a ride home after school?"

"No. No, thank you. You guys go ahead." Throwing his backpack over a shoulder, he headed for the classroom exit.

Toward his back, she called, "Answer your damn phone the next time I call!"

Justin ignored her. Or at least he pretended to.

It was 3:30. Justin had managed to survive to the end of sixth period. School was over, and he had no intention of catching the bus for a ride home. He wasn't sure how long Mr. Babar typically worked, but he'd wait around just the same. Then he'd follow him to his car, or follow him to his home if he didn't drive.

chapter 7

Loham Babar

Babar didn't reach the gap in the old Wrigley Factory's chain-link fence until around 4:30 that afternoon. Prior to leaving the high school, he'd first needed to mop the floor in the girl's bathroom, in Building 5—a *vomit mess* from a new strain of flu going around. Now within the old factory's littered, overgrown grounds he continued to walk, hunched over and limping, for a few more paces. Once out of street view, he straightened to his full height and walked normally, with purpose and self-assurance.

Always leery of interloping humans possibly lurking around within the darkened factory confines, Babar stopped every so often to listen for any out-of-the-ordinary noise. All was quiet. He walked through five separate graffiti-covered corridors before emerging out onto the main factory floor. Here, in spite of the posted asbestos signs, the space vessel would not be found easily by junkies or by squatters looking for shelter, or by partying teenagers either. The massive generator flywheel, positioned sub-level and almost as large as the factory's main floor, was once hidden beneath timber joists and oaken floors that had rotted away decades before. Babar had fashioned-out multiple cross beams to lie atop the generator room's sub-flooring. Pilfering intact sections of flooring—from other areas of the factory—he somehow managed to piece together a new floor. Then, tossing debris onto the area, creating an eight-foot-high mountain of rubble, further obscured all signs of what lay below.

Babar retrieved a key, hidden atop a nearby overhead beam, and unlocked a rusted, albeit still functional, door lock. Hinges complained as the door swung open. Closing and re-latching the door behind him, he descended the staircase into the pitch-black void below.

Once again, Babar listened intently for out-of-the-ordinary sounds. As he took two steps to the left, his hand—reaching out into the darkness—found the light switch. The sub-level room was instantly illuminated beneath a dozen or so hanging light bulbs. He was standing fifteen meters below the sub-level flooring he'd fashioned out a month earlier. The space was large—approximately fifty meters wide by sixty meters long, roughly half the size of a typical football field here on Earth.

Dank, cinderblock walls surrounded the entire space. A generator and a looming iron flywheel completely dominated the room's far end. Situated midway, in this sub-level space, was the damaged Stinger. The agile warship, relatively small in size, was approximately seven meters wide, twenty meters long, and eight in height. It was powered by dual, wing-mounted, anti-matter powerplants. The vessel typically accommodated a crew of fifteen or less. The Stinger had two levels, accessible from an aft entry hatch, which led into a small one- or two-person airlock. The bow of the vessel was somewhat bulbous, affording a boomerang-shaped, wrap-around windshield at the bridge. Integrated, though not in the least hidden from view, were the ship's weaponry systems. Multiple plasma cannons and rail-gun turrets abounded, leaving little doubt that this indeed was a scrappy little warship.

Babar took in the sleek vessel, his eyes drawn to the specific areas he had repaired and others still needing work. The damage incurred from the pursuing Empire Rage-Fighters had been the least of it. Colliding with no fewer than three SUV-sized asteroids had caused most of the damage.

Procuring adequate replacement materials had been among Babar's biggest challenges. Composed of exotic lightweight elements, the Stinger's hull was robust enough to withstand whatever was thrown at it, be it space debris, high radiation levels, or extreme ranges of temperature—though of course, direct plasma fire was a different story. That was what augmented shields were for. Just one more item on his to-do-list that would need repairing.

For eighteen months, Babar had been hard at it—he had repaired at least sixty individual hull breaches, two porthole windows, and a starboard-side wing strut. Currently, he was attending to the spaceship's internal issues. The environmental system was being temperamental. The on-board AI seemed to be operational, but was acting 'quirky,' and the primary Zyln-strap coupling needed further attention. At his current rate of progress, the Stinger would be space-ready within four to five weeks' time. Still, a lot could happen in that timeframe—damage to some ship system than he hadn't anticipated. Or the Empire, undoubtedly still looking for him, could home in on his present location on Earth. Though he'd been careful in that regard—keeping the vessel's comms systems offline and the powerplant shut down for the most part, the anti-matter would still have left a definitive signature trail. Eventually, they would find him. He knew it was just a matter of time.

Babar walked around the perimeter of the Stinger, his eyes studying every nook and cranny, every aspect of the ship. This vessel was his lone connection to his life back on Calunoth. A full two years had passed since he'd left his home world. Two years since he'd last seen his wife and their three little ones. He found it painful thinking about them, what they were doing now, and if they believed him either dead or forever lost in space. He also avoided thinking about Magistor Pietra—his best friend and liege. As Noble-Fist to the aristocracy, Babar had always found solace in the fact that he had one supreme purpose in life—to protect his Eminence and the Dow Dynasty. *So what is my purpose now?* Babar mused, remembering the ball of fire flaring off the starboard wing some year-and-a-half prior.

Babar climbed the short gangway, aft of the vessel, then walked in and out of the airlock. To his right, was the Stinger's primary hold area. Passing through the open hatchway, his eyes took in the two, nine-foot tall, stasis-tubes. Illuminating a bright bluish glow, he regarded the body immersed within each. Molecularly frozen in quantum time and space, Prince Markus Pietra suspended in one, and Princess Lena Pietra in the other. Dressed in white stasis suits, their eyes were open, their mouths slightly agape.

Both were alive—although brain activity was negligible—two healthy, mindless, bodies. The Stinger's power grid had been damaged during the attack. Subsequently, both stasis-tubes had languished three full days without power. Babar looked into Prince Pietra's unfocussed eyes, then said, "I am sorry, young Markus ... not only did I not protect your father, I failed to protect you and your sister. Far worse, Calunoth and the Dow Dynasty may have lost their last beacon of hope." Babar wondered how long it would be before the Empire reached the core Dynasty worlds, before Calunoth sovereignty was in peril—or was that already the case? Was the majestic Cristine Castle already under siege from Empire disrupter brigades?

Ting ting ting ting ...

The sound was ever so slight, coming from the bridge. Babar turned his head and listened. *Motion detector alarms?* Hurrying from the hold, he maneuvered through narrow passageways and eventually entered the Stinger's bridge. The soft alarm was working in cadence with a blinking warning light. Tapping on the console brought multiple local-vicinity video feeds up. A dark shape could be seen moving about the factory's first-floor level. Babar leaned closer to the virtual display, narrowing his eyes. The form walked into a golden swath of setting sunlight. "Damn it!" It was the scar-faced boy. Babar searched his memory . . . *Justin. Justin Trip*. He adjusted one of the feed's zoom levels, zeroing in on the boy's face. Apart from the fact this meddlesome teenager should not be here and had obviously followed Babar, there was something far more intriguing about the situation.

He'd seen the boy walking around the school before, but had always primarily noticed his scars, and had somehow missed the impossible appearance of the face beneath them. Until just now, as he held the faces together in his mind— the boy in front of him, and the prince just a little ways away within the stasis tube. *They could be brothers . . . twins, even.*

chapter 8

Harrage Zeab

Pinterthor War Ship, Deep within Frontier Space

For three weeks now, Harrage Zeab, Chancellor of Broudy-Lum StarStation, had been on a special assignment for Emperor Chi-Sacrim. Zeab could almost hear the emperor's thunderous parting directives, "This was your screw up, Chancellor. Find that Dynasty Stinger . . . bring me back Babar's head in a fucking bucket! Now get out of here!"

Three of the Empire's finest medium-sized destroyers were under Zeab's authority, although not under his direct command. It was a distinction Fleet Commander Admiral Grishlund took every opportunity to mention. The admiral was old—far too ancient to still be holding command, in Zeab's opinion. Today, the old coot was wearing his typical, oversized black uniform. Hanging limply off the admiral's rickety old shoulders, his uniformed breast was adorned with colorful, albeit frayed, ribbons and metals. Unruly wisps of white hair topped the pale pate of his skeletal-like head. His sunken, beady eyes that never seemed to settle longer than a moment or two surveyed the bridge, like a predatory bird.

Zeab wanted to be home, back in his finely appointed apartment within Broudy-Lum StarStation. The living condition on any warship was little more than barbaric, but even worse when confined within a 1,300-crew destroyer. His own quarters upon the *Pinterthor* were bleak, and he could swear he once saw a deck-scart skittering up a bulkhead in the middle of the night.

"We are officially entering Dynasty space, Admiral Grishlund," a young ensign relayed from his bridge post.

"Continue on course," the admiral said back, turning his attention to Captain Poot. "Instruct the *Prowess* and the *Mortise* to engage stealth-running."

Zeab, sitting atop one of three command chairs, let out an audible sigh as he checked beneath his fingernails for any new bits of grime.

"You have something to add, Chancellor?" the admiral asked, without looking at him.

Zeab tore his attention away from his splayed-out fingers. "Yes . . . yes, actually I do. There is no reason to think Babar would have escaped to the frontier worlds. There's nothing out there. No, Admiral, Babar would have headed directly for the core worlds . . . if not for Calunoth, itself."

"And the wake signature that we've been tracking? We know that vessel is damaged, requires repairs," the admiral said.

"That could be the signature of any number of Dynasty Stingers," Zeab said back.

"Doubtful . . . this signature is unique. Sensor readings tell us it emanated from the OB5 asteroid belt," Admiral Grishlund said, shaking his head. "The odds that signature wake came from some other vessel are infinitesimally small. Continue on course, Captain," the admiral ordered.

Zeab rose to his feet, joining the admiral and Captain Poot, who were standing at the bridge-hub—a raised oval command center positioned several steps down from the rest of the destroyer's twenty-crew bridge. Local virtual space was projected above the ten-foot- long console table.

Zeab asked, "And what is this planetary system you've dragged us to?" as his eyes took in the three unimpressive, lack-luster stars, and a medium-sized, tan-colored world. The readings told him that it was Proxima Centauri, positioned within the Alpha Centauri star system. "Just one more turd of a planet stuck in the middle of nowhere," he added.

"Captain . . . Dynasty Patrol . . . inbound!"

Captain Poot manipulated the projected feed and zoomed in on eight patrol vessels. "They see us?" he asked.

"Yes, sir," the ensign replied.

"Even with stealth-running?"

"Yes, sir," the ensign replied more apologetically.

The captain looked to the admiral, who turned to Chancellor Zeab. "This is your assignment. We flee now, we won't be returning any time soon. There'd be a Dynasty fleet waiting for us next time, I can assure you of that."

Zeab considered the admiral's remarks. He was right. But Zeab was somewhat surprised to be asked to make the decision. Clearly, Admiral Grishlund didn't want later ramifications coming back at him, biting him in his geriatric ass. Chancellor Zeab licked his already-moist lips. Glancing past the admiral at the captain, he ordered, "Go to battle stations, Captain Poot. Show me what your destroyers are capable of."

A klaxon blared overhead as the bridge crew scurried about, readying the ship for battle. "All eight vessels are Fast-Attack Corvettes, sirs," the ensign said.

Zeab watched as the console projection, altering perspective, showed eight small patrol vessels zooming into view from around the mud-colored planet. They immediately split off into three groups.

"We have a lock on three of those Corvettes, Captain."

Captain Poot, a short and stocky man with bushy muttonchops, gave the order: "Battle Command ... fire three mid-range torpedoes ..."

Zeap felt tingling vibrations in his feet as each missile shot forth, out from integrated silo slots located along the underside of the *Pinterthor's* fuselage. But half the distance to their selected targets, the three torpedoes exploded.

"Captain ... tell me this is not indicative of your best

offensive measures," Zeab said, exchanging a quick look of concern with the admiral.

Ignoring Zeap's remark, Captain Poot spat out a new flurry of directives to his crew as a group of enemy Corvettes began closing in on the *Pinterthor*.

"They're firing—explosive rail munitions!" the ensign shouted out.

"Divert more power to the portside shields!" Poot yelled back, as they watched the fast-approaching small ships. A blaze of bright projectiles arced across the spatial divide, flaring even brighter when they struck the *Pinterthor's* portside shields.

"Shields taking a beating!" one crewmember yelled out from the other side of the bridge. "Losing shield integrity! Recharging capacitors overloading. "

"Do something!" Admiral Grishlund ordered, glaring at the captain.

Zeab said, "I suggest you order twenty to thirty Rage Fighters to also get into this fight, Captain . . . and I'd convey that same order to the *Prowess* and the *Mortise* too . . . they don't seem to be faring that much better than the *Pinterthor.*"

Seeming less than thrilled at taking combat advice from the chancellor, still, the captain did exactly as Zeab suggested. Within three minutes, close to seventy Rage Fighters could be seen entering into the conflict from all three Empire destroyers. Soon, darting in and out of view behind the attacking Dynasty Corvettes, they looked like a furious swarm of angry insects. The well-trained pilots quickly gained the upper hand in the fierce battle. Green plasma fire could be seen everywhere.

A sudden massive fireball captured everyone's attention. Three additional fireballs followed suit.

"Corvettes . . . not ours," Captain Poot said. "Just took us a little time—we've got this handled now."

Zeab leaned in closer to the admiral. "Three of the Empire's finest destroyers . . . leave it to the Dynasty that we're outplayed by a few Corvettes."

The admiral stared at the projected feed, at the raging battle now waging before them. "Evidently, Dynasty technology has . . . well advanced."

"No, Admiral, I suspect your ego hasn't come to terms with the well-known reality . . . Dynasty tech has always been a step ahead of the Empire's. Sure, they may not have our numbers of warships, but what they do have, simply, is better."

Visibly flustered, the admiral said, "Well . . . we shouldn't need to deploy fighters . . . not for eight *shitty* Corvettes."

A crewman said, "Captain, the *Mortise* has taken direct hits to the stern . . . propulsion is offline. Multiple deck breaches, with casualties, perhaps reaching into the hundreds."

As if sensing an easy kill, Dynasty ships converged en masse on the now-ailing destroyer.

"The ship is lost . . . use it as bait," Chancellor Zeab said.

"Bait? what are you talking about?" Captain Poot spat back. "There's close to fifteen hundred souls aboard that Empire ship!"

"Do you want to join them? Their destiny is already a foregone conclusion. Fire two Tyron Nukes, maybe three, into the fray. Be content that both the *Pinterthor* and the *Torrent* will survive the day."

The captain stared at Zeab in dismay, sickened by his suggestion.

"Do as the chancellor suggests, Captain. Do it now . . ." Admiral Grishlund commanded.

Captain Poot, momentarily hesitating, reluctantly gave out the order: "Battle Command, fire two Tyron Nukes . . . target the *Mortise* mid-ship. Ensign, issue orders for our Rage Fighters to return back to the *Prowess* and *Pinterthor*. Instruct the *Prowess* to head away from the *Mortise*."

Two large missiles shot forth, holding parallel trajectories toward the ensuing battle ahead. "Helm . . . get us the hell away from here," the captain shouted, his voice heavy with distain.

Zeab watched the two fast-moving missiles converge on the *Mortise,* and on the encircling, attacking Corvettes. He could hear multiple, frantic distress calls coming in from the *Mortise's* bridge command. The fiery flash from the combined Tyron nuclear explosions was blinding. Blinking hard, it took a moment for Zeab's eyes to readjust. When he looked at the projected battle scene again, little was left to see, only space debris. Primarily remains of the *Mortise.* No enemy vessels were visible.

The bridge crew had quieted, the overhead klaxon now silent. Captain Poot stood at the bridge-hub console, with his head hanging low, clearly distraught at having to give out such horrific orders.

Chancellor Zeab focused on the admiral, who did not look

all that disturbed. In fact, he stared back at Zeab with an odd, somewhat bemused, expression. "Perhaps I've underestimated you, Chancellor Zeab."

Zeab had heard similar remarks before, was often under-estimated. "Captain ... Admiral ... let's now resume our hunt. There's a certain Stinger's wake signal still out there waiting to be found, no? Since we're here, we'll continue reaching out with our long-range sensors. Stingers leave behind them a wake of alpha-emitting radiation and gamma particles ... if it's out here, we'll pick up its trail."

chapter 9

Prince Markus Pietra

Wrigley's Chewing Gum Factory, Bridgeport, Chicago—Gun Ship Hold

Markus languished within a constant haze of confused, undefined thoughts and feelings. Here, wherever *here* was, provided minimal sensory input. Sure, he knew he was floating. Often wondered if he even had a body. *Am I dead?* Was this present state of being to become his eternity? Over the preceding months, he'd been able to resolve one definitive aspect of life as he now was experiencing it—that he was abiding within a perpetual dream state. He knew, though he didn't know how he knew, that such had not always been the case. It was a source of near-constant frustration and anxiety for him, because he still had clear memories. In fact, Prince

Markus Pietra's only life-saving grace was these memories— memories of his past life. That recall was his only respite from horrific, torturous, undefined monotony. And sometimes, through these recollections, he felt he was close to penetrating the veil between then and now—the curtain separating consciousness from unconsciousness, reality from lifelessness . . .

How old am I? Markus wondered. Mentally, it was like wading or trudging through knee-high paste, how slow his mind seemed to work. *Perhaps seventeen? Eighteen?*

One memory spoke to him more than any other, although this recall of when he was a mere boy within the kingdom was unwelcome, somehow drawn into his consciousness like water into a sponge. Dread weighed heavily on Markus now. Anger flared within him, which inevitably, like so many times before, would soon turn to guilt, then self-incrimination. Twelve years old at the time, he was the leader of the pack. Home on break from boarding school, they were rueful youngsters with far too much time on their hands. It was the cyclic warm season, known as Harvest-Gather.

Back in ancient times, before modern technology and AI robotics, the outlying townspeople toiled in their fields, bringing into town their agricultural bounties, which later would be portioned out to their shared society cumulative. Even today, it was a festive time of remembrance and thanksgiving. A celebratory parade where, in ages past, long-legged Tranga-beasts had pulled great timber-hewn wagons piled high with everyone's combined harvests, weaving through the realm's majestic countryside.

Today, the wooden wagons had been replaced with enclosed hover-carts. Both the tranga-beasts, and the piled-high-wagon harvest, were simply artificial projections. Although certainly real looking, they were artificially produced just the same. Hundreds of real people lined both sides of the long cobblestone road. And off in the distance, the six tall, sapphire-colored spires of Cristine Castle were visible to the eye, no matter where one stood within the realm.

Bossy and impatient with the other four, Markus, whether consciously or unconsciously, embodied the worst of his father's leadership qualities.

"Let's go, already. What are we waiting for?" chubby little Thorman Smatt asked, revving up the power output on his kneeler. Kneelers were what most teenagers sped around on these days. As the name implied, one kneeled upon the anti-gravity transport scooters. Kneelers came in a wide variety of models. The most basic, little more than a thin platform, had handlebar controls, and an under-mount G-thrust powerplant. Other kneelers, like the wealthy boys within Markus's click possessed, were more powerful models, capable of moving at dangerously high speeds—and they had remarkable maneuverability.

"Shut up, Smatt . . . we go when I say we go," Markus ordered, glancing around at the others. Ballard, tall and self-assured, was the closest Markus had to a best friend. Also part of the gang was Mahlnie Ringfind, Ballard's sister. The only girl in their group, she was someone Markus had feelings for—to the point his heart actually hurt. She wore her straw-colored hair longish, which often obscured her expressive, emerald-green eyes. And when close enough, one could see the tiny freckles sprinkling the bridge of her small upturned nose. Why he went out of his way to insult her, belittle her, Markus didn't fully understand. Another in their pack was Brill Maxtore. Slight and quiet, he was unobtrusive, to the point Markus sometimes forgot he was around.

"There!" Mahlnie said, pointing toward the crest of the distant rise. The first of the lumbering-along parade wagons was coming into view. A distant cheer from the crowds underscored her observation. Soon, the parade would reach the elevated observation seating where his father and mother sat, as well as other dignitaries, and those in the military, like Admiral Tike, who oversaw the realm's Space Flight Academy. In less than three years, Markus had every intention of being among those entering the academy's freshman class. As the Magistor's son, and a prince, his place there was already assured. Today's demonstration would be the proverbial icing on the cake. By publicly showcasing what he could accomplish on a mere kneeler, he'd convince the military of how suited he'd someday be sitting within the cockpit of a FareCat Fighter craft. Maybe even a Stinger gun ship!

"Okay, if you don't want to get yourself flattened out, stay away from the G-thrust powerplant that's on the underside of these wagons. The magnetic polarity of your kneelers can suck you right in," Markus said, making eye contact with each, one at a time. "So everyone knows what to do, right? Or do I need to go through it again for all you morons?"

"Ugh, we're not stupid, Markus . . . we got it," Mahlnie said, knitting her brows together. "Let's get on with it!"

Markus's temper flared, as it often did, when anyone asserted their will over his. But he let her bossiness go unchallenged—this time. The plan, *his* plan, was to disrupt the festivities. The five kneelers would weave in between and circle the parade wagons, demonstrating their maneuvering skills. Hell, it should be a lot more entertaining than watching a bunch of ridiculously slow-moving hover-wagons inch past them. But mostly, it would give Markus the opportunity to impress Admiral Tike.

Markus, his eyes narrowed, watched and waited. The timing had to be just right. Get there too early, and it all would be for nothing. Arrive too late, and he'd simply make a fool of himself.

"Go!" Markus yelled, cranking his kneeler's accelerator control as far as it could go. His kneeler sped out and away from their hiding place among the low strand of trees. As he swooshed ahead onto the cobblestone road, the rushing wind on his face felt incredible. Glancing back, he found the four others desperately trying to catch up. Snickering, he thought, *That'll be the day,* but then slowed enough for them to assume their pre-arranged positions behind him—two to the left and two to the right.

Three-quarters of the way up the hill, Markus yelled, "Here we go. Follow my lead. Do what I do . . . follow-the-fucking-leader time. Even you four idiots can manage that, right?" Markus, glancing to his left, tried to catch Mahlnie's eye. He had to admit this was more than just impressing crusty old Admiral Tike—he wanted to impress her too, perhaps even more so. But she didn't look at him. Didn't acknowledge him at all.

Infuriated, Markus raised his chin in defiance and accelerated his kneeler forward.

"Hey!" Smatt yelled. "We're supposed to do this together. Come on, Markus!"

Up ahead, the towering leading parade wagon was moving slow and steady down the grade. Markus had forgotten how monstrously huge these things were. Each wagon carried a different, colorful projected display on top. The lead one had harvested Dally stalks, with comical, integrated, animated faces. The stalks jumped and danced in unison to the beat of the raucous broadcasted music.

Markus smiled. He'd timed their approach perfectly. The lead wagon was just approaching the observation platform. He gunned the accelerator and within seconds was close to the parade. Giving the impression he was about to careen into the lead wagon, he swooped left at the last moment, missing the projected-upward team of Tranga-beasts by inches. As preplanned, Mahlnie did the same, only veering to the right instead. Back and forth, the rest of Markus's parade intruders rocketed by—just missing the lead wagon.

The prince, suddenly pulling back on his kneeler's controls, ascended up and up, then initiated a backward barrel roll. He heard both yells and curses coming from the crowd below, which was to be expected. Completing another maneuver and momentarily standing upright on his kneeler, he stood hundreds of feet up in the air. Then hunkering down low, he leaned forward and dove his kneeler down at a sharp, death-defying angle. In the airspace around him, Markus could see his fellow cohorts enacting their own aerial tricks—although none compared to his own masterful maneuvers.

With the raised observation deck directly below him, Markus angled his descent toward the trailing parade wagons. Slowing, then leveling out, he swooped mere feet above the crowd. As he made a U-turn between two wagons, the two leading Tranga-beasts reared up and shrieked. Smiling, Markus came around the rear of the parade and cranked the accelerator as far as it would go. Nearly losing his balance, he smiled as he held on for dear life. Flying close to the ground now and running parallel to the line of the immense parade wagons, Markus needed to be careful not to be pulled into any of the G-thrust powerplants. He could feel their continuous tug— *how easy it would be to be sucked in and pulverized by those magnetic counterforces.* He leveled out for his approach, in position to rocket right past the observation deck some fifty meters away.

Up ahead were the long, reflective gold capes worn by his parents—the Magistor and Magistra. Just beyond them sat the admiral, attired in a smart, light-gray uniform with a matching officer's cap. Five seconds to go and Markus would be right in front of them. He turned his head, so they'd be able to see his face—his defiant smile.

No longer watchful of where he was going, Markus caught

sight of *something* out the corner of his eye. Startled, he saw another equally fast-moving kneeler headed right toward him. Frantic, Markus knew there wasn't time to stop or ascend higher—he'd surely hit the observation deck's overhanging roof. No, he'd veer to the right, just as he'd been taught. In dicey situations like this, always veer to the right. And if the other rider had a brain—did the same thing—all would be okay. The last fraction of a second in time seemed to slow to a crawl. Within that split second, he recognized the oncoming rider; saw her straw-colored, blown-back hair; her frantic, wide-open, emerald green eyes. *Oh God—Mahlnie.* Markus had no time to think—no time to even hope for a good outcome. As he veered right, Mahlnie veered right also. They missed hitting each other by a hair's breadth.

Only when he'd passed by her, their combined speeds easily one hundred miles per hour, did he realize she wouldn't have enough space to clear the parade wagons. He heard that *sound*. A sound he would never ever forget. The sound of a kneeler and its rider being drawn in . . . then crushed beneath the incredibly powerful downward forces of a powerplant.

chapter 10

Justin Trip

Wrigley's Chewing Gum Factory, Bridgeport, Chicago

Justin crept through the darkened, debris-strewn factory hallway, doing his best not to make too much noise. It smelled of rot. Reflective dust particles hovered in the air like minuscule aerial drones. He'd followed Babar here, waiting outside the school for the school janitor to complete his work before heading out after him. Staying a block back, he'd kept to the shadowed side of the street. Babar had taken extra care, ensuring no one was watching as he slipped through the opening in the chain-link fence. Justin found it interesting that Babar had returned to the old Wrigley building that overlooked the street where he'd been beaten—where Harland had been killed.

Emerging out onto the factory's main floor, Justin once again was tempted to leave. Whatever Babar was up to and was doing here, it probably wasn't on the up-and-up. Late-afternoon sunlight streamed into the factory through a line of high, narrow windows. The factory floor was immense. Justin could easily imagine a number of large machines churning out thousands upon thousands of individually wrapped sticks of gum, day in and day out. What remained today on the cement floor was only a mountain of crap, piled high in the middle of the room. Taking another look around, he shrugged. *It was a mistake to come here.* Ready to leave the same way he'd entered in, he stopped short, his breath catching in his chest. The silhouette of an unmoving man stood a mere ten feet away. Dark shadows kept him mostly hidden, almost impossible to see. But Justin recognized the school overalls he was wearing.

"Uh . . . Mr. Babar?"

A long moment passed. "You should not be here. Why have you followed me?"

"You saved my life."

Mr. Babar stayed quiet.

"I wasn't sure what was real, or what I imagined . . . I was hurt, lying there on the sidewalk. Maybe I just imagined some things."

"Maybe you did."

"Yeah, and maybe you didn't hurdle an eight-foot-high fence, and move about like a Ninja . . . but you did save my life. You used that metal pipe against Harland. I know—I saw that much of it."

"I acted impetuously."

"He was going to kill me. I have zero doubt about that, and . . . you saw him. I was about to have my head bashed in."

"Why are you here?" Babar asked.

Justin, wanting to ask Babar the same thing, said, "The gang . . . Harland's brother. They won't stop till they get revenge. They've been camping out in front of my house at night. I think they might have confronted my mom, but she's not talking about it."

"A job for the police."

Justin snorted, "Yeah . . . that's a joke. There's nothing they can do. Not for one lone kid."

"Again, why are you here, boy?"

Justin, not exactly sure why himself, only knew that he was desperate. "Show me how to defend myself. Show me how to . . . to stay alive. And keep my mother safe."

"Me? A high school janitor?"

"A high school janitor that pretends to have a limp. That whole hunchback routine . . . it's fake. Don't forget, I've seen you in action. Seen you move."

"And why would I do this for you? Out of the goodness of my heart, because I am such a nice guy?"

Justin, his lips pursed, shook his head. "No, none of that. How about because I'll keep your secret about what you have hidden down below?" Actually, Justin didn't have a clue what was below the pieced-together flooring they were now standing on. But he'd figured it out enough to connect the dots: the makeshift flooring, the doorway behind Mr. Babar, and the dimmed light emanating up from what he surmised was a stairwell.

The janitor stepped forward, now walking fully into the light. He was a far larger man than Justin had ever considered. He'd disguised his physique almost perfectly.

"Threatening me . . . you believe that is a sound pursuit? A good idea?"

Justin considered his present situation. Alone here, in an abandoned factory, his yells for help wouldn't be heard by anyone. And the large man standing just in front of him was capable of strewing overwhelming violence. "You've already proven yourself to be, um, I don't know . . . *cool,* I guess?"

"Seriously? You are going with that?" Babar asked.

Justin had to smile. "Look, I'm desperate. I don't care what you're up to. I don't care if you're a bank robber or an arms dealer. I don't give a shit. But I know I'm fucked if I don't get help."

Babar seemed to reconsider what was said. Eventually, he exhaled a slow breath and raised his chin. "The price for what you ask will be high."

"Price? What kind of price? I have . . . no money. And if you are some kind of perv—"

"Shut up, boy. You insult me."

"Okay, then, what price? I'd rather not do anything that will put me in jail—don't think I'd last too long in the big house."

Mr. Babar seemed to find that funny, and stifled a laugh. "It would mean leaving here . . . your home, perhaps for an extended period of time. To be honest, I haven't had much time to think about it. But you would be helping me. Me, and many others."

"Wait . . . so let me get this straight. For you to help me, teach me how to defend myself and keep that gang of killers away from me and my mom, I'd have to go off somewhere—with you?"

Mr. Babar stared at Justin, his eyes boring into him with such intensity that Justin had to look away. "Maybe this isn't such a good idea. I . . . I should go." He took three strides toward the same corridor he'd first entered through, then suddenly halted. The janitor had somehow crossed the room's expanse without making a sound. He should have been huffing and puffing, yet he was breathing normally. In a blur of motion, Mr. Babar stepped forward, passed Justin, then swept him off his feet. Landing hard on the floor, Justin gasped for air. The sole of Babar's boot was now pressed against his exposed throat. The sudden ambush had taken about two seconds.

Justin struggled to breathe. Raising both palms up, he managed to croak out the words, "Yeah. Teach . . . me . . . how . . . to . . . do . . . that shit."

Babar raised his boot, then crouched low beside Justin's vulnerable, prone form. "Let me make this perfectly clear for you. I do not wish to harm you. That is not who I am . . . I am not that kind of person. But, if necessary, I will. I have far too much at stake. Obligations. Sacrificing your life, my own life, is of little consequence in the full realm of what I must do."

Babar, was looking weirdly at Justin again, seeming to analyze him—his face.

"Okay . . . but it's the whole thing—me having to go somewhere with you. You have to admit it sounds a bit creepy. Right?"

Babar stood and extended a hand down. "Stand up, boy."

Justin took the big man's hand and rose to his feet. Uneasiness seemed to be present in the man's overall demeanor; some internal conflict perhaps. "What's going on? What are you thinking about? You worried I'll tell someone about this place . . . your hideout? Because I won't," Justin promised.

Mr. Babar glanced back toward the slightly ajar doorway. As darkness settled in, the light within the stairwell seemed to increase.

With his back to Justin, the man said, "Trust . . . hmm, I am not accustomed to having to trust anyone on this world."

"Okay . . . um, well, I'm basically pretty honest. Maybe too honest, some would say. So, are you going to help me, Mr. Babar?" Justin asked.

Babar turned to study him. With doubt and some vulnerability showing in his eyes, he said, "You can just call me Babar, Justin . . . and the truth is, I need your help as much as you need mine. Unfortunately, for me to explain all of it to you, I have to risk more than you can possibly imagine."

"Risk? I assure you, I'm no risk to anybody. That's the problem—I'm no threat to anyone at all."

Babar said, "I'm going to show you something, if you will let me. Something that will change your life forever."

"That sounds ominous. Is it like taking a red or blue pill type of thing?"

Babar didn't seem to catch the Matrix reference.

"Okay, sure, show me," Justin said. "Like I said, I'm dead the way things are anyway."

Babar headed toward the inner doorway. *Of course*, Justin thought, *whatever the man wants to show me must be below . . . down at the bottom of that creepy stairwell.*

chapter 11

Justin thought about the lame excuse his mother had offered up to explain the bruise on her cheek. And he thought about the gang of MP140s—hanging out in front of his house at night—and the fact that he, whether intentionally, or not, was at least partially responsible for the death of Lewis's brother, Harland. And how his world seemed to be spinning out of control. He needed to change the death-spiral trajectory he was on, needed to do *something*. From the top of the narrow stairwell, he watched as Babar descended down the steps below. Ignoring the warning bells going off in his head, he followed after him.

Finally emerging into a large basement, of sorts, Justin took in the poorly lit area. The surrounding cinderblock walls looked moist—tinged a moldy bluish-green. A rusted-out generator with its gargantuan metal flywheel loomed high in the dilapidated factory cellar. But Justin wasn't focusing on any of that. What he was focused on was what clearly was a space-craft of some kind. More accurately, what had to be a talented hobbyist's rendition of a spacecraft. Justin knew Trekkies and the sort did this sort of this. Idled away time—days, weeks, months—working on elaborate models like this. But on closer scrutiny, his awe at what some hobbyist had accomplished here wasn't adding up. Sure, there were scaled fabrications, reproductions. But this . . . Justin was suddenly feeling uncomfortable. It was one of those moments when you'd look back and say to yourself, that was when things changed—when everything came undone.

As positive as he'd been moments before that this was a hobbyist's dream project, he was now just as certain that this was, in fact, a real spacecraft. It was big, taking up a good portion of the factory's cellar. It was also very cool-looking—*badass*. Matte black for the most part, there were eye-catching metallic gold highlights here and there along the ship's hull and two stubby wings. The bow of the vessel was rounded and blunt-nosed. From where he stood, it looked as though the entrance to the ship was at the rear, the aft of the ship.

He tore his attention away from the ship, seeing Babar now standing before it, his arms crossed over his chest.

Just then, Justin felt his cell phone vibrate in his pocket. He ignored it.

"This is a Dow Dynasty Defender-Class Stinger. An intergalactic spacecraft capable of Zyln propulsion—what you would call FTL," Babar explained.

Justin, not knowing how to respond, said, "Uh huh . . . Well, traveling faster than light is impossible, at least according to Einstein." Once again, his pocketed cell phone vibrated, and again he ignored it. It was something he would regret for the rest of his life.

Babar shrugged. "Do you really want me to explain it to you? Get into all the science?"

Justin shook his head no. He didn't care about the science at the moment. "Is it real?"

"What . . . you think I made this? That I worked all day, slopping a mop around hallways and bathrooms, then came back here at night and assembled this ship out of spare parts, scraps . . . rubbish lying around in here?"

"Well, putting it like that does sound a bit far-fetched."

"Justin, I realize this is overwhelming. It would be for anyone. But I assure you this is indeed a spacecraft, and—"

"Please don't say it," Justin said, offering up a pained expression.

"I am what you would call . . . an alien."

"Shit! You just had to go there, didn't you?" Justin replied. He honestly didn't know what to believe right then.

Babar smiled. "You are free to leave, Justin. I will not chase after you, nor will I harm you."

Justin, having a hard time focusing his eyes away and off of the spaceship, asked, "So that accent I thought was . . . like Pakistani, or Indian . . . is from where you come from?"

"That's right. I am from a distant star system, a world called Calunoth. Calunoth is the ruling hub for the Dow Dynasty. Thousands of worlds come under our protection."

"Protection? Protection from what?"

"Conflicts in deep space are not that different from what

is going on here on Earth. War is constant. Celestial coalitions, such as the Dow Dynasty, are always fighting over one thing or another. Disputed territorial boundaries, or even more basic aspects, such as freedom from an oppressive government body—such as that of the Empire."

"That's your enemy? This . . . Empire?"

"The Demyan Empire, yes."

Justin wasn't buying any of it; sounded way too out there, literally. He was certain there was a much simpler and more believable explanation, but he played along just the same. "And Earth? How do humans fall into this dispute?"

"The Sol system is considered a backwater planetary system, out in the middle of nowhere—frontier space; outlier civilization. Kind of a no man's land."

"Okay, sure, that sounds plausible. *Not!* Um, so why are you here? Working as a janitor at my high school?" Justin's eyes moved past the spacecraft to another area of the cellar. An ancient, black-leather couch with dingy tan stuffing coming out of the cushions, like a gutted Orca whale lying on its side. He saw a flat screen television on a rickety TV stand with shelves beneath packed with DVDs. Apparently, Babar was into old 60s Westerns—*The War Wagon, The Good the Bad and the Ugly,* the original *True Grit.* There were two hot plate burners sitting upon a makeshift counter and a refrigerator that would have looked old even back when Clint Eastwood started in his spaghetti westerns.

Babar stared silently at the teenager for several beats. "You don't believe anything I've told you, do you?"

"I don't know what to believe."

"Well, it's a long story. Leave it to say I was being chased. My ship was damaged, and I needed to stop somewhere and make repairs."

"Chased by this Empire?" Justin asked.

"Yes, by the Empire. I stole something ... took it back, rather. Something stolen earlier from the Dow Dynasty. Something more precious than you could ever imagine. Something irreplaceable."

"What was that?"

Babar hesitated before answering, then said, "At this point, it would be best to just show you," gesturing to the spacecraft behind him. Observing Justin's uncomfortable, somewhat fearful, expression, he said, "But if you are too frightened—"

"I'm not frightened!" Justin spat, his sharp outburst only confirming that he indeed was just that.

"You came here for a reason—for my help. I agreed to do so, but there are conditions on receiving such help. If you no longer require it ..."

"No, I need your help! Let's go, show me what you need to show me."

Before taking another step, Babar said, "You can't speak of this. Any of this. Promise me."

"What? That I visited an alien, plus his spaceship hidden in a basement? Sure, I can promise you that. I most definitely am not going to mention this. Who would believe me? I'm already a social outcast. I assure you, your secrets are perfectly safe with me."

Justin followed behind Babar to the aft end of the vessel. A short upward ramp led to an opening—to some kind of hatchway. Babar, not waiting for him to ascend up, disappeared into the ship.

Justin, proceeding slowly up the short gangway, entered the vessel. The compartment was small—about the size of a large shower. *An airlock*, Justin thought, continuing on. He found Babar waiting for him, within the passageway just beyond.

"Later I will give you a full tour, if you like. But first . . . the reason I invited you onboard." Babar turned right, then continued several paces, to where two passageways converged. He stopped and waited for Justin to catch up, his swiveling head trying to take it all in—the indirect lighting shining upon brushed metallic bulkheads; the black deck plates beneath his feet; tight cable bundles, running across the ceiling overhead and shimmering with colorful bursts of iridescent light—or energy. He no longer had any doubts that this was, in fact, a real spacecraft. Making a tight fist, he dug a fingernail into his own palm until the pain was too great. He wasn't dreaming.

"In here, please," Babar said, standing aside so that Justin could enter a hatchway leading into another compartment. "This is my vessel's primary hold area."

Justin was taken aback by how large the area appeared—perhaps because it was kept so dark in here. Almost all of the space's ambient lighting was being generated from two eight- or nine-foot-tall tubular containers. Both, glowing emerald green, were made of glass, or some glass-like material. Inside each tube was a liquid—evident by the tiny air bubbles percolating upward in a constant flowing pattern. Stepping closer, he suddenly realized that a single form floated within each container. Justin took several steps closer again to the tube on his left. No doubt about it—a submerged body floated within it. He shot a puzzled glance toward Babar, now at his side, who gave back an encouraging chin gesture, prompting him to move even closer.

Standing no more than a foot's distance from the glass, Justin waited for the slow- turning form to face forward—to face them. Viewed from the side, the person looked human enough: a young male, wearing some kind of form-fitting white bodysuit. Turning more, now facing them, he saw the boy's eyes—although open—were unfocussed, his mouth somewhat agape. His hair swayed and flowed within the invisible liquid currents. Justin gasped. "He looks just like . . . me!" Unconsciously, Justin placed several fingers along the side of his own face and touched the scar tissue marring his cheek. "Except . . ."

"The resemblance is quite remarkable," Babar said. You could be brothers, even twins."

"Who is he? Why is he in this tube thing? Is he still alive?"

Babar seemed hesitant to answer, as if doing so would be physically painful. He said, "He is from the Dow-Dynasty, where I come from . . . where this ship comes from. He is Prince Markus Pietra, heir to the throne. His father, Gunther Pietra, was the Magistor. What you would call a king. His mother, Tammera Pietra, the Magistra, was queen. Both are now dead. The ship carrying their stasis tubes was destroyed eighteen months ago."

Justin's eyes next moved to the stasis tube on the right. Within its glass walls floated another teenager—one who also looked human. A girl. "His sister?" he asked.

"Princess Lena Pietra. Yes, his sister. A year younger than Markus."

It didn't go unnoticed by Justin that the girl was beautiful. Her long, light-colored hair swirled about the top of her head like a glowing halo. She indeed did seem to possess a regal bearing of some kind—high, delicate, cheekbones, a small nose, and eyes, he imagined, that would have shone blue within normal lighting. Her skin looked smooth, even creamy. Justin's gaze turned downward, leaving her face. She was rather petite in size, but not delicate. Although she was slender, he could see the curve of her apple-sized breasts as he took all of her in. He imagined she was spirited—perhaps even a bit spoiled. Strangely enough, he already felt some kind of protectiveness towards her. He asked Babar, "Are they alive in there? They look alive."

"I told you, we were fleeing the Empire. Fleeing from a squadron of Demyan Rage Fighters. We were outnumbered, twenty to three. It wasn't long before our three Dow-Dynasty Stingers began fleeing... attempting to make it back to Dynasty space." Babar appeared to be back there—back in time, remembering.

"That's when the king and queen died. Their—what did you call them—Stingers, were lost?" Justin asked.

Babar nodded, back in the present moment. "It was a miracle I survived. This Stinger was heavily damaged from multiple plasma strikes, and further damaged after being struck by several small asteroids. With the hull breached in multiple locations, my crew all perished. I alone survived by sheer chance. Made it here, to Earth. Ever since, I have been making ship repairs."

"You still didn't answer me . . . are they alive?" Justin pointed to the tubes.

"This Stinger lost all power while up in space for a span of time. These hyper tubes must be kept circulating, or . . ." Babar turned his eyes away from Princess Lena Pietra. "To answer your question, yes, they are alive. Although neither one has any significant brain activity, they are not what you would call 'brain dead' . . . close to it, though."

Sadness for their hopeless state struck Justin. A tightness forming in his chest and in his heart. He didn't know these two aliens and, other than looking like the boy, he had no connection to them. Why, then, did he feel so moved? Blinking away the accumulating moisture in his eyes, he asked, "What now? You can't let them float there in these tubes indefinitely."

chapter 12

Lewis B. White

Outside of 3612 S Marshfield Avenue, Chicago

Lewis was late to the party, having had business to attend to several blocks over. One of his whores had killed a 'john' there—left him in the Bart Motel, Room 53, with his trousers bunched-down around his ankles. A small paring knife, buried to the handle, protruded out his left eye socket. Apparently, from what GG-Guns—one of his foot soldiers—had conveyed, Mandy, the whore involved, had felt disparaged when the john had commented on her abundance of facial moles, something Lewis knew Mandy was sensitive about. Without his brother Harland around to assist him, Lewis was dealing with an increased level of this kind of minutia.

Not a single hour went by without Lewis experiencing a wide range of heart- wrenching emotions: loss, frustration, and more than a little guilt—and self-recrimination. Knowing that he'd put Harland in that situation in the first place didn't help any, because every emotion he was feeling, inevitably, still led to renewed thoughts of hatred and revenge. Revenge aimed at the boy, Justin Trip, who lived at 3612 S Marshfield Avenue, where Lewis and seven of his crew currently loitered in the dark—directly across the street.

Having dealt with the messy situation over at the Bart Motel, Lewis waited for GG-Guns, now on his way, who carried the bottles in the trunk of his eight-year-old Chevy Malibu.

"How sure are you that the boy and his mother are in there?" Lewis asked, gesturing with two fingers. "Pass the puff."

Coby, short and stout—always high and half-lidded—passed a doobie the size of a thumb over to his boss. Lewis took a long drag and held it in. When he next spoke, an escaping cloud of white smoke enveloped his head.

"Been here watching the house every night, for days now," Coby said. "Kid stays hidden for the most part. Has no life other than school. Guess he's got no place to go . . . and doesn't like being out and about, I imagine, count of his face being butchered like that."

Lewis inhaled another toke then passed the still-glowing doobie back to Coby. A twin pair of car lights swung slowly around the curve at the far end of the street, momentarily lighting up the cluster of similarly dressed MP140s that were either standing on the sidewalk, or leaning against one of several parked cars. The maroon Chevy Malibu slowed as it approached. Passing them by, it pulled over to the curve. GG-Guns climbed out and directly went to the back of the car. Using a key, he let the trunk swing wide open, then left it that way as he headed over to where Lewis and Coby were standing.

Lewis queried him, "Mandy?"

GG said, "Taken care of . . ."

Coby, distressed, looked from GG to Lewis. "No! Really?" He looked ready to cry. "Grew up with the bitch. We were tight; off and on."

"Yeah, well . . . she was also crazy. None of us were safe around that hyped-up tweaker. She had to go," Lewis responded, with zero emotion in his voice. He noticed a closed curtain shift across the street, someone peeking out.

"Told you. They're in there," Coby said, looking self-righteous.

Lewis peered up at the dark sky. A moonless night. "We'll give it a few more minutes. Everyone grabs a bottle. Light, toss, then *amscray* out of here . . . got it?" Lewis spoke loud enough for the others to hear.

Coby asked, "Won't they just dash out the front door when the place starts to burn?"

Lewis didn't answer right away. Several moments passed before he slowly nodded. Pulling a worn, but well maintained Glock 17 from the back of his waistband, he racked the slide. "I'm counting on it."

Coby moved over to GG Gun's low-riding Malibu. Digging deep into his left front pants pocket, he retrieved a genuine

Zippo lighter. Lewis, upon hearing the sound of bottles clinking together, nodded his go-ahead to Coby, whose other hand now held one of the brown glass bottles. The MP140s were lined up single-file as they typically did at the Golden Corral, over on Central Avenue, on Tuesdays and Thursdays, at the all-you-can-eat buffet. Coby flicked his lighter, lighting the gasoline-saturated rag protruding from the full bottle's pierced metal lid. It immediately ignited, flaring brightly in the contrasting darkness of the night.

The others, wasting no time lighting up their own Molotov Cocktails, immediately tossed them upward. Arching high overhead in the night sky, they almost looked like a short-lived meteor shower. Most of the thrown quart-sized bottles landed on the roof of the small, two-story house. Several crashed through the home's two oversized front windows. One after another, more fireball explosions erupted. In just a matter of seconds, the entire house was ablaze with high-reaching flames.

Lewis—detached, thinking about his dead brother—heard sounds of nearby car engines starting up then speeding away. Soon he was alone. His crew, scattering fast, were already a block away. He raised his Glock and stared at the front door, waiting for it to fly open. He waited for both the mother and son to flee, perhaps tumble, coughing, onto the front lawn. The entire house was now engulfed in flames, as neighbors opened their front doors in alarm. Frantic, they were yelling out. But still, the watched door remained shut, and Lewis was denied his just revenge. He narrowed his eyes, both hatred and seething anger consuming him.

Then motion—the next-door neighbor, a man ... no, a large teenage boy with dark hair, running toward the burning house. Without hesitating, the boy kicked in the front door and rushed inside. Ten seconds, twenty seconds, thirty seconds ticked by. Lewis could hear the sound of distant sirens approaching. Motion again: the young neighbor, coughing and staggering, was back outside, carrying someone on his shoulders in a fireman's hold. Dark smoke still rose off his clothes—recently extinguished flames. It was the damn mother across his shoulders—gagging and choking and coughing. The boy carried her over to his own yard then laid her down on the grass. The front porch light illuminated one side of her scorched and blackened T-shirt.

Lewis brought his attention back to the targeted house next door. If Justin was still inside, then he was probably dead by now, little more than charred remains. He'd planned to shoot him, to have the opportunity to make momentary eye contact. One split second when the kid would realize that justice was being served.

Lewis realized he was being scrutinized by an old man, who was pointing a crooked finger in his direction. *Time to go.* He'd done what he'd come here for. *This was all for you, Harland.*

chapter 13

Justin Trip

Babar said, "These two youngsters, Markus and Lena, they are all that remain of a royal family that was adored . . . revered. You need to understand, this is a turbulent time within Dow Dynasty space. Four long years without the Pietra family's presence has been an eternity for a people that relied day-in and day-out upon the guidance of their sovereignty. Through millennia of countless wars, one catastrophe after another, the Dow Dynasty looked to their Magistor and Magistra . . . but now the Dynasty is like a boat without its rudder. Gunther and Tammera have been missed. Dissention throughout the realm is becoming more and more prevalent. Efforts to protect against Empire aggressions are failing. Each day, I come here and pray that either of these heirs to the throne miraculously shows new signs of brain activity."

Justin, feeling his cell phone vibrating again, rechecked it. It was getting late, well after midnight—why would he be getting a text message from Garrett? Probably just confirming he'd be giving Justin a ride in the morning. He slipped the phone back into his pocket, his eyes drawn to the sleeping princess. "You said that in order to help me, with the hoodlums, you wanted something from me first."

Babar looked reluctant to speak—to say what he had to say.

"Just spit it out. What do you want?"

"I need you to come with me. To venture into space with me, in this ship."

"Me?" Justin laughed. "I'm literally the last person anyone picks to do anything. Including softball or volleyball in PE." Yet he could tell by the expression on Babar's face that he was dead serious. No, it was more than that. He was desperate. Justin, suddenly nervous, glanced about the hold while trying to make sense of things. Only then did he look at the stasis-tube, at the teenage boy floating within it.

The boy, Prince Markus Pietra, looked shockingly similar to himself.

"Oh no . . . no *fucking* way, Babar."

"One year of your life. That is all that I ask of you."

"No! And it's a ridiculous idea, anyway. Look, I get it. Your Dynasty needs hope restored. But there has to be a better plan than me pretending to be some kind of royal prince. And by the way, how is it that us humans look so much like you . . ."

"Parians. We are Parians. And I cannot explain that. I know of no other sentient life within the galaxy that shares such a close genetic code as humans do with Parians"

"Fine. But did you forget that there is one definitive difference to my ... specific appearance?" Justin gestured to the scar tissue along the left side of his face.

A sudden coldness flashed from Babar's eyes. "I cannot force you to help me. Help my people. You are free to leave. Please do not speak of this to anyone. Soon, I will be gone from here. I just need a bit more time to complete my repairs."

Justin was surprised—he'd expected Babar to push his plan a little harder than that. Perhaps lay a guilt trip on him. State how he could be the single cause of untold deaths and suffering, or something like that. But he said none of that. "I guess I'll see you at school ... sorry, man, but I have a life here. My mom's here."

"I understand, Justin—"

Justin's phone again vibrated—it had been pretty much non-stop for several minutes now. "Hold on," he said, pulling the phone free of his pocket again. He didn't recognize the number. "Hello?"

"Justin! Oh God ... you have to come fast. Hurry!"

"Who is this?"

"Aila ... Garrett gave me your number. Justin, it's your mom. She's in the hospital. She's hurt pretty bad."

He tried to make sense of what she was saying. How would his mom be hurt? His heart missing a beat, his mind flashed back to the gang who'd been congregating out in front of their house. He pushed those thoughts away and tried to think. Of all people, why was Aila the one calling him?

"Um, I don't have a car ... I ..."

"Where are you? I'll come get you."

* * *

Within five minutes, Aila's little Ford Fiesta came rocketing toward him in front of the Wrigley building. Seeing him, she braked hard. Reaching over, she opened the passenger side door. "Get in!"

She stomped on the gas pedal before Justin had the door shut. In the process of buckling-up his seatbelt, he noticed a distant amber glow in the night sky, then watched the flashing lights of a fire truck as it crossed over Ashland Avenue into the residential area. He could smell smoke. "What's happening?"

Aila stared straight ahead. Brow furrowed, her eyes glistening, she shot a quick glance toward him. "Okay, I'm just going to spill it out real fast-like." Taking a deep breath, she continued, "They torched your house. Yes, your mom was inside, and yes, she is alive, but she's hurt pretty bad. Burns covering 30 percent of her body. She's in the ER, at the hospital. Oh god, I'm so very sorry, Justin."

"They? You mean Lewis? He burned our house down? Hurt my—"

"She's going to be okay. That's the important thing. After . . . surgery."

"She needs surgery?"

Aila nodded. "Skin grafts and such."

"Fuck!"

"I'm so sorry."

"Who got my mom out of the house? Who saved her? The fire department?"

"No. Garrett. He went into the burring house and brought her out. She apparently was asleep in the front room."

Justin grimaced, feeling guilty that he'd thought the worst of Garret being in a relationship with Aila. Something that was none of his business, and so much less important than what was happening now. "Is he okay?"

"Not really. He went back in again. Looking for you. But he's in better shape than your mom. May not need surgery."

"May not need surgery?" Justin stared up to the car's dingy roof liner. How was it possible that so much was happening all at once?

"At least maybe the police will get involved now," she said. "They better . . . that gang crossed a line. Nobody messes with the Tuffys and gets away with it."

Justin stared at her. Aila, looking back at him, took both hands off the wheel to raise her fists in the air.

"Garrett's name is Tuffy. Garrett Tuffy."

"Yeah . . . that's right."

"And you're a Tuffy too?"

"You didn't know my last name?"

Justin shook his head and chewed on the inside of his cheek—thinking.

"Wait. You didn't think . . ."

"I didn't think anything," he retorted back, a little too defensively.

"Garrett's my cousin. We moved here so my dad could be

closer to his sister and brother-in-law. That's why I hang out so often next door to you."

"Yeah. Right. I figured it was something like that." Justin shrugged, like it was no big deal, though his mind was reeling.

"Hold on! I'm pulling up to the ER entrance now . . . you go on in, and I'll park," Aila said, breaking hard behind an ambulance that had its rear doors open.

The hospital doors opened wide as he approached the ER. Inside was pure mayhem, as doctors and nurses and attendants scurried around. Sounds of multiple telephones ringing, heart monitors beeping, and gurney wheels squeaking across lino-leum flooring. Every examination bay was occupied with a patient.

"Mr. Trip?"

Justin eyed the two men standing before him. Both were dressed in rumpled suits. *Cops.* They looked serious. "May we have a word with you? It won't take long."

"No . . . I need to find my mom first. It'll have to wait." He dashed off, peering into each exam room. In one, an elderly black woman, an oxygen tube up her nose, was coughing. A small boy, lying in another cubicle, was getting his ankle wrapped up in an bandage by a nurse. In another, a man with severe burns on his arm was being treated by a doctor.

"Young man!" a woman called after him. "You can't be in here."

Justin figured she must be the admittance nurse—maybe she evaluated the level of trauma a person suffered, directed patients to the various exam bays. He kept walking on, checking out each cubicle. "I'm looking for my mom. Kilian Trip. Can you take me to her?" he asked the nurse.

The nurse, flustered and irritated, looked at her clipboard. Glancing up, she said, "Son, your mother's been transported up to the fifth floor. To surgery. There's a waiting room up there."

"Justin?"

Spinning around, Justin saw Garrett, lying on a gurney. Both his hands were bandaged, as was an exposed shoulder. The admitting nurse turned back, hurrying toward the admittance desk where two gurneys were being rolled in by EMTs.

Approaching Garrett, Justin took in his appearance. His hair was dusted with white flecks and his cheeks blackened with soot. "You look terrible!"

"I'm okay. I'm real happy to see you, though. Thought you were dead—that you were upstairs in your room. I couldn't get up there, the fire was everywhere."

"You saved my mom's life. Thanks! You're like a badass hero. Guess that's how you burned your hands . . . your shoulder?"

Garrett shook his head. "No, did that helping my parents and brother out of our own house."

"Your house?"

"Look around, dude. The whole block is burning. Those bangers of yours just murdered three people. I thought it was four, till Aila got you on your phone."

Justin nodded back, though not liking that Garrett had called the MP140s *his*.

The two detectives were back. "Son, we must speak with you. I realize this is a difficult time, but . . ."

Justin said to Garrett, "I'll be back. Thanks for saving my mom and for trying to save me." He turned, facing the detectives.

"My name is Detective Chad Roach, and this is Detective Juan Gomez."

"Hi," Justin responded. "Can we do this up on the fifth floor? I'll be seated in the surgery's waiting room up there. But first I need to check on my mom." Justin hurried off, leaving them for the second time.

chapter 14

Justin Trip

University of Chicago Medical Center

Justin, sitting within the drably furnished fifth-floor waiting room, was told a doctor would be out to speak to him shortly. Three others were there too. A Latino couple in their late-twenties who, from what he'd overheard them say, were there for Tomas—their young son undergoing kidney surgery. And a red-haired woman sitting alone in a far corner, who was knitting a long blue scarf. Justin didn't know her story, though she often glanced toward him—or more accurately, toward his nervous, bouncing left leg. He crossed his legs and tried to calm his mind, to not think the worst. His mother, lying on an operating table in a room just across the corridor, maybe barely clinging to life. Their house now gone, burned to the ground. He'd spent much of the late night within the confines of an alien spaceship. It was all too much. Justin closed his eyes, forcing himself to take a few long deep breaths in. He concentrated on thinking only calming thoughts, but it wasn't working.

Justin pulled out his iPhone. The perfect diversion—catch up on his portfolio of penny stocks. Basically, 'penny stocks' were dinky companies, priced in the range of $10 million to $100 million in valuation. Though that sounded like a lot of money, on Wall Street it was mere *peanuts*. The stocks typically sold for less than five bucks a share. He'd last glanced at his stocks' value mid-day in class; not much had changed prior to the market closing. But there was a new private company, one named SlapTac, that he'd had his eyes on this past week. Located in Silicon Valley, they made athletic shoes that incorporated a wide range of body-sensor technology. They now were going through an IPO.

Justin's finger hovered over the Buy button as he first checked on the company's market capitalization one more time. *Good, it was still strong.* The opening offered price was six dollars a share. Going ahead, he placed a buy order for five hundred shares—$30,000, the most he'd ever spent on a single stock purchase. He was feeling bold. His all-too-predictable life had become anything but that in recent days. This was the one thing he felt confident about, the one thing he had some semblance of control over. Justin made a mental note to stay on top of this one. The market, showing more volatility than usual, could easily go upside-down quickly.

Startled, he glanced over to see who'd plopped down next to him.

"Any word?"

"Uh, no . . . not yet. You know . . . you don't have to wait with me. I'm sure you have—"

"Shut up! Of course, I'm here to wait with you," Aila said, a tad too loudly. Noticing the woman knitting in the corner glaring at her, Aila glared back and mumbled, "Mind your own beeswax, lady."

Justin asked, "What's going on with Garrett? Is he . . . okay?"

"Yeah, first- and second-degree burns, mostly on his hands. He'll be bandaged up, mummy-like for a couple of weeks. I was with him when the doctor told him there should be no long-term complications."

A dark-skinned woman wearing scrubs entered the waiting room. Scanning the inhabitants, her eyes eventually locked onto Justin. "Mr. Trip?"

Justin and Aila stood up together. "Yes, I'm Justin Trip."

The woman, who looked to be of Indian descent, said, "I am Doctor Anand." A tiny diamond glistened beside her left nostril. "We are currently treating your mother. She sustained burns on one side of her torso, as well as the back of one arm—"

"How bad is it?" Justin asked, cutting her off but dreading her answer.

"Please do not be overly concerned. You look terrified.

Things are not as bad as we initially thought. She mostly suffered second-degree burns, which is a good thing. Any skin grafts will be minimal."

Relieved, Justin saw the two detectives, Roach and Gomez, hovering out in the corridor.

"Let me deal with them," Aila said, already storming away.

"When can I see her?" Justin asked the doctor.

Dr. Anand said, "She will be in surgery for another hour at least. Afterward, she will be heavily sedated. Best if you go on home then come back in the morning."

Justin didn't want to mention that he no longer had a home to return to; no longer possessed anything personal, other than his iPhone, the backpack holding his laptop, and the clothes on his back. He nodded, "Thank you, but I'll probably just hang out here, if that's okay."

"Yes, of course. Please, again, do not worry. We are taking excellent care of her."

He watched her leave, expecting her to disappear back through the double-doors marked Surgery. But she instead joined Aila and confronted the two detectives. "Absolutely not. Listen to me . . . leave the young man alone. Leave the fifth floor. Mr. Trip has more to worry about right now than answering your questions. Please go, off with you both!"

Justin sat down, thankful for Aila and the good doctor running interference for him. As others drifted into the waiting room, he soon overheard what the present situation was like back on Marshfield Avenue. The fire was still going strong, with at least twelve homes already destroyed. There had been three deaths. An elderly couple in their bed—a fallen overhead beam had trapped them there, where the fire overtook them. Also a little girl, who'd been saved, but had run back into her burning house to save her kitten.

Leaning forward, elbows on his knees, his face buried within his palms, Justin contemplated what he should do next. He pictured killing Lewis, in a number of creative ways: a baseball bat to the head; shooting him right in the face with a gun; cutting his throat from ear to ear with a kitchen knife; or hacking him to pieces with a jungle machete—even *better*. Justin, cloaked in hatred, became aware that someone's arm was draped over his back. He breathed in the soft scent of Aila's perfume. Other than his mother, no one had shown him any real affection before.

"You're coming home with me. My mom is already getting the guest room ready—"

"No. I can't." Standing up, he glanced about the surgery's waiting room that no longer had any available, non-occupied, seats. He hurried out into the corridor.

"What?" Aila asked, following close behind him. "It's okay . . . please, let me help you. You have nowhere to go. Your house is—"

Justin stopped short, frustrated and antsy to get away from the hospital. "I know. My house is ashes. Already got the memo."

Aila winced.

Oh God. The most beautiful, amazing girl he'd ever met—could ever hope to befriend—he'd rebuffed her again with another callous comment. "I'm sorry, Aila. I'm an asshole. Please . . ."

Aila placed a finger over his lips, "*Shush!* It's fine. I think I can be overly nurturing. Been told that before."

Justin stared back at her. Really studied her. "Why are you being so nice to me?" He touched the side of his scarred face, almost without realizing it.

"Pity? You think I pity you? You might want to give me more credit than that, Justin." Aila looked angry—angry and hurt.

He wanted to say the right thing back to her, but he didn't know how to talk to girls. He'd never had much in the way of practical experience. Instead, he merely shrugged, which, he realized, came across as being callous. *Shit!* "I have to go. I have something I gotta do." Offering her a weak smile, he headed toward the bank of elevators.

"Wait, damn it!" Aila caught up to him as he hurried in. As the door began to close, she jumped inside. "Where are you going?"

Justin shook his head. "Look, I have to go away."

"Where will you go? When?" she asked, with an incredulous expression.

"Not right away . . . but soon. Like, in a month."

Aila raised her brows.

"I can't tell you. And trust me, you wouldn't believe me even if I did."

"What about your mother? You're going to just leave her?"

Reaching the lobby level, the elevator swooshed open and

Justin stepped out with Aila at his side. "She won't be safe as long as I'm around here. The MP140s won't stop. Not until I'm either gone from Chicago or dead. As for my mom, she'll be well taken care of, I assure you. I have some money put away."

"I already know that. Everyone does. You're like some kind of teenage millionaire. Something to do with stock investments."

Justin thought about that. *Everyone knows?*

"Come on! You're on that phone of yours like 24/7. We see you tapping away on that app, Justin. There's a ton written about you online—blogs chronicling your success, the 'boy wonder' that never gives an interview."

Justin was well aware of the many social media and web postings about the wealthy, albeit hideous, teenage hermit. His identity could have been leaked by kids or even teachers at school, he wasn't sure. And he did have a good many online day-trader compadres who'd have no hesitation blabbing about his successes. He'd made it a point not to read any of it, not to let himself get distracted. It didn't seem to matter that it would be a violation of journalistic ethics, if not law, to publish a minor's name or information without his or his mother's consent—in the past year alone, his mother'd had to change their home phone number three times. He'd changed his own cell phone number at least five times, as reporters, journalists, bloggers, and random people just being assholes relentlessly pursued him.

As they approached the lobby's entrance, the doors automatically slid apart. He stopped and looked earnestly at Aila.

"Thank your mother for me, for readying up the guest room and everything else. But I have a place to stay, at least I think I do. I won't be back at school either, Aila. Not with what I have to do next."

Aila stared back at him, her eyes searching his eyes—for anything. "I know you don't know many people, Justin. Where will you go—"

"I'm not a lost puppy. I don't need rescuing. Honest, I'm okay. And I have a feeling my life is about to change. That the Justin Trip you know, or think you know, needs to become someone else."

Aila shook her head. "You know that makes no *fucking* sense, right?"

"I know that, but I need it to be true." He looked at her and in that moment, he desperately wanted to kiss her. *No . . . that would be a big, BIG, mistake!*

But suddenly emboldened, and ignoring his inner trepidations, he leaned in and kissed her cheek. She seemed surprised, but he was pretty sure that was a smile on her face.

Smiling too, he headed out into the night. *Did I really just do that?*

chapter 15

Justin took a CTA bus, billowing dark smoke from its tail-pipe, from out front of the University of Chicago Medical Center, on a route that took him within a mile of Ashland Avenue. It was one or two in the morning by the time he arrived at the hidden tear in the chain-link fence that ran around the old Wrigley's Gum Factory. He retraced his steps taken earlier. Making no attempt to keep his arrival a secret, he made even more noise than necessary. The last thing he wanted to do was surprise or startle Babar. He'd seen what physical damage the alien was capable of.

He was halfway down the narrow stairwell when he heard ruckus sounds emanating upward from below. The banging and clanging noise was so loud, he was tempted to turn around—maybe take Aila up on her offer to stay at her house. Persevering downward, he eventually stepped into the factory's sub-level basement, where he found Babar, shirtless, swinging a twenty-pound sledgehammer. His upper torso was slick with sweat as his muscles flexed and bulged beneath the glare of a hanging light bulb. This was not the first time Justin had a hard time correlating Babar to that hunched-over, crippled guy who maneuvered a fifty-gallon trash bin all around his high school.

Babar shot Justin a quick glance over his shoulder. "Be done here in a minute," he said, then resumed his high overhead whacks. Justin peered around Babar in order to get a better look at what he was hitting. What appeared to be a big metal stake, or spike, was being driven farther and farther down into the cement foundation.

Babar finally ceased his hammering and turned to face Justin. "I'm sorry about your mother. Your house."

"You know about that?"

"I could smell the smoke down here. By the time I arrived over there on foot, the whole block was in flames. I queried a fireman . . . got more of the details."

"Did he tell you Lewis and his gang did it?" Justin asked. "Did he tell you three people are now dead? Dead because of me. Because I walked home that night, got his brother killed."

Looking perturbed, Babar merely rolled his eyes. Apparently, it was a gesture not exclusively used by Earthlings. "I'm not going to stand here and listen to you play the victim, boy. You and I both know that what happened to that gangbanger was his own doing. You humans have a saying I like—live by the sword, die by the sword. The lifespan of a Chicago gang member is more often calculated in months from the point they join, not years. Anyway, *fuck* him. He had no moral compass. All living, sentient, beings must make a choice. One can either strive to better his *Harmah*, his relative sphere of influence, or ravage his relative sphere of influence. Good and evil co-exist."

Justin asked, "What's with all the hammering? That spike."

"This is for you."

"Me?" Justin laughed out loud. "What need do I have for a metal spike driven into the floor?"

Babar stared down at his handiwork. "What I need is for it to be hammered the rest of the way in." Flipping the long-handled tool up in the air, he grabbed it by its business end, extending the handle toward Justin to grab onto. "Go on, take it!"

Justin did as told. Confused, he stood still, not sure what to do with the thing.

Babar said, "You have come to two decisions. First, to learn how to defend yourself; how to protect both you and your mother from Lewis and his group. Second, you have mentally reconciled leaving your Earth world to assist me with my task within the Dow Dynasty."

Justin shrugged. "I guess . . ."

"What is with that thing you do with your shoulders?" Babar asked, looking perturbed. Mimicking him, he exaggerated how Justin kept raising and lowering his shoulders. "This is . . . what is the phrase you use . . . namby-pamby? Yes, namby-pamby. Are you so weak of mind that you cannot make a decision, either one way or another? Instead, you prefer to reveal your lack of mental fortitude? I do not like this shrugging-thing you do. Please do not do it again in my presence."

Justin was tempted to do it again, just to spite him. But he supposed Babar was right, about all of it "Okay, so you want me to—what, hammer that spike?"

"Yes. You are weak, like a small defenseless child. First, we must build up your physical muscles. Next, we can work on your mental shortcomings. Only then will you be prepared to go up against those who wish you harm. Warriors—those living on Earth and those living beyond." Babar, gesturing toward the heavens above, added, "What awaits us in the distant stars."

Justin, after taking a firm hold of the sledgehammer in both hands, found it difficult to raise it over his head. *Shit, this thing's heavy.* "I'm not going back to school. I'm living here with you 'till we go." Making pathetic attempts at striking the spike, he added, "You too should quit your job . . . concentrate instead on getting me ready."

"Hit it again. Harder. Put your back into it."

Justin tried again. And this time he did a somewhat better job of it.

"I work to eat. The food replicator is inoperable . . . on my list of things to repair."

"Don't worry about that. I'll give you enough money to buy what you need."

Babar, mentally reconciling the offer, said, "Yes, I like this idea . . . would allow me time to make repairs much faster."

"And train me, too," Justin demanded. "I want my training to be a priority, or we can forget the whole thing." Swinging the hammer higher this time, putting his back into his downward swing, he still missed the spike completely. "*Fuck*!"

chapter 16

Justin Trip

Wrigley's Chewing Gum Factory, Chicago

Awakened, Justin gasped in sudden agony. *Where am I?* Glancing around him, he remembered. He had hammered that damn spike for what seemed like for hours. He couldn't remember ever being so tired, so physically spent. Every muscle in his body so aching with pain, and he wanted to scream.

Justin, looking about the small compartment, figured it wasn't that much larger than a jail cell—maybe eight feet by eight feet. His backpack, lying on the floor, was alongside the bunk. The surrounding four bulkheads were a glossy, metallic light blue. Other than a closed hatchway door, some kind of fold-down desk surface, and the bunk he was lying upon, there was nothing else. As he readjusted his position, turning more onto his side, fresh pain shot through his entire body— limbs, torso, back, and neck. He couldn't remember how he'd got there—had Babar carried him? *I'm so pathetic . . . God, how embarrassing.*

Justin's thoughts turned to his mother. *I'll go and see her this morning.* His next thoughts were about their former home— now little more than a mound of ashes—then about his collection of shoes. They were so much more than just that; for him, they were a symbol of success. The jargon for his prized kicks included: bathing apes, kicks, kickers, scooby-doos, dookies, creepers, sambas, airs, biscuits, Jays, boats, feet-whips, coke whites, trainers . . . yet now they'd be nothing more than clumps of charcoal. He wondered if they were insured. He didn't know much about such things. He knew homeown-er's insurance covered the house burning down, but expensive shoes? Personal items? Had his mother told the insurance company about his collection? He let out a breath—none of this even mattered right now.

Babar, entering. "Tine to get up. Much to do today."

"I hate you," Justin said.

"That's fine."

"I hate your stupid face."

Five minutes later, Justin dragged his aching body from his bunk. Padding shoeless, he made his way down the main passageway in search of the bathroom. Finding it, and after some serious detective work, he figured out how to use the toilet—energy-based, not water-based. After relieving his bladder, he noticed there was the equivalent of a shower within the compact space as well. As he flushed the toilet, the bowl briefly glowed blue, making static-electric, crackling noises. Fortunately, there was a faucet tap—running water was available to wash his hands under. All in all, alien bathrooms didn't appear to be significantly different from those found on Earth.

Exiting, Justin found Babar coming down the passageway. "I will give you a tour. The vessel is small, so it won't take long." Twirling a finger in the air, he added, "Turn around, and let's start forward . . . at the bridge."

Justin led the way, down what he figured was the ship's main conduit, running the length of the vessel, then stopped several paces in front of a closed hatch.

"I have programmed your bio-signature . . . your DNA, into the central AI. Move closer and the hatch will slide open automatically," Babar said.

Justin, doing as told, watched the hatch silently slide sideways into the bulkhead. Stepping into the bridge, he found the area compact, not much larger than his sleeping compartment. A wraparound window lined the front of the room. Virtually every inch of space was filled with technology. There were four primary seats here where they were standing, plus two smaller ones which looked like they could be folded down. A table-high console ran around the perimeter of the bridge, yet nothing seemed to be turned on or operational. Justin said, "Looks complicated."

"It is," Babar said. "You will learn what each one of these

bridge sub-systems do, and how to operate them, before we leave Earth."

Justin, glancing all around the bridge. He had his doubts about that.

"Come, we will now head up to the top level."

Justin followed Babar into a small alcove, not much larger than a coat closet. Progressing through it, they exited out the other side. Justin stopped and stared around the passageway they stood in. For a moment, he thought they had emerged back into the same hall they'd just left through. But now, noticing slight differences—like hatchway doors located at different locations and a slightly higher ceiling—he realized they somehow had emerged one flight up. "Will I learn how we just did that, too?"

"You will be provided any necessary knowledge. Do not concern yourself. That will be the easy part."

Justin realized the hatchways slid open only when faced head-on. Simply passing by a hatchway did not trigger it to slide to one side. Babar provided him a brief explanation of what each passed compartment was used for. First was a small medical bay, then an armory of sorts, holding multiple rows of assorted weaponry. "That's a lot of guns," he said.

"The nominal crew capacity for a Dow Dynasty Defender-Class Stinger is fifteen," Babar said. Justin nodded as he perused the assortment of weaponry. He assumed they were energy rifles of some sort. Babar next showed him where the mess was situated, with its adjacent kitchen. A number of integrated microwave, oven-sized appliances lay along one bulkhead.

"Food replicators . . . still not operational," Babar said.

His remark prompted Justin's stomach to gurgle. "How about we hit the Dunkin' Donuts down the street after the tour?" he suggested.

"You need to pay more attention to what you put into your body."

"Well, maybe we can make a stop at the supermarket, instead. After hammering most of the night away, I need calories."

"You will be properly fed, Justin—a diet I will personally take charge of, for your optimum health and strength."

Justin didn't like the sound of that; he was picturing a plate full of broccoli and cauliflower. "Should I give you some money? I have some cash . . ." Unslinging the pack from his shoulder, Justin unzipped one of the pockets where he kept his wallet.

"Yes. I have already informed the high school that I will no longer be 'slopping a mop' there, as you so tactlessly put it earlier."

"Really? You quit?"

"Yes. We have much to accomplish in a short amount of time."

They had already discussed much of this, but hearing Babar had taken such definitive action reinforced this new reality for Justin. Soon, he would be traveling into space. Impersonating the kid floating comatose in that hyper tube—the prince, the heir to the throne. *Oh God . . . what on earth have I gotten myself into?*

Justin said, "Our agreement is that you show me how to deal with Lewis and his crew. I have a score to settle."

"Revenge is—"

"Please, I don't need a lecture, or some platitude on the evils of revenge. The guy burned down my house and put my mother in the hospital."

"I was only going to say that revenge, in my experience, is often a healthy and necessary endeavor. One that will work well with your training."

"Oh, okay, that's good." Justin, opening up his wallet, withdrew about half of the bills. "Here's five Benjamins . . . if you need more, let me know."

Babar took the bills and studied them. "Thank you. This should make the next few weeks more . . . comfortable. I will purchase necessities at the market later today."

Continuing on with the tour, Babar showed Justin the Environmental Systems compartment, and then, finally, the brains of the craft—which he referred to as the Neural Center—where the Neural Dome was located. Inside this aft compartment was a circular dome, one that appeared to be more organic than machinelike. It was taller than Justin and approximately seven feet across. Babar gestured he should follow him through an opening along one side. Once inside, Justin could see various parts of the fleshy dome lit with tiny flashes, bursts of light coming on here and there within one select area, below a translucent surface. Justin reached out a hand to touch it.

"Do not touch the membrane! Not ever," Babar scolded.

"Okay. Sorry, uh, looks like synapses in there," Justin commented.

"A good analogy," Babar said. "Normally, this dome would be 100-percent aglow, with trillions of intellectual processes taking place, but now, no more than 10 percent of the Neural Dome is operational." He turned to Justin. "This is where I will be spending much of my time over the next few days. Like with those two hyper tubes, the disruption in the power supply has taken its toll here as well."

"But it can be repaired?" Justin queried.

"It can repair itself. I just need to accelerate the process."

Leaving the ship's artificial intelligence area, which didn't seem all that artificial, Babar led Justin down a narrow, perpendicular hall. He pointed to a low, three-foot-square access panel located on the bulkhead. "This is the conduit to the starboard anti-matter powerplant, mounted at the end of the wing assembly just beyond. There is an identical wing powerplant configuration located on the port side."

Heading back toward the bow of the vessel, Justin saw something he hadn't noticed earlier. Shiny and black, about a foot-and-a-half wide and a foot tall, and egg-shaped, the device was snugly tucked into a small alcove. "What's that?" Justin asked.

Babar glanced at it. "The one crew member, other than myself, to survive. RP9, a drone-bot; it's on my list to reactivate. Maybe later today."

"Are we done with the tour?" Justin asked.

"Yes. Although we still have much to do."

"Okay. But first I need to go to the hospital and see how my mom's doing."

chapter 17

Justin Trip

University of Chicago Medical Center

An hour later, walking through the lobby doors of the University of Chicago Medical Center, Justin headed for the front desk, pretty sure his mother was up on the fifth floor somewhere. Still, he needed to check first, in case she'd been moved.

"Good morning," an overly cheery, middle-aged woman said, as he approached the counter. Her brass nameplate read Pricilla Stark. Her gray hair was worn in a tight bun atop her head, her lipstick a bright red color. Justin noticed she'd colored outside the lines of her mouth—perhaps to make her lips seem fuller? Or maybe she'd just hurried this morning getting ready for work.

"Morning. I'm looking for Kilian Trip's room."

Startled, noting his scarred face, she self-consciously made eye contact with Justin, who was used to this reaction. "Are you a family member?" she asked.

"Yeah, her son."

The receptionist tapped at her keyboard, then read something on her monitor. "Here we go . . . Kilian Trip. She is on the sixth floor. In our Burn and Wound Center. You'll have to go up there to see if they'll let you in to visit her."

"All right, thanks."

Justin, going up in the elevator alone, took the opportunity to stretch his back, turning his torso to one side then the other. He'd noticed, when leaving Babar's spacecraft, that another four metal stakes had been partially driven into the concrete floor. He'd considered not returning—getting a room at a Motel 6, instead—but he'd made an agreement and needed to follow through with his end of the bargain.

Reaching the sixth floor, Justin followed the directional signs to the Burn and Complex Wound Center. At the counter was a male nurse, wearing light-blue scrubs.

"Who you here to see?" the nurse asked, without looking up.

"Kilian Trip . . . I'm her son."

"You have a cold? Recovering from the flu, anything like that?"

"No."

"Any kind of virus?"

"No."

"Don't touch anything. Patients are at risk for infection. Doctor's with her at the moment."

"Okay. Um, should I wait here?" Justin asked, looking around for a place to sit.

"No, head on over. He'll send you away if he doesn't want you there." The nurse gestured off to Justin's right. "Go on, her bed is down that way."

In addition to individual treatment stations, Justin noticed the burn center had four enclosed rooms, their floor-to-ceiling windows facing toward the nurse's station. Every bed within the burn unit was occupied. One of the patients was so heavily bandaged that Justin couldn't even make out if it was a man or a woman. Pained moans emanated outward through the plate-glass window. Justin forced himself to look away. He had little doubt that whoever lay within there, the odds were the patient was one of his neighbors, victim of the same fire. Like a sodden wet blanket, new feelings of guilt weighed heavily on his back and shoulders. But his feelings quickly turned to anger. *I'm going to kill you, Lewis . . . maybe not today, or tomorrow, but soon.*

A sweet, antiseptic, hospital odor permeated the ICU. He next passed a treatment unit whose curtain was only partially closed. Peering inside, Justin found his mother sitting up in bed—a doctor, tablet in one hand, was speaking to her.

"Justin! Come in . . . I've been worried sick about you." Her face showed her concern. Grimacing in pain, she reached out her hand to him. "Come here, sweetie."

On seeing his bandaged-up mother, looking so small and vulnerable, Justin found it nearly impossible to breathe. His vision blurred as tears brimmed his eyes. Raw emotion, only moments before held firmly in check, now bubbled-up to the surface, out of control. He hurried to her bedside to receive a one-armed embrace, now bawling uncontrollably. A sudden memory flashed within his mind—memories of being a lost, despondent, six-year-old at K-Mart, eventually reunited with his mother.

"Hey, hey, hey . . . I'm fine! Honest, sweetie, I'm going to be okay."

Justin, who'd buried his head deep into her pillow, felt her kiss the top of his head. And just as quickly as that, the raw deluge of emotions engulfing him dissipated. He stood up straight, suddenly feeling stupid, and self-consciously aware of the doctor's presence nearby. Sniffling, he swiped at his runny nose.

The physician plucked several tissues free from a box on the table. Handing them over, he said, "Hi Justin, I'm Doctor Kline. Your mother has several pretty bad burns. Mostly first- and second-degree burns, but a third-degree burn too, along her upper left torso. Last night we operated on her, performing a single skin graft. Taking skin from her upper left thigh area, we transplanted it to an area on her ribcage."

Justin, letting out a held-in breath, nodded. "Sounds painful."

Kilian glanced at the hanging IVs. "Morphine drip ... but yeah, it's going to hurt for a while. Tell me, honey, where did you stay last night?"

"Um, with a friend."

Kilian's brows drew together. "What friend?" She knew Justin was only a step away from closing down.

"Actually, the high school janitor," Justin responded back, not thinking.

"What? A janitor? That sounds creepy, to say the very least."

"No, it's fine. His name's Mr.—his name's Babar. He has a nice family, and they live nearby. Anyway, I couldn't stay with Garrett. His house—"

"I know. The whole block's gone."

"I'll let you two talk. Nice meeting you, Justin," the doctor said, disappearing through the gap in the bedside curtain.

"He saved your life. Garrett, I mean ... you know that, Mom?"

His mother nodded, blinking away fresh moisture from her eyes. "Garrett was discharged an hour ago. Came by with his parents to check on how I'm doing. The girl, Aila, was with them."

Justin felt half his face grow hot when she added, "You know ... she's his cousin, not his girlfriend."

"Yeah, I know," he said back too quickly. "And don't look at me like that."

"She said she gave you a ride, asked if you had a girlfriend."

"Mom, can we drop it?" he said, forcing his facial expression to show only annoyance, instead of hope.

"I don't want you staying with—"

"Babar."

"Whoever. The school janitor. My sister's on her way here now. You'll get a hotel room—"

"Mom, stop! Can you please just listen to me?"

"What?"

"You're going to be a patient here for a while. Right?"

"At least a week. They need to watch for infection—"

"I'm going away. Maybe for a long time."

His mother stared at him, suddenly speechless.

"I'm leaving you enough money to buy a new house. Don't argue with me about that. Seven hundred and fifty thousand dollars will be deposited into your checking account by end of day tomorrow. Plus, you'll have free access into my account should you need more."

"Just stop . . . I don't understand. Where are you saying you're going—and without my permission?"

"First of all, I don't need your permission."

Even before his words passed through his lips, his mother was squeezing her eyes tightly shut, a pained expression on her face. "Oh god . . . Today's your birthday. Your present. It was under my bed," she whispered.

Justin smiled, "What did you get me?"

"New pair of kicks . . . the Marque Le' Fonts you were eyeing the last few weeks."

"Way too expensive, Mom!"

She shrugged. "I feel bad, sweetie. You have nothing to open. Eighteen is a very special year. You're a man now."

Yeah, one who only moments ago was bawling tears into your pillow.

"Now what's this about you going away?"

He'd been thinking about that. What bullshit story to come up with—one that would be believable to his mom. Justin replied, "Well . . . I've joined the service. The Marines!"

"Seriously? Since when have you ever been even the slightest bit interested in military service? Not that there's anything wrong with that. But, Justin, I just don't . . ." She looked away perplexed, shaking her head. Frustrated, she said, "What about college? What about finishing fucking high school?"

Justin rarely ever heard his mother swear. It took something monumental for her to rise to that level of anger.

"It's all part of the program. I'll be getting my GED—and college, too, eventually. Mom, I need to make some changes in my life, to stop being such a hermit. I also need to get far away from the MP140s. Come on, they leveled an entire street because of me, Mom." He saw she wanted to argue with him, though clearly recognized there was truth in what he said.

"Well, we can talk about all this later. You've dropped a lot on me in a short amount of time."

"I know. Sorry, Mom, I'll be back . . . I'm still not leaving town for a while."

She only nodded, deep in thought.

Justin kissed her cheek. "I'm going to put an even million into your account. Go hog-wild, Mom. Get us a nice house. I don't want to come home to some ghetto-hut."

"We'll talk about it later." She offered up a weak smile. "I'm tired. Drugs kicking in. Come see me later, okay?"

"Tomorrow." Justin turned, ready to leave.

"Sweetie?"

"Yeah, Mom?"

"Happy birthday. I mean it. Do something nice for yourself today."

Justin, recalling the addition of those new stakes awaiting him at the factory, said, "I'll try. Thanks."

chapter 18

Prince Markus Pietra

Mountains on Calunoth—Order of Relian High Priests.

Four-and-a-half years earlier.

S oon after the accident, when Markus was still twelve, he was sent away. Sent off to the desolate mountains of Calunoth where, hopefully, he would learn humility. Find some measure of kindness in his rebellious heart. Initially, the Relian High Priests, in the Shan Bahn Mountains, hadn't wanted to take in the sour-faced boy. Only after weeks of pleading by Magistra Tammera Pietra had they finally acquiesced. On rare occasions, those of sovereign blood were permitted within, to be trained outside of the priest's religious order. But Markus Pietra needed to prove himself worthy, in order to stay. What the Relian High Priests did not know was that Markus welcomed whatever hardships they could burden him with. Beyond his own self-hatred, Mahlnie was never far away from his thoughts.

Markus quickly discovered he no longer was recognized as a prince within the Shan Bahn Mountains. In fact, for months, he was treated little better than a stray dog. And, like a stray dog would, he rebelled—disrespecting both priests and other students alike. He expressed his inner torment the only way he knew how, through utter alienation of any he came in contact with, inflicting upon others what he felt deeply within himself. His shoulders, and the backs of his legs, would carry the many scars from spin-reed beatings the rest of his life. But forcing humbleness and humility into him—through beatings and rough punishment—was unsuccessful, for the most part. As were their daily, high-order spiritual teachings. Although he somewhat liked these quiet, introspective periods, they did little to alter his dark, brooding countenance.

Markus was issued worn, frayed, hand-me-down, silken robes. Called a *Tasarra*, the garment was named after the saffron-colored dye used in its making. It was during his assigned periods of meditation that Markus finally learned to rein in his inner rage. Although he despised most of the religious order's priests, he found he could somewhat tolerate both Master Shornha and Master Clearr.

Much later, introduced to the ancient fighting techniques of Relian Wham Dhome, Markus was able to push beyond the limits of his physical abilities. Pain and exhaustion rarely deterred him. He had an innate will to persevere through obstacles intended to both hamper and discourage young students. But for Markus, such hardships emboldened him even more. As days turned into weeks, and weeks into months, then into years, he eagerly consumed the intricate fighting techniques with a kind of desperate hunger—one that both intrigued his priest teachers and made them uneasy. Markus was ever the first one to withdraw to his simple sleeping den, which was more like a thatch-covered timber hut open on three sides to the elements. At night, as he rested upon his worn floor mat, draped over his back and shoulders was a frayed pelt, some kind of animal hide. It was never adequate in keeping him warm at that high mountain altitude.

Halfway into his third year of tenure, Markus was allowed to compete within the Ring of Ten Fires. Here, situated within the central stadium, massive dark bronze caldrons blazed brightly with tall flames that were never allowed to be extinguished. Some seventy feet overhead, the flag of the Relian Order, its crest a saffron-colored open palm on a field of green, flapped and snapped in the high mountain winds. The site was where weekly hand-to-hand and edged weapons combat competitions took place. To date, Markus was undefeated, going up against students of a similar age within the Ring of Ten Fires. Even the Relian Wham Dhome masters found the young warrior to be a cunning, relentless adversary. All the while, Markus attributed his growing successes there to Mahlnie. In his mind, she was the one deserving either the praise, or accolades, bestowed upon him. Concerned, the high priests would periodically ensure that the boy-prince sometimes lost too, either at the hand of an older, more accomplished student, or against the expertly trained hand of a master priest. Markus was never allowed to become too confident in his abilities—to become overly full of himself.

Upon the anniversary of Mahlnie's death, Markus, now finished with the day's lessons, received word by messenger. Unsealing the scroll, he began reading, recognizing his mother's neat, hand-written words upon the now partially unfurled scroll. He would be leaving the religious order the next morning. Some part of Markus longed to go home. He missed his mother and father terribly. He even missed his annoying younger sister, Lena. Strange, considering they'd never been close. In fact, they had fought constantly, like two rabid slog-banshees with their tails knotted together.

Markus continued reading on, which evoked competing emotions of sadness and exhilaration within him. No, he would not be returning home to Cristine Castle—too soon for that. But due to his father's influence, and the forgiving nature of Admiral Tike, he had been accepted into the freshman class of the Dow Dynasty's elite Space-Flight Academy this year, his fifteenth.

* * *

To say his attendance at the academy was controversial would be a gross understatement. The teenage boy carried the calamity of young Mahlnie Ringfind's death with him wherever he went.

To many there, the privileged, arrogant prince was little more than a murderer. Mahlnie's death, as the daughter of a wealthy dignitary, plus the discord that followed, had placed the Dow Dynasty's ruling sovereignty in a terrible light. Markus, not sure how much money had been paid under the table to allow his attendance at the academy, knew it must have been substantial. But he couldn't have cared less—to fly FareCat Fighter crafts, or to be a part of a Stinger gun ship's bridge crew, was all he'd ever wanted.

Delivered to Grindhold Space Station by a young, recently graduated academy cadet, Markus didn't know what to expect. He did what he was told to do and went wherever he was told to go. But all hope he'd had of simply blending in was quickly dashed due to his noticeable, cleanly shaved head from the years spent at the strict religious order.

The space station, a formidable-appearing structure outside, had eighty-eight separate levels. Everything was over-sized—bulkheads and expansive windows towering thirty feet overhead, where high-arched ceilings were a jumble of criss-crossing pipes, cables, and air ducts. Within minutes of being dropped off, Markus was directed to the forty-fourth level, where hundreds of new cadets were being ushered from one line to another. Over the course of several hours, he was first examined by a medical bot, then tested—both psychologically and intellectually—by military personnel. Verifications were made, via random Q-and-A tests, that he'd received the necessary MemSnap learning modules, which every child received over the course of their lives. Thus far, Markus did not recognize anyone from Cristine Castle, nor from its nearby rural sur-roundings, but that was to be expected. The Dow Dynasty was vast. Any number of planetary systems sent their young cadets to Grindhold Space Station—although there were a number of other space academies that served the same purpose—to train young boys and girls to become part of the elite Dow Dynasty Space Force.

By mid-day, Markus hadn't made friends so much as new acquaintances—those who shared their nervousness, unpre-pared for their new life here. He learned there were close to three thousand attendees at the academy, and that of the five hundred freshmen recruits now entering, half would be cut loose within the first few weeks. By the time the rest gradu-ated, at age eighteen, only a mere 20 percent of those who'd enlisted would still remain. By mid-day, Markus was mentally exhausted. He realized that life spent within this space station would be challenging. Prior to arriving, he'd come to relish the quiet mountain sanctuary among the Relian High Priesthood, free to feel the cool breezes on his face, smell the big cauldron fires, and looking up, see Calunoth's two sister suns high in the sky overhead. Here, everything he saw was in a monotone, metal-gray in color.

The final admittance line led to a dispensary, where each cadet was handed their standard-issue kit. Each kit contained two uniforms, undergarments, a belt, boots, a cadet cap, and a cuffcom unit—assembled by procurement bots earlier. Even the cuffcom units were, supposedly, pre-programmed—personalized for each individual cadet prior to issuance.

Markus grabbed ahold of the curved, thin, rectangular slice of blue-tinted crystal and placed it atop his left wrist. Over the last several minutes, he'd watched as a number of recruits had done the same thing. Using the thumb and forefinger of his other hand to slightly compress together both ends of the crystal, he watched as a semi-transparent, three-inch display band quickly encompassed his entire wrist. Although he knew the thing was only energy-based, the device felt actually real, felt solid. Tapping on the cuffcom's face, he watched as a series of text lines begin to scroll across it. Instructions for what he was to do next.

Leaving the dispensary, slinging his duffle bag over one shoulder, Markus suddenly felt the skin on the back of his neck bristle. He was being watched—a cultivated sensory observation he'd learned from his years at the religious order. He scanned the open floor space. A hundred similar-appearing boys and girls were rushing this way and that, a blend of unfamiliar faces. But across the expanse, just leaving after his psych evaluation, was none other than Ballard Ringfind—once his best friend, and Mahlnie's brother.

chapter 19

Justin Trip

Bridgeport, Chicago

Having officially turned eighteen, Justin wasted no time downloading one of the more popular ride-sharing apps and scheduling a pickup out in front of the hospital. He had some business to take care of that morning—a trip to his bank, where he'd ensure his mother had adequate funds in her account to purchase a new house or anything else she might need for the next year or so that he'd be gone. After that, he'd find a Kohl's or a J.C. Penney for several changes of clothes. Then he'd find a supermarket—he needed toiletries, especially a toothbrush.

It was just after two o'clock in the afternoon when Justin's Uber driver dropped him off down the street from the Wrigley's Gum Factory on Ashland Avenue. Even though it was still daytime, he was conscious of having so many overstuffed retail bags, along with several grocery bags clutched in his hands and hanging down from his arms. Ensuring no one was around, he wasted no time ducking between the gap in the fence and hurrying inside the old building.

Earlier, he had taken a detour down Marshfield Avenue. One side of the entire block was little more than smoldering ruin, looking like a war zone. He'd told the driver to slow down when he reached 3612.

"Oh boy . . . pretty bad, what happened here," said the older man, wearing a worn and frayed Cubs baseball hat. "You know anyone who lived here?"

Justin said, "Yeah . . . me."

The driver had looked to the pile of shopping bags next to Justin. "Real sorry, young man. Maybe see if the app will compensate you for the ride? I wish I could."

"Nah, but thanks just the same."

Now, he descended the stairs and found Babar at work on the starboard wing powerplant. The housing had been removed, and the inside mechanical workings were exposed. Babar, holding a piece of equipment in one hand that Justin didn't recognize, said, "Justin . . . I hope you are ready to start your training. It is already late in the day."

"Yeah, sorry. Had some things to take care of. But yeah, I'm ready. More than ready."

"Set down your purchases and help me reposition this drive casing."

Justin did as told, moving to one side of the metal casing, and together they hefted it up.

"Hold it up there in position while I fasten it in place," Babar said, now using a small power tool to drive small clasps (the equivalent of alien screws, Justin surmised) into various holes located around the metal casing.

With the power plant all buttoned up, Babar turned his attention to Justin's shopping bags.

"I'll go store these things in my quarters . . . is that okay?"

Babar nodded. "Make haste young man, we're burning daylight."

Yeah, thanks, John Wayne, he wanted to say. "I'll be right back." Moving around to the stern of the ship, he eyed the four metal stakes in the concrete. His muscles still hurt from yesterday's hammering. He was tempted to slow his pace, but he didn't. The vision of his burned-to-the-ground house was still vivid in his consciousness. No, he'd do what he needed to do to make Lewis pay. He'd drive a hundred metal stakes into the floor if he had to.

He found his quarters and put the bags on his bunk. Before heading out, he looked about the small confines. This would be his home for the foreseeable future. Leaving, he decided to make a quick detour into the ship's primary hold area. He wanted to see the reason, or object, of his forthcoming trip into space. He entered the darkened space and stopped in front of the first stasis tube. The boy was half turned away from him. Justin noticed now that, although they did look remarkably alike in terms of their facial structures, their anatomies were not all that similar. This Prince Markus was muscular. Hell, Justin could see the guy had well-defined biceps and pecs. Shit, he had an actual six-pack beneath that formfitting suit.

As if influenced by some invisible gravitational force, Justin's attention was pulled to the other stasis tube. And there she was. Her lithe form was facing him, her long blonde hair swirling around the top of her head. Her eyes were open. It saddened him that she, like her brother, was brain dead. *What a shame,* he thought. And then he saw it. Or had he? A momentary flicker of something. The briefest of moments where her eyes narrowed. There was something—intelligence? Recognition?—in there, behind those pretty eyes. And just as quickly, it was gone. Justin stared at her for several more moments, watching as her form pivoted away from him. His eyes took in the rest of her. Like her brother, she too was in amazing physical shape. His eyes lingered, traveling the length of her. She had the most incredible rear end he'd ever seen. Not too small and not too big. Curved, and he was certain just looking at it, as firm as volleyball—

"We have much to do today," a voice exclaimed several paces behind him.

Justin was startled by the intrusion. He spun around to face Babar, feeling as if he'd been caught doing something he should. A creepy peeping tom—a nighttime stalker lurking outside a pretty girl's window. "Sorry, I just wanted to see them again."

He nodded. "I don't blame you for that, boy."

"You know, for an instant, I thought I saw..." Justin

stopped mid-sentence. "Never mind. Probably just my imagination. What's up for my training? More hammering?"

"Perhaps later. I need to, uh . . . expedite our timeframe."

"Why? What's happened?"

"More of the Neural Dome has regenerated. Ship systems are coming back online, including the OCI . . . the Organic Cognitive Interface, which allows the crew to communicate verbally with the Neural Dome."

"Okay. And why does that expedite our timeframe?"

"The OCI has informed me that the ship's long-range sensors are back online. That's the good news. The bad news is that two Empire vessels are en route to the Sol planetary system."

"How long before they reach us?"

"Maybe a week."

Justin thought about that. "Just curious . . . how, again, does a ship travel across the galaxy faster than the speed of light, defying the laws of known physics?"

"Actually, the laws of physics cannot be defied within a lone, single dimension. Your scientists are just now exploring the relation of time and space to virtual, quantum states. How about we postpone this discussion for another time? Soon, you will have many answers to such questions."

Justin nodded without knowing what he meant. "Anyway, we had an agreement, though. A week . . ."

"I will keep my end of the bargain. Now that the OCI is operational, much of your training will take place on the upper deck in close proximity to the Neural Dome. At least on the mental training side of things."

Justin was visibly irritated. "In a week, I'll be gone. But my mother will still be here. She'll want to stay here, in her neighborhood. I cannot risk Lewis getting to her. And in a week, I won't be able to deal with him. Hell, as things stand, I couldn't go up against an eight-year-old little girl." Justin held up an arm and flexed a near-non-existent bicep. His mind flashed to the tuned-up muscular bodies of the prince and princess floating within their respective stasis tubes, and it infuriated him more.

chapter 20

Justin entered the vessel via the aft hatchway, several strides behind Babar. They were greeted by a kind of omnipresent, surround-sound, pleasant woman's voice. Justin didn't understand the language. Babar said, to no one in particular, "OCI, speak Earth American English for our guest."

"Apologies. Welcome back, Loham Babar, Noble-Fist to the aristocracy. Greetings, young visitor . . . Justin Trip, student, and adopted son of one Kilian Trip."

Babar spoke over his shoulder as he moved forward down the passageway. "She's still reinitializing . . . in time she'll forgo the formal receptions."

Justin said, also to no one in particular, "Hello. Nice to meet you, um . . . what's her name, Babar?"

"We're not big on giving inanimate objects names like people here on Earth do."

He thought about that. He said, "Really?"

There was no immediate reply. Ten seconds later, she spoke.

"Apologies, but guests do not have the administrator rights necessary to impart official nomenclature."

Babar and Justin passed into and out of the forward lift. Justin didn't like Babar's bemused, seemingly all too superior smile. Justin said, "Well, even though I'm just a guest here, I think she should have a nickname . . . I'm sure you know what a nickname is."

"I know what a nickname is, yes." He looked annoyed at the distraction. "Fine, how about we refer the OCI as Ocile . . . O, C, I, L, E . . . that work for you?

Justin smiled, "Yeah . . . hey, nice to meet you, Ocile."

Babar stepped aside to let Justin enter the Neural-Center. Justin audibly gasped. The entirety of the Neural Dome was now aglow. Thousands upon thousands of synapses were flashing, firing, deep within its translucent membrane.

"Go ahead . . . enter the dome," Babar said.

Justin did as asked, but this time the experience had a far more intimate feel to it. He was aware that this, whatever the hell it was, was indeed alive. He was an organic being now deep inside of another organic being. His being here, within it, was so much more than, say, a mechanic working under the hood of a Dodge Minivan.

"Let's have a seat," Babar said.

"Like, here on the deck? Right here?"

Babar sat down, crossed his legs, and looked up to Justin. "Sit."

Justin did as asked, taking a seat and crossing his legs. He looked up and all around. He hadn't realized how amazing the colors were. Like a surrounding sky with hues of aqua blue, pink, and violet. There were flashes all about them, like synapse sparklers—this was truly one of the most beautiful things he'd ever seen. Ever experienced. So immersed in it all, he hadn't realized Babar was speaking to him.

"Justin—you need to listen to me now."

"Oh, sorry. What?"

"We are at a crucial, pivotal juncture."

"Okay . . ."

"One where soon, turning back will no longer be an option. What I'm saying is, you can still change your mind. We can stop this. You leave here now and live out your life—"

Justin saw the seriousness on Babar's face. That and concern. So, Justin did what Babar was asking of him. Contemplated what going forward would really mean. Was he really ready to do this—become someone different, embark on a journey to somewhere unimaginable?

He said, "No. I'm not going anywhere. Just tell me what I'm supposed to do."

Babar, looking more serious than Justin had seen him, was inspecting his face, his features. The alien's eyes were boring into him, "Where I come from, on my world of Calunoth, which is the hub of the Dow Dynasty, we as a species are considerably more technologically advanced. But our evolution was not so dissimilar to that of humans here on Earth. As you can see, humans are similar to my species, to Parians. Our DNA is 99.92 percent identical."

"So that's what you are? Your genetic species . . . is Parian?"

"That's right. And this Neural Dome that surrounds us, it too is a genetic match to Parian DNA."

"Okay . . ."

In time, within the next seventy-five years I would guess, the acquisition of advanced knowledge here on Earth will no longer require twelve, or sixteen, or more years of one's life. School, such as it is now, will no longer be necessary. In fact, it would be considered a colossal waist of valuable time."

"I could have told you that now," Justin said.

Babar ignored his joke. "Within a single strand of DNA, an immense amount of data information can be stored. Your scientists are just now unlocking the fundamental mechanics of such science. But it will be years before they progress from experimenting with linear storage techniques to sequencing the near-limitless aspects of *quantum* molecular DNA applications. Think organic packets of information, where there's a transfer of zettabytes of information into a subject. I'm talking transfers taking place within picoseconds or even femtoseconds."

"I get it," Justin said. "Yeah, silicon chips will soon be a thing of the past. And we still have a long way to go before we're as advanced as you, um, Parians are. Got it."

Babar smiled, but the smile did not reach his eyes. "For you to accomplish the things you want to accomplish here, before we leave, and for you to be of use to me in space, you will need to fundamentally change. I'm talking DNA. Genetically."

Justin thought about that. He didn't like the way that sounded. "Like, change from being human to something else?"

"That is correct. You would no longer be 100 percent human."

"Well, what would that be like for me? Like, a third arm growing out of my forehead?"

"No. Of course not. But you would be, well, something new. A hybrid. Part human, part Parian."

"And my body wouldn't like, reject, this alternate DNA?"

"No. Not in the least."

"And you would introduce these new, *learnings,* into my body, my physiology, somehow?"

"More or less. Via a device called a MemSnap. We have found that the best method for introducing new or altered DNA memories into a subject is via a virus. Through the respiratory system." Babar held up a small, square item about a half-inch thick and no larger around than a postage stamp. He positioned the thing under his nose and, using his thumb and forefinger, squeezed it together. It audibly *snapped.* A bright blue mist shot forth and lingered beneath Babar's nose like a self-contained cloud. He breathed in sharply, making a sniffing sound in the process. He wiggled his nose and blinked his eyes a few times. "That's it. The virus has been introduced into my physiology. MemSnaps contain an immense amount of knowledge. For instance, you could gain the know-how for piloting this vessel." Babar clicked his fingers. "Just like that. You could have full access to in-depth knowledge that you never had to learn through any of those rudimentary methods you're used to."

Justin said, "And this is how people typically learn on

Calunoth? MemSnaps, depending on the type of information they require at the time?"

"That's right. But it is tightly regulated. There are limits to what the brain can handle. And we are careful what children are allowed to learn at various points in their development. Typically, trained physician specialists administer the process. This is all commonplace throughout much of the Dow Dynasty—for thousands of worlds, actually."

"Yeah, I get it. Okay, I'm good. Let's do it."

Babar held up a palm. "Hold on. There's more. And here's where you may still want to back out of this agreement."

"Go on, but I've already agreed to you making me into some kind of alien hybrid. What could be bigger than that?"

Babar looked reluctant to continue. Then he said, "Markus . . . Prince Markus Pietra. I wish to attempt something, well—something that is illegal. Unconscionable. Outlawed throughout the galaxy."

"I take it I'm not going to like this part of the agreement."

"Perhaps not. But it will be essential for my plan to work. And without doing this, I foresee the potential fall of the Dow Dynasty. I foresee great misery and death to millions if not billions of people."

"So, you're going to guilt me into doing this?"

"Feeling guilt would be your choice."

Justin breathed in the musky air within the Neural Dome. He wondered what Ocile thought of all this. "All right. Tell me the rest of it."

"My people are demoralized and floundering without their

sovereign leaders. A civilization void of hope will not, cannot, prevail over the powerful Empire. I fear the Dow Dynasty could fall, and fall soon."

"You've already mentioned that."

"So you will become Prince Markus Pietra."

"Yeah, we talked about that, too. We look a lot alike. I'll be an imposter—"

Babar was already shaking his head, "No, more than that. You'll be, partially, him. You'll have some, many, of his thoughts . . . his memories."

"Shit . . . that's weird. That's really weird."

"It is the only way this can work."

"Well what about my own thoughts. My own memories?" Justin asked, not liking this latest development.

"What about them?" Babar asked.

"What will happen to my memories and thoughts?"

"You'll still have them. You'll still be you. Well, I'm fairly certain you will."

"Fairly certain! You're not sure?"

"This, what I'm talking about, has not been done. At least not for many years. Whatever experiments were undertaken, all those years ago . . . that data has been destroyed. Banished from the realm's archives forever."

"Obviously not. Babar, you're asking me to die and let someone else take over my . . . beingness."

"No-no-no, that is not what I'm asking. You will still be you. You will still be Justin. In charge of your thoughts, your life. You'll be *Justin* with another aspect to himself. More memories.

You'll have more abilities. But not Markus's personality—not his spirit. I would not do that to you. Trust me on that."

Justin looked past Babar toward the hatchway, "I thought the prince was brain dead. How—"

"The prince's brain is, in fact, no longer functioning. Damaged beyond repair. That does not mean all or some of his memories are completely gone." Babar looked contemplative. "Think of it this way . . . it's like an artist who's long dead, but their paintings, and the impact of their artwork, still exist. Or how the people and tools used to construct a wonderful old building no longer exist, but that structure is still there."

"I get it. So . . . what? You're going to inject me, somehow, with his memories?"

"With the help of this Neural Dome and OCI, yes, a transfer of the prince's memories, both cognitive and muscle, will be introduced into your physiology, into your brain. You will have capabilities far beyond any human here on Earth."

"And just giving me a few MemSnaps wouldn't be enough?"

"No. MemSnaps can certainly give you specific root knowledge. But we're talking about two separate things. You must become, at least to a certain degree, the prince. And there is only one method for obtaining his core thoughts and memories."

Justin thought about that. He didn't like this, any of it. But he saw no way around it. "I guess . . . if there's no other choice," Justin said.

"Via this neural dome and with OCI as the interface, it will be transferring what is salvageable from the prince. It may be some or a lot of his memories. This is not an exact science, as I've discussed.

"That's the illegal . . . the banished aspect. Right?"

"Yes."

"How does all this relate to what *I* want, what I need out of the agreement? Dealing with Lewis and the MP140s? Ensuring my mother will be safe while I'm gone?"

Babar's smile now reached his eyes. "Prince Markus Pietra . . . he is, was, a champion in the ancient fighting techniques of Relian Wham Dhome. An elite combat teaching. Think of it as a kind of Kung Fu on steroids. Exclusive to our Relian High Priests in the Shan Bahn Mountains on Calunoth. Only those of sovereign blood were permitted to be trained outside of the religious order. Markus Pietra . . . he was trained in those ancient fighting techniques."

"And I'll have those memories?"

"Hopefully," Babar said, but looked hesitant.

"What?"

"The muscle memory. That may be an issue. Getting your body to do all that your mind expects of it . . ."

chapter 21

Babar got to his feet and placed a firm hand on Justin's shoulder. "I'm going to leave you now. So, one last time, Justin. Are you on board with this? With what's about to happen to you? There will be no rewind here . . . no redoes with this."

Justin didn't need to think about it. What choice did he have, anyway? Yes, of course he wanted to protect, his mother. Of course, he wanted to enact revenge for the shit storm caused by Lewis and his crew. But it was the millions or maybe billions of lives he might affect out there in space that now made this so much more important. Something occurred to him then. Perhaps it was silly—then again, perhaps not. How did Justin know, for sure, that Babar was on the right side of things? All he really knew was what Babar had told him. That this Empire was bad, and this Dow Dynasty was good. But doesn't every-one think the side they're fighting for are the good guys?

What he did know though, what he had seen demon-strated, was that Babar was a decent, honorable person. What it came down to was that he'd have to go with his gut. For some reason, he trusted this outsider, this alien man. He simply believed Babar had his best interests at heart—though perhaps he was being naïve.

Justin said, "How long will this take? What am I supposed to do?"

Babar headed out of the Neural Dome, and once outside the membrane, Justin heard his muted response. "I have no idea . . . we're breaking new ground here, boy. I'll check in on you in a while." With that, he was gone, and Justin was alone with the dome. He said, "Ocile . . . are you still there?"

"Yes, Justin. I am here."

"Are you, um, okay with what we are about to do?"

"An interesting question. As of right now, I do not have an equally interesting answer. Please, lie back. Make yourself as comfortable as one can be lying on hard metal deck plates."

He did as asked and tried to slow his increasingly rapid breathing. His mind was racing. He, this version of himself, was about to change—forever. In a sense, he was about to die. Would there even be a rebirth? Babar said it himself— they were breaking new ground here. That meant he might not survive this—*whatever* it was. He might actually die. He stared up to the top of the dome. The colors had changed. The aqua blues, pinks, and violets were now navy blues, reds, and golds—a breathtaking and mood-altering transformation. His fear had abated into something else. He searched for the right word. *Fatalism. What will be will be . . .*

Out of the corner of his eye, he saw movement above his legs. Slowly extending down from above was a kind of protrusion of the dome itself. An organic, reaching tentacle—no, actually more like a stalactite, thicker at its base and thinner as it reached farther and farther down. More movement. Another stalactite was reaching down toward him, above his chest. Now, dozens of them above his body were reaching down toward him. *Oh fuck.* He glanced toward the opening in the dome—the exit. He'd forgotten to ask one important question. "Ocile?"

"Yes, Justin."

"Is this going to hurt?" He waited for the reply to come. It was a simple question. Yes or no. *How long does it take to say either yes or no?*

But as that first pointed stalactite reached his lower right leg, the answer became all too apparent. He screamed. It was as if a white-hot lightning bolt had penetrated his flesh—had driven itself into the bone. Fleetingly, he had just enough time to consider what was to come, the innumerable other white-hot lightning bolts soon to arrive. He screamed in anticipation. "Help!"

Excruciating was an inadequate word to describe such agony. Fortunately, something in his brain flipped the right switch, and he soon blacked out. His last waking thought was of the physical revenge he'd get on Babar for not warning him.

* * *

Babar, back at work within the narrow crawlspace leading to the Starboard wing's powerplant, heard the boy's high-pitched screams. He grimaced. Babar had wondered if the procedure would be uncomfortable. Now he had his answer. But it wasn't long before it was quiet again and he could concentrate on the task at hand: a loose power coupling. What he hadn't shared with the boy was the latest updates provided by the OCI. Those two Empire ships were making far better headway toward the Sol planetary system than he had figured earlier. Just as his ship's long-range sensors had picked up on their unique energy signatures, they too, undoubtedly, would have picked up on his vessel, situated here on Earth—or at least that it was here within the planetary system somewhere. The Dow Dynasty's technology had always been better, more advanced, than that of the Demyan Empire—although of late, with the Empire's encroaching expansion into Dynasty space, and the subsequent acquisition of new technologies that came with that, he wasn't sure how long that inequality of technology would last. Babar had a good hunch that it would be Harrage Zeab, Chancellor of Broudy-Lum StarStation, at the command of those two war ships. Not only had Babar and his team stolen back the four stasis tubes, he'd damaged Zeab credibility in the eyes of Emperor Chi-Sacrim. That brought a smile to Babar's lips. A small consolation, considering Babar had also failed so magnificently. Magistor and Magistra Pietra were dead. The prince and princess were as good as dead. Hopefully, news of this disaster had not reached Calunoth—ignorance was preferable to the true reality. With luck, he would be able to change that reality. The boy had little notion as to his true importance. He might just be the Dynasty's last hope of holding back the Empire's advances into Dynasty space—despite their technological dis-advantage, the Empire's resources were unmatched.

"Loham Babar, Noble-Fist to the aristocracy . . ."

Babar rolled his eyes at the OCI's constant use of his formal title. "Call me Captain or Captain Babar, OCI. Now what is it?"

"Justin has awakened."

"And the procedure . . . was it a success?"

"Yes, to the degree the young human has survived the ordeal, physically. As to his mental condition, that is indeterminate at present. Too little in the way of relatable comparisons. What would be considered a success? The human being sane? Or perhaps simply being a functional organic being? Or—"

"Fine, I get the point." Babar replaced the power coupling's cover. "Test this juncture connection for me, will you?"

"It is now operational."

Babar collected his tools and test devices, placed them into a satchel, and back-crawled out of the wing access's narrow channel. He squirmed feet first out from the access hole until he was standing on the passageway deck. It was then he heard the heavy breathing behind him. Without turning around, he said, "Justin?" He waited.

"I'm . . . going . . . to . . . kill . . . you!"

Slowly, Babar turned around.

chapter 22

Lewis B. White

Mount Hope Cemetery, Chicago

Lewis stood alone. He held a folded white handkerchief in one hand—routinely having to swipe at his eyes. The tears just didn't fucking stop. He'd purchased a new suit for the occasion. He'd spent two g-notes on the Armani threads and Dylan Gray dress footwear—nothing less would have been appropriate. Not for Harland. There would be no church memorial service—nah, this would be it. And Mount Hope Cemetery hadn't been his first choice. A bit *scruburbs* for his taste. There was a morning mist, appropriate for the somber occasion. He looked out across the span of rolling green—headstones as far as the eye could see. People were still hurrying from nearby parked cars. Considering this funeral had been organized quickly, the attendance wasn't bad.

Lewis brought his attention back to the dark mahogany coffin suspended on an aluminum lift rack, there above the open grave. Beneath it, faux grass lined the hole to disguise the true reality—that this elongated box would soon be lowered into the cold Chicago soil where bugs and worms and all kinds of crawly things would eventually find their way into the casket. Into his brother's lifeless corpse. Again, his anger began to stir within, like fire beneath a kettle, hot steam building and building and building—shit needed to escape. No, it needed to erupt.

The eight rows of folding metal chairs were almost filled now. Everyone wore black. There was no new-age, wear-what-you-want bullshit for a Chicago morning glory—people wore their best, and they wore black. He heard sobs all around him, the soul-crushing soundtrack of the day. His and Harland's mother sat nearby with her best friend, Jen, on one side and fat Aunt Bunny on the other, embracing her. Their consoling was doing nothing to ease Mama's pain. Her sobs only grew louder.

Lewis saw that the service was about to begin. Minister Manford was here, futzing with his robe and glancing leerily at the assemblage. It wasn't unheard of for rival crews to pay their own kind of respects. Hell, funeral drive-byes, guns blaring, were half-expected these days. Maybe not today, though. The cops, out among the distant headstones and standing between the trees, were all around here in force. He'd heard a couple of Chicago detectives within the Criminal Gang and Homicide Division had been assigned specifically to the arson case. He knew them—Detectives Roach and Gomez. They'd never pinned anything on him, and this fire would be no different.

About to take his seat next to Colby and GG, Lewis saw that there were several attendees huddled together on the outskirts, almost unnoticeable there in morning haze. Two notably white faces among the mostly black crowd. He narrowed his eyes. "Fuck me . . ." It was that girl. That same teenage girl who had been there at the side of the road. Who'd stood and watched Harland, dying in front of the truck, his blood flowing all over the street. She'd been at the hospital too, visited Justin's mother. This white girl meant something to Justin. *His girlfriend?* He leaned over and whispered into GG's ear.

"Now? I want to be here for this . . . for Harland!" GG said, loud enough for others around them to overhear.

"Do it. Follow her when she leaves. Then grab her!"

chapter 23

Aila Tuffy

Mount Hope Cemetery, Chicago

"This is a bad idea," Garret said, pulling his watch cap down farther to cover his exposed ears. "Nothing good will come from us being here."

Aila could hear the minister's distant baritone voice, reading a verse she recognized from Romans 8:35, 37–39. "Who will separate us from the love of Christ?"

She tore her eyes away from the distant proceedings. "How can you say that? I saw the boy, Harland, die on that street, Garret. I saw the life leave his eyes. I'm sorry if this is inconvenient for you. But we're all connected with this, whatever *this* is . . ."

"What this is, is unsafe. An MP140's funeral is by invitation only . . . and we're not on anyone's list, I assure you." Garret momentarily placed a hand in his jacket's right-hand pocket.

"What's with your pocket-checking every few minutes?" she asked.

"Nothing."

"What do you have in your pocket?"

"Don't worry about it."

"Garret!" she scolded in a hushed voice.

"Seriously? Did you think I'd come here without . . . protection?"

Aila stared up at him, and he noted the disappointment in her eyes.

"I'm not going to ask where you got that. Your mother would shit if she knew you had it," she said.

"Where do you think I got it? She keeps it in her bedside table . . . you obviously

haven't lived in Chicago long enough to know everybody keeps a loaded gun in their house."

Aila thought about that. They'd been here a few months now, and the transition had been tough. With her mother dying of breast cancer two years prior, and her father losing his job back in Toledo, the two had ventured to Chicago. Her dad was working now as an HR manager for a tractor manufacturer. But the real reason they'd come here was for her father to be closer to his sister, Garret's mom.

"Fine. Let's just go. I've seen enough," she said.

"Good."

Staying close to each other, crossing over the private street that bisected the cemetery grounds, they hurried toward Aila's Ford Fiesta. Since they'd been late arrivals, they weren't boxed in like some of the other cars. Most were crowded together, in what had become little more than a parking lot.

They weren't the only ones leaving early, Aila noticed. Two black guys—one tall and broad-shouldered, the other short and stout (and struggling to keep pace)—climbed into an old Chevy Malibu and started the engine.

Aila asked, "Still no word from Justin?"

Garret shot her a sideways glance. She'd asked the very same question a half-hour earlier.

"Well, he might've texted you. Just saying . . . it'd be nice knowing if he's okay. I mean, where's he staying? Where does he go?"

"I don't know," Garret said. "I'm not the kid's keeper. His mom says he's staying—"

Aila cut in, "With the janitor. Um, that Mr. Babar . . . which makes no sense. The guy's like, anti-social. Creepy, if you ask me. Nobody knows where he lives."

"Let it go, Aila. I'm sure Justin's just fine. Don't get all stalker-like."

"Shut up! It's nothing like that," she said back, although it kind of was. She'd been infatuated with the boy ever since her first week at school here. The boy everyone talked about behind his back. *Scarface*. But she saw more than the scars that dominated one whole side of his face. She saw someone who, in spite of what he faced due to his disfigurement, was kind and insanely smart. Yes, he was shy, keeping mainly to himself, but he *owned* who he was. She'd had boyfriends back in Toledo, rarely sat home alone on weekend nights, but she'd never been in love—hell, she was only seventeen. But she felt *something* for Justin that she couldn't explain. There was no one she'd rather be with. And it was driving her batshit crazy not knowing where he was now.

Reaching her car, Aila pulled out the keys from her pocket and unlocked the passenger side door for her cousin. A slow-moving car was approaching. The car, that same Chevy Malibu, stopped and idled next to them. Aila glanced over at the driver, ready to tell the guy to keep driving, that she wasn't interested. Instead, her breath caught in her throat. All she could see was the muzzle of a gun pointed her way.

"Hey, pretty young flicka . . . how 'bout we go for a ride?"

Garret said, "Hey, man . . . we don't want any trouble—"

"Keep your trap shut, waspy boy. Both of you get in now, or die."

The shorter stout guy sitting in the passenger seat snickered. "We know where there's still an open grave."

* * *

A few hours had passed since they'd first arrived at this garage. Aila figured it was some kind of chop shop. An assortment of expensive-looking, undoubtedly stolen cars—all in various stages of disrepair—surrounded them. The three entry metal bay doors were closed. High up, late afternoon sunshine attempted to penetrate in through a row of grime-covered windows. She and Garret sat closely together upon an automobile's tattered bench seat. She could still taste blood in her mouth from the last time Colby had slapped her face. Moving her bottom jaw back and forth, Aila wondered if it was broken. It sure felt like it.

Garret said, "I'm telling you . . . you have to believe us. We have no idea where he is, I swear. Please . . . please, believe me."

Aila stole a glance toward her cousin. They'd been far rougher on him than on her. No open-handed slaps, just fists—hard punches to his face and body. Twice he'd been kicked between the legs. He'd cried out in pain. Both of them had sobbed, begging to be free.

Aila now raised her head and took in the group's hard, expressionless faces. The MP140s were truly an ethnically diverse, equal-opportunity bunch of lowlifes and probably killers. Definitely killers. For a few hours, she and Garrett had just sat there, but when the other four arrived, things got ugly. The six guys were probably not much older than her. Maybe one or two were in their twenties. She'd learned all their names in the short time they'd been here. There was Colby, GG-Guns, Trev, Dadda Bing, and Cuppa. Also Lewis. She said, "Lewis . . . it wasn't Justin that hurt your brother. It was Mr. Babar . . . the high school janitor. I saw it happen. I was there!"

But Lewis, not listening, was messing with her smartphone. She'd given him the access code the second time he'd backhanded her. The way his fingers were moving, she could tell he was scrolling through her photos. Every so often, he'd pause to make a comment to Colby or GG. Both were looking over his shoulder. She thought about the pics, taken at East-Harbor State Park. She and Lidia, sitting together on beach towels, posing in their bikinis. She suddenly felt a chill. The big one, GG, was eying her. She didn't want to think about what was coming—what they were going to do to her. It was just a matter of time. And then they'd kill her. For sure they'd kill her. Kill both of them. She hoped they'd kill Garret first, before they did anything horrible to her.

"I'm sorry, Aila, I should have protected you better," Garret said.

"Shut the fuck up. You only speak when spoken to . . . got that?" GG said, stepping up closer, looming over the two of them.

"Fuck you," Garret said, through split and bloodied lips.

Aila noticed that one of Garret's front teeth was missing. Her heart sank. He should have kept quiet. His hands were tied behind his back; they'd used what was left of her bra to bind his wrists. Yet they'd left her hands unbound, since there was nothing she could do to them—they knew it, and she knew it.

GG didn't strike Garret again right away. Instead, he just stood over him, his fists white-knuckled and clinched.

Lewis, holding up Aila's smartphone, said, "Hold on, GG . . . I want to get a good angle on this. Make a movie for our homeboy, Justin . . . I'll text it to him. Whatcha' think of that idea, Aila? Think he'll appreciate my movie-making skills?" He then stepped sideways so both Aila and Garret were in the frame. "Oh yeah . . . that's the money shot. We'll be a regular—what's that white director's name, made ET and all that shit?"

"Steven Spielberg," Colby said.

"Yeah, that's the motherfucker I'm thinking of. Steven, fucking, Spielberg."

Knowing they were being recorded, that Justin would see this video, made it so much worse. Aila closed her eyes as fresh tears rolled down her bruised and battered cheeks. She said, "I'm sorry, Justin . . . please don't watch this. Please . . ."

"Quiet, missy—he'll watch it. He'll want to see what's coming up later. Hell, he'll fucking wear out the rewind button, girl!" All six of his cronies laughed.

"Okay, GG, go ahead and punish that smart-mouthed cracker boy now."

Aila, not wanting to see it happen, found she was looking right at Garret when the punch came. She heard the crack, his nose breaking. Blood spurted—so much blood. Garrett, hit hard, was propelled off the bench seat onto the oil-stained concrete floor. Aila reacted without thinking. As the crew of MP140s cheered, seeing such a colossal blow come from GG, she threw herself atop her cousin, trying to cover his fallen body with her own. Placing her hands on his ruined face, attempting to stop the oozing blood flow, she cried out, "Stop! Don't hurt him . . . he's done nothing wrong. Oh please, please, please, please . . ." Looking back over her shoulder toward Lewis, she stared into the tiny lens of her smartphone. And again, she knew Justin would soon be watching this. Lewis, smiling, wore a big toothy grin on his smug face. She sobbed into Garret's chest, felt it rising and falling, his strained breathing. And then she heard his whispered, barely audible words, "Gun ... my gun ..."

She froze. Oh my god, where was it? Was it in his left-side jacket pocket? No, It was in the right one ... definitely the right. She hugged her cousin even tighter—making a bigger show of it—of how desperate she was. Crying louder now, she slipped her hand all the way around his body. *There!* She felt it. The hard bulge. The gun was there, beneath the thin fabric. She gave a silent prayer that no one would notice as she slipped a hand into Garret's jacket pocket. *Ah!* She had it—her hand wrapping around the handle of the pistol. She felt dizzy as adrenalin coursed through her blood stream. A kettledrum thundered in her chest—go, or not go? Pulling the gun free, she pivoted her body around until she faced Lewis, the barrel of the gun pointed at his face.

Ignoring the smartphone, Aila stared straight into Lewis's eyes. "Stop recording, asshole." The gun was slippery in her hand, Garret's blood making it near impossible to keep a proper grip on the thing. As she rose onto her feet, nearly losing her balance, she brought up her other hand to help steady the weapon—but it too was a bloody mess. The gun slipped sideways as she tried to tighten her hold, so she concentrated instead on keeping her finger lodged on the trigger. *Fuck!*

"Hey, little lady, just calm down ... no need to be pullin' out daddy's bang bang, right? We're all friends here, right? Just having some fun." Lewis was still filming, but his smile wavered some behind the held-up phone. Only then did she notice all the others had somehow pulled their own weapons. *When did they do that?* Five pistols were aimed at her. Aila, desperate, knew things were entirely out of control, that this was it. She was going to die ... like right now, right there. She was going to be blown away in this dingy, shitty chop shop, and there was nothing she could do about it. If she lowered the gun, gave into these *fucking* hoodlums, they would kill her anyway. But first, she knew they'd rape her. All of them—one after the other—while Lewis recorded it. Chronicled each sadistic action for everyone to see—for Justin to see. The gun slipped. Once again, she was losing her grip.

Lewis raised a free hand toward his cohorts. "Hold on ... she's no killer. Sweet thing's just scared. We just be talking here, right, Aila? Things got a little out of control. I apologize. Take a breath. We'll all take a breath ..."

"Fuck you ... there's no more talking. You're an animal. You're all animals. And I know I've already lost. I'm already dead." Turning the pointed gun away from Lewis and fumbling with it, she pointed the gun's barrel toward her own head. Muzzle to temple. *I'm not like them. I'm not a killer.* Her entire body was shaking now, her hands trembling uncontrollably. She tried to swallow. Tried to think.

"No, girl! Easy does it ... we all are going to put our guns away." Lewis, jutting his chin out toward his crew, ordered, "Put your fucking shooters away!"

Aila glanced down at Garret. Tears brimming in his eyes, he shook his head. "No, Aila."

Aila's mind no longer raced, coming to terms now with what was happening here, what it was she had to do. But she didn't want her father to see her dead body like this—one side of her head blown apart—so she quickly repositioned the barrel of the gun. Arms straight out, and her thumb positioned on the trigger, she pointed the gun instead at her chest, aimed directly at her heart. She closed her eyes. The pistol slipped again, a little wonky within her grip, causing her to exclaim out, "Damn it!" as she pulled the trigger.

She didn't expect the sound to be so loud. Then darkness . . .

chapter 24

Justin Trip

Stinger Gun Ship, Wrigley's Chewing Gum Factory, Chicago

He came at Babar with one thing in mind—retribution. Someone was going to pay for what he had gone through. Pain, agony, fucking torment to the point Justin had wanted to die—for it to just be over with. Babar hadn't mentioned any of that. He hadn't prepared Justin for the reality of the situation. He swung, a haymaker punch that Babar easily pivoted away from. Justin stepped in and punched upward—this time an upper cut to Babar's jaw. The alien man moved out of its way with little effort.

"You left me up there in that—that—that torture chamber! I was dying. Didn't you hear my screams? My calls for help?"

Babar took a step back as Justin swung again. "Heard some of it. I was inside that wing channel, can't hear much in there."

"You didn't think to like . . . check on me?"

Babar thought about that for a moment. "No. To be honest, there would have been little I could do. Once the procedure had started, it pretty much had to run its course."

"I hate you!"

"I understand. You need someone to blame."

"Damn right I do. You! Fucking alien freak!"

Justin, seeing that last comment made Babar chuckle, said, "You think this is funny?"

"A little."

"Why? There must be something wrong with you. You're a sadist, that's what you
are."

Babar nodded. "Other than being angry, having your feelings hurt, how else do you feel?"

"I don't know. Same, I guess."

Babar took a tentative step closer while looking at him like a doctor would look at a patient. Taking in his true physical condition. Then the alien's eyes settled on one specific area—the left side of Justin's face.

Feeling self-conscious, as he often did when people stared or gawked at his disfigurement, Justin placed a hand on that side of his face. To shield his ugliness from public view.

Babar's brows arched upward—questioning.

"Why you looking at me like that? Stop it . . . it's creepy." Justin didn't like to be looked at. In fact, he hated it. It was humiliating. He felt his face go hot with embarrassment. *Wait. My face . . . is hot. My entire face.* Now his hand was touching his skin. He probed for the all-too-familiar scar tissue—the ridges and valleys that had dictated the course of his life as much as a river does for a boat or a road for a car. But the ridges and valleys were gone. He touched the other side of his face, thinking perhaps the scars had somehow moved from one side to the other in that god-awful procedure. But no. Both sides of his face were smooth. He looked at Babar. "How . . . ?" He ran back down the passageway to the bathroom and looked in the mirror—turned his head from left to right. "I feel like I'm someone else."

Babar stood in the open hatchway. "OCI . . . Ocile was able to fix your face. I imagine much of the pain you experienced was due to her making those alterations."

He thought about that—his facial scars, which had always been a part of who he was. And the constant reminder that he wasn't like anyone else at school, or probably anywhere else. They were a symbol of where he'd come from, of the explosion that had taken his mother's life, leaving her dead and him terribly disfigured for life. Or so he'd thought.

"I don't know what to say. It's . . . kind of weird." He looked at Babar's reflection in the mirror. "Thank you?"

"Don't thank me . . . my intentions were self-serving. For you to look like the prince, as much as possible, those scars had to go."

Babar left, and Justin looked at himself again. *Weird.* Down the passageway, he heard Babar say, "It is time to begin your training,"

The alien man was waiting for him outside the ship. He was holding the twenty-pound sledge again.

"Oh, come on, really? That again?"

Babar ignored Justin's whining. "Strike the first stake. Hard as you can. Put your back into it."

Reluctantly, Justin took the hammer and approached the take. Babar had driven it about a third of the way into the concrete. He widened his stance, positioned the head of the hammer over the top of the stake, and then raised it over his head. He brought the business end of the hammer down with as much force as he muster.

Bang!

Strange, how good that felt, Justin thought. And not just mentally, at having an outlet for so much pent-up aggression. But physically, too. Sure, his muscles had complained, hurt a bit as expected, but it was different than before.

"Now the next one," Babar said, gesturing to stake number two.

Justin didn't understand. Not until he glanced back down to the metal stake. The stake that had been driven all the way into the concrete floor. "Woah." He pointed to it. "You must have gotten it started for me."

"Yeah, pound the next one," Babar said.

Justin repeated the maneuver when he approached the next stake. He widened his stance, positioned the head of the hammer over the top of the stake, raised it high over his head, and swung it downward.

Bang!

Justin stared down at the stake. This time, he'd pounded it to below the surface of the floor. A small crater encircled the top of the stake. Without prompting, Justin moved to the next one and pounded it in as well.

Bang!

And then the last one.

Bang!

He looked over to Babar. "How was that possible? How did I do that?"

"You didn't do that . . . Markus did."

Confused, Justin shook his head.

"I chose this exercise for a reason. Prince Markus was particularly fond of it. He spent years perfecting this drill. What you just experienced was muscle memory. His, not yours."

"Well, the kid was strong . . ."

"Sure, he was strong. But that's not what drove those spikes into the concrete, Justin. It was years of practice. Placement of the hammer head just right. Utilizing a maximum amount of concentrated force—a precision downward strike without unnecessary exertion."

"Earlier, when I was punching you . . . trying to punch you. How come—"

"How come you didn't connect? Punched like a small child?"

"I guess, yeah."

"Both the physical and mental transition will take a number of days, maybe weeks, to be fully realized. Give it time. But it is imperative we maintain a rigorous physical training from this point on. Justin . . . we leave here within a week's time."

About to protest, Justin stopped as a black, egg-shaped orb exited out from the back of the ship. RP9, a drone-bot, as Babar had described it, made no sound as it hovered in close to Babar. They communicated in Babar's alien language, and whatever the drone-bot was saying, Babar was getting more and more disturbed. "No!" he shouted, as he ran toward the aft end of the ship, hurried up the gangway, and disappeared inside.

Justin followed, as did RP9. He found Babar within the main hold area. He stood in front of Markus's stasis tube. Within the green glowing liquid was a terrible sight. The young prince was disintegrating. It was as if the liquid had turned from water to hydrochloric acid.

Tears brimmed in Babar's eyes as he stood there with his palms on the curved class. "I'm sorry, my prince . . . I have once again failed you and your family."

Justin stood there, not knowing what to do or say. When Babar finally looked over to him, he had composed himself. "Even more now than before, your presence within the Dow Dynasty is essential."

"What happened to him, Babar?"

"The quick answer . . . he died. What you're witnessing now is the stasis tube's automatic response. A cleanse cycle. What is left of his body will be gone within the hour." Babar lowered his head and brought his fists together over his chest. His lips moved as he recited what Justin surmised was a silent prayer.

Justin moved to the other tube and took in the princess's angelic form. "Babar?"

"If you're going to ask if the same thing will happen to her . . . the answer is yes. It could be a month from now or a year. It could be tomorrow."

Justin saw that RP9 was approaching them, but this time, its intended destination appeared to be him.

"Master Trip . . . may I speak with you?"

Master? Justin glanced toward Babar, who was in deep thought in front of the princess's Hyper Tube.

"Uh, sure . . .. what is it?"

"Within your quarters . . . your communications device. It has been signaling for close to an hour."

Justin looked at the friendly, and oddly formal-sounding drone-bot. "Must be my mom calling me. I should go see what she wants." He shot Babar another glance before heading out of the hold. Moving down the passageway, he was briefly annoyed that RP9 had just entered his quarters without asking.

He heard his smartphone ringing as the hatchway slid sideways into the bulkhead. He dove for the phone. "Mom?"

"Oh God . . . Justin. It's just terrible. Horrible. I'm so, so sorry."

"What are you talking about? Are you okay? Your burns—"

"No! Not me. Haven't you watched the news? Heard what happened."

"No. I'm pretty much living in a cave, Mom. Just tell me what's happened. You have me worried."

There was a long silence before his mother spoke again. "Justin, there's no easy way to tell you this. So I'm just going to say it. Garret and Aila have been shot. Their bodies left on the bank of South Fork Chicago River . . ."

It was as if his body had been electrocuted. Shocked senseless—paralyzed. "Wait . . . Dead? Mom, are they dead?" *Of course they're dead*, he thought. Two bodies found on the side of the fucking river.

"Garret is dead, honey. Aila, miraculously, is injured, but it's not life threatening. A bullet hit her in the upper chest, but it completely missed her heart."

Thank God, he thought. *She's alive. Lewis. Fucking Lewis did this* . . . "She's there, in the hospital . . . where you are?"

"Yes, I think so . . . she's probably still in the ER. Her father came by a few minutes ago. He's beside himself with worry about his daughter. He just popped his head in, wanted to know what I knew about the situation. And if the MP140s will still be coming after his daughter. Anyway, from what he said, she needed a fair amount of stitches. She also needs bed rest—that and probably counseling. Such a terrible ordeal . . ."

"Okay, Mom, I'm on my way to the hospital now."

chapter 29

Justin Trip

Bridgeport, Chicago

He was halfway to the hospital, sitting in the back seat of his Uber ride, when he felt his back pocket vibrate. He took out his phone and saw there was a new text message. It was from Aila, which under the circumstances, didn't seem possible. He tapped to bring up the full message and saw all their previous texts back and forth. He saw the latest text, one added a few minutes earlier.

Aila: An eye for an eye . . . bro

Justin saw that there was a video icon beneath. Justin's finger hovered over the screen. He tried to focus, but panic was overwhelming his mind, making it hard to breathe. He felt as if he was drowning—suffocating in dread. He tapped the video icon.

Yelling broke the silence within the SUV, and Justin fumbled to lower the volume. The driver had said her name was Kadisha, and he saw her large brown eyes looking back at him in the rearview mirror.

"Sorry," he said.

She smiled and put her attention back on the road.

Just loud enough for him to hear, there were multiple male voices, laughter, a kind of party atmosphere. The video was jumpy, panning too fast to make out any faces. And then he saw her. Aila's terrified, swollen face looking into the camera. Garret was seated on the other side of her. He looked to be unconscious, but it was hard to tell—both his eyes were swollen to grotesque proportions, two slits probably impossible to open. The camera moved, and Justin could see Aila's shirt was torn open, revealing her exposed chest. She was saying something. Pleading. He heard his name, "I'm sorry, Justin . . . please don't watch this. Please?"

"Quiet, missy—he'll watch it. He'll want to see what's coming up later. He'll fucking wear out the rewind button, girl!" Justin heard Lewis's crew laugh in unison.

"Okay, GG, go ahead . . ."

Justin watched the entire clip. Sadness and compassion for his friends was soon replaced with stone-cold hatred for Lewis and his pack of thugs. Eventually, the video played to the end, where he'd watched Aila do the only thing she thought she could under the conditions. She knew what they were about to do to her, so she flipped the gun around. He watched as she fumbled with the gun—her hands still covered in Garett's blood. The she closed her eyes and, using her thumb, she pulled the trigger. The video went shaky, losing focus as she dropped to the ground.

"Sir?"

Justin looked up.

Kadisha had partially turned in her seat. "We're here. University of Chicago Medical Center . . ."

He hurried through the hospital's automatic entry doors and a nearly deserted front lobby. The same woman he'd talked to before, Pricilla, was seated at the front desk. She looked over to him and then did a double take with a look of astonishment. Justin looked away, uneasy with being scrutinized. He'd see his mother first, then see if it was possible to see Aila. He doubted it. Within the stillness of the elevator, his mind flashed back to the video—blood misting from Aila's shoulder, and the way her body had just dropped, like a marionette with it strings all cut at once.

The elevator doors slid open on the sixth floor, and without stopping at the nurse's station, Justin headed directly to where his mother was being treated.

"Justin . . . isn't it?"

He looked up to see Dr. Kline, his mother's doctor, standing three paces in from of him. "Uh, yeah. Hi, Doctor. Is my mother . . ." Justin gestured to the closed curtain off to the right.

The doctor continued to stare, his lips parted, as if the words he'd been about to vocalize had been plucked from his mouth. Again, with the look of astonishment, he nodded and absentmindedly pointed, "Yes . . . go . . . go on in."

Justin looked in through the gap in the curtain and saw that her eyes were closed. She must have felt his presence there, for she opened her eyes and turned her head. She smiled and reached her arms out. "Get over here, Justin."

They hugged, and he felt there was more strength in her embrace. He knew then she was going to be alright. With all the shit happening in his life—all the death and violence—his mother would be okay.

When she finally released him, he stood looking down at her. But her smile was gone. Her eyes had done wide—an expression of horror looked back at him. "Oh my God! Justin . . . your face . . . your face! What happened?"

And then he figured it out. Pricilla in the lobby, Dr. Kline two minutes ago, and now his mother—all not understanding how it was that he no longer had scar tissue covering half his face.

"Mom . . . it's okay. I promise. I'm still me. I'm fine."

"But . . . how? It's impossible." She was shaking her head while her mind tried to make sense of what she was seeing.

He pulled up a chair and scooted it in close to her bedside. He took her hand in his, all the while trying to come up with something that would explain why he was no longer so terribly disfigured.

She'd regained her senses and was now pushing herself up into a seated position. "So, what? You're saying this is some kind of miracle? Spontaneous supernatural healing? I've read about such things, but always knew there had to be more to the stories. I'm an RN ... these things simply don't happen in the real world." She placed the palm of her hand on his cheek. "So, I'm having a real hard time believing this. Honestly, I cannot believe this." She stared back at him, dumbfounded.

He wanted to tell her she'd nailed it. That God, or Jesus, or Mohammed, or Allah had done this, but he didn't want to lie to her. He'd be leaving soon, in a matter of days, or maybe hours, and he needed to tell her the truth. Of course, she wouldn't believe him—no way. But then again—"Mom, I need to tell you something. And I want you to promise to listen to me. Don't like, freak out. Don't call for the doctor to bring me a strait jacket. Can you do that?"

She gave him a quizzical look. "I promise. And I don't think you've lost your mind."

"Well, just wait." He started at the beginning. From when he was walking home from school several days ago—when Harland was moments away from bashing his brains in with a long metal pipe. He told her about Babar and the old factory. He told her about the spaceship and the two stasis tubes. He told her about the Neural Dome and the procedure that had transformed his face. And finally, he told her about the promise he'd made. That soon, within days, he'd be leaving Earth. When he was done, he leaned back in his chair and looked at her. From her expression, he had no idea if she believed all of it, some of it, or none of it.

She seemed to be choosing her next words carefully. "You know that all sounds ... ridiculous. Crazy."

"You said—"

She raised a hand to stop him from talking. "I believe you. Every word of it. I can't remember you ever lying to me, Justin. And there is no feasible explanation of what could have changed your face like that. Yeah, aliens from another star system sounds a bit out there, but it makes as much sense as any other explanation."

She took a deep breath, and continued. "But no, you're not leaving here. You're going to college . . . your life is here."

"It's just for a year. Think of it as a gap year. Going abroad to get some real-life experience under my belt." He laughed, and she did too. He could tell she was trying to come to terms with the idea. She looked at him, serious now. "I'm sorry about Garret. I know you really liked him. Looked up to him."

"I'll miss him, Mom. Garret had nothing to do with any of this. They didn't have to do that to him. To both of them."

"Don't let yourself get consumed with hate, sweetie. Don't become so driven by revenge that you lose yourself." She looked away. "Maybe it is best for you to leave for a while. Get away from that gang and all the evil that surrounds them."

Justin wanted to tell her that by the time he left, Lewis would no longer be breathing, but he kept that to himself. "What do you know about Aila? Her condition?" he asked. He'd purposely avoided the subject till now. If she was at death's door, perhaps moments from dying, he didn't think he could stand it. His heart might just split in two.

"Surprisingly . . . she's doing pretty good. Physically, anyway."

He looked at his mother. "That's impossible. I saw the video Lewis sent me. She shot herself in the chest. In the heart!"

"Yes, and no. Apparently, and I'm getting this second hand from her father, she tried to shoot herself in the heart, but her hands were a slippery mess. Apparently, she wasn't able to get a good grip on the gun. She ended up shooting herself in the shoulder. More like what they call a graze, really."

"I know what a graze is, Mom."

"I imagine they'll kick her out of the ER as soon as they think she's stable enough to go home." Seeing the relief on his face, she added, "I know she'd want to see you. Go on down there, Hun. I'll call down and see if they'll let you in. I think I still have some pull around here."

He stood and exhaled, feeling he could truly breathe for the first time in hours.

"I still can't get over looking at you. Amazing," she said.

He nodded and turned to go.

"Justin?"

"Yeah, Mom?"

"This Mr. Babar fellow . . . I need to meet him. You're not going anywhere until I talk to him. Until I better understand all this."

"Okay. I promise."

* * *

Aila was, in fact, still in the ER. He peered in through the open curtain to make sure she wasn't asleep or being attended to by a doctor or nurse.

"Justin?"

She was sitting up in bed. A bandage could be seen across one shoulder beneath her hospital gown. He covered the left side of his face with one hand as he approached her bed. By the time he reached her, tears were already streaming down her cheeks.

"I'd hug you if it didn't hurt so much to move my arm." She sniffed and looked toward an adjacent countertop. Justin plucked a tissue from the dispenser there and handed it to her. Taking it, she winced. She blew her nose and looked up at him. Her face was a rainbow of colors—yellows and greens, but mostly reds and purples. She looked worse than she had in the video. The beating that she'd survived had been horrendous.

He said, "Aila, I'm so sorry I've caused all this. Brought this nightmare into your life. And Garret . . ." The words caught in his throat and he fought back tears of his own.

"Don't be an idiot. This is all on that fucker Lewis and that gang. The police are looking for him. They assure me they'll get him, eventually."

"He sent me the video you know . . . from your phone."

"Sorry you had to see that."

She was looking up at him. Both were uncomfortable with the abrupt silence. "You know, you don't have to do that. Cover your face like that. Not for me."

He shrugged. "Look, I have to go. Things I need to do today."

"Oh . . . alright. Can you come see me at home? In a day or two?"

"Maybe. I'm just glad you're okay. Well, you're not okay, but . . ."

She laughed. "I know what you meant. I'm not going to die, at least. My injuries are, somehow, relatively superficial. I'll be discharged within the next few hours. " She went quiet for a moment. "You know, they didn't . . . do anything to me." Her eyes flicked down to her lap and then back to his.

"I'm glad. Um. I should go. Look, can you do me a favor?"

"Sure. If I can," she said apologetically.

"There's some things I told my mom. Explained to her. Things I can't get into now with you . . . but I want you to know. You probably won't believe them. Not at first. But eventually you will."

"That sounds ominous. Just tell me. My dad's over in the cafeteria—he doesn't do well in hospitals."

He lowered his hand to expose his face. "As I said, there's a lot to explain."

She stared at his face, speechless. She shook her head, her expression a mix of confusion and something else he couldn't read.

"As I said, you'll want to talk to my mom." He placed a hand on hers and gave it a squeeze. "I'm so glad you're okay, Aila. You have no idea." With that, he left, knowing he may never see her again.

chapter 26

Prince Markus Pietra

Grindhold Space Station— Space-Flight Academy

Three years earlier ...

They stared at each other across the concourse for several moments before, to Markus's utter surprise, Ballard offered up a casual wave. Markus looked to his left and right, making sure Ballard wasn't waving to someone else. But that wasn't the case. To his further surprise, his childhood friend was crossing the distance—headed his way.

"I didn't recognize you ... not at first, anyway," Ballard said coming to a stop several paces in front of Markus.

Markus nodded, but was unable to speak. What could he possibly say after what he'd—

Ballard pointed to the top of his own head. "Your hair . . . all chopped off."

"Oh, yeah . . . priests chopped it off at the order."

"I wasn't sure you still wanted to join," Ballard said, gesturing to their surroundings.

Markus shrugged. "I think it's all I've ever wanted . . ."

He saw Ballard giving him the once over again.

"You've gotten bigger. Like, brawnier. Guess the priests made you exercise a lot, huh?"

"Pretty much non-stop. Exercise, meditate, eat, shit, sleep, repeat . . ."

Ballard laughed at that. "So, guess you have some cool fighting skills, but you'll be behind with any kind of flying proficiency."

"You've been flying? What have you been flying?" Markus asked, already envious.

"Nothing all that impressive. Last year, parents bought me a used DawnSlicer."

Markus knew a DawnSlicer was a one-person aircraft capable of low to medium atmospheric flight. Teens often modified them for greater speed and, in some cases, even adapted them for short-term, low-orbit space entry. "Stock configuration?" he asked.

"Nah . . . it's souped up. My dad worked on it with me over the last few years."

Markus wondered if his own father would have done

something similar if things had turned out differently. Probably not—hell, he was the Magistor of the Dow Dynasty—but perhaps Babar would have. "Well, I'm more than a little jealous. A kneeler was the closest thing to flying I ever—" He stopped mid-sentence. How could he have been so stupid? To bring up kneelers. The object of Mahlnie's death. He felt his face go hot. He looked away, unable to meet Ballard's penetrating gaze.

"You know, I don't blame you, Markus. Wasn't your fault," Ballard said.

Markus forced himself not to get all teary-eyed. He thought, by now, he had gotten to the point he could better manage his emotions.

"You warned us . . . all of us," Ballard continued. "Stay away from the underbellies of those fucking wagons."

"None of us . . . Mahlnie . . . wouldn't have been there. Causing trouble, if it wasn't for me. So it is my fault. You should hate me. You should want to—"

"Oh, I did, for like a long time. I miss my sister every day. But then, I don't know. I thought about how you must feel. What it had done to your life. Shit. And you were totally in love with her. We all knew it. Joked about it behind your back. So, I know you suffered. Suffered, like the rest of us."

Markus's eyes filled with tears and he tried to blink them away.

"I'm surprised you don't have like, bodyguards . . . realm security around you," Ballard said, changing the subject.

He shook his head. "I think my father issued some kind of order . . . that I wasn't to be treated any different than anyone else. So far, you're the first person who I think knows who I am."

"You're an idiot," Ballard said, making a face. "Oh, sure, people are going out of their way not to be conspicuous about it . . . but everyone knows exactly who you are. Mostly the officers."

Markus scanned the hordes of other teens rushing this way and that. Sure enough, he saw several kids doing double takes at seeing him standing there.

"Your instructors . . . they're going to make your life extra miserable. You know that, right?"

For some reason, that made Markus laugh. "It'll be nothing compared to what I've been through for the last few years, and I have the scars to prove it."

An announcement blared overhead. Immediately after completing the check-in process, recruits were to head off to their assigned training squads. Earlier, Markus had been told that he was to join his fellow recruits within the Blue Cutlass barracks.

"I'm with Yellow Saber," Ballard said, looking proud. "You?"

"Um, Blue Cutlass. You know anything about them?" Markus asked.

Ballard laughed so hard he bent over with his hands on his knees. "No way . . . that has to be a mistake."

"No. Why? What's wrong with Blue Cutlass squad?" Markus asked, not finding this funny in the least.

"It's like the worst. You have your idiot tards and

imbeciles ... not to mention your hooligans, delinquents, and your troublemakers. It's the worst squad you could possibly have been assigned to. Shit, you'll be lucky to graduate now from that pack of misfits ... sorry."

Markus thought about that. He had little doubt this was his father's doing. "It's okay. Maybe I can rise above all the riffraff."

"Well, you never know. I guess our squads will be competing against each other. Nothing personal, but you're going to be shit on by all the other squads. Be the butt of all the jokes." Ballard became serious. "You know, you might be able to transfer out. Be assigned to another squad. Maybe mine! You being the Magistor's—"

"Nah ..." Markus cut in, "Blue Cutlass is where I'm supposed to be. And hey, don't underestimate what a bunch of misfits can accomplish if they set their minds to it."

Ballard shrugged, then glanced over his shoulder. "I gotta go. Sure I'll see you around. Take care, Markus."

He watched as his once-best friend head off. He let his eyes rise to the top of the surrounding bulkhead where, overhead, much of the concourse was encircled by transparent metal-glass. Out there, beyond, was open space. He could see an assortment of various spacecraft. Several were heading in, preparing to dock. Others were engaging their aft thrusters and powering away. Three smaller crafts flying in formation rocketed across the expanse. He saw they were sleek-looking Stinger Class gun ships. He wondered how long it would be before he'd be allowed onto the bridge of one of those little warships. Soon, he hoped.

chapter 27

Justin Trip

Bridgeport, Chicago

He'd gotten the same Uber driver for the ride back to the Wrigley's Gum Factory. After giving Kadisha the address, he relaxed some—laid his head back against the headrest and was soon fast asleep.

Fifteen minutes later, Kadisha was tapping on his knee, "Hey . . . Justin, we've reached your destination."

He looked around, blinking sleep from his eyes. "Oh, yeah, thanks." For the first time, he noticed that Kadisha had equipped her SUV with handicapped mods, whereby the brake and accelerator controls were accessible on the steering wheel.

Once he was out on the darkened street, he gave Kadisha an extra two-hundred-buck tip via the Uber app. He looked about—all was quiet. The factory's shapeless silhouette was a foreboding presence, like a black hole against the star-filled night.

He found his way into the building, through the dilapidated hallways, and over to the stairwell. Peering down into the pitch-black void, he wondered if Babar had forgotten to turn on the light down there. He slid his phone from his pocket and tapped the flashlight feature. By the time he'd reached the bottom of the steps, the light flickered out. It had been a while since he'd charged his phone—*shit.*

He crept into the sub-basement space with his arms extended out in front of himself. The darkness was absolute. He stopped and listened—he hadn't so much heard something as sensed something. "Babar? You here . . . you screwing with me?"

An azure-blue cone of light suddenly appeared ten paces in front of him. Some twenty feet above, at the pinnacle of the cone of light, was a dark, egg-shaped object—RP9. Now, taking shape within the cone of light was a three-dimensional form, a person. No, a warrior. Although Justin was aware that this indeed was a hologram, the detail was amazing. Justin's eyes were drawn to the weapon, some kind of sword, being held high over the warrior's head. The guy looked to be a cross between a Japanese Samurai and a Roman gladiator, helmeted and with strategically placed protections, chest, sleeves, chins, and loin guards. But apart from those area, his exposed and pronounced muscles made it dramatically clear that this dude was colossal. An Arnold Schwarzenegger on steroids—Justin, at close to six feet tall, was at least a foot shorter.

Justin said, "Babar . . . this isn't funny."

"Prepare to defend yourself, Justin," Babar said, his voice emanating from above—probably from RP9.

"You're kidding, right? A joke?"

"You'll find a *Cinnichan* blade at your feet. Best you retrieve it now."

Reluctantly, Justin did as told—finding the sword by feeling around for it on the floor. Once his fingers had brushed against it, like the cone of azure light and the big warrior, it too illuminated via its own cone of light. He saw that it was being generated from above—from RP9. It was a hologram.

"Babar . . . how is it I can feel it? Like it's actually real."

"Directed auricular soundwaves. Pay attention, boy. Your opponent's blade will feel just as real when it cleaves your head from your neck." And with that, the hologram warrior came alive.

Justin backed up several steps, "Uh, I think we skipped a few steps, Babar . . . like the whole learning how to defend myself, part."

"You already know all that you need to know. Prince Markus Pietra had a long run . . . I believe it to be twenty undefeated matches, before he encountered a most resounding, decisive, loss with this same exercise. No one's perfect, not even Markus. But few were better."

"Okay . . ." the hologram was swinging his sword around in some kind of show of agility. His blade made *swishing* sounds as it sliced through the air.

"He awaits your attack, Justin."

"Did I mention I haven't experienced much, or any, of the prince's memories?"

"You're not remembering, not like a memory. You're knowing, like you know how to walk or how to take a piss. Don't think about it. Just let your mind do it. Engage . . . do it now!"

Justin looked at his opponent, noted his two-handed grip, the way he stood with his knees slightly flexed, the method in which he kept his sword horizontal albeit high overhead. Also, how upright and rigid his back was. The warrior continued with his fancy sword twirling.

Approaching the hologram, Justin twirled his own sword in a fast blur of motion—first to the left, then to the right, and then overhead. *I have no idea how I just did that . . .* He came at the warrior head on, then at the last second dodged left while ducking. He'd anticipated, *somehow*, the trajectory of the warrior's blade—which barely missed his head. Justin spun low to the right and let the momentum of his body ratchet his sword around fast. His blade sliced through the warrior's legs just below the knees. He toppled over as holographic, blue-hued blood sprayed into the air. Flailing on his back, Justin wasted no time—driving the point of his weapon into his opponent's windpipe. But Justin instinctively knew, this battle was far from over. He centered himself into what was referred to as Targe-le-con, the standard fighting stance of the Relian Wham Dhome elite combat teachings. In a momentary flash of memory, a glimpse of a past that wasn't his own, he recalled training with the Relian High Priests high up in the Shan Bahn Mountains on Calunoth . . .

One, two, three new azure cones of light appeared within the cellar. Three big warriors, just like the first. This time, they did not wait for his attack. And this time, he knew, they would be playing for keeps. He noticed now that they were, actually, slightly different from one another—each having a slightly differently shaped ornamental top of the helmet thingamabob. One was triangular, one was square, and one was circular. What Justin didn't know was why he couldn't wipe the smile from his face. He let out a primal yell in a language he didn't understand and attacked the one he had mentally named triangle-bob. Their swords clanged together as both attempted head blows. Four more clangs as they anticipated each other's strikes. He sensed the movement of one of the others at his back and dove into the darkness beyond any of their illuminated holographic cones.

He suspected this training session would have certain filters in place—such as the opponents not having super-human abilities, like the ability to fly, go invisible, or see in the pitch-black darkness of the building's sub-level basement. Justin moved in the outlying darkness with stealth and agility. His feet made no sound as he circled around the three warriors. Every so often, one of them would swing their weapon or suddenly stab outward into the dark. They'd communicated something to one another and had moved into a three-way back-to-back stance. Justin darted forward, feigned toward circular-bob, and then stabbed at square-bob. His blade found flesh between the warrior's chest and sleeve guards. He grunted in pain—a nice touch, Justin thought, as he attempted to spin away back into the darkness.

But circular-bob was right there on his retreat, catching him across the back of his shoulders with a swinging blade. The pain was enough to stagger him. Blood streamed down his back As much as Prince Markus Pietra may have had a high pain tolerance, Justin did not. No longer being directed by Markus's muscle memory, Justin looked back to his opponent. He was surprised to see that the hologram had been halted mid-strike. The blade of his sword was fractions of an inch from Justin's neck. If left undeterred, it would have indeed cleaved his head from his neck.

The overhead light came on. One by one, the three combat warriors faded away. Slow clapping came from atop the spacecraft, where Babar stood. "A pathetic display. The Relian High Priests would have turned away in disgust."

On his hands and knees, Justin was only half listening to him. He had never felt this kind of pain. He realized his hands were situated in a pool of his own blood.

"Get yourself into the medical bay. We'll take a ten-minute break."

"Break? It'll take me weeks to recover . . . I need stitches, time to heal."

Babar laughed. "I said get up and head to the medical bay."

Justin saw that RP9 was now hovering at his side. He placed an arm over the top of the bot and felt it rising, lifting him up to his feet. It took some doing, but eventually he was stumbling his way up the ramp, moving through the airlock and into the passageway beyond. By the time he turned into the awaiting medical bay, he felt as though he would pass out. Justin felt hands—no, claws—take hold of his two upper arms and lift him up, face-down, onto the table. He remembered seeing these articulating robotic arms, collapsed and stationary against the bulkhead, when he'd been given a tour of the ship. Now they were busy attending to his wound. Something was being sprayed across his gaping wound—it was cold but soothing. Something pinched his forearm, a needle maybe. He didn't feel too awful. A little sleep. Perhaps some recovery time on his bunk—

"Up! Let's get out there and try it again. Up! Up!"

Justin looked back toward the entrance to the Medical Bay. Babar was standing there with his arms crossed over his not-insubstantial chest.

"Are you crazy? I've just been injured . . . I lost buckets of blood."

"You'll find your wound has been mended, the lost blood replaced with an infusion of a fluid that adapts to your DNA profile."

Justin clenched his teeth and heaved himself up on the table. He waited for the searing pain to come. But there wasn't any. He flexed his back and shoulders—still, no pain at all. He assessed his overall well-being and, if he was being honest with himself, he felt better than he had all day.

RP9, which had remained at his side for the entirety of the

medical procedure, was suddenly moving, lights flashing upon its top panel. An overhead klaxon began to wale.

"On no . . ." Babar said, hurrying down the passage.

"What is it?" Justin yelled after him.

Babar replied, "It's the princess!"

chapter 28

By the time Justin reached the primary hold area, his mind had played out several scenarios, none of which were good—such as the princess, like her brother, having died unexpectedly, her body already in the process of dissolving. Or, that what meager signals had been coming from her cerebral cortex had ceased—and she truly was brain dead.

Entering the hold, he stopped and tried to make sense of what he was witnessing. Babar was frantically tapping at a nearby console while shouting a series of unintelligible curses. Inside the right-hand stasis tube, Princess Lena Pietra was fully awake and looking desperate to get out. Her palms went from pushing outward on the inside of the glass to making fists and pounding. She was yelling, screaming at Babar—Justin could just make out the sound of her muted yells.

"Can't you just drain the thing?" Justin said, coming to Babar's side.

"No, it doesn't work that way! There are protocols, safety guidelines."

"Is there anything I can do to help?"

"Yes, shut up and let me work!"

Justin stood back and watched the desperate princess inside her tubular prison. Her eyes met Justin's; momentary confusion was replaced by pleading, desperate looks. "She's dying in there!" he said. Then he saw the droid-bot hovering nearby. "RP9 . . . can you open that tube?"

"Safety protocols require—"

Babar, seemingly just now becoming aware of the hovering bot, yelled, "RP9, I order you to open it—fire plasma bolts into the top of the stasis tube! Do it now!"

A series of bright energy pulses streamed forth from the droid-bot. The stasis tube's glass exploded outward into thousands of tiny, glistening pieces of glass. A tidal wave of liquid poured out onto the deck, quickly swamping the hold. The princess, now on her knees, was coughing and struggling to catch her breath.

The angelic form who'd previously floated within the stasis tube, her hair a halo of suspended gold around her head, now looked more like a drowned rodent. Her wet hair hung over her face in dark, limp strands. Snot dripped from her nostrils. She then threw up an ungodly amount of green sludge and groaned. Babar was at her side, his hand on her back in a comforting gesture. He looked over to Justin. "Best you wait outside . . . take RP9 and resume your training."

The princess was now lying, curled up, in the bottom of the tube. Her eyes met Justin's, and once again he saw her momentary confusion.

"Um . . . come with me, RP9. Let's do what Babar says."

Outside the ship, Justin's mind was all over the place. The implications of this latest development were, well, big. With the princess now awake, and seemingly having her cognitive abilities (although he wasn't one hundred percent sure about that), there didn't seem to be the same need for him to travel to this Dow Dynasty place. They would have their actual, real heir to the throne to lead and motivate their masses. He had to admit it, he was feeling relieved. The prospect of leaving his mother and his home for an indeterminate period of time had been a tough pill to swallow.

What hadn't changed, though, was his need to deal with Lewis and his cronies. And for him to do that, he needed to be a hell of a lot more dangerous than he currently was. He spotted RP9 hovering high up over the top of the ship. The lights within the basement dimmed and then went out completely. He felt the acceleration of his heart rate, the tensing of his muscles. His mind flashed back to the video clip Lewis had sent him. Anger, hatred, and thoughts of revenge coursed through his mind all at once. He saw Aila's battered face. He saw Garret's body on the concrete, and Aila trying desperately to shield him with her own. He saw her shoot herself in an attempt to kill herself. He swallowed and cleared his mind of emotions. He knew he operated best when he thought analytically. Wasn't that how he'd amassed a small fortune buying and selling penny stocks? He thought about the video clip again and tried to remember how many gangbangers had been there.

Although their faces were kept out of frame, he'd seen their legs. Including Lewis, there were seven of them.

"RP9 . . . I'll be going up against seven, um, adversaries. Can you project that many?"

"Affirmative. Although, your earlier training session—"

"Seven, RP9. No more, no less. Let's get started," he said, in a tone more confident than what he was actually feeling.

The first cone of azure light was directed down to Justin's feet. His holographic weapon would be lying on the concrete. Before snatching it up, he thought about Markus. Thus far, he had had little internal interaction with the prince. Sure, there had been muscle memory aspects, and an ability, a *knowingness,* for fighting. But none of the prince's actual memories had infiltrated his mind. His biggest fear had been an inner conflict, whereby two minds would struggle for dominance—who would prevail and take supremacy? But none of that had happened, thus far.

Justin, about to pluck the sword from the ground, hesitated. It wasn't a sword. It was a spear—or a kind of spear. He knew, somehow, that it was called a *Lanchot.* An ancient Dow Dynasty Legionnaire's assault weapon. Close to seven feet long, the thing was extremely lethal in the right hands. The staff was made from the wood of an Ortillian sapling tree, dried and hardened in a kiln for no less than seventy-five years.

How the hell do I know all that?

But the knowledge just kept coming. The tip of the weapon was called the crown—a circular metallic construct that banded together around the hilt of a curved and pointed, twelve-inch-long cutlass sword. He snatched up the incredible weapon and ran toward the back of the ship. One right after another, azure cones of light pierced the darkness around him, emanating from RP9 above.

Justin bounded onto the gangway, only to use it as a means to leap up and onto the starboard-side wing. From there, he sprang up to the top of the gun ship. Although he'd reached the strategic high ground, he'd also made himself an easy target. He was already diving onto the hull when a *Lanchot* shot past him, missing his head by inches.

Justin called over his shoulder, "RP9 . . . being able to see their cones of light makes this too easy."

RP9 must have done something, because he no longer saw any of his opponent's cones of light. Nor did he have had any idea where they currently were. The basement was back to being pitch black. *Good!* Justin crab-walked forward, toward the bow of the ship.

It wasn't his eyes that detected the figure climbing up the front of the ship, it was the hologram's labored breathing. The training opponent crested the hull and stood. Although RP9 had done an admiral job suppressing his overhead cone, at this close proximity, the holographic figure was partially visible, a silhouette of blurred edges. Justin saw the hulking figure surveying the lightless scenery. Still lying on his stomach, Justin waited for him to move past. Then, Justin was up on his feet and driving the *Lanchot* into the combatant's back. As it slumped forward, as dead as a holographic training combatant could be, Justin saw two more silhouetted figures moving toward the bow.

No . . . wait for them. Don't give away your position. Justin had heard his own inner voice too many times to count. A lifetime's worth. This was not that. Markus's voice spoke with a certain kind of arrogance that Justin instinctively didn't like. Actually, he hated it. It had a kind of superior snarkiness, the kind that came with privilege and over-doting parents. And in an incredible disorienting fashion, the voice sounded much deeper than his own.

And so, the prince speaks, Justin thought. He crouched down on one knee and waited. Once close enough, he sprang to his feet while spinning his *Lanchot* overhead twice—letting its weighted end gain momentum. He didn't so much see his opponent's head being cleaved from his body, more like felt the clean decapitation through the staff of the weapon.

Duck!

Justin did as told. As the blade swish by overhead, a breeze fluttered his hair. *That was too close.* Justin thrust out sideways but missed. *Shit!* He leaped to the right, knowing his opponent was already making another move on him. That was when he felt something pierce into his abdomen, right below his sternum. He'd been skewered—a fatal strike that there would be no easy fix for within the medical bay. He dropped to his knees, retching—his hands clasped over his belly in an instinctive reflex response intended to keep his insides from spilling out.

The overhead hanging lights came on. The individual azure cones of light became visible again, and Justin could see where each of his five remaining opponents were standing. They were all around him—each poised to strike, their individual *Lanchots* mere moments from thrusting or slicing at him. Beyond the circle of seven-foot-tall holographic warriors was Babar.

"That was a pathetic display of ineptitude. A mere two out of seven combatants? Come on! Really?"

But Justin wasn't listening to Babar's reprimand. He was inspecting his mid-section. He was looking for the blood and guts that should have been pouring out of him, feeling for the death blow that was sure to have ended his far-too-short life. But his abdomen had not been torn open. He was not injured. He looked up to Babar, who was now right before him. "Ouch. That fucking hurt!"

"Yes, I imagine it did."

"How . . . I don't understand."

"Technology. Just as we can construct these amazing training combatants, we can fully characterize the physical effects of being injured."

"Then why, before . . ."

"Because fear is a great motivator. So no, you cannot be killed during these exercises, but on certain occasions, I will ensure the necessity of a trip to the medical bay when you make stupid mistakes."

The training combatants around him dematerialized, one by one. The pain in Justin's abdomen was less, but by no means all gone. Babar extended a hand down to him. Justin took it and hefted himself up. "The princess? How is she doing?"

"Sleeping in the medical bay."

"Did you tell her . . . about her parents? Her brother?"

"Yes. Best she deals with both her physical state as well as her emotional state now. And as you could imagine, she is devastated."

"And me? You told her about me?"

"As much as I could. It was a lot to convey in so short a time."

"Well, I'm just happy you now have a true heir to the throne. Someone that can better lead your people. I hope you will still train me . . . to deal with Lewis and all."

Babar looked down at him with a perplexed expression.

Justin said, "You don't need me anymore, right? Wouldn't I just get in the way?"

"Oh, I get it. You think you can now squirm your way out of your commitment, eh?"

"No. That's not what I meant."

"The princess, as much of a part of the family as she was, loved and revered by all within the Dynasty . . . she cannot, will not, take the throne."

"Why not?"

The voice that answered was not Babar's. "Because I am not a blood relative."

Justin spun around to see Princess Lena Pietra approaching. "I was adopted by Magistor and Magistra Pietra as an infant. Royal blood does not flow through my veins."

She came to a stop five paces away. She was wearing a new uniform, and her hair was almost dry, but still a bit of a mess. Her eyes were red and swollen and, if Justin was reading her expression correctly, her contempt, hatred even, for him held no bounds.

chapter 29

Justin Trip

Wrigley's Chewing Gum Factory, Chicago

"**Y**ou should be resting," Babar said.

"And you need to stop making decisions for me in my absence." She glared back at Babar.

"Please. My intent has always been for your benefit, Lena. You know that."

"I am Princess Lena, and your lack of formality is an insult," she spat. Her eyes shifted to Justin. "So, this scrawny human is your intended savior? The one person who can unite all the realm?" She snorted and took a step closer, observing Justin's face now with more scrutiny. "I suppose he does hold a certain resemblance to my brother," she said, continuing to look at him, "Okay, he looks a lot like him. A whole lot like him." She reached out a hand and gripped Justin's bicep. "The only exception . . . he's most definitely scrawnier. He'd be a pathetic excuse for Markus."

"You know that I'm standing right here, right?" Justin said. He'd been insulted his entire life, so he could take whatever she handed out; he just wanted her to know he wasn't a complete doormat.

"What is the operational status of this gun ship?" she asked Babar while still looking at Justin.

"All primary sub-systems are operational, but—"

"Flight ready?"

"Close, but—"

"We leave immediately. I want to go home."

Justin and Babar exchanged a glance.

"I have made a commitment. To the boy. There were . . . stipulations I agreed to."

"What kind of stipulations?"

Babar said, "Combat training, to start—"

Not wanting her to know his personal business, Justin said, "Look, it's a long story, and to be honest, it's not any of your business. If you want to leave here without me, you two can go . . . I'm fine with that."

"You indignant shit!"

Her tight-fisted jab to his face came without notice. But Justin hadn't been caught totally off guard for it. He caught her fist as one would catch an inbound baseball. Momentarily impressed with himself, he realized it was Markus's muscle memory that had influenced his quick reactions. He continued to hold her small hand in his grip.

"Let go of me! How dare you make physical contact with a royal subject!"

Justin held back a laugh. "Oh, sorry, so so sorry, esteemed untouchable Princess Pietra... how could I have been so thoughtless?" He dropped her hand and bowed his head in mock humility. His smile only seemed to infuriate her more.

"Babar, we will leave him here. Fire up the propulsion system. We're leaving!" She strode off.

Babar didn't make a move to follow her. When she stopped several paces away and turned to look back, her face was several shades of red darker. "You dare to disobey me? To disobey the princess of the realm?" She glanced up and saw RP9 hovering overhead. "RP9, you will restrain Babar. Lock him in the hold!"

The drone-bot stayed where it was.

"I'm sorry, Princess Lena... RP9, currently, will only take orders from either myself or Justin."

"Him! He's nobody! An ignorant fool, incapable of understanding the complexities of our people's situation. He's not even from Calunoth!" She closed her eyes and bit her lip.

Once more, Babar and Justin exchanged a quick glance. Babar spoke softly to him, "Lena... the princess, is not from Calunoth, either."

In that moment, seeing her standing there with her arms crossed over her chest, her pouting lips—she looked almost vulnerable to Justin. The princess blinked away tears.

Justin said, "I'm sorry..."

Babar said, even quieter than before, "Don't buy her act . . . she is a master of manipulation."

She'd heard Babar. Her expression changed in an instant, and once again her eyes were full of malice. She laughed, but it was a laugh without humor. Her eyes narrowed, "Putting your faith in this boy will be your undoing, Babar. All our undoing." With that, she headed toward the stern of the ship.

Justin looked from her retreating form over to Babar. "She's . . . horrible!"

Babar smiled. "You have no idea. She can be spiteful, insolent, selfish, and cruel."

"Terrific."

"But she can also be generous to a fault, loyal and sweet. Princess Lena is an amazing young lady. At least for a while, though, you're going to be the subject of everything that has gone wrong in her life. Warranted or not. Remember what she's lost. Both of her parents, her brother, any semblance of normalcy in her life. She's hurting. She's suffering. We will give her space. Let her deal with her pain alone . . ." Babar's words were cut short. Both Babar and Justin watched as Lena crested the curved hull, only this time she was clutching a length of rebar in one hand. Justin figured it was about six or seven feet long. Approaching, the princess twirled the metal rod left, right, and then overhead. It was a magnificent show of dexterity. She stopped twenty paces away and bowed toward Babar. He bowed back, inclining his head.

She thrust the makeshift spear up and forward, yelling out some kind of war cry. Then the weapon was twirling again as she spun around, her opposite hand extended outward like a knife. She kicked forward and then jumped and kicked high into the air with her opposite foot. She landed soft into a crouch, then thrust the rebar spear backwards into an imaginary adversary. Then she was up and spinning again, thrusting, twirling, kicking with the kind of agility and grace Justin hadn't thought possible. He saw her momentary glance their way, a fleeting smile on her lips, and then the seven-foot-long length of carbon steel was streaking through the air—a spear there would be no time to dodge or duck away from. It sailed right between Babar and Justin, heading for a torn and faded poster on the wall. With a deafening *clang*, the iconic WWII Rosie the Riveter was struck between her eyes. The end of the spear continued to wobble and vibrate in place.

Justin's mouth gaped. "That was beyond cool."

Lena didn't acknowledge Justin's comment. Instead, she was looking at Babar. "I will assist with the idiot human's training. Anything to move this misery here along." She waited for Babar's response.

Eventually, he nodded. "But I will preside over his training. You will take direction from me, Lena. Understood?"

She shrugged and rolled her eyes, now back to being the insolent princess again. *God, she's irritating*, Justin thought. *Irritating and beautiful,* he further admitted.

The rest of the day was pure misery. Justin had never been much of an athlete, having preferred the comfort of his bedroom and sitting in front of his computer or TV, or simply admiring his collection of cool kicks displayed on glass shelves.

But he was now experiencing as close to a hellish existence as he could have imagined. While Babar, for the most part, had retreated back into the vessel to finish up final ship repairs, Lena was taking out all her frustrations on Justin. The drills seemed to be out of some kind of medieval playbook. At one point, she had him doing handstands—in fact ordered him to walk that way for close to an hour. His head became so full of blood, he found it hard to see straight. Then he was climbing the massive, rusted out flywheel, going up and down the thing like a kid playing on monkey bars.

"Now double-somersault to the other side... move it, move it, move it!"

Justin, gasping for air, did as told. If it hadn't been for Markus's infused muscle memory and overall transmuted athleticism, he knew none of this would have been remotely possible.

Then it was back to the combat holograms, only this time Lena had taken control of their programming. All kinds of weapons were swapped out during the various exercises. Knives, swords, *Lanchots,* and then more contemporary weapons used for current-day Dow Dynasty warfare. Energy weapons, both pistols and rifles. Lena explained they shot magnetically clustered bursts of raw plasma. Although these weapons were actually little more than holographic simulations of the real thing, getting hit with simulated plasma fire was indeed painful, although thankfully not lethal.

The more exhausted Justin got, the more tormented he was sure he looked—the more content Lena seemed to be. This was clearly some kind of grief therapy, at his expense. But all Justin had to do was think of his mother being carried, burned and moaning, from their now-torched home, or Aila and Garret within that garage being tortured, and Justin was back in the game. He'd endure whatever Lena handed out. And along the way, he hoped that it would irritate the bitchy princess.

Having just completed a battle scenario with five holographic warriors along with Lena herself, each of them equipped with nothing more than their fists and feet to battle with, Babar appeared, exiting the ship and striding down the gangway. "That's enough for tonight, Princess. The object is to train the boy, not kill him."

Her hair was wet with perspiration. Her chest was heaving from the many hours of physical exertion. She had unzipped the front of her uniform enough to expose her cleavage. The tops of her glistening breasts heaved up and down with each lungful of air. She noticed his gawking stare and zipped up her uniform in an over-dramatic fashion. She glared at Justin with contempt.

"How's his progress with the training?" Babar said.

"For one thing, he's lazy. Second, he has the coordination of a pregnant flap-whamp back on Calunoth. Seriously, Babar, was this pathetic excuse for a human really the best choice you could have made here?"

Babar closed his eyes, looking to be counting to ten. Then he opened his eyes and looked at the princess—but not with anger or even irritation, but with pity. Both Babar and Justin knew that what she was dealing with on the inside would take a long, long, time to heal.

"Both of you get something to eat. Justin, you need a shower. And I suggest you do some stretches before hitting your bunk. Tomorrow you'll feel like you've been run over by a truck."

Lena headed off toward the ship. Babar was about to follow after her, when he asked, "Um, is there a way I can charge my phone here? I don't like being out of contact with my—"

Babar cut him off with the wave of a hand. He spotted RP9 hovering nearby and said, "RP9, charge up the boy's phone, will you?" Babar didn't wait for an answer, heading out after the princess. He too looked tired.

The drone-bot hovered in close. "Process complete."

Justin slipped his phone from his back pocket. Periodically, he'd texted his mother as well as Aila for updates. Lewis and his MP140s were still out there and he knew they weren't going away anytime soon—or ever. But it had been a number of hours since he'd last checked in. He now inwardly cursed himself for getting so caught up in things here at the factory. He saw the little battery icon showed it was now fully charged. He felt it start to continuously vibrate. He saw multiple messages were being downloaded—text as well as voice. Twenty-three in all. *Shit, someone's really trying to get ahold of me.*

chapter 30

He'd expected the messages and calls to have been from his mother, or maybe Aila. But that wasn't the case. Several calls and texts were from Detective Chad Roach, and most of the others were from Detective Juan Gomez. At first, they seemed content to simply ask for a call back at Justin's earliest convenience, but the messages soon gained in urgency. Justin played the last voice message, this one from Gomez. "Justin, it is imperative that you call me back as soon as you receive this voice message. There have been several . . . developments, you need to be aware of. Leave it to say, you are in grave danger. Both your mother and Miss Tuffy have already been taken into protective custody."

Justin checked the time on his phone—it was quarter to midnight. He dialed detective Gomez's number. It was picked up on the third ring.

"Gomez . . ."

"Um. Yeah, this is Justin. Justin Trip." He heard the scratchy sound of the mouthpiece on the other end being covered, but Justin could still hear Gomez saying, "It's him . . . kid's alive."

"Justin, where are you right now?"

"I'm here, in Chicago."

"This is no time to be a smart ass. Specifically, where are you so we can send a cruiser to pick you up?"

"What exactly is this about, Detective?" Justin said, avoiding the question.

"This is about Lewis B. White and the MP140s . . . apparently a city-wide bounty has been offered for your capture. You and those close to you."

"How many of these MP140s are there?" Justin asked.

"Best estimate puts the number close to one hundred. Could be a bit higher than that. But Lewis's immediate local crew is small, maybe seven or eight."

"But a hundred in total? That's an army . . . there's a fucking army coming after us?"

"We can protect you. This isn't our first rodeo, Justin. Contracts or bounties like this are usually constrained within the gang personnel themselves, and we tend to let them settle their own scores internally. But we have means to protect you, Justin. Now, for the third damn time, where are you?"

Justin was having a hard time hearing the detective over the noises coming in off the street outside. Like a damn parade, or maybe a riot. *Shit!* Were they already there?

"Detective . . . I'm afraid it's already too late. They've found me. Please keep my mom and Aila safe." He wasn't going to tell

Gomez where he was. Babar, the ship, the princess, could not be discovered. He hung up the line.

He saw Babar running toward the stairs. He yelled, "RP9 . . . cut the lights! Protect the ship at all costs!"

Justin hurried after Babar and caught up to him on the ground floor heading down a dark corridor. Justin said, "They've found me."

"No shit. You must've told someone about this location."

"No! I wouldn't do that." And then he remembered the Uber driver. Kadisha. She'd dropped him off right out front. "Unless the rideshare driver—"

"Shhh . . . It doesn't matter now. Let's see what we're dealing with," Babar said, opening a side door and slipping outside.

Justin followed, staying low and close on Babar's heels. They moved to the remnants of a half-demolished brick outbuilding and peered around the corner. From this vantage point, they were about fifty yards from the street. He saw dozens of gang-bangers out there, congregating in various-sized groups around blazing bonfires out on the street. There certainly was a festive atmosphere. Hooting and hollering and cursing filled the cool night air. Every so often, someone would lob a brick or some-thing toward the factory. Justin had expected to see an ocean of black hoodies, and their trademark black baseball caps—the MP140s' standard attire. Although there were plenty of those, there were clearly other gangs here too, clustered mostly by race—some Latino, some Asian, some Black, and even an all-White gang, which he assumed were skinheads. An assemblage of Chicago's worst. Lewis hadn't simply put up a bounty within his own ranks, but across all Chicago. Justin wondered just how much money had been offered up for his capture. "There's an awful lot of them out there," he said.

Babar didn't comment.

"Can't we just leave . . . take off in your ship?"

Babar looked frustrated in the dim light. "Another couple of days would have been better. But yes. Though I'll need an hour, minimum," Babar said.

"I don't think we'll have that much time," Justin said, pointing to the group of MP140s. they were already heading toward the chain link fence. It wouldn't be long before they'd be searching the factory.

Then he saw Lewis. He was in the lead. He jumped onto the fence and climbed to the top. Straddling it, he said something to his crew. One of them pointed to a nearby asbestos warning sign. Lewis cursed at him, his exact words unintelligible. Begrudgingly, soon they all began to climb the fence.

"I need to get back to the ship. Make sure you stay low and out of sight," Babar ordered before scurrying off toward the side entrance.

Justin held back a moment to watch the situation. Virtually all of the gangs were now headed for the fence. He turned to follow Babar inside, but then stopped. He looked back to where Lewis and his crew were standing, waiting for the last to jump down from the fence. He counted seven of them, as he'd expected. *When will I ever have this opportunity again?*

Instead of the heading for the side entrance, he stayed low and scurried along the side of the building. If he hurried, he just might be able to catch Lewis and his crew before they found a way inside.

You're not ready for this . . .

Justin considered the inner voice, the one that was not his own. He ignored Markus's warning. Watching the various other clusters of gangs, he saw they were moving slow. Some were standing on the outside of the fence. Others had made it over but were huddled together in the dark. And others were now making the trek across the span between fence and building, but looked hesitant at approaching the looming, broken-down structure.

Lewis and his crew had started making a racket. They'd found a potential opening, perhaps formerly a window or a door, covered by a gray and splintered sheet of old plywood. Justin saw that the other crews were looking for different, less labor intensive, ways to enter the building.

Suddenly, gunfire erupted from somewhere inside. Justin stopped and listened. It had come from the south end of the building, on the ground floor and on the opposite end from where the ship was located. The maniacs were shooting at shadows, or more likely each other. For some reason, Justin found that funny. That was, until, he realized there were close to two hundred of them around here, and each well armed. A disorganized army, but an army just the same.

Having reached Lewis and his crew, Justin kept out of sight within a three-foot-wide darkened alcove. He saw that they'd managed to pry open the plywood wide enough to squeeze through. One by one, they turned sideways, and in they went.

Justin waited a few moments before poking his head in and looking around. Voices echoed and bounced around from all directions. Someone in another area of the ground floor had lit a length of timber and was using it as a torch—its moving amber glow created long, dramatic shadows. Justin saw that Lewis was headed toward a stairway that led up to the second floor.

"Dadda Bing! Get the fuck off my ass... you're close enough I can smell your dank breath."

Justin saw the last one ascending the stairs slow down and hold back a moment. Obviously, this was Dadda Bing. Justin crossed the trash-cluttered space to the base of this stairwell and fell in behind the MP140s' straggler. For a brief moment, Justin considered what was about to happen. That afterward, nothing would ever be the same. Having found a foot-long length of rebar outside, he gripped it tighter, feeling the individual ridges along its cold, hard steel. He timed his steps to coincide with Dadda Bing's. He could just make out the back of the guy's head in the dim light. This was no boy. In fact, he thought he saw flecks of silver. Justin, having second thoughts for a moment, forced himself to think about his mother's burns, Aila's bruised and beaten face, and Garret's dead body lying on that chop-shop's concrete floor.

They were halfway up the flight of stairs. Up ahead, it sounded like Lewis and the others had already stepped out onto the second floor. It was now or never.

chapter 31

Justin Trip

Wrigley's Chewing Gum Factory, Chicago

Don't screw this up, human . . . the inner voice said.

The last thing Justin wanted to deal with at this moment was Markus. He'd been assured that the prince's influence would be restricted to physiological muscle memory, maybe a few abstract actual memories, but nothing more than that. So how was it that the arrogant prince seemed to now be barking off comments to him on a regular basis? *Shut up, Markus!*

Justin leaped up two more steps until he was right behind Dadda Bing. He saw the gangbanger's head start to turn—perhaps he'd heard a stair creak, or maybe felt a slight breeze against the back of his neck. Justin reached up and around, placing his left palm firmly over Dadda Bing's mouth while simultaneously driving the length of rebar into the man's back. The stab was made at just the right angle, and Justin knew the sharp and jagged end of the makeshift weapon had pierced into Dadda Bing's heart. How he knew that, he wasn't sure.

The man stiffened and died. Justin let his now-dead weight fall backward into his arms. Taking care not to make any noise, he eased the body down onto the steps. About to leave him there, Justin leaned down, reached around the body, and found the Glock semi-automatic pistol wedged into the back of Dadda Bing's waistband. After three years of hard hours playing Grudge Kill, on his Xbox 1, he was more than a little familiar with handheld firearms, even if only from a virtual standpoint. He released the magazine and confirmed it was fully loaded. Replacing the clip, he eased back the slide and saw the glint of brass—there was a round in the chamber. *Idiot. Good way to blow a second hole in your ass.*

Justin bounded up the stairs, taking them two and three at a time. He wasn't worried about the noise; they'd be expecting the last of their crew to be coming along. He heard them moving on—they hadn't waited for Dadda Bing. The second floor was somewhat better illuminated, since there were open areas along the outside wall. He saw the bonfires down on the street were petering out now, but still aglow.

Shit! Another crew, this one larger, maybe twenty or so, was coming the opposite way. Chides and insults went back and forth between the MP140s and whoever these other guys were. They were white, and every one of them had their base-ball caps flipped backward on their heads. They wore their pants hung low, making an exaggerated *pouchy* area below their collective asses. It was a fashion statement that just didn't work. In fact, instead of these guys looking badass, they looked ridiculous—comical.

Justin waited back within the stairwell for them to pass before sprinting after Lewis's crew. He'd already mentally come to terms with what he intended to do. That he was going to kill all of them, each and every one. He found them standing in a circle, the cherry glow of a joint being passed. Ganja smoke rose in the air. He raised Dadda Bing's Glock and pointed it at Lewis's crew.

"Where the fuck is Dadda? Don't tell me that lard ass has gotten himself lost . . . mother fucker's living proof that a man can live without a functioning brain."

"That's cold, Colby . . . real cold."

Justin move fast and with surprising stealth. He was certain Markus had a lot to do with that. Without being noticed, he approached the circle, creeping in close behind Lewis.

Lewis said, "Enough . . . I'm paying ten G's for that crack-erboy . . . we're wasting time here." Perhaps he felt the presence behind him, or maybe it was something else that made Lewis suddenly turn around. Either way, looking more than a little surprised, Lewis came face to face with one person he was searching for. His mouth stretched into a broad, toothy grin. "Well well well, if it isn't my good buddy, Justin Trip. Huwee . . . I have to give it to you, man. You're batshit crazy.

Lurking around here in this stank-ass factory like this. But I like that. Crazy's cool."

The five others moved to Lewis's sides. No one moved for their weapons. Justin reminded himself that he had fifteen rounds at his disposal. Even if he missed a few times (and at this range, with his new skills, that would be doubtful), he'd be able to take all of them out. Hell, they'd lined up for him like stationary targets—like Coke bottles along a fence rail.

"That's a nice piece you got there. You know how to use it? You wouldn't want to hurt yourself," Lewis said.

"Wait... isn't that Dadda's piece?" the short and stocky banger said with a cinched together brow. "See the big gouge there along the left of the barrel? Dadda dropped it that time riding shotgun. Dropped the thing right out the window onto the street."

That brought laughter from all six of them.

Lewis said, "Don't tell me you got ahold of Dadda Bing's gun. If there was one gun in the whole wide world you wouldn't want to grab, it would be Dadda's. It's a piece of shit. The mechanism, it's all fucked up inside. Jams like you wouldn't believe."

All six nodded their heads in concession.

Justin said, "Why don't we make this just between you and me, Lewis? You want a chance for revenge? Here I am. Tell everyone else to go... no one else needs to get hurt."

Lewis looked to be considering that. Then he shook his head and scratched at his chin. "I'm afraid it's not up to me. A lesson needs to be taught here. We live by a code. You understand what a code is?"

Justin was only partially listening to the man. Over the last few moments, the others had moved in behind him. The other crews as well. Only five or six lit torches illuminated the second-floor space, but the murmur of dozens of voices told him there was a full-blown crowd assembled here.

Lewis took several steps closer. His hands were raised to waist-level. "You killed my brother. You have to answer for that."

Justin considered mentioning that he didn't even remember much of that night. And how much he was responsible. But that would be futile. "So, you're really willing to take the chance that Dadda Bing's gun is going to jam? With me being eight feet away from you? I will pull the trigger."

"You think this the first time I stared down the muzzle of a Glock?"

Chuckles erupted from the ranks.

This is a clusterfuck of epic proportions... what were you thinking? Justin had to agree with Markus's inner voice. How could he have gotten himself into this situation? Even if he did kill Lewis, he would be dead where he stood mere seconds after.

Movement. High up there in the murky recesses of the factory ceiling was something small and dark. A reflection off of one of the torch flames danced upon its glossy black surface. Relieved, he determined it had to be none other than RP9 hovering, staying out of sight. He wondered if Babar was nearby too. *Is that enough of a rescue team?* He doubted it. Sure, Babar was some kind of highly trained combatant in his own right, but these dozens of armed gangbangers had made mayhem and murder their preferred form of weekend entertainment. Time was up.

Justin said, "I'm sorry about your brother. Honest. But it was an accident. What you did . . . killing Garret, hurting my mom and Aila . . . not to mention burning down my house. My neighborhood. People died, Lewis. Don't you think we're, like, even? Isn't all that enough?"

Lewis pursed his lips. His eyes went cold—hatred stared back at him. Justin knew then that Lewis would never stop. He wouldn't stop until Justin was dead, along with everyone he cared about. Justin pulled the trigger.

Click!

chapter 33

Justin Trip

Laughter erupted from all around. It would have been funny to Justin as well, if it hadn't been so pathetic. Lewis offered Justin an *I told you so* expression as he reached back for what Justin could only assume was his own gun. Justin pulled the trigger again. *Click!* And then again. *Fucking Dadda Bing moron!* On the fourth pull of the trigger, the gun fired. *Bang!* Between the nearly deafening noise and the unexpected recoil, neither of which could be accurately portrayed in a video game no matter the hardware, Justin nearly fumbled the gun. Everyone went quiet, and then he saw what everyone else saw. Yes, Lewis was pointing his weapon directly at Justin. But there was a blood-red dot about the size of a pencil eraser right between Lewis B. White's eyes. As the gangbanger fell sideways, the back of his head came into view—blown apart by the exiting 9.mm parabellum round. When Lewis hit the floor, he was deader than dead. In the span of fifteen minutes, Justin realized, he'd already killed two people.

It seemed as if everyone was reaching for their weapons now. Justin dove for the shadows. Gunfire erupted. Several rounds splintered the floor mere inches from his face. He rolled backward and felt something sharp, most likely a nail that had impaled his side. Still gripping Dadda Bing's piece of shit Glock, Justin fired toward the forest of moving legs. *Bang! Bang! Bang!* He couldn't decide if he was more amazed that the gun had successfully fired again, or that he'd actually struck two of them—seeing them fall, he could tell that both were MP140s, with their black hoodies and caps.

Then multiple guns fired at once, rounds clattering into nearby walls and into the floor, several whizzing by in the air close enough for him to hear. He closed his eyes—flattened himself onto the floor and waited for the inevitable.

He probably wouldn't have noticed it, if his face hadn't been lying there upon the floor. A rumbling. A machine-like vibration emanating from somewhere down below. *No! The ship*—it's engines, drives, whatever the hell they were called, were coming to life. Babar and Lena were getting out of here and, evidently, leaving him behind.

Two unexpected things happened then. First, bright blue energy bursts, plasma fire, rained down from above. RP9 had apparently decided to join the fight. Agonizing screams erupted. Almost immediately, Justin could smell burning flesh and hair. At least now, he was no longer the object of anyone's gunfire. Now, muzzles were aimed high—a hundred guns fired

GUN SHIP

upward. RP9, moving lightning fast, proved to be an impossible target. The second unexpected thing to happen was having someone manhandling him up to his feet.

"Get up!" Lena yelled.

Justin did as told, but quickly realized there was a short length of two-by-four jutting out from his side. Pain coursed through his ribcage.

Lena moved to support his wobbly weight by getting Justin's arm up and draped over her shoulder. Both of them looked up just in time to see that GG-Guns, big and mean as a rabid dog, was charging fast. Lena high-kicked him in the face. Stunned, eyes having lost focus, GG remained standing. Annoyed, Lena cursed something unintelligible. She let go of Justin just long enough to drive an elbow into GG's throat while spinning low and sweeping his legs out from beneath him. Even before the big guy hit the floor, she was back in time to steady Justin again. "Come on . . . we don't have time for any of this nonsense."

Those that hadn't been hit by RP9's plasma fire couldn't get out of the factory fast enough. Justin heard desperate yells and the clattering of fast-moving feet within the stairwell.

"Hold on!" Lena said, stopping to see what was clinging to Justin's side. "Oh, you have something . . ." She wrenched the pieced of wood from his side. "There . . . problem solved."

Justin tensed and stifled a scream, though the sounds still came out strangled. She got his arm over her shoulder again, and together they hurried toward the second-floor stairs. Something blew past them at head-level. It was RP9.

Halfway down the stairs, Lena said, "Is this how it's always going to be with you? You getting yourself into trouble and me saving your ass?"

Justin couldn't make any promises in that regard.

"Who cares . . . we need to get the hell out of here, and fast!"

He felt his side was wet. Blood had streamed down his leg and was sloshing into his shoe. They'd reached the main level and together headed toward the stairwell that led down to the basement. "You got yourself a *MemSnap* memory enhancement thing . . . right?"

"Yeah, shut up and move!"

"What's the hurry? They've gone—no way any of those guys will step foot in this factory again."

They turned the corner for the stairwell and headed down once again. She glanced up at him. "We're not leaving because of a few gangbangers, Justin. We're leaving because they've found us . . . two Empire ships, inbound to Earth."

As they reached the basement, there was a cyclone of buffeting winds. Disturbed debris fluttered about all around them. The Stinger's engines were racing, both glowing hot. Babar was on the gangway, motioning for them to hurry it up. "We have to go . . . Now!"

Justin wanted to slow down. To talk about this a moment. He hadn't said goodbye to his mother. Nor to Aila . . . how could he just leave Earth? And so suddenly. Realistically, would he ever be back?

"Move it!" Lena yelled, now forced to practically pull him

toward the ramp. Babar ran down, lifted Justin up, and tossed him over his shoulder like he weighed nothing.

"Wait!" Justin heard himself yell, but nobody was listening. No sooner had they cleared the aft hatchway than he heard it slide shut with a suctioning *thunk*.

"Were you shot? How many times?" Babar said, hurrying down the central passageway.

"No. Not shot. Put me down . . . I can walk."

Babar turned the corner, and suddenly Justin was seated back within the medical bay. Babar yelled for the medical robot to attend to Justin's injuries, and then was gone—heading toward the bridge.

The articulating robotic arms were moving. He felt his clothes being sliced away from his body and his injuries being sprayed with some kind of cleaning solution, then wiped dry. He was sprayed again—this time it was more of that skin replacement stuff. He felt his stomach lurch. Like an elevator ascending fast, the ship was rising, pivoting, and then he heard the sound of it crashing up through the factory sub-floor. *Shit . . . this is really happening.* The vessel jerked and jostled, and he reached out for something to grab on to. He heard the two drives wind up, and then there was an even louder, more thunderous racket. The ship had torn through or maybe clipped the building's roof. Soon, all was quiet. He no longer felt he was being held down from intense G-forces.

Ship's inertia dampeners kicked in . . . should be smooth riding from here on out.

It was the inner voice again—Markus.

Lena cleared her throat from the entrance. Casually leaning against the threshold, with arms crossed over her chest, she said, "You should get dressed. That and get some sleep. You're going to need it."

Her bemused smile and quick once-over glance reminded him he was as naked as a newborn infant. He tried to cover his privates, but it was too late.

She snickered, turned, and headed off. "Nothing I haven't seen before."

chapter 33

Loham Babar

Earth's Upper Stratosphere

With Babar alone on the bridge and situated at the helm console, he throttled the ship higher and higher into Earth's upper stratosphere. He listened to the soft purr of the two anti-matter drives. A quick glance down to the control board offered Babar the operational status of this Defender-Class Stinger gun ship. Virtually all the primary systems and most of the sub-systems were back online. Notably, comms was now operational. When he'd entered Earth's atmosphere those eighteen months ago, most of the systems had been in the red. He glanced down again:

Powerplant Starboard Drive: Green — **Powerplant Port Drive:** Green

Helm Control: (*Nav*) Green

Environmental Support Systems: Green

Forward Shields: Green — **Aft Shields:** Green

Neural Center: Neural Dome Processing at 85%

Weapons: Pivoting Plasma Cannons: Forward (2) Green — Mid-Ship (2) Green — Aft (2) Green — **Pounders:** (2) Green — **Onboard Missile Ordinances:** Yellow (75%).

And the final readout, Stealth Running, was also a solid green.

Babar wondered, for the thousandth time, how this Stinger gun ship had been tracked here to Earth. Here, within this small desolate corner of space. How long could a ship's trailing radiation wake even last? He considered that for a moment. This was an area of the cosmos that experienced virtually no space traffic—there would be little to no disruption from other vessels. Again, he asked himself, could a damaged gun ship's radiation wake have been been tracked all the way from that OB5 asteroid belt? Possible, but it seemed highly unlikely. To do so, it would take a long while, which could explain why they were just now arriving. Truth was, he might never know the answer.

All in all, the gun ship was in surprisingly good shape.

Minutes prior, breaking through that factory's makeshift sub-floor and then clipping part of the factory's rooftop apparently hadn't caused any damage. These little Stingers were about as tough as any Dynasty, or even Empire, war ships in operation. Sitting there within the ship's bridge, he reflected on what he was leaving behind on Earth. He'd come to care about humans and the planet in general. At times, he even felt he was one of them. If he was being honest with himself, yeah, he'd left a bit of a mess, and he felt bad about that. But in comparison to what was coming—what the Empire was poised to do, all too soon—the stakes were far higher for the thousands of Dynasty worlds now in jeopardy.

He heard someone enter the bridge behind him. Princess Lena plopped down in the adjacent seat. He saw her looking out through the forward starshield window as they cleared the upper atmosphere and officially entered space. She turned her gaze to Babar.

"What now?"

"Now we go home," he said.

"I see that comms are now operational . . . you know, on Calunoth, they may not know, at least for sure, that mom and dad are—well, dead."

"I don't know, Princess. It's been almost two years, and I have no idea what's what."

"You nervous? You know, telling them about Magistor and Magistra Pietra? That it's just me. Me and . . ."

Babar exhaled and shook his head. "How is he back there, anyway?"

"Okay, I guess. Can I ask you something?"

"Yes."

"What the hell were you thinking? That boy … sure, he looks like Markus, but he's not even close to ready to … to *be* him."

Babar nodded. "Some things didn't work as I'd hoped. I'd expected by now for far more of the prince to have surfaced. That the boy would be better able to draw upon that."

"And that's not happening?" she asked.

"Well, he does have a fair amount of Markus's muscle memory. He did quite well during his physical training, the battle simulations."

"I guess I have to admit that much," she said reluctantly.

Babar continued, "But when I asked him about other thoughts or recollections, Justin says he's had little of those. Other than an occasional judgment or opinion he said weren't his own. But I suspect that's recently changed, at least to a degree. More than once, I've spotted Justin talking to himself. Experiencing inner conflicts. I suspect the procedure has manifested unexpected, and unexplainable, results. Memories are one thing … Justin dealing with Markus's personality traits would be another."

"Then how can we possibly consider taking him back with us? If it's discovered what you did—hijacking Markus's memories—you'll be imprisoned, or worse, executed!"

Babar tapped a new heading into the console. "I did what I thought was … necessary. Remember, at the time, you were still floating within that stasis tube and there was little indication you'd be waking up anytime soon, or ever."

"I guess we'll just have to work with him," she said. "How long before we reach Dow Dynasty space?"

"Eight days," he said. "I should probably contact Dynasty High Command."

"Maybe we should shove the kid out the aft airlock, first."

Babar shot her a disapproving glance.

"Kidding. Well, kind of kidding . . ."

"You keep calling him a kid . . . he's older than you are, Princess."

"We're the same age, almost exactly."

They sat in silence for another few minutes before she said, "It's time, Babar."

Babar said, "Ocile, open a channel to Dynasty High Command."

"Establishing a connection," the pleasant female voice came back.

"Ocile?" Lena said with brows raised.

"I gave the Neural Center's Interface a name. Actually, it was Justin's idea. I didn't see the harm."

She rolled her eyes.

A series of static clicks and pops filled the cabin. "Connection made . . . channel open," Ocile said. "Expect response delays due to distances between Communications Repeater Stations."

Babar was used to intergalactic communications delays, just as anybody who traversed space would be. Throughout Dow Dynasty as well as Empire space, there were millions of these CR-Stations, strategically positioned for optimally boosting and relaying ship-to-ship, or planet-to-ship, voice and video messaging. While standard comms would allow for near-light-speed transmissions, that would be dreadfully slow across interstellar distances. No, to communicate across many light years, the CR-Stations' ability to open and synchronize artificial micro-wormholes between one another was the only way to cut those times down to mere seconds. Even with this technology, there were noticeable conversation delays.

"This is Dynasty High Command Officer Corfu...identify yourself. You are utilizing an unauthorized comms identifier." The voice seemed far away and none too happy at the violation.

Babar and Lena exchanged one last look before he answered. "High Command, this is Dom-Dynasty Stinger designation 222156890. This is Loham Babar—Noble-Fist to the aristocracy."

Babar could detect the disbelief over the light years of distance. The static and pops were the only indication the channel was still open.

"If... you are indeed, Babar—Noble-Fist to the aristocracy... you must know, you were assumed deceased, close to two years ago."

"More than you know. But it is the truth. For eighteen months, I have been hiding... making repairs to my ship. Only now have I been able to reenter space."

"I apologize, but your identity will need to be confirmed. Although voice verification does seem to confirm you are who you say you are. Please disclose the status of others onboard your vessel."

Once more, Babar and the princess exchanged a look. "My crew was killed in its entirety while battling Demyan Empire forces within the OB5 asteroid belt."

"Then . . . you are alone. The prince and princess . . ."

"They both are alive. Here with me onboard." He'd said it. There would be no taking it back now.

"That is . . . amazing, welcome news, sir."

Babar could hear the emotion in Officer Corfu's voice. " Prime Minister Yansle will be . . . overwhelmed with joy. This, this is a momentous day. And their parents will of course, be thrilled by the news. Truly a momentous—"

Lena stood, glowering at the forward console, her anger displayed in both expression and posture. "This is Princess Lena . . . you are mistaken! Both Magistor and Magistra Pietra were killed, their Stinger destroyed by Empire Rage-Fighters."

Babar actually heard the officer swallow. "Princess . . . Princess Lena?"

"Yes, it is me."

"I assure you, we have news that your mother and father are, in fact, alive. Not unlike your own situation, they have not been able to return to Calunoth. Apparently, the Stinger they were aboard was indeed *nearly* destroyed when two Empire fighters collided almost upon them . . . but that lone Stinger, crippled as it was, escaped. Made it to a fringe planet bordering Empire space. Reports are, your parents were extricated from their respective stasis tubes. But I must tell you, we have had no direct contact, only sporadic transmissions from their vessel's RP9 unit. We do have their coordinates, though. And ensuring that their location remains secret has been a top priority."

"They cannot find another way to leave? It can't be safe for them to stay there." Lena asked.

A new voice came on the line. "As far as we know, no attempt to flee that world has been made . . . as of yet."

"And who are we addressing?" Babar asked, but he already knew that voice. That arrogant, superior tone.

"Apparently, their ship's Zyln capabilities were damaged during the asteroid battle."

Babar said, "Yansle . . . Nimb Yansle," making no attempt to hide his contempt for the individual.

"It is Prime Minister Yansle . . . and hello to you, Loham, it has been a long time. I was certain you were long dead. So nice to find you still alive."

Babar wanted to scoff at that, but said nothing.

Yansle continued, "Although the realm rejoiced with news of the Magistor and Magistra's survival . . . thus far, any attempt to rescue them has been futile. Such a dangerous and remote area of space."

Lena said, "So, they've just been left there to languish in hostile territory? Who made that decision?"

"I did, Princess. You have all been gone for some time now. Much has changed within the realm. Please remember, it had been years since the loss of our beloved royal family. I'm sorry, but no longer is the realm governed as it had been. Chaos, near-riotous conditions prevailed. It was necessary for martial law to be enacted throughout the core worlds. The constitution amended."

"Wait ... What!? What are you talking about?" Lena said.

"It only made sense, with the terrible loss of, well, all of you ... it was soon decided a more watchful and less lax government was needed. Again, the unrest was growing by the day, by the hour."

Babar said, "So now, you're the Prime Minister. You always were an ambitious sort, Yansle. How fitting, you now being a dictator with so much power. I had warned the Magistor about you ... that you cared little of our Dynasty's thousand-year constitution. So, the perfect opportunity arose for you. A gift laid at your feet. Tell me, Yansle ... how long did your coup take? Perhaps you were already prepared for the opportunity?"

"I don't have to listen to this insolence. You should be mindful of who you are speaking to ... that is, if you ever want to return to Calunoth."

"Let me guess," Lena interjected with a wry smile. "You've taken up residency within the royal palace."

There was no need for Yansle to reply. The answer was obvious.

"So now, of course, you've seen fit to simply let my parents languish there in Empire space. The last thing you'd want is for them to return, to challenge your new autocracy."

"Watch your tongue, Princess ... many lives have been lost attempting to reach your parents. Parents, mind you, we have no direct confirmation are still alive. But numerous tactical missions have been deployed."

Babar would have wagered his left hand that it hadn't been Yansle who'd deployed those operations. There must have been many still loyal to the constitutional monarchy. But that was a matter for another time.

Lena's face reddened, her eyes burning with rage. "Then send the Realm Guard . . . the Fifth Fleet!"

"To do so would be considered an overt act of war. A war we are already trying to avoid. We must tread carefully during these precarious times."

"Prime Minister Yansle, my father would be ashamed at your cowardice . . . treading carefully? That is not how you rule the known galaxy, by placating to the Empire's whims."

Babar placed a hand on Lena's arm. "Take a breath. Best if I take it from here."

Prime Minister Yansle continued, "I am sending you their transmission coordinates over a secure channel. I am sorry, I wish we could do more. With that said, it is splendid news you are alive and safe. That our beloved prince and princess . . . and you too, Loham Babar. Please know that the three of you were posthumously awarded the Honorary Medal of Tchahn. Loham, you were already a hero to all within the Dow Dynasty. The fact that the three of you are alive . . . well, this is—"

Lena said, "You can take those medals and shove them up—"

Babar broke in, "Prime Minister, thank you. We look forward to the receipt of those coordinates. And now, we can continue on with Officer Corfu." He sat back and looked up to the still-standing Princess. Her eyes were unfocused. He guessed she was mentally somewhere else—perhaps thinking about the last time she had seen her parents alive—reconciling this new reality. It would take some time.

Officer Corfu was talking again. "I apologize . . . I know this is all, um, a lot to absorb. Please understand, the Empire . . . their attacks of late into Dynasty space along the outer realm, frontier space, well—our forces are dwindling. Morale is low . . ."

"Send me the secret coordinates of the Magistor and Magistor. Do so as soon as you can, Officer Corfu."

"Yes, sir . . . sending now."

"What did I miss?" came a voice from behind. Both Babar and Lena turned to see Justin entering the bridge, wearing a new uniform. For the first time, he noticed they were no longer on Earth. "Holy crap . . . we're in space."

chapter 34

Justin Trip

Justin had been listening from the passageway outside the bridge. He considered everything he'd heard. Of course, it was good news that the Magistor and Magistra might still be alive. The expectation for him to conduct himself as the real sovereign son and take on those immense responsibilities that would come with ruling this Dow Dynasty may no longer be an issue. Perhaps returning home to Earth sooner rather than later just became a whole lot more likely. So why was he so bothered? So, frustrated with himself? Babar's procedure had apparently failed, or maybe only marginally worked. He still had little access to Prince Markus's memories—other than the obscure comment he received now and then.

Both Babar and Lena glanced back to him as he entered. Babar said, "Eavesdropping is impolite, boy."

"Sorry . . . I didn't want to intrude."

"Uh huh," Lena said, heavy with sarcasm.

Justin was mesmerized by the blur of starlight out the forward spacescreen. "Maybe we'll see Saturn or Jupiter?"

"Wow, he knows his own planetary system. We have absolutely nothing to worry about, Babar," Lena said with more sarcasm. She continued on, "Yeah, we're passing the orbit of Jupiter, but despite your elementary-school solar system charts, the planets aren't lined up straight and all convenient like that. And anyway, we're traveling faster than light so you wouldn't see it anyway. So much for the procedure..."

"Why is it my fault the procedure was a bust? That doesn't mean I can't learn. Can't you just load me up with the memories I need...those MemSnap things?"

"Doesn't work that way," she said, shaking her head. When she looked back to him, clearly annoyed, her features softened somewhat. "Think of MemSnaps as textbooks in a pill. But there's no pill for one's personal memories...their experiences. And even if there were, it would be illegal to dispense them." She shot a disapproving glance toward Babar.

Babar said, "Take a seat. Listen, and learn. When we have time, I'll get you the necessary MemSnap for you to be of use to us. Till then, keep quiet."

Justin sat in silence for as long as he could. "You really know how to defend yourself, Lena," he said. "I suppose Markus was like that too?"

She exchanged a quick glance with Babar. He said, "You may as well bring him, and me, up to speed."

She turned in her seat to face Justin. She looked as though

she was choosing her words carefully. "Years ago, my brother was involved in an incident of sorts. More of a stunt gone terribly wrong. One of his friends was killed. Someone Markus cared for more than he'd even admitted to himself. Her death was a big deal. It rocked the foundation of the realm and cast the sovereignty in a terrible light. Look, Markus was already considered an arrogant, self-centered shit. So, he was sent away. To the Shan Bahn Mountains on Calunoth, where he would be watched over by Relian High Priests. And, hopefully, learn to quell his foul temper. Learn to play well with others."

"How'd that go?" Justin asked.

She shrugged. "Who knows? Markus was a master of deceit. But at least he didn't kill anyone, and he mastered Relian Wham Dhome."

"Relian what?"

"Relian Wham Dhome... it's the ancient martial arts taught by the High Priests."

"And how is it you know how to fight the way you do?"

Babar glanced her way, also looking curious.

"I too attended the order atop the Shan Bahn Mountains on Calunoth. The Magistor and Magistra were incensed, couldn't understand why I'd want to do such a thing. Go there. But as much as I've always clashed with my older brother, I guess I also wanted to be like him. Anyway, it was about ten miles from where Markus was. This one was strictly for females and female priests. I wasn't there quite as long as Markus had attended his order, and Markus had moved on to the academy by then. I guess about two years into my stay, I was pulled out.

It was supposed to be a temporary break. The royal family was going on special holiday. All four of us—Mom, Dad, Markus, and me. I didn't want to go, and my brother was furious at having to leave the academy—even for a few weeks. But apparently, the royal family needed some good optics... positive public relations."

"Doesn't sound so bad... spending time with family after such a long span away from each other," Justin interjected.

Lena ignored the comment. "We were en route to visit several important Dow Dynasty planetary systems. Hopefully shore up waning support within distant worlds bordering the outer reaches of Dynasty space... what we refer to as the frontier zone. Areas influenced heavily by the Empire."

She looked over to Babar. "There'd been a last-minute rescheduling and Babar, who was the Noble-Fist to the aristocracy, wouldn't be traveling with us. When we came out of Zyln, we found that our accompanying security detail of eight warships hadn't made the jump with us. We were alone in quasi-hostile space. While attempting to make contact with our escort fleet, we were attacked. Within minutes, we were boarded and taken prisoner. The last think I remember was being tossed within that hyper tube and feeling the thing being pumped full of that green sludge. You were there when I woke up... you both were. That was when I learned my family was dead. Or rather, Markus was." She looked down, pensively.

"I'm sorry. I guess I'm a reminder of what you've lost... with your brother and all."

"Don't flatter yourself. You may look like him, but you're

little more than a pathetic replica. An aimless child incapable of much of anything from what I've observed thus far."

"Come on, Lena . . ." Babar said.

"It's *Princess* Lena . . . and it's true. He's far more trouble than he's worth. Why you had to conjure up that my brother Markus was still alive, I have no idea!" she said, raising her voice and looking frustrated.

"Because, at the time, I thought all of you were dead!" Babar protested. "The Dynasty was in desperate need of their sovereign family. Bringing back Markus, or what you call this pathetic replica, was intended to reunite a disheartened realm. One that the Empire was increasingly attacking. I didn't know your mother and father had, somehow, survived, and I certainly never imagined you'd eventually awaken from that hyper tube."

Both Lena and Babar looked angry and frustrated.

"We on Earth have a word for this," Justin said.

They both looked at him curiously.

"Clusterfuck . . . it's a clusterfuck."

Both Babar and Lena smiled.

"I don't think the MemSnap we sniffed included that particular . . . um, vernacular," Lena said. "Look, I'm sorry I called you a pathetic replica. I'm sure you have many admiral qualities. You've picked up some of my brother's muscle memories . . . I saw that during your practice trainings."

"You don't have to apologize. I don't get my feelings hurt all that easily."

"Good. Because I probably won't be very nice to you in the future. For as long as you're with us."

"Whatever. Don't worry about it. Since we're talking about the future, how long do you think I'll be playing the part of Markus, now? When will I be able to go home?"

Both Lena and Justin looked to Babar.

"We'll have to see. Perhaps figure out a convenient way for you to be . . . killed off. Then get you back to Earth. Since you've received little of Lena's brother's memories, you're more of a liability at this stage. So sooner rather than later. Around others, keep your mouth shut. Don't make this any more of a clusterfuck, as you put it, than necessary."

Lena nodded disapprovingly at Justin. "I'll take him back to medical . . . load him up with more MemSnaps . . . what he needs to learn about the ship and realm history. Anything else?" she asked Babar.

Babar glanced at him. "He's spent a number of years at both the order atop the Shan Bahn Mountains on Calunoth and the Dynasty's Space-Flight Academy. Get him as much deep-learning as we have onboard. It'll have to do. Oh, and the various languages Markus would be familiar with by now."

Lena stood and gestured for Justin to stand. "Up you go," she said.

"Hold on to something," Babar said. "I'm kicking us into Zyln."

Justin glanced up just in time to see the star field beyond the starshield window blur into a composite of stretched points of light. He felt his stomach lurch and the bridge sway beneath his feet.

chapter 35

Aila Tuffy

University of Chicago Medical Center

A ila sat in her bed a few more minutes, thinking and worrying about Justin. She replayed their last conversation one more time. *I can't just sit here.* Immediately, she got herself up and out of bed, found her clothes and shoes, and proceeded to get dressed. Her shirt had been literally cut off her and was a bloody mess—so she improvised by simply tucking her hospital gown into her jeans. It looked sort of stupid, but she didn't care. She glanced out through the open curtain, knowing her father would be back any second. She hurried out of the examining room and moved toward the ER's exit. Within a minute, she was standing alone in an elevator heading upward. She'd find Kilian Trip's room and get the full story from her.

An hour later, having listened to what Kilian recounted from Justin earlier, she sat back in the bedside chair, shaking her head.

"I know ... it sounds crazy," Kilian said. "Aliens? A spacecraft hidden within that old factory? But I know my son. He's never lied to me. So, he's either delusional or ..."

"Or it's the truth," Aila said, finishing her sentence.

Kilian said, "There's nothing you can do. Find your father and go home. Rest. Your body needs to heal, Aila. Don't worry, I'll keep you appraised of what's going on."

"There you are," came a stern voice to her left. "I've been looking all over this damn hospital for you, young lady. Security personnel are going floor by floor. What were you thinking, leaving the ER without telling me?"

"Sorry, Dad ... I just had to get out of there. Needed to talk to Justin's mom."

The furrow of his scowl lessened some when he glanced over to Kilian.

"I'm sorry if she's bothering you," he said.

"No, it's fine. It's been nice having the company," Kilian said.

Aila stood and moved to join her father. She looked back. "He's not delusional, you know."

Kilian nodded. "I guess that's what I'm afraid of."

* * *

Hours later, at home and lying in bed, staring at her bedroom ceiling, Aila had come to a decision. She glanced over to the clock on her night table. It was after midnight. The house was quiet—she'd heard her father retreat to his room around nine o'clock. Earlier, she'd had some soup and taken a shower before saying goodnight to him. He was still upset. The whole ordeal had taken its toll on her dad and she felt bad—god, these last few years …

She swung the covers off of herself and proceeded to get dressed, taking care with her injured shoulder as she pulled on a sweatshirt. She filled her school backpack with a few necessities, including a change of clothes and a flashlight. Once downstairs, she grabbed her father's car keys from the hook in the foyer. Being careful not to make any noise, she opened the front door. She looked back, up to the top of the stairs. Her dad had been through so much. The loss of her mother. Today's craziness. She was tempted to close the door and return to her bed. Instead, she stepped outside and closed the door behind her. Her father's old Plymouth sat in the driveway where they'd left it hours earlier. She hurried to the driver's side door. *Sorry Dad …*

A bit later, she pulled to the curb in front of Wrigley's Chewing Gum Factory, having had to maneuver around what looked to be the remnants of several still-smoldering, bonfires on the street.

She sat there in the dark, willing her pounding heartbeat to settle down. *This is too crazy … fucking crazy. Girl, you must have a death wish!* She opened the Plymouth's door and got out. She swung the door and it slammed closed way too loud. She looked about the darkened street feeling as though she was being watched—perhaps by some of the same bangers who'd abducted and beaten her earlier. Had killed her cousin. *What am I doing here?* She unclenched her fists—tried to relax. The old factory loomed high in the darkness.

It took her ten minutes to find a slit in the fence large enough for her to slip through. From there, she eventually found a way inside. She was glad she'd remembered a flashlight as she proceeded down one dark and beyond-scary hallway after another. It wasn't lost on her that others had recently been here. It looked as if someone had peed off in a corner, something yellow pooled there on the floor.

She had no plan, nothing thought out as she headed up the narrow stairway to the second floor. Because some of the outer walls were open to the outside here, she could see more of her surroundings. Most of the walls were bare to the open studs, and the floor was gouged and splintered wooden planks. She moved with care—it would be easy to step on a nail, or fall through an open hole. She entered an open area where trash was everywhere and the place stunk. She followed the layout of the facility while shining the beam of her flashlight into every nook and cranny, half expecting to see someone's face staring back at her at any moment. She veered left and stopped. Something dark was on the floor up ahead. She hesitated before continuing—perhaps it was just another stack of wood scraps. She'd seen several of those here. She took another few steps. It wasn't a stack of wood It was a person. A person lying perfectly still on his back.

Turn around and get the hell out of here! She ignored her inner voice and stepped closer. It was a black man—she took in the MP140s garb. She moved the beam of her flashlight over the body, letting the light illuminate his face.

"Hello, Lewis," she said aloud. She saw the red bullet hole between his eyes and a trickle of blood that had run down one side of his face. "I only wish it hadn't been so quick, you piece of shit."

She heard a faint scuffling sound farther into the building. She audibly gasped as she frantically swept her flashlight into the darkened gloom beyond. *There!* Another body lay on the floor about twenty feet away. Her thoughts immediately turned to Justin. *Movement!* A leg, no, an arm moved. "Justin? Is that you?"

Taking tentative steps now, she proceeded forward. She scanned the floor for something to use as a weapon. Spotting a length of two-by-four, she knelt and picked it up—not letting her flashlight waver from the prone body. She approached slowly while raising the two-by-four. Her shoulder hurt where she'd had stitches, but she ignored it. And then she saw who it was. He was even bigger than she'd remembered him. She saw he'd raised his head, and his two eyes were staring back at her. GG-Guns. He looked to be hurt. *Good.* She wanted to finish the job, but wondered how she could both hold on to the flashlight and beat him to a pulp with the two by four at the same time.

It was then that they came out of the darkness. Ten, no, eleven, no, twelve of them. They were dressed in uniforms, and upon closer inspection, she saw they each carried a kind of pistol in one hand. She raised the flashlight's beam into one of their faces.

The man was not a man. At least not like any man she had ever seen. Sure, he had two eyes, a nose and a moth, but the nose was where the chin should have been and the mouth was where the nose should have been. Not hideous. Not grotesque. Just weird. *Oh my . . . these, most assuredly, are aliens.*

Three of them approached at once. Aila heard herself try to yell for help—but it was more of a squeak than a yell. She dropped the two by four. She dropped the flashlight. Everything went dark.

chapter 36

Harrage Zeab

Pinterthor War Ship, High Orbit over Earth

Zeab watched as the *Pinterthor's* drop-shuttle, one of six, crossed in through the bay's blue-glowing energetics boundary—the threshold between the harshness of cold, open space and the warship's environmentally and gravitationally controlled flight bay. The small craft slowed and ceased its forward progress—then, pivoting on its horizontal axis forty degrees, it gently descended down onto the deck in between in-line drop-shuttles number two and number four.

He already knew Babar's Stinger was gone—had left the confines of a crumbling terrestrial structure on Earth within the last hour. Only now, obviously repaired, the gun ship would not be leaving such an easy trail for them to follow. The stinger's radiation wake would be properly disrupted and scattered, making the *Pinterthor's* tracking sensors useless.

What he did know was that Babar was still alive. He knew his vessel was now fully operational. So now what he needed was verifiable intel. Such as, were the prince and princess still alive? Had Babar successfully extracted one or both of them from their stasis tube confinements? Had Babar reestablished coms back to Dynasty space? It was a long shot, but he hoped the two abducted humans would be able to answer some of these questions. If not, perhaps they would have other usefulness. Perhaps as a means for a future bargaining. He wouldn't know until the two were properly interrogated.

Fleet Commander Admiral Grishlund stood at his side. Stooped and out of breath from his jaunt here to the flight bay, Zeab had to give the old coot his proper due. He was as hands-on an officer as any he knew. The admiral's career, like Zeab's, hung in the balance of retrieving one or two, if they were so fortunate, Dow Dynasty brats. And of course, lest he forget, Emperor Chi-Sacrim's other not-so-subtle directive. "Bring me back Babar's head in a fucking bucket!

The admiral cleared phlegm from his throat before speaking. "This blue planet . . . they call it Earth. I suggest we stake a claim on it. A gift for the Emperor."

Zeab waited for the shuttle's aft hatchway to open. *What the hell is taking so long?* He shot a glance to the Admiral. "Technically, this is Dynasty Frontier Space."

"I am well aware of that, Chancellor. But, it is only a matter of time before that will be remedied."

Zeab wondered if Admiral Grishlund had more definitive knowledge than he did concerning the possibility of an out-and-out war. Sure, Dynasty and Empire fringe skirmishes had been going on for decades. And the Empire had been making substantial spacial territorial grabs of late. But actual war? Zeab smiled. If he couldn't play this old relic, then he himself should think about retiring.

Zeab said, "So, I take it you have been briefed? I didn't think you had been cleared for—"

The old officer abruptly turned toward him. "I am an admiral, a fleet commander, Chancellor . . . of course I have been briefed! Why you have been, well, that is not so clear to me."

"Emperor Chi-Sacrim relies heavily on my council. You must know that, Admiral. War . . . he does not take the prospect of it lightly."

"Nor should he. But it is time. Well past time. Strike while the Dow Dynasty is in disarray. While their beloved sovereignty remains broken."

Zeab nodded as if this was all old news to him. He watched as the shuttle's uniformed ground patrol were now, finally, descending the shuttle's aft gangway. Two prisoners, both with their hands bound, were being escorted in the direction of where Zeab and the Admiral stood.

"I'm surprised you have accompanied us on this . . . expedition, Admiral. Knowing what is coming. Surely, as the commander of the third fleet, you would want to be there, with your—"

"I agree, Chancellor," the admiral interjected. "And I made that same point to the emperor. But he assured me, no offensive engagements would be initiated prior to Lark's Call."

Zeab nodded. Lark's Call was the Empire's preeminent yearly celebration. Two weeks of the year where all Empire subjects were required to give thanks, not to mention substantial tiding offerings, to the Empire's government body. It had started back when the Demyan populous was introduced to intergalactic space travel by a visiting, seemingly friendly alien named Pahll Lark. He and his contingent had arrived from a neighboring planetary system.

Promising global stability, prosperity, and the end to all wars, the populous would soon hand over all governmental control to Lark and his minions. Quickly gone were the once democratic and free societies that inhabited Demyan. And his invasion of what he coined "heathen worlds" had not stopped with that planet. Anointing himself Emperor of all known space, now three centuries ago, Emperor Pahll Lark's legacy of total intergalactic dominance had continued until they stumbled across, many light years' distance away, another, perhaps even larger galactic force known as the Dow Dynasty. It was a monarchy by nature, and its worlds were not subjugated as the Empire's were. In fact, there was a long and stringent submission process to even be considered for acceptance into the realm and all the benefits that come from such inclusion— including protection from the realm's six warship fleets, and even more importantly, the profitable trading rights with other Dow Dynasty members.

The uniformed patrol of fifteen came to a stop several paces in front of them. The highest-ranking soldier among them, called a Gallant-Arms, slapped his chest in salute and said, "Prisoners delivered without incident, sirs."

Zeab took several strides forward. He wanted to get a better, up-close look at these two Earth beings. One was clearly female, the other a quite large male, who was of a different race. Zeab already knew this Earth planet had a number of races—as did many worlds within the galaxy. He studied their grotesque faces, not dissimilarly as he had studied the sovereign Pietra family's faces, sometimes for hours on end, within the Enclave, back on Broudy-Lum starstation. As he had then, he now pondered how—how, with the juxtaposition of their mouths and noses, could their anatomy possibly function?

The female glowered back at him. "Why are we here? What do you want with us?"

Zeab was somewhat surprised he understood her words, this barbaric fringe world language. Obviously, at some point, he'd sniffed a MemSnap containing the associated linguistic DNA storage.

"Before I answer any of your questions, you must first answer mine. Those are my terms. You are free to decline, whereby I will have Gallant-Arms Fraing here separate your head from your neck."

The sound of metal scraping against metal brought the female's attention over to a short sword being unsheathed by one of the uniformed soldiers. Before the female could answer, though, the larger Earth being spoke. "Hey, hey ... I'll tell you whatever you want to know, man. Just ask. No need to be pulling no blades here."

"Excellent!" Zeab said, smiling, then splaying his hands out wide in a friendly gesture as if welcoming a long-lost friend. "So glad we avoided the whole decapitation business ... so messy. Certainly not how our new Earth friends should be properly welcomed into the Empire."

"Empire? Are you serious?"

Zeab was already tired of this skinny female. "Please, tell me your name."

She stared up at him for a long few moments before replying, "My name is Aila ... and this soon-to-be traitor to all humanity is GG ... GG-Guns is his stupid name." She glowered at the black-skinned Earth being.

"Aila and GG-Guns," Zeab repeated.

"Just GG is fine, man ... keep things casual. What people call you, dude?" GG asked.

"I am Chancellor Harrage Zeab. Pleas, call me Chancellor."

"Well you're not going to get away with this, Harrage whoever the fuck you are."

What a little starburst this Earthling was, he thought to himself. He had to give her her due—she was no coward.

"Such disrespect ... I shall terminate this vulgar creature myself!" the admiral said from behind them, with more acrimony than Zeab thought the old fleet commander possessed.

Zeab said, "Young Aila is clearly upset. Perhaps after an

adequate meal and some rest, she will be more affable. Ready to converse like a civilized representative of her beautiful world."

Now, GG looked both perturbed and perplexed, "What's this bunkass bullshit? I just said . . . I'll give you all the 411 you want. So, where's *my* alien snitzel . . . *my* ET panda express? Not sure why I'm being disrespected here."

Zeab had no idea what the human male just said. He saw the corners of Aila's lips curl upward into the briefest of smiles. *These are strange, complicated beings,* Zeab thought. He contemplated letting the admiral just kill them. *Soon.* First, he needed what, if any, information they had on Babar and that gun ship of his. He looked up at the one who called himself GG. "Tell me, what does . . . 411 mean?"

chapter 37

Justin Trip

Stinger Gun Ship, 700 million miles from Earth

"Why are you slowing down?" Justin said, standing at the back of the bridge.

When Babar didn't immediately answer, Lena did for him, "Behind us . . . long-range sensors have detected two Warships have entered Earth's high orbit." She looked over to Babar, "Though it's not our problem. We have our own, far more pressing issues."

"Wait a minute . . . warships? What kind of warships?"

Babar said, "Destroyer-class. The *Pinterthor* and the *Mortise* . . . both formidable Empire vessels. Even just one would be far more than this little gun ship could manage."

"Wait, you're telling me the Empire is here? And what? They're going to attack Earth?"

"Doubtful. The Empire is looking for this Stinger. For me. They'd have no reason to fire on your world," Babar said.

"He's right," Lena added. "Although, you can bet they'll be tagging Earth for later inclusion into the Empire. It's what they do . . ."

Babar shot Lena an annoyed look.

"Turn this ship around!" Justin said.

Babar looked over his shoulder. "No."

"Turn around. I've changed my mind. I'm not helping you . . . take me back to Earth."

"You made a promise . . . now it's your turn to keep your end of the bargain."

"I won't do it. Go back and help—do whatever you can to save Earth. That or I'll never, ever, help you."

"Absolutely not!" Lena said. "Your Markus experiment didn't work anyway, Babar. The human will be useless to us . . . more of a liability, in fact."

But Babar continued to stare at Justin—clearly weighing his options.

Justin said, but this time to Lena, "So . . . if things were reversed, are you telling me you'd just let your own home planet come under attack from Empire forces?"

"That's different. Not close to the same thing."

"How so?" Justin said staring her down.

She let out a long breath and turned her gaze out the side

window. "Is there anything we can do? Without getting ourselves killed in the process?"

Babar was busy tapping at his console. He looked to be considering something. "Well, it seems both vessels have been in a recent fight. Sensors have picked up hull damage, some of which looks to be significant."

"To both warships?" Justin asked.

Babar nodded, still tapping away. Justin could hear a faint female voice emanating from the console. After a full minute, he turned in his seat. "We might live through one fly-by. One surprise stealth-running offensive attack. It'll be dangerous. OCI calculates our odds at about even that we'd survive."

"Forget it!" Lena said letting out an exaggerated teenage gasp. "Sure, you want to drop him back home, that's your prerogative. But risking all our lives taking on Empire warships? No way!"

But Babar was looking at Justin. "That's my offer . . . one pass. If that's not good enough, I'll take the princess's suggestion and drop you back in Chicago."

He thought about that. "Can we make sure they follow us and don't stay back there near Earth?"

"I assure you, boy, if, and that's a big if, we survive, we will have two war ships hot on our tail. With luck, I've the repaired propulsion system will hold and we'll lose them once we engage the Zyln-strap. But I'm all out of guarantees."

"Okay, I can agree to that," Justin said.

Both Justin and Babar looked to the princess. She didn't meet either of their eyes, continued to stare out through the forward spacescreen. Eventually, she said, "Just don't get us killed . . . I'd like to see my parents again. Make it back home."

"Sit down and strap in, Justin," Babar said as he took the controls in hand. "Things are about to get real exciting here."

Justin did as asked and watched as the big Parian man expertly piloted the little gun ship into a backward barrel roll, leveled out, and then accelerated back the way they'd come. G-forces momentarily pinned him to his seat. Justin felt exhilarated by the maneuver. Now, looking at Lena, he wanted to tell her to swap seats with him. Tell her that he was the one with true flight experience here. *Where's that coming from?* He thought, and then knew precisely where it had come from—*Markus.*

They returned at what appeared to be a much-higher speed, though it still felt excruciatingly long as Justin paced, considering the situation back on Earth. Finally, they dropped out of Zyln, and after a couple more impatient minutes, Justin looked up as Lena shouted.

"There!" She pointed straight ahead.

Justin, momentarily memorized by Earth's captivating beauty, shortly after saw the two distinct shapes in what he surmised was a high orbit. As they approached, the warships grew in size—looking even more formidable. Along their hulls corresponding to the various deck levels, hundreds of tiny lights twinkled from porthole windows. It occurred to Justin that this really was a crazy idea. A guppy attacking two blue whales. Babar was slowing their approach.

"How far out are we?" Justin asked.

"Coming up on two hundred miles from their orbit."

"What are we doing?"

Lena shot him an annoyed look.

Babar said, "I need to run a few simulations . . . pipe down."

Projected between Lena and Babar, but still close to the console, a 3D holographic representation of Earth, the two warships, and their gun ship, had taken high-res form.

"Now that's cool," Justin said.

"It's just a simple Holo-Sim," Lena said.

Justin watched, captivated, as the tiny version of their Stinger approached and then shot forward, shooting between the two war ships, all the while firing energy weapons as well as projectiles—rail guns. The *Pinterthor* and the *Mortise*, almost immediately, began to return fire, although it looked to be a fairly lack-luster response. Then he got it—of course it would be lackluster—it would be all too easy for the two mammoth warships to damage each other being in such close proximity to one another, and with the flight path Babar was planning.

Babar said, "See . . . Ocile has calculated the damaged and most vulnerable sections of the enemy hull locations for us."

Babar used his hands to swing the perspective around of the Halo-sim. Then magnified the perspective view from between the *Pinterthor* and the *Mortise*.

"See, these jagged outlined areas in shades of red and orange . . . they depict the exact areas where hull damage occurred from whatever earlier battle they endured."

"And the darker areas that are more red? Those show the more significant damage?"

"He sure is a sharp one," Lena said, rolling her eyes.

Babar ignored her jab and continued, "Ocile has now computed the most effective flight path for us, along with the timing for firing missiles . . . allowing for trajectories that will cause the most damage. The princess and I can concentrate our efforts manning the plasma canons and rail guns."

"What do you want me to do?" Justin asked. "Are there *virt-stick* controls here at this station I'm at?"

Both Babar and Lena stopped what they were doing and looked at him. "How did you know what to call the weapon controls?" Babar asked.

Justin shrugged. He didn't know how he knew.

"Well, you can try shutting up and staying out of the way," Lena said activating her own *virt-stick* controls at her station. Babar followed suit, bringing up his own *virt-stick* controls.

"Do they know we're here? Are we showing up their sensors?" Justin asked.

"No . . . but as soon as we make our move, they'll catch sight of us." Babar looked at Justin and then to Lena. "Here we go. Ocile . . . take us in. Attack!"

chapter 38

G-forces drove Justin hard back into his seat prior to the inertia compensators kicking in. Almost immediately, the gun ship was upon the prows of the two warships and then just as quickly swooping into the narrow space between them. One moment, harsh sunlight was streaming in through the forward starshield; the next, they were rocketing into deep shadow. It was as if two immense chasm walls were flanking their port and starboard sides.

The 3D projection model rotated and updated as they progressed. The *Pinterthor's* and *Mortise's* most vulnerable hull sections strobed red as targeting vectors resolved in real time. Every weapons system suddenly came alive, and Justin knew precisely what was what—the repetitive and heavy recoils coming up through the deck plates were missile ordinances being fired off. The two big pounders, projectile-firing rail guns, came alive with an earsplitting clang, and finally, all six rotating plasma cannons could be heard from up atop the little ship. Outside, the black of space had come alive—like a Fourth of July extravaganza, ablaze with multiple streams of golden targeting tracers and countless blue plasma bursts, along with the short-range missiles, with their incandescent amber exhaust making their way across the divide—locked on-course to their specified targets.

The first magnificent fiery eruption came from the *Pinterthor's* forward starboard side. A plume of expelled atmosphere sprayed forth along with indeterminate debris. There were bodies there too. A lot of bodies. Arms and legs flailed for several moments before freezing in the vacuum. Space was a harsh and cruel environment.

Two more explosions occurred on the *Mortise's* port side—more spewing atmosphere, debris, and bodies. That was when the two colossal warships began to return fire.

Bright, crimson-colored plasma bursts seemed to be coming from every direction. Almost immediately, the temperatures within the small bridge edged up.

Lena yelled above all the noise, "Shields already down to 50 percent!"

Both Lena and Babar were busy manning the Stinger's plasma cannons.

"Activate my station! Give me the two aft cannons!" Justin yelled.

Babar glanced back at him with an unsure expression.

"Do it . . . I know what to do!"

With that, the console and two virt-stick controls hovered right there front of him. Taking one in each hand, Justin joined the fight. His thumbs triggered the firing action and he felt a tactile response, from the virtual controls, along with the patter of gunfire. Justin couldn't keep the smile from his lips. His eyes were glued to the holographic 3D battle model; somehow, he was able to determine which two streams of plasma fire were derived from his cannons.

The Stinger had wreaked surprising damage upon the enemy vessels. One seemingly catastrophic explosion after another followed in their wake. As each missile found its mark, the resulting explosion illuminated the gun ship's bridge like repetitive camera flashes. And the successfully targeted areas on the *Pinterthor's* and *Mortise's* projected 3D model's flickered out.

Approaching the mid-ship area of the two warships, Justin noticed things were getting more than a little warm within the confines of the bridge.

"Shields down to 30 percent . . . outer hulls starting to overheat," Lena said.

Justin could see the same readings, the entire ship's telemetry, but found Lena's verbal announcements strangely comforting.

"We've got company!" Babar said.

Justin looked up and saw them through the starshield. Five, no six, enemy Rage-Fighters. "Only six?" Justin said.

"I made sure to take out both ships' flight bays first thing, so not sure where even these guys game from. Perhaps a training shoot—"

"It doesn't matter! They're big trouble for us," Lena said, cutting Babar off.

"Leave them to me," Justin said. "This is what I was trained for. I want all six cannons. Do it, now!" he demanded.

Babar and Lena didn't hesitate. Babar said, "You have all the cannons!"

Justin went to work. A part of him was back within the academy's battle simulators, another part later, when he'd sat within the cockpit of a FireCat fighter during live battle sims. No one had scored higher than he had—not within his own academy squad, nor any of the others. In a battle situation, it was as if a switch got flipped. He became an intuitive, high-functioning, killing machine at the controls. Tapping at his control board, he brought up a separate virtual bounding box tracker for each virt-stick control.

The fighters came at them head on, then split apart mere meters in front of them, three per side.

"They're coming around . . . flanking us," Babar said.

"Shut up and let me concentrate!" Justin snapped back. He watched as the sets of three Rage-Fighters were positioning for their simultaneous attacks. "This isn't going to work—give me help helm control!" Justin said, his voice even and self-assured.

This time Babar did hesitate.

"Don't do it!" Lena yelled. "He's just a kid . . ."

"You have the helm," Babar said. "Hope you know what you're doing."

So did Justin. *Or was it Markus?* He banked the Stinger hard left, throttled forward into a downward reverse-barrel roll, and then banked hard right. He'd positioned the Stinger right in behind three of the fighters—undoubtedly surprising them in the process. He let loose with all six plasma cannons at once.

One, two, and then three Rage-Fighters exploded right in front of them. Justin cranked the controls, avoiding hitting their remnant space debris. "Three down ... three to go," he said.

"Yeah, well they're coming up on us fast from our stern!" Lena said.

Justin held their current course. He even slowed a bit.

"What the hell are you doing?" Lena barked, spinning around in her seat to glare at him. "They're right on us ... do something! We're taking it up the tailpipe—our shields are just about gone!"

Justin ignored her—waited, waited, waited, then flipped the Stinger up horizontally like a ready-to-turn pancake. Again, he did the reverse-barrel roll routine and again throttled forward. Streaks of bright crimson plasma fire shot by both side windows. As he came out of the next tight maneuver, the gun ship was approaching them from below and to the left. Justin's thumbs engaged the Stinger's plasma cannons. All three rage fighters exploded at the same time. Neither Babar nor Lena said anything.

Again, Justin eyed the virtual 3D battle model. Only five vulnerable hull area remained highlighted—one on the *Pinterthor* and two on the *Mortise*. Apparently, Ocile had continued firing more missiles, even during the course of the looping, dodging, dog-fight moments before. *Impressive.*

A massive explosion erupted from the stern area of the *Mortise*—one unlike any of the others thus far.

"We need to get out of here," Babar said.

Both Lena and Justin watched as the warship seemed to take on a strange inner glow.

"She's going critical . . . internally, already engulfed in fire. Any moment, her engines will erupt and we'll be atomized right along with her. Get us out of here, Justin!" Babar said.

He gunned the Stinger's dual engines. At first it seemed as though they weren't moving at all—as if were stuck in place. But it was an optical illusion. The *Pinterthor* was moving along right with them at the same pace. Justin glanced down to the console—they had put close to a hundred miles between themselves and the doomed *Mortise*.

Then she exploded.

Momentarily, it seemed as if another sun had appeared in space behind them. The blast was so bright, Justin had to squeeze his eyelids shut.

He blinked—he knew there was still another warship to contend with. Expecting to find it still out his port-side window, he was surprised to see it hadn't kept up.

"Taking back helm control," Babar said. "And good job back there."

"I think you and I both know that wasn't me . . ." Suddenly exhausted, Justin let out a long breath and leaned his head back. He felt his heart rate slowing. The spiked hit of adrenalin in his bloodstream was now normalizing.

Babar, keeping the Stinger a good distance away from the

Pinterthor, was circling the big, clearly crippled warship. Bright flashes here and there, like electrical discharges, made for an eerie scene. Justin wondered if this once-formidable warship was soon to follow in her sister's path.

Babar said, "OCI . . . provide status of the enemy's weapons systems."

"Ship-wide weapons systems have been destroyed or significantly damaged."

"And propulsion?" he asked.

"Marginally operational. Taken off-line for crucial repairs."

"Good, so she's no threat and not going anywhere anytime soon . . ." Babar said.

Lena said, "OCI, how many survivors are there?"

"There are 207 organic life forms still present, 205 of which are consistent with Horthian DNA."

Lean said, "Those are Empire lifeforms . . . probably from the areas around Demyan."

Justin considered that. "What about the other two? So they aren't Horthian DNA?"

Ocile replied, "Correct. Both human. A male and a female. Both are being held within the *Pinterthor's* high-security corridor. What you would call the ship's brig. I have verified contact with one of them is possible."

The three of them exchanged perplexed looks. Justin said, "Just how would we do that? Communicate with one of them."

"Archaic technology, wireless personal communications devices which receive their signals from land-based towers. A 'cell' is typically the area of several kilometers around a tower in which a signal can be received—"

"Hold on, Ocile ... you're telling me one of them has a cell phone? And it's turned on?"

"That is correct."

"And—you can communicate with that kind of signal?" Justin asked.

"Of course, rudimentary."

"Do it. Call the phone on that ship."

chapter 39

Aila Tuffy—
Shortly before the battle

Demyan Empire Warship, Pinterthor—Earth's High Orbit

Aila sat upon the cold, hard, metal bench with her arms wrapped tightly around her pulled-in legs. *This can't be happening,* she told herself for the tenth time. She was being held within an approximately ten-foot-by-ten-foot, glass cage—a prisoner. And she wasn't alone here. The big gang-banger, GG-Guns, was sprawled out on the deck, dozing. Fear and uncertainty had turned to anger. She thought about stand-ing up and kicking GG in the balls. She pictured herself doing it—she'd put all her weight into it. Maybe kick him two or three times, consecutively. It was because of him, and Lewis, and those other vicious losers, that her cousin was dead. And now she was a captive—a captive stuck here with him!

Aila and GG had been escorted over to a fast-moving elevator and then through a maze of interconnecting passageways. Eventually, they had been deposited here, to this glass-enclosed jail cell. And here she sat, staring at the now-snoring gangbanger on the floor. She had a number of questions. How the hell had GG-Guns just fallen asleep given the circumstances? When would Zeab come to speak with her again? *What am I supposed to do if I have to pee?* There was a white cube-like thing in the corner. *Is that a toilet? Am I supposed to know how to use that thing—and use it, like, right here in the open?*

The bench beneath her vibrated, then jostled her body more vigorously. An alarm sounded from somewhere overhead, a klaxon blaring four times, then pausing, then four more. She stood and approached the enclosure—placed her palms on the glass and stared out. "Hello? What's happening?"

The floor beneath her shook harder—it was like an earthquake. *But how is that possible?* This was a massive spaceship. *What could possibly cause ... Oh no ...* It was faint at first. The sound of distant, repetitive explosions. Explosions that were now getting louder and louder. The jail cell began shaking to the point Aila had to lower herself down to the floor. GG's unconscious form rolled this way and that like a floppy, dead carcass. Suddenly, Aila was in the air sideways, her back careening into the seat of the metal bench. She screamed out, feeling a sharp pain where her ribcage took the brunt of the hit. More explosions erupted around her, even louder now—and like a ragdoll, she was tossed to the other side of the cell. For another five or six long minutes, it continued like this—where at any moment, she was sure the next blast would land right on top of her and GG-Guns.

When the ship finally stopped shaking and the explosions had stopped, she was on the floor, the back of her head lying next to GG's. His eyes were wide open. His mouth agape. It wasn't until he blinked, that Aila was able to confirm he was alive.

"What's happening?"

She rolled onto her side, and wincing with pain, got herself up into a seated position. GG-Guns appeared terrified. She smelled the acrid odor of warn urine—the young man had pissed himself.

Aila stood, finding that her balance was somewhat off. She took a tentative step away from him, and then another. Only then did she look down at him. She stood two paces away from his easily size-twelve shoes. She didn't hesitate. She didn't even have to think about it. She took one, then two steps, and drove the toe of her right shoe into GG-Guns's testicles. Was it all she'd imagined it would be? *No.* So she kicked him twice more.

For another ten minutes, she sat on the hard metal bench, watching GG curled up into the fetal position, groaning and moaning—his tear-streaked face frozen in agony.

The ship had clearly been attacked. And it seemed it had come out on the wrong side of things. *What now . . . are we just going to die here, trapped in this little room, GG and me?*

"What is that?" she said, trying to wrap her mind around

a sound coming from GG-Guns's back pocket. Then she knew what it was—"Nuthin' But A G Thang." GG's phone was playing an old Dre and Snoop rap ring tone. But how could he be getting a phone call here—up in space? That would be impossible.

By the chorus of "It's like this and like that, aha . . . and it's like this and like that," Aila was on the move. She'd watched as GG attempted to reach for his back pocket. She dove, but he got to it first, bringing the phone to his ear. He raised his foot, kicking her away.

GG said, "Hello. Who is this? I need help!"

chapter 40

Justin Trip—Present Time

Gun Ship, orbiting Earth . . .

Justin listened to the clicks and pops as the connection was being made. The ringing phone sound filled the confines of the bridge.

A man's deep voice answered, and Justin responded. "Who is this? Who am I talking to?"

"I need help . . . I'm being held here—in a damn jail or something."

"And you're on a spaceship?" Justin confirmed.

"Yeah! It makes no sense . . . no sense at all!"

"Okay. Tell me your name?"

"Gordon Gerber. But everyone calls me GG . . . GG-Guns. So, are you gunna help me or what? Who you?"

Justin's eyes narrowed hearing the name. The last time he'd

seen GG was him laid out on the factory floor. "Tell me who's there with you, GG. Who's the other person?"

"Um, her name's Alliyah or something."

"What? Aila? No."

GG said, "Look, you need to call NASA. Get me the hell off this—"

"Put her on. Hand Aila the phone," Justin said, his mind racing—trying to connect the dots. How was it possible she was onboard that ship? How was it possible either of them were?

"Hello? This is Aila ..."

It was like being zapped by an electrical shock, hearing her voice. "Are you okay, Aila? Are you hurt?"

"Justin?"

"Yes. We're close ... coming for you. Are you hurt?"

"Hey! Wait a minute ... we're doing no such thing," Lena said defiantly.

Aila said, "No, I'm fine. GG could use an icepack for a bruised ball sack, though. We're locked some kind of glass prison cell."

"Hold on a sec, Aila ..." he said.

"What can we do?" He put his attention on Babar. Justin already knew where Lena would stand on the situation.

Babar, still piloting the gun ship around the perimeter of the *Pinterthor,* had called up several new projection readouts. He said, "Virtually every one of the ship's systems is either heavily damaged or destroyed. Environmental support is no longer producing breathable atmosphere. But what's most concerning—the propulsion system, at some point, will go critical." Babar looked back to Justin. "The ship's going to blow up . . . soon."

"I heard that!" Aila said.

"We need to get away from here, now!" Lena said.

Babar said, "Ocile . . . can you access what's left of the *Pinterthor's* network?"

"Affirmative."

"And the security latches for the ship's brig?"

It was several moments before Ocile spoke again, "Disengaged."

Babar asked, "Is the flight bay accessible?"

"It can be . . . one moment . . . Complete."

"Good, show me the quickest escape route from where Aila is situated to the flight bay."

Justin could now see multiple small craft escaping the doomed *Pinterthor* via the flight bay.

Babar said, "Zoom in."

Ocile had projected a 3D holographic internal layout of the *Pinterthor*. It zoomed in to show precisely where Aila and GG-Guns were being held, along with a highlighted green path that led to the flight bay. "Ship's lifts are off-line. I have indicated the stairwell to their closest proximity."

Babar examined the model. "Can you send this image to Aila? To her communication device?"

"Complete," Ocile said.

Justine said, "Aila . . . you see it? What we just sent to your phone?"

"Um, yeah . . . just trying to make heads or tails of it." She sounded like she'd put the phone on speaker mode.

Lena rolled her eyes and let out an exasperated breath.

"Give that to me," came GG's voice. "Read maps like that in the Army."

"You were in the Army?" Aila asked.

Justin was more than a little surprised by that admission, himself. He heard shuffling sounds and fast footfalls. They were making their way through the ship's passageways.

Babar had navigated the gun ship to the *Pinterthor's* bay opening. It was a glowing blue energy field, undoubtedly designed to allow for smaller ships to pass through while keeping the larger ship's atmosphere contained. But the energy field was faltering—blinking on and off.

"Babar . . . don't do this," Lena said. "You have an obligation to protect sovereign subjects, at all costs."

A running count-down clock was now being projected above Babar's station. Justin didn't need to ask what it was for. They had just twelve minutes to pick up Aila and GG and get themselves the hell away from here.

Babar looked at Lena with tired eyes. "Princess, your lack of compassion never ceases to amaze me. We're going to at least try to save that human. You can report my conduct to the Magistor, if we get out of this mess." Babar piloted the Stinger in through flight bay's energy field.

Justin hadn't been prepared for the crazy pandemonium happening within the ship. Multiple fires were burning, and the air was thick with soot. Even through the Stinger's hull, he could hear a repetitive klaxon alarm. Surviving crew members were hurrying to board the few remaining shuttles. He saw why there had been limited Rage-Fighters confronting them out in space—at the far section of the bay, a whole portion of the ceiling had fallen from their attack, blocking what looked to be hundreds of parked fighters.

There was another vessel though, sleek, with a reflective, mirror-like hull. A contingent of uniformed officers, along with several well-dressed dignitaries, were making a mad dash to the craft's lowered gangway.

"You see him?" Lena said.

"I see him . . . but he's not our priority right now."

"Chancellor Harrage Zeab is not our priority? The one responsible for our capture . . . the one responsible for Markus's death!"

"What's happening here?" Justin asked.

"Stay out of it," Lena said.

One of the scurrying dignitaries had noticed the gun ship's arrival into the flight bay. He stopped, hands on hips, and stared up at them. Justin could almost feel the hatred emanating up from the fancily dressed alien. Closer now, Justin saw his face more clearly. His features were all screwed up. That his nose and mouth were transposed. The alien turned and ran for his ship—he had an impressive, long black ponytail.

"Blow that ship up, Babar, or I will!" the princess demanded.

Babar's thumb was poised over his virt-stick controls.

"There! Aila made it to the flight bay!" Justin said, excited. "You can't fire . . . she's too close."

Babar looked conflicted. Justin looked at him, horrified. *Is he actually considering Lena's demands?*

"Just land this thing and pick her up, Babar . . . it's the right thing to do," Justin said.

But Babar was already maneuvering the gun ship around and descending. Out the side window, Justin saw both Aila and GG-Guns looking around—not knowing where to go.

"I'm going to kill him!" Lena said.

Justin saw that this chancellor guy was standing at the still-open hatchway on his ship—watching their decent onto the deck. *Is he taunting us?* They were close enough that Jason could see he was smiling. He gave a kind flippant wave and disappeared into the ship. Immediately, it was ascending up into the flight bay. It's aft thrusters engaged, and the ship was heading for the exit.

The countdown timer read four minutes. The gun ship set down onto the deck.

Babar said, "Go . . . get them onboard!"

By the time Justin appeared at the top of the Stinger's ramp, he saw Aila and GG running toward him—the noise level within the bay was near-deafening. He waved for them to hurry. "We gatta go! Come on!"

Aila was all-out running, while GG looked to be having a tough time of it, winded and limping. Up the ramp Aila came, and right into Justin's arms. Her embrace felt wonderful. But in his mind's eye, he saw the countdown timer ticking down to the final minute. "Go on . . . head inside!" he yelled over the clamor.

GG had made it to the bottom of the ramp by this time, but he was struggling. Sweat glistened on his face, and he stopped to catch his breath.

"No time for that! Up you go, come on. The ship's going to blow any second."

Comprehension settled onto his features, and he laboriously strode up the ramp. Justin got ahold on his arm and did his best to man-handle the big guy upward. "That's it . . . almost there . . . yup, go right into the open hatch."

Justin followed him into the airlock compartment and turned to close the hatch. Three crewman, eyes wide and frantic looking, were ascending the ramp. He'd made the decision to let them onboard. To save their lives. But the hatch suddenly slid shut before they could reach the hatchway. He could still hear their desperate yells for help from outside. He spun around to see Princess Lena standing there. She'd been the one to engage the aft hatch.

"Get yourself strapped in, Justin. We'll be lucky if we make it out of here alive as it is."

As if on cue, the Stinger began to shake. A rumbling noise that coincided with amplifying vibrations let them both know that time had run out.

chapter 41

The G-forces within the now-accelerating Stinger caught the three of them off guard. While GG was on the deck, grasping for anything he could get ahold of, both Justin and Aila were driven back into the nearest bulkhead. He took her hand in his, and together they staggered forward along the main passageway. By the time they'd entered the bridge, Justin saw they were clearing the bay's energy barrier. Babar gunned the propulsion system, and the Stinger rocketed away from the *Pinterthor*. He saw the countdown timer above Babar's console was no longer ticking—anyone still onboard the ill-fated Empire ship was living on borrowed time.

"Sit down! Strap in!" Lena yelled.

Aila looked confused as Justin helped secure her seat belt. He understood Lena's words in her own language just fine, but he realized that of course Aila wouldn't be able to. As if on cue, RP9 was hovering in front of her. An articulating arm emerged from its reflective obsidian shell; a small postage-stamp-sized square device held within the small claw.

"What's this?" Alia ask looking unsure.

"Something to help you understand when I say shut up," Lena said.

It was then the *Pinterthor* blew up.

First came the flash of light through the side windows and forward screen, quickly followed by a wave of debris, the fragmented remains of the vessel, shooting by them at incredible speed.

"Shields are falling—but holding," Babar said.

Justin saw that Lena was looking back at him. Her impertinent stare said it all. They'd cheated death by mere seconds.

"What the hell is she doing?" Lena said.

Aila had unstrapped herself and was now down on all fours.

"Aila?" Justin said.

"The hovering thing dropped it?"

"Dropped it?"

"Whatever that little thing was."

RP9, too, was hovering down near the deck as well, searching alongside Aila. Suddenly, the drone-bot made an almost imperceptible sound as it plucked the little device from a crevice—where the deck and bulkhead came together. Aila took the thing from RP9's outstretched claw and, taking her seat again, held it up—showing it to Justin.

"Are you going to tell me what this is? How do I know it won't hurt me? Change me into something weird?"

"No one's putting a gun to her head . . . she can stay stupid for all I care," Lena said.

Again, Aila looked at Lena with confusion.

"It's called a MemSnap ... it provides you with, um, necessary know-how. For things that would take you a lot of time to learn on your own, like languages and such. There are various others you can take too, like for learning this ship's functionality. Learning that will be absorbed into your physiology via a DNA memory transfer. I've taken several myself. Pretty much insisted when I first came onboard."

Aila looked at the small device. "How do I ..."

Justin took it from her. "When I tell you too, breathe ... or more like sniff in fast." He squeezed the device right under her nose, and it made an audible *snap* sound. "Okay, sniff in!"

She hesitated, then did as told. "Wow ... has a bit of a kick to it." She blinked repeatedly then looked around the bridge. She shrugged. "It didn't work. I don't feel any different."

"Are all humans this stupid?" Lena asked shaking her head.

Aila's eyes widened in shock, and then anger. She'd understood.

GG-Guns was suddenly there, standing at the hatch, breathing hard. "Where are we? And who are they?" he said pointing to Lena and Babar. "Wait ... isn't that the broom-monkey guy from the high school?" He pointed to Babar.

"Never mind," Lena said, "That answers my question. All humans are idiots ..."

Justin said, "RP9, how about you get GG here one of those MemSnaps too?"

"I want to go home ... take me back to Chicago," GG-Guns said, sounding more like a five-year-old than a full-grown man.

"The sooner the better," Lena said. "The both of them need to be dropped off."

"Quiet!" Babar responded, leaning forward and listening to a frantic-sounding verbal broadcast emanating out from his console. Babar looked over to Lena, concern on his face.

Lean shook her head. "We have to go . . . now. How far is it to the Danspair system?" she asked.

"We're actually not that far. Three days at a high Zyln Speed. Probably closer than any other Dynasty vessel," Babar said. "But that's deep within Empire space."

Justin looked from one to the other. "What? What's going on?

"Magistor and Magistra Pietra . . . they've been in hiding for some time now, it turns out. Like us, unable to make it back to Dynasty space, to Calunoth. But they've been discovered and are on the run. They need help."

"Just go, Babar!" Lena said. "Minutes count . . . seconds count!"

"Sorry," Justin said, "looks like you're both going to be with us for the foreseeable future. How about I show you the ship?"

"I'm not going anywhere with him," Aila said.

Justin didn't blame her. He looked over to Lena, who nodded. She'd show GG around on her own—hopefully, not out the airlock. He momentarily considered kicking the man out himself. *No . . . I'm not that person. Not when it's not for my own survival.*

GG-Guns said, "Look, what happened to your cousin,

your mom . . . I didn't do that. But I could have done more to stop it. I—none of us thought Lewis would go that far."

"So, you're saying you're only guilty by association?" Aila said, without looking up at him.

GG shrugged. "I know I'm guilty. I'm just saying . . . things got out of hand, and if I could go back and change things, I would. I'm sorry."

"Well, that won't bring Garret back. Or that little girl. I don't understand how killing people has become so easy for you . . . the MP140s and the like."

"I've never killed anyone. You don't know my story, girly. You don't know me. You think just because I'm black that I'm a killer?"

"It has nothing to do with you being black, or any other race, it's because you're a gangbanger!"

"Well, I'd be dead if I wasn't part of a gang. It's how things work in cities like Chicago. It's reality!"

"Not my reality," Aila shot back.

Justin and Lena exchanged a quick, tense look. Babar was staying out of it—was content busying himself at the helm. Things were heating up, and this was going to be a long few days. Justin said, "Maybe we should table this for now—"

"No!" GG said, still standing there—towering over everyone. "We need to talk about this first. You think I grew up dreaming of the day I could be inducted into a gang like the MP140s? *Phht!* I had dreams. I had hopes for a different future. Different life. I played football in high school, you know?

Running back. Got a scholarship to LSU, full ride and everything. Hoped to play in the NFL, someday."

Justin watched the big man's face. Saw the raw emotion there as Gordon Gerber's mind went to another time and place.

"When I was a boy ... I don't know, maybe I was twelve or maybe thirteen, this was back when my Pa was still alive. He used to wake me up, often late in the night. He'd be all excited ... like hardly containing himself. You see, he'd make these crazy bets. Bets with other boy's fathers ... all over the fucking neighborhood, sometimes neighborhoods miles away."

"What kind of bets?" Justin asked.

"I was fast, man. We're talking world-class, poised to go to the Olympics fast. My dad would get me dressed and he'd drag my sorry ass to a street sometimes five or ten miles away. One, two in the morning, and there'd be a crowd there waiting. Sometimes several races would take place ... boys my age with their dads. Money would be exchanged, bets made. My Pa would take me out to the middle of the road ... few cars were out that time of night. And he'd give me a little pep talk. Tell me that the family's rep was at stake. That I was running for us getting do respect. As if he was running along with me ... which I guess, in a way, he kind of was.

"Anyway, a hundred meters down the road was the finish line. A guy with a stopwatch and a few others waited there. I'd get lined up with the other boy. Usually older than me, sometimes a lot older. Didn't matter. Never mattered ... then someone would say, 'On your marks, get set, go!; I'd run like a maniac. I'd leave the other boys in the dust, usually reach the finish line while they were humping it past the halfway mark. It's just the way it was. "

Justin saw tears welling up in the young man's eyes. "And you won. Won the race."

"Yeah, I won. Always. Can't remember losing more than once or twice. Pretty sure my Pa kept food on the table with those late-night bets. God, I loved those times."

"What happened?" Aila said, now looking at him for the first time.

"Things were good for a long time. All through high school, I stayed out of trouble. I was a star football player well into my senior year. Kept my grades up, too. My whole life was on track . . . my future was golden."

Aila said, "What changed?"

"My Pa—he was killed. Killed because of me. The Vice Lords . . . apparently, Pa had shot his mouth off bragging about me to the wrong people. Pissed them off for real. So, they blew him away. It was a drive by. He was getting out of his rickety ol' work truck right there in front of our house." GG looked at Justin and then to Aila. "I was sitting in the passenger seat. Got shot myself—a stray bullet splintered my ankle. Ten-second burst of gunfire, and I'd lost my father and lost any hope of playing ball at LSU, or a later career.

"And then the Vice Lords found out I'd survived. I was a witness, and I knew it was them. I was dead . . . knew the cops wouldn't be able to do anything. And Lewis and his crew were there for me. It was his brother, Harland, who killed the three

Vice Lords responsible for that—for killing my Pa. They didn't do it for nothing though. I was locked into that gang for life."

"I'm sorry that happened to you. But, I don't think that excuses you for what you did, or didn't do," Aila said.

"Not looking for no excuses . . . just understanding. Things—people, aren't always what they seem."

She asked, "How old are you?"

"Turned nineteen two weeks ago."

Aila's shrug was almost undetectable. An uncomfortable silence prevailed for a full minute, before Justin said, "You two want to see your quarters . . . get the grand tour?

Aila stood. "Sure, why not."

chapter 42

Onboard the Stinger Gun Ship—en route to the Danspair System

Over the next two days, everyone had settled into a kind of routine.

RP9 spent much of its time in one corner of the medical bay, manufacturing a variety of MemSnaps specific to Babar's stringent instructions. It was here that Justin was seated upon the med-bed, watching the little drone-bot diligently going about its various tasks. He saw that both of RP9's little articulating arms were extended outward. Justin marveled at how nimble the little claws were, possessing far more dexterity than, say, a person would have.

Justin asked, "What's that machine do, exactly?"

About the size of a Keurig coffee machine, RP9 had been manufacturing the tiny MemSnaps non-stop for over an hour now. Every so often, Justin heard the *psssst* of pressurized air being injected into another little tab.

"The machine is referred to as an Expander . . . referring to the expansion of a host's mind."

"Okay . . . tell me, where's all the raw information, come from?" he asked, peering around the bot's small form.

"The knowledge base is derived from the Neural Dome, of course."

That made sense. Stupid question—the organic onboard AI seemed to have an endless capacity of knowledge. "And a virus is used, somehow?"

"Yes, various recombinant viruses. The Expander synthesizes viruses, each having been engineered to express foreign transgenes that have a broad tropism, allowing gene expression in a wide range of host cells."

"Uh huh, cool . . . I see," Justin said, not really understanding. He continued to watch in silence.

* * *

Over the course of the journey, Justin, Aila and GG inhaled more MemSnaps as needed, attaining higher aptitudes toward everything from using the onboard bathroom, to getting properly suited up into an environment suit, to operating the food replicators and the airlock, to providing basic maintenance or repairs to faulty onboard sub-systems—including environmental, navigation, and even the weapons systems. At first it seemed beyond strange to Justin—one moment he was clueless about one thing or another, the next he was an expert. Learning packets of information that would have taken years—hell, a lifetime—within minutes.

The thing was, you didn't fully know you had any of this new learning until you mentally tried to access it. All Babar had to do was ask if any one of them, for instance, would adjust the starboard wing gyros for him. And though they hadn't been thinking about it a moment before, hadn't been aware of the knowledge, they would—as if the information had always been there in their minds.

This made Justin think of Earth—out of all the technological advances the Dow Dynasty could offer society there—hover crafts, medical magic to cure virtually all disease, even intergalactic space travel—none of that would have as much of an impact as the ability to absorb virally delivered, pre-packaged knowledge.

It was the other knowledge, that which had come from Markus's brain DNA, that was giving him trouble. The prince's inner voice was becoming more and more noticeable within Justin's mind. Babar had warned of this—that, for a while, there may be a kind of power struggle within him. And that it would be up to Justin to stay strong—to corral Markus's forceful thoughts and impulses. In time, Babar assured him, things would balance out—an equilibrium would take place. Until then, he'd need to hold fast to his own inner rudder—stay the course of Justin, not Markus. One thing was clear to Justin—making this procedure illegal had been a smart move. He could see how one could go stark raving fucking mad if unprepared for this inner conflict.

There was another kind of distraction onboard the gun ship, which Justin was finding just as difficult to deal with—Aila. He hadn't been sure what to expect with her being here, onboard. He'd thought, *just maybe*, things would keep progressing from how they had seemed to be going back on Earth. But that hadn't been the case.

It wasn't that she was particularly cold toward him—more like indifferent. She'd thrown herself into this situation so entirely, so completely, that there didn't seem to be any room for anything else. Not only had she taken to this space travel adventure like a duck to water, she seemed to love everything about it. Seeing her, passing her in the passageway, the entire crew eating together in the mess, or hearing her quietly singing to herself as she sat within her quarters with their respective hatch doors open—it was unbearable. *God, I've got to get a grip.* Right then, he made himself snap out of it. It was time for him to concentrate, instead, on the job at hand.

His mind turned to GG-Guns. Clearly, GG would rather have been back in Chicago, but he seemed to be making the best of things. As much as Justin wanted to hate the guy, for what he'd done, what the gangster had been part of it, he was finding it difficult to do so. GG's interactions with Aila had been limited. She and GG had been cordial thus far to one another, but clearly, they would never be best of buds. As for Princess Lena, she continued to be a dynamic whirlwind of expressed emotion and the primary cause of crew contention.

He'd heard GG call her a crazy-maker, and the term certainly fit. Lena was Babar's right-hand person—along with being the ship's taskmaster. She took being bossy to a whole new level. But Justin didn't really mind—he had his own multiple issues to contend with.

It was close to two in the morning of the third day when Justin awoke from a disturbing dream. It wasn't one of his own—it had taken place on Calunoth. Getting back to sleep was useless, so he got up and headed forward. The bridge hatch door was open, and although the cabin lights within were substantially dimmed, he saw movement. Entering the bridge, Justin eased down into the co-pilot's seat. Before them, out the starshield window, were a million points of light. More than that. Until this moment, he had never felt so small and insignificant. The expanse before him was both awe-inspiring and humbling.

Babar glanced his way. "Couldn't sleep?"

"Bad dream."

Babar continued to stare forward.

"I wanted to ask you . . . is this such a good idea? Me being here. The Magistor and Magistra will undoubtedly know that I am not their son."

"I too have been ruminating on this. There is but one course of action. I will tell them everything. It will be up to Magistor Pietra to administer my punishment."

Justin didn't know what to say to that.

"How he and his wife will react to you, I cannot say. I would be lying to say you too, are not in danger of reprisal.

Yes, I broke a number of Dynasty laws, some of which are punishable by execution. But you too will undoubtedly face their wrath."

Justin didn't want to think about that—especially since there was nothing he could do about it.

"How are you doing? Getting along with the others, being onboard this gun ship?" Babar asked, changing the subject.

"Doing okay. I've never been a part of a team or crew. Always pretty much a loner. So that's kind of different. I think I like it enough."

"RP9 get you situated with your phone?"

Justin smiled, "Yeah ... in a big way." Ocile had magically configured his and GG-Guns's iPhones to communicate back to Earth at multiples of Zyln Speeds. It turned out much of both Dynasty and Empire space was saturated with small Accelerator Stations—basically, Communication Repeaters. Like interstellar switchboards that received incoming laser light-based communication streams and sent them back out, filtered and boosted, at well past the speed of light. They used a kind of point-to-point micro-wormhole tech that he wasn't fully up to speed on yet. But even with all this highly advanced, faster-than light technology, there were still delays. It was often best to avoid annoying, pause-filled voice calls and just send emails or texts. He'd already been able to send and receive texts from his mom. Justin was aware GG-Guns was texting far more than he was—clearly he had more friends. Aila periodically borrowed Justin's phone to communicate to her father and friends. Other than Justin's mother, no one really understood, or believed, that these texts were coming from space. It was all beyond strange.

Justin tapped the icon for his E-Trade Pro App. It was the lone other app that he'd asked RP9 to try to get working. Earlier that evening, the bot had exhibited rare enthusiasm, telling him the app, albeit slow with data downloads from Earth, was now fully operational. Prior to leaving home, he'd purposely avoided checking his accounts. He now thought about SlapTac again. After investing that $30,000, he purposely hadn't checked his account since. There was an excellent chance he was upside-down. He'd be able to cover it, sure, but losing money was one of his least favorite things. He checked his current balance.

"Something wrong?" Babar asked, seeing Justin's furrowed brow.

"No . . . just not sure if there's been a mistake. An investment I made prior to leaving. Bought a cheap $5 stock, a bunch of it. My account . . . this can't be right."

"How much is in it?" Babar asked.

"$234,000 . . . the IPO price has settled around $39 dollars a share." He didn't mention he already had another $3,000,000 saved from previous investments.

"I know little of such things there on Earth. Although, it does sound like a good time to sell, no?"

Justin was already doing just that. He tapped the SELL button as well as the secondary, Are You Sure? Button. He smiled, "Now that's cool."

"Making money?"

"Yeah, well, that too, but making money so many light years away from Earth . . . here in deep space."

But Babar wasn't listing to him. He was tapping at his console and not looking all too pleased about something. A new 3D holographic console projection appeared between them. "Long-range sensors just picked them up," Babar said.

Justin looked at the triangular formation grouping of multiple spacecrafts. Warships?"

"Yes, those are most definitely warships. What you're looking at, Justin, is the Empire's prized Crimson Fleet . . . three hundred of their most advanced and powerful warships."

"Let me guess, they're also headed toward the Danspair System."

"Looks that way."

"Who'll get there first, them or us?"

"Us . . . maybe, but we'll have to step on it."

chapter 43

Onboard Stinger Gun Ship—en route to the Danspair System

The next day, Justin hung out exclusively with Babar. Both GG and Aila had been given their own individual check-lists of tasks to accomplish for the day. Justin saw little of either, since Justin and Babar's work was mostly confined to within the Neural-Center—where the Neural Dome was situated. Babar was busy trying to gain more speed from the two Zyln engines. As it turned out, to do that, he'd need to come at the problem from the ship's AI. Here, Justin spent much of his time playing gofer, handing Babar a particular tool or measurement device upon the alien's request. In trade, Babar answered Justin's unending questions.

"So, it's all based on what you call Zyln technology . . . and Zyln physics."

"Correct," Babar said. "Hand me that silver calipers . . . no, not that one, the one next to it."

"Everyone uses this Zyln tech?" Justin could only see Babar's legs, since the other half of him was hidden beneath one of the Neural-Center's consoles.

"Yes . . . it's the basis of all intergalactic travel among all the Dynasty worlds . . . and probably those of the Empire as well."

"What makes it so special? I imagine there's more than one technology—"

Babar cut him off. "What it provides for is . . . more or less a means to cheat the rules of natural physics. The ability to jump to multiples of light speed, we call Zykn Speed or Z-Speed. It requires immense amounts of antimatter energy to artificially construct wormholes, creating the ability to calculate event horizon start and end points via quantum mechanics calculations, then literally splice multiple quantum realities within the space-time medium." Babar glanced over to Justin. "Got all that?"

"Sure, no problem . . . space-time medium, event horizons. Yup. Got it." Justin rolled his eyes.

Babar slid out from beneath the console and looked up to him. "Being allowed to exist in multiple, corresponding realities all at once . . . that's what's important. An intergalactic spaceship moving at multiples of the Z-Speeds of light, actually travels through these artificially created wormholes within surrounding causal bubbles, and sometimes within bubbles within bubbles—each tied to their own quantum realities. What use would space travel be, if upon a three-week journey, a space-faring individual discovered their homeworld had aged centuries or even millennia while gone? No, FTL space travel is about far more than speed, it is about quantum synchronizations—joining aggregate realities. Again ... doing so takes two vital components—immense amounts of energy and immense amounts of computational quantum power. The energy aspect is actually the simpler of the two—we have contained antimatter-fusion reactors, one per Zyln Drive unit." Babar gestured with his chin toward the glowing mass of flickering synapses. "Computational power comes from our Neural Dome here, along with Ocile, the interface you're familiar with. This living, organic AI is the intelligence that makes the physics—or better stated, the distortion of physics—all come together." Babar laid back down, ready to slide back beneath the console.

"So how fast can this Stinger, or any ship, go? And can a bigger ship, like one of the Empire's warships, travel faster through space? Or does that slow them down, take more energy?"

"No, size makes little difference in that regard. If a ship has something equivalent to our Neural Dome, then we all can go the same speed. Measurement-wise, Zyln or Z-Speeds are divided into five primary levels, with Z-Speed 5 being the fastest."

"Okay, how fast is Z-Speed ... 1, I guess? The same as the speed of light?"

"No, not exactly. There's a metrics involved," Babar said.

"Alright, so let's say we needed to travel 120 light years. At Z-Speed 5, how long would that take?"

Babar thought about that for a moment, doing some math. "About 6.35 Earth days."

"So how come there's no Z-Speed 6?"

Babar looked to be losing patience. "*Uhg.* I'm sure RP9 could manufacture an appropriate MemSnap . . ."

"Would rather just get it from you, if you don't mind."

"Fine, but this is your last question. I have a lot more work to do here. Let's see . . . at Z-Speed 5, the Neural Dome, any Neural Dome, will have reached their intellectual boundaries. They are unable to mathematically go beyond the complexities of adding any more quantum realities and interconnecting synchronizing threads. Even attempting to go any faster could yield catastrophic results. Although, many have tried."

"All unsuccessfully?"

Babar pursed his lips. "I honestly don't know." Back beneath the console now, Justin could hear the alien talking to himself, or, more likely, to Ocile.

Babar slid back out again. "I need to shut down the ship."

"Now? Here . . . in space?" Justin asked, a little confused what had changed so suddenly.

Babar sat up and then got to his feet. "We need to reach a Z-Speed 5. Unless we shut down both drives, recalibrate, and then reinitialize . . . 4.3 is the best we'll manage."

That didn't sound like much of a difference. But then it came to him. "The scale—it's logarithmic? Like how me measure earthquakes?

"Exactly."

Justin thought about that. It might add weeks to their travel time. "How long will this take, this reinitialization thing?

"Six hours—five and a half if things go perfectly . . ."

"How does that impact our getting to the Danspair System in time?"

"I don't know . . . but we have no choice in the matter. Tell the others we'll be shutting everything down."

chapter 44

Onboard Stinger Gun Ship—
Approaching the Danspair System

The deep-space shutdown took only four hours and ten minutes. Once the little Gun Ship had been reinitialized, with the propulsion system properly aligned and synchronized, Babar was able to achieve a full Z-Speed of 5.

The crew worked long shifts over the next four-and-a-half days. In time, the little vessel's upper and lower decks were cleaned and polished to the point they sparkled. And Babar's now-perfectly-synchronized dual antimatter Zyln drives practically purred. He had instructed his small crew to get themselves showered and had issued them all new jumper-style uniforms.

Now, Babar and Lena sat at the two forward helm seats, while Justin and Aila sat behind. GG-Guns sat on one of the fold-down jump seats at the aft section of the bridge. They'd come out of Z-Speed fifteen minutes prior, and no one had spoken since. The view out the forward starshield window was both beautiful and mesmerizing.

It was only been the second planetary system Justin had ever witnessed, and this one was very different from the Sol system—and breathtaking. There were three close-proximity Sun-like stars, and a tight cluster of six planets that filled the view before them. An intertwining band of golden-colored space dust was catching the light from the three stars—creating a glimmering-sparkling scene that even a Hollywood CGI team couldn't have rendered to such a level of mystery and beauty.

"Which of the planets are we headed to . . . where Magistor and Magistra Pietra are holding out on?" Aila asked.

"The fourth world out from the three-star cluster. It's called Opalla," Babar said.

Each of the six worlds was unique in its own way, but only the fourth world looked somewhat similar to Earth—a blue planet with azure oceans and fawn-colored continents. Strangely, the swirling white clouds appeared restrained entirely to the lower hemisphere.

GG-Guns said, "And that Empire fleet? Looks like we beat them here . . . how much of a lead do we have?"

"Seven hours," Lena said. She turned around in her seat, "So we have six-and-a-half hours to find my parents, get them onboard, and be far, far away from here."

Babar said, "I have the coordinates of their last comms transmission there on Opalla. But there's no guarantee they are still there, or even still on that world." Babar looked up, "Ocile, provide a visual of the terrain location of that last transmission."

A projected hologram came to life—one that depicted a sandy-colored terrain and what looked like an ancient city. A dozen tall, majestic spires pierced high into the sky—while massive, wind-damaged surrounding walls, many of which had crumbled and fallen over time, encircled the city. It was a city that must have been, possibly centuries past, a hub of commerce and vitality, but looked now to be little more than a ghost of what once was.

A flashing, bounding red box depicted one small, mud-colored structure. "There . . . the last known whereabouts of your parents," Babar said.

"Are there other, local inhabitants, around?" Justin asked.

"Hostiles?" GG added.

Ocile picked up on the questions, and now the hologram showed numerous indications of habitation. Dozens of green icons spread over the entire landscape.

Lena said, "No way to determine if any of those are—"

Babar said, "No . . . onboard sensors can't make the determination of if any two of those are your parents from this distance. Ocile will keep scanning and update us if that changes"

"So, what's the plan?" GG asked.

Babar manipulated the hologram, expanding the area where those last comms had emanated from. "Interesting . . . there seem to be structures beneath the city."

"Yeah, another city below this one," Lena said looking closer.

"What are those tiny red dots on some—actually, most of

the green icons?" Aila asked, pointing to those located on the above-ground terrain.

"Ocile has updated. Those individuals are armed ... they carry some form of weaponry or another. That doesn't mean they'll be hostile to us, especially if we get in and get out."

"That's mostly everyone who has a weapon" Justin added.

"I believe down there, in that city below the city, is some kind of vehicle or even a spacecraft," Babar said, inspecting the hologram.

"How would it have gotten there?" Lena said.

"Tunnels ... you can see them now, faint as they are."

"They must be incredible," Justin said. "Several seem to run all the way from the distant mountains into the city."

Babar smiled and leaned back in his seat. He closed his eyes. A minute later he said, "Ocile, tell me about the atmosphere on Opalla."

The AI interface listed off the chemical elements that comprised the world's atmosphere: "81.5% nitrogen and 17% oxygen; 0.98% argon and 0.1% carbon dioxide, with trace amounts of other gases, and water vapor."

Babar shook his head, looking annoyed. "A little low on the oxygen side of things ... everyone, let's get suited up into an environ-suit."

Standing up, Justin noticed Aila had lost her self-assured demeanor. In fact, she looked downright terrified.

GG headed aft toward the airlock compartment where the environ suits were stored. Aila followed behind and then Justin behind her. "Hey, you okay?"

She glanced back at him. "I'm not a soldier. I've never even held a gun. The thought of shooting, or God forbid, killing someone . . . I don't think I can do that."

Justin was about to say something motivating, or maybe supportive. But instead he said, "Probably best you stay behind, then. Maybe hang out here on the ship . . . keep guard. Being scared is nothing to be ashamed of."

He saw her back go rigid. "I didn't say I was scared. I said I didn't want to shoot anyone!"

"Uh huh . . . well, just let Babar know you'll be staying behind. I'm sure it's fine."

She spun around on him, fury in her eyes. "Are you intentionally trying to piss me off? Because if you are—" It was then she saw Justin's smile. "Fuck you, Justin . . ." she said, continuing on her way aft. He had caught her smile prior to turning back around. She said, "Maybe I'll shoot you for practice."

By the time they were all suited up into full-body environment suits, they'd been instructed by RP9 to head over to the onboard armory. Babar was there checking, one by one, the battery levels on five energy rifles laid out on a central metal table. He handed GG-Guns one of the weapons. "You'll get three hundred high-powered plasma bolts before you lose power. Sounds like a lot, but it goes fast in the midst of battle. I'm sure your time in the Army taught you that."

GG grunted something unintelligible as he took the rifle. Hefting it, looking it over, he said, "Huh . . . I know how to use this . . ."

Lena said, "MemSnaps, genius" and snapped her fingers. "We all do."

Babar handed Aila her weapon but kept a hand on it, making her have to pull harder to take it. He said, "You sure you want that?"

She shot an annoyed glance toward Justin.

"I have ears . . . pretty good ones, too. Justin didn't say anything to me about you not wanting to shoot a weapon. I heard you myself."

"I'll do what I have to do. Don't worry about me," she said defiantly.

"I'd rather she stayed onboard the Stinger . . . she's a liability." Lena picked up a rifle from the table without looking at Aila. "Do us all a favor, little girl, and stay behind."

Babar said, "No. We're all going . . . RP9 will stay back to protect the ship. We'll stay together. If anyone shoots at us, we return fire. We do a quick recognizance of whatever is down there. If we don't find Magistor and Magistra Pietra, we get out, fast. Any questions?"

No one replied.

"Good, head on back to the airlock. We should be approaching Opalla's upper orbit by now."

There was just enough room for all five of them to cram into the airlock. A voice in Justin's head said, *I already died once . . . how about you try not to get this body of yours ruined.* Before Justin could react, a translucent visual scene was there on his HUD. Undoubtedly, Babar was transmitting this same feed to the rest of them, too. The gun ship was descending down through Opalla's atmosphere. Coming up from below was the ancient city. The ship banked, veering away, and was now headed toward a distant ridgeline.

Justin took in all the status indicators on his HUD, as well as the tiny row of four live helmet-cam feeds of the team. He saw that Aila's face still looked terrified. He looked at her actual form, and she was turned away from him—he wanted to console her, perhaps place a hand on her shoulder, but resisted the urge.

Babar's voice was in his ears. "Ocile's found us an entrance into that tunnel. Hold on, we're about to make some quick maneuvers here."

The Stinger suddenly banked and altered course. Everyone was abruptly thrust up against the port-side bulkhead. Justin was leaning hard into Lena, who was next to him.

"Get off of me, you big Guntha!" she yelled, pushing him off of her.

The ship righted and Justin regained his stance. "What's a Guntha?"

"It's like an ape, I guess . . ." she said. "Found in the jungles on Calunoth.

"But they're uglier and stinkier," Lena added, without the slightest humor in her voice.

Justin felt the ship suddenly drop, and then change directions once more. The HUD video feed showed that they were now inside a tunnel. The interior was comprised of massive, stacked stone blocks, darkened with age and moisture. The Stinger's outside running lights illuminated their forward progress. Justin estimated there wasn't much clearance beyond either of the stubby wings. Ocile was piloting the ship, and was doing a remarkable job. He guessed they were traveling at close to one hundred miles an hour. He had the feeling they were heading deeper below ground but couldn't be sure of that. His eyes leveled on his HUD's mission timer. It was down to five hours and fifty-two minutes. He wondered what it would be like once the Empire showed up within this system.

Markus's voice was back in his head. *Hey, scrawny human . . . be prepared. There's a good chance one of you won't be coming out of this alive.*

Justin's anger flared. "And how would you even know that? How about you just shut up. Keep your opinions to yourself."

Both Aila and Lena turned to look at him. Aila said, "Who are you talking to?"

"Don't ask," Justin said fuming.

"Get ready everyone," Babar said. We're approaching the site. And be aware, according to Ocile, there's two small craft down here, not one."

chapter 45

Onboard Stinger Gun Ship— Approaching the underground city

The Stinger exited the subterranean tunnel into an expansive cavern of immense size. High above, the cave-like ceiling was easily a half-mile overhead. It was clear now, they had indeed been diving deep below the exoplanet's surface— potentially descending miles, Justin thought. The feed on his HUD showed a city not so dissimilar to the city above ground. Here too were tall spires and sand-colored structures worn and crumbling from time and the elements. The Stinger slowed as they approached the nearest outer wall. The gun ship turned 180 degrees on its axis before landing thrusters were engaged and the Stinger set down.

Babar raised one hand up. "Those ships are approximately two kilometers' distance away. An easy walk. I want two teams. GG, Justin, and Aila . . . you're Beta Team. The princess and I, we're Alpha Team. No one wanders off alone. Stay on comms. Everyone got that?"

Everyone agreed.

"Good. Ocile . . . open the aft hatch and lower the gangway."

As the hatchway door slid to one side, Justin was surprised to feel a breeze buffeting the pant-legs of his environ-suit. A twirling dust devil rose up from the bottom of the ramp. It was light enough to see out there—dusk-like. Justin wondered where the ambient light was coming from. He then realized it was from the iridescent, almost-glowing, swirling dust particles themselves. This was a place that never got completely dark, nor got completely light.

Babar reached the ground first. "You'll see on your HUDs, one ship is positioned directly ahead on the other side of this wall here. The other is off to the right. Ocile is having trouble with her scanners down here. So, if there are any lifeforms present, she's not picking them up . . . not yet, anyway. Beta Team, you check out the vessel on the right. And check in regularly."

GG-Guns, Aila, and Justin stood and watched as Lena and Babar trotted off toward an area of the wall, which was easily thirty feet tall, that had crumbled and allowed an ingress into the city.

The three of them followed, GG taking up the lead. He said, "This place gives me the creeps. How could anybody have lived here? Live in a cave like this, like miles below ground. It ain't natural."

The moved as a group toward the opening in the wall.

GG, big as he was, had to turn sideways to slip through. Next was Aila. Before she too went through, Justin reached out and touched her arm. "Okay...level with me. What's going on? What's changed between you and me?"

He saw her face, partially illuminated within her helmet. She was looking down, contemplating her response. "I...I didn't know before coming on this trip how you felt about her."

"About who?" Justin asked.

She now looked up to Justin. "Lena, the princess. I didn't know you were like...in love with her?"

Justin laughed. You're kidding, right? The princess? She has to be the meanest, bitchiest...nah, you're way off base, Aila."

"Yeah? Then tell me, Justin why is it you never take your eyes off her? Just now you couldn't stop staring at her ass!"

Justin was honestly dumbfounded. How could she be so off base. *Watching her ass?* Had he? Maybe, he may have been, but...

"Just deal with it, Justin. All this"—she gestured with one hand to their surroundings—"will make for amazing stories I can tell my children or grandchildren someday. But they won't be yours. I'm ready to go home. I miss my dad." With that, she slipped through the opening in the wall.

Justin wanted to argue with her. Somehow prove to her that everything she'd said wasn't true, was ridiculous and off base. But was it? No...Lena had so captivated his mind it was hard to think—hard to do anything. And, for the life of him, he couldn't understand why. Sure, she was beautiful, and smart, and athletic, and like no one he'd ever met before...

GG-Gun's baritone voice filled his helmet. "You coming? Did you not hear we have a mission . . . and not much time to complete it?"

"Coming, had to tie my boots," he said, then remembered the boots they'd all been issued didn't have laces. He ran to catch up to them. Alpha Team was already out of sight.

chapter 46

Exoplanet Opalla—
The Underground City of Molhan

J ustin caught up to GG and Aila, who were making slow, steady progress up some kind of winding, dirt, road. It was getting steep, and by the time they'd reached the top of a rise, he could see most of the underground city from this vantage point. "Huh, it's an exact duplicate of the city above, down to the individual mudbrick structures and the dozen tall spires."

GG said, "The other vessel . . . it should be just around the next bend. Be ready."

Justin had the same HUD feed as everyone else, and he already knew that. But GG was in military mode, constantly looking left and right for hiding enemies—it was as if he were back in the Army infantry, back in Kabul or Kandahar.

Aila, on the other hand, was walking with her head down— she seemed to be deep in thought. Justin felt like a jerk. She was the last person he'd ever want to hurt. *Maybe best to let a little time pass before talking to her again*, he thought. But then she was walking next to him, looking up to him.

"Have you given any thought to what you'll say? If Magistor and Magistra Pietra are in that ship? How you're going to handle being here? The whole imposter thing?"

"Not really. We talked about it . . . Babar was going to do all the explaining."

She made a face. "Good luck with that. Look, there's the ship." She pointed.

Coming around the bend, Justin saw that it was close in size to the Stinger, but boxier. Less sleek.

"Wait!" Aila said. "GG, isn't that the same shuttle as—"

She wasn't able to complete her sentence, as just then, six armed soldiers approached, coming at them from all sides. Interestingly, none of them wore environment suits.

From the ship, striding down the ramp, was a lone figure dressed more like a dignitary than a soldier. He wore his dark hair pulled back into a ponytail. Justin recognized him from the flight bay of the *Pinterthor*. His long cape billowed out behind him—caught in a flurry of subterranean breezes.

"Chancellor fucking Harrage Zeab," Aila said. "I thought we were rid of this guy . . ."

Strangely, Justin was a tad relieved this wasn't the ship with the Magistor and Magistra. Although, this clearly wasn't good either.

One of the soldiers yelled for them to drop their rifles. They complied and raised their hands. Waiting for Zeab to arrive,

Justin couldn't help studying the strange faces of the soldiers, with their transposed noses and mouths. For a moment, he wondered how they would kiss, then came to the conclusion it probably wouldn't make much of a difference.

The chancellor, wearing a mischievous smile, stepped forward, looking more than a little pleased with himself. "Please, please, put your hands down. We're old friends here, no?"

GG, fists clenched, looked ready to take a swing at him. Justin caught his eye and shook his head.

Zeab turned to look at the ancient city. "We arrived here an hour ago. Then we quickly moved to recapture Magistor and Magistra Pietra. As you know, I'm sure, their damaged vessel is not far from here. Unfortunately, we found that no one is aboard that Dynasty Stinger. The Emperor will be displeased with the news. He was so looking forward to having the entire royal family in its entirety . . . back within the Museum of Calico and exhibited in all their glory." He licked his already wet-looking, wormy lips, while eyeing Justin. "Young Markus, I must say, you look . . . somehow different out of your stasis tube."

Hearing footsteps from behind, Justin and the others turned to see Babar and Princess Lena approaching from around the bend. Six additional Empire soldiers had them at gunpoint.

"Ah! Princess Lena, Babar, so good of you to join us."

Lena looked to Justin, Aila, and then GG. "They were waiting for us when we left the other ship . . . surrounded us before we could even react. My parents weren't there ... the ship was deserted."

"If they are alive, which I doubt, we'll find them," Zeab said. He looked at Babar, narrowing his eyes as if trying to figure something out. "The Emperor is most interested in you, Babar. A hatred beyond anything I've seen before."

"Good, the feeling's mutual," Babar said, looking pleased with Zeab's revelation.

"What is that about? Some history between you two am I not aware of?"

"Let's just say I took something that belonged to the Emperor a long time ago. Something he desperately wants back."

"I know he wants your head in a bucket ... and, unfortunately, I have no intention of disappointing him."

Babar looked unconcerned. As did Lena, which was a little odd.

"Do you know the story of this place?" Zeab said, gesturing to the dimly illuminated city beyond.

Aila said, "No ... and we don't care to hear it."

"Now now, don't be indignant, young human. The crumbling city above is called Jarhan. Two thousand years ago, it was alive and thriving. A highly religious society, where they lived by a strict moral code. A polarity of right and wrong society norms. Good and evil. Not so different from your own Christian beliefs, they believed in a heaven and hell. But their version of it had nothing to do with an afterlife. No ... their heaven and hell were realized, actualized—here, with this subterranean city, which is called Molhan. Jarhan above and Molhan below. They look identical, yes? But Molhan was a hellish place. A place for deviants. A place for killers and molesters. And unlike the hell you're familiar with, where a kind of justice is enacted, no such thing happened here. The bad, the evil . . . they were content to be here. Perhaps those inhabitants were even encouraged to do their worst. Unlike Jarhan above, there were no rules here . . . it was do unto others and fuck the rules." Zeab looked up at the towering spires. "They say the ghosts of Molhan still inhabit this dark place—that just coming here curses one's life for eternity."

"You would have been right at home here," Aila said.

Zeab contemplated that. He tilted his head and said conspiratorially, "Perhaps . . . but I think I would have found a way to move back and forth between the two cities." He smiled up at GG-Guns. "Such a large, muscular one you are. A fine human specimen.

GG clearly was not used to being ogled in such a way. "Come closer, you alien freak . . . I'll snap you over my knee. Leave you in the dirt paralyzed . . . let you drool and suffer for a while before I stomp your ugly head beneath my boot."

"Oh my, such an imagination this one has. Brutish and creative . . . yes, I think I like this one. I will put you in chains and make you my pet."

"Enough," Babar said. "What now? Or do you have more historical trivia to tell us?"

"No, you are quite right . . . we should be going. Seems there are local inhabitants hereabouts. Armed nomads and such. We will confiscate your Stinger. Soon, within the hour, I expect the Empire's Crimson Fleet will arrive in local space. You will be taken onboard as my guests. Guests that will witness the inevitable end of the Dow Dynasty."

"What are you talking about?" Babar said. "You and I both know ... a long time ago, the Empire and the Dow Dynasty had reached a common understanding. That war between our two superpowers would only ensure our mutual destruction."

"Oh yes, that was true. At one time. But so much has changed since you've been gone." Zeab feigned weariness at having to explain something so commonly known. "It is your own Prime Minister Yansle who has altered the destinies of our two civilizations. Negotiations that have led to numerous high-level decisions. Did you know new commerce has resumed between our realms? And, just recently, prisoner exchanges. But most importantly, no longer does your Royal Fifth Fleet patrol this far out in frontier space. Your prime minister has demonstrated surprising trust in our burgeoning, new-found friendship." Chancellor Zeab's expression changed. He now wore a dark, malevolent, smile. "He is an arrogant idiot, and it will be the downfall of your realm."

"The Crimson Fleet ... you intend to attack," Lena said making no attempt to hide her contempt.

Justin had been listening, as well as strategizing. At this moment, he felt more at one with Markus than at any previous time. Now, hyper-aware of his surroundings, these armed aliens surrounding them, a kind of action plan had formed. Markus had asked for Justin to step aside in this moment. To become more of an observer than the dominant one. Justin acquiesced and watched as his body's musculature, somehow, altered—readied into Tarl-le-con, the warrior's fighting stance. Now, memories that were not his own filled his mind. Memories of the elite combat teachings from Relian High Priests high in the Shan Bahn Mountains on Calunoth. His years mastering Relian Wham Dhome.

Babar was looking at him. The corners of his mouth twitched upward.

chapter 47

Markus

Exoplanet Opalla— The Underground City of Molhan

There were twelve armed hostiles here to deal with, not including the Chancellor. Not an insubstantial number. But Markus had trained for this. There was a formation of two groupings, a kind of oblong figure eight—actually, more like an infinity symbol. He mentally numbered each opponent, so he'd be able to keep track of who was who in the midst of what was to come. And he'd have to be careful not to harm any of the friendlies in the process. Again, he'd trained for this—and against far-more-skilled adversaries. Unconsciously, Markus had already made a number of micro-decisions. Which adversary had become lax, which gun muzzle had dropped and no longer was pointed in his direction? Which foot would he strike with first, second, and third? Would he spin left or right—would he go for that gunman's vulnerable kneecap or go for the kill by crushing the larynx? No, the initial attack would come at Chancellor Zeab. That would be the most disruptive, fractious, first move. Off to his right, he saw that Zeab was talking, being expressive with his silly hand gestures, now in mid-sentence—speaking about one thing or another of little importance.

Go time.

Markus moved like the wind. Forceful, yet nearly unseen—undetectable. He spun, and the heel of Markus's left hand drove up into Zeab's nose with sufficient force to crush cartilage and send splintered bone fragments deep into sensitive sinus cavities. Even while the chancellor's knees were buckling, blood spurting, Markus's right foot was already thrusting forward toward the unprepared gunman number one, directly across from him. The abrupt kick slammed his chin upward, like a pile-driver, breaking his neck with an audible crack.

Markus was aware on an abstract level that 1.5 seconds had now elapsed. No one had had time to react as yet, with one exception—*Babar*—and now he too was on the offensive. *Good.*

Markus jabbed his right fist hard into gunman two's right ear, followed by a lighting-fast flurry of four more punches to the face. Down he went. Babar was on the move and had taken out two adversaries within the other elliptical formation. A gunshot, energy pulses, erupted from one of the weapons.

No time to think about that. Markus leaped and sent a devastating right side kick to the head of gunman three. *Movement.* Gunman six was raising his weapon, pointing it toward Aila. Still in the air, Markus used his already-spinning body's momentum force to bring an elbow down, at an angle, aimed toward the gunman's temple. He missed—*shit*—instead hitting his eye socket, but making a clean orbital fracture in the process. Markus felt the thrill of battle. That wonderful exhilaration as more and more adrenalin coursed through his blood stream— Justin's bloodstream. How incredible it was to be alive again. To be a living, breathing participant instead of that dormant, lifeless thing he'd become.

Markus battled on. He punched and kicked with a killer's ferocity even he hadn't known he possessed. The big human, GG-Guns, had joined the fight and, of course, so had Lena. She moved almost as fast, as effectively, as Babar had. Markus had forgotten how she too had been taught by the priests. Had mastered, to some degree, Relian Wham Dhome.

At the seven-second mark, the remaining Empire gunmen had recovered enough from the shock of the situation to become lethal in their own right. They had raised their weapons, placed fingers upon triggers. Markus knew from the start that this was going to be a dicey situation. One where survival was doubtful. But he had taken out a good number of enemy combatants. He and the others had fought bravely, honorably.

Bright blue plasma pulses streaked through the air. Markus had no doubt that, any second now, he would feel a white-hot bolt pierce his body—well, actually, it would be Justin's body. *Sorry about that . . .*

Suddenly, bodies were dropping to the ground around him, one after another, the Empire soldiers being taken out with precision fire from the terrain beyond. Within seconds, all that remained standing were the five of them. GG had a blackened scorch mark high on his shoulder, while Princess Lena had a bloody nose. Other than that, they had come through the ordeal unscathed—which was remarkable considering the odds they'd faced.

Babar said, "It must be the locals . . . those armed nomads—" But his words fell silent at seeing who it was who was actually now approaching. They were disheveled, dirty and worn, but those were undoubtedly Dow Dynasty uniforms, Markus thought. Then he saw the one leading the contingent of the twenty or thirty armed fighters—a head larger than the others, muscular and broad of shoulder, he was none other than Magistor Pietra himself. Markus felt his heart race as he took a step forward, where he and his father momentarily locked eyes. Then Markus felt himself falling. Not so much physically, but inwardly. As if his very psyche was being pulled from one reality to another—a tunnel effect where he fell deeper and deeper into that all-too-familiar place. A place of obscurity—a place of limbo.

chapter 48

Justin Trip

Exoplanet Opalla— The Underground City of Molhan

Justin's consciousness had resumed its dominant place within his psyche. And as frightening as the altercation had been, to be in the midst of such danger and violence with the Empire soldiers—what had been truly alarming, once again, was his total loss of control. His loss of self. Justin realized now how easy it would be for him to be irrevocably supplanted by Markus.

Lena yelled, "Father!" as she ran into his open arms. A part of Justin wanted to do the same—an echo of Markus's emotions felt deep within.

Next, Babar was embracing his lord—whereby backs

were mutually and enthusiastically slapped hard. Justin, Aila, and GG-Guns stood by, silent and watchful. They observed the ruckus and the joyous reunion. Watched as tears filled Lena's and Babar's eyes. Eventually, the one thing Justin had been most apprehensive about was now happening. Magistor Pietra approached the three of them. His eyes darted between Aila, GG, and Justin, but inevitably steadied onto Justin. The Magistor's expression was unreadable. His hair, a mix of blonde and gray, was a wild mess, his beard an unkempt tangle. Most striking, though, were his eyes. Even in the dimness, Justin could see that his blue eyes were so light, they didn't look real. Now, standing before him, this mountain of an alien man staring down at him—Justin nervously looked away. He looked to find Babar, to perhaps gain some inkling of what he should say or do next.

Deep and resonating, the man's voice was just as intimidating as he looked. "So, you're the human . . . the Earth boy, who helped bring my daughter back to me. Helped to reunite me with my friend Babar. You are Justin."

It was a statement, not a question.

Justin, bewildered, said, "So . . . You know? Who I am?" Then he added, "Um, what I am?"

"Yes, and yes."

"How?" Justin's eyes found Babar standing several strides away alongside Lena—both had been watching the exchange.

Babar said, "I made contact with my lord several days ago. The princess and I both have had a number of discrete intergalactic communications with him. Conversations in a language you would not have understood, nor would any potential listening Empire eavesdroppers."

"Boy, Justin," Magistor Pietra continued, "I've had little time to grieve the loss of my son. We were never close, but the loss is still very difficult for me. You know, you look much like him. It really is quite remarkable. And the way you fought just now . . . I don't think I've ever—"

"That was Markus . . . all Markus, sir. He shows up like that, unexpected."

"Yes, I was informed of Babar's . . . unconventional experiment. One that in any other circumstance would demand his quick execution." The Magistor shot Babar a disapproving scowl. "But these are most desperate times."

Justin said, "I'm sorry about Markus. And I know me being here is, um, weird for you. Actually, not real sure what I'm supposed to do now. Maybe I can get back to Earth soon?"

"Eventually, perhaps. You're here, and I'm going to make good use of you. Sorry if that sounds crass, but if I'm going to take back my throne—"

"Wait. You're going to take back your throne?" Aila said, then looked embarrassed for her outburst. "It's just . . . there's so few of you here. Isn't there an Empire fleet coming this way?"

Princess Lena said, "You shouldn't address Magistor Pietra without being spoken to first."

"It's alright, Lena, and it's an excellent question." Magistor Pietra looked down to Aila, "There's much you do not know. Plans that have been in the works, well, for some time now." He looked up to the cavern's distant ceiling, "In high orbit around Opalla, there are close to one hundred Dynasty warships. Loyalist crews of the realm that know just how dangerous Prime Minister Yandle's motivations truly are. They see through his seemingly close ties to the Empire." The Magistor looked between the three of them. "They are deserters from Dynasty fleets. And they have found their way here to this far corner of space. Their warships . . . many of them are old. Many are barely spaceworthy. But all have been fitted with the latest cloaking technology . . . a technology that should, effectively, help us to evade Empire long- and short-range sensors. Princess Lena's mother, the Magistra, is there now and awaits our return to space. She looks forward to meeting each of you."

GG-Guns spoke for the first time. "One hundred old, barely spaceworthy warships against an opponent of three times that many? That doesn't sound like a well-constructed plan to me."

The Magistor laughed—a deep, hearty sound that echoed off the surrounding city walls. "Honesty. I appreciate your bluntness . . . GG-Guns. Saying it like it is. Refreshing, when so many around me are reluctant to be so candid. But rest assured, my ramshackle collection of warships do not need to defeat the Empire's esteemed Crimson fleet, only delay its further progress into Dynasty space. Those ships move under the guise of establishing inter-galaxy accord and friendship, but the Crimson fleet has a far more malevolent, malicious intent. No, I have it on good authority that Emperor Chi-Sacrim has chosen this moment in time to attack their one true rival within the galaxy."

"So, we delay this Crimson fleet—what happens then?" Justin asked.

"The Dow Dynasty is vast and made up of many individual self-sustaining planetary systems, galactic societies with their own governments, but under the rule and protection of the Dynasty. But there is one expansive planetary system, called the Corthinian-Muan—a society a thousand years older than that on Calunoth—that has chosen to stay independent of both Dynasty and Empire influences. They are highly advanced in their own right, and recently, I made an alliance with the Corthinian-Muan parliament. They have little affection for the Empire and see great insecurity in a Dynasty-Empire alliance. One hundred of their most modern great ships are en route to Opalla, as we speak."

There was a long moan, followed by a croaking sound.

The Magistor glanced toward the individual now attempting to get up onto all fours. "If it isn't Harrage Zeab, Chancellor of Demyan Empire's Broudy-Lum StarStation . . ."

Lena was the first to move—springing on to Zeab's back, as if she was going to ride him like a pony. She took his chin in one hand and place her other at the back of his head—clearly, she was going to snap his neck.

"No," her father said, raising a palm. "If the chancellor wishes to keep breathing, he can be of use to me still."

Lena forced Zeab's face upward and looked into his eyes. "I would have killed you. Are you going to help the Magistor, or do you want me to put you out of your misery here and now?"

In a raspy voice, he said, "Just tell me what you want me to do."

Lena looked at him, disgusted. She dismounted. Then, as an afterthought, she spun around and kicked him in the face. Zeab screamed something as he curled into a ball, cradling his now twice-ruined and bloodied nose.

Justin saw the Magistor and Babar had stepped away, talking in low tones. Babar abruptly said, "No! Absolutely not. My place is here . . . as Noble-Fist."

His lord smiled and placed a comforting hand on Babar's shoulder. "It must be you, my friend. With no one else would I entrust such valuable cargo. Everything we do here . . . the sacrifice of so many in battle. It will all be for naught if you do not complete your mission."

Eventually, Babar, looking solemn, nodded his agreement. "I will not disappoint you, my lord."

GG said, "I have a feeling we're not going to like what's coming next."

chapter 49

Justin Trip

Battle Cruiser, Victory's Flight— High Orbit Around Exoplanet Opalla

Justin walked in lockstep at the side of Magistor Pietra. The old warship's corridors were wide, allowing for an assortment of hurried crew pedestrian traffic to move in both directions as easily as if they were walking on a busy Chicago sidewalk. Here, there was an assortment of curious-looking alien life forms—crew members from various worlds all across Dynasty space. It took all of Justin's willpower not to gawk at the strange and sometimes bewildering-looking individuals. Justin brought his attention to the tired-looking ship's interior. Sporadic patches of rust could be seen on the arched structural girders—a massive ribcage running the lengths of this old warship.

"She's old ... like me," Magistor Pietra said, stopping to give the structural support an affectionate pat. "But she has good bones." It wasn't the first time the esteemed leader took an extended beat to look into Justin's eyes—perhaps seeking some indication his son Markus was there too, within.

They continued their trek aft, toward the ship's midship section. "I'm going to speak frankly to you. I'm going to tell you what I did not have the courage to tell my wife or daughter. Not even Babar knows everything."

Justin stayed quiet. He had a feeling he wasn't going to like what was coming.

"The five of you will be leaving here within the hour. You'll be taking that little Stinger gun ship to Calunoth, back to the heart of the realm. To the royal castle there. You will have two passengers. One of which will be Chancellor Zeab."

"And the other?"

"That will be Magistra Pietra."

"She's not staying here with you? At your side?"

The once-lord of all Dow Dynasty space stopped and turned to Justin. "Look, the Corthinian-Muan fleet will not arrive here in time. I will not survive the coming battle. That is my destiny. All those who have chosen to stay and fight will, undoubtedly, die here defending our great and wonderful Dow Dynasty. For all of us, it will be an honor to do so."

"I don't understand ... why does it have to happen here?

Couldn't you draw the enemy fleet back toward the incoming reinforcements, for example?"

"There are many options available. I assure you, greater minds than yours or mine have exhaustively calculated all of the options. But what is crucial is that this precarious rag-tag rebel force see that this ship—that I, am leading this fight. That I'm not backing down. No, *Victory's Flight* must remain the tip of the spear."

Justin could see the Magistor would not be faltering on this point. "And the Magistra . . . Princess Lena? They don't know?"

"Do you think they would leave here if they did?" he said with a sardonic expression.

"And Babar?"

"Oh, he may have his doubts, but no, he does not know for sure."

Justin had more questions but settled on the two he felt were the most important. "Will Magistra Pietra even be welcomed back into the castle? And what's with bringing Chancellor Zeab along with us?"

He smiled, "One is the answer to the other. No, my wife would not normally be welcomed by Prime Minister Yansle or by his castle guard. Not since the coup. But seeing the Emperor's emissary accompanying her will suffice to gain her entry. Yansle fears the Emperor—he will not take action against the Magistra if he thinks her presence is preordained . . . a part of some kind of Empire politics. But Zeab, with his vaulted position within the Empire, will need to be convincing . . . that she's there for, let's say, new high-level negotiations. There are still many star systems within Dynasty space with deep loyalties to the royal family. Yansle, if he's smart, will see an opportunity to use the Magistra to shore up new support within the realm. Zeab and the Magistra just need to buy us some short-term time."

"Short-term?" Justin said.

"The five of you have shown to me you're an effective team. Under Babar's command, you, Lean, GG-Guns, and Aila will assist my wife to regain her proper throne."

"Assist how?"

"You will assassinate Yansle at your first opportunity. You will take out all those within his guard that oppose me."

Justin thought about that. So now he was to be an assassin. A killer, a hired gun. But he'd come this far, and wasn't this the logical conclusion of what he'd been tasked to do? "I'm in . . . I'll do what I can. But I can't speak for Aila or GG-Guns . . . this isn't their fight, sir. They may just want to go home."

"I can arrange that. I can spare a shuttle . . . it would be a slow voyage, several months."

"I'll talk to them."

"I'm counting on you to keep most of what I've told you in confidence, son."

The term of endearment was not lost on Justin, and just briefly, he wondered if Markus had heard it too. The inner answer came to him instantaneously. As if far away or under-water—it was as if Markus was trying to get to the surface, to physically reach out to his father. Justin, feeling a little guilty, pushed him back down.

"You can count on me, sir. You can count on all of us."

"Good . . . I know I can." The Magistor looked as if he wanted to say something else.

"Sir?"

"I'd like to . . . hug you. If that would be alright."

Justin felt his face flush. He'd no sooner nodded and was engulfed within so powerful an embrace it forced the air from his lungs. A moment later, he was released and allowed to breathe again.

The Magistor was already striding away. Justin turned to see he'd been deposited in front of the ship barracks where he, GG-Guns and Aila had bunked the previous night. He stepped toward the hatchway, and it slid aside with a pained sounds of metal scraping against metal.

Both Aila and GG-Guns were sitting upon their respective bunks, looking bored.

"Finally! Where have you been?" Aila said looking annoyed.

GG looked perfectly calm, like he had nowhere else to be. He got right to it. "We're leaving."

"This ship?" Aila asked.

Justin nodded. "Within the hour."

"Good, this rickety old barge creeps me out. Smells bad, too," Alia said.

"You have a choice to make. Both of you. Give it some thought, okay?"

"Just get to it," GG said.

"There's a shuttle they can spare. It's old, like all the other vessels in this fleet. But it can take you back to Earth. Would take a couple of months, but you should be safe enough. Return to your families, your lives."

A crease had formed between Aila's brows. "You said take you...like you wouldn't be coming with us."

"I'm not going back to Earth. At least, not now I'm not."

"Are you shitting me?" she said.

Justin didn't answer.

"They're giving you an opportunity to go home now... why not take it? You've—we've done our part." She slapped her hands together in a job-well-done gesture. "It's time to pack up and leave."

GG-Guns, looking curious, said, "Where you off to? What's up with that?"

"A mission. We're taking the Magistra back to Calunoth to reclaim her throne. And we're going to kill Prime Minister Yansle, among other, um, duties." Justin couldn't help but smile seeing GG-Guns expression. "You want to come along? We can use your help?"

"Who is us?" he asked.

"Babar, Lena, and me. Oh, and Chancellor Zeab as a prisoner. Taking the Stinger. We leave within the hour."

Justin already knew GG would be going with them. As strange as it was, the big gangbanger was now as much a part of the team as Justin was. Justin didn't look directly at Aila, but he could see her out of the corner of his eye. She was fuming, ready to go ballistic.

"So...you want GG-Guns to go with you on this thing, this mission, but not me? Is that what you're saying?" Aila said, hands on hips and barely containing her anger. She didn't realize that both Babar and Princess Lena had entered the barracks behind her and were watching as things progressed.

Justin shrugged. "It'll be dangerous. You've said it yourself; you don't know if you can risk life and limb for people you don't know—"

"I never said that! Now you're putting words in my mouth. Why don't you let me speak for myself?"

Lena spoke from behind her, "Well, you better hurry it up. We're leaving . . . like right now. Personally, I think you should hop on the shuttle and never look back."

Aila spun around to see the two of them standing there—Babar looking bemused, Lena looking contrite, with her arms crossed over her chest.

"I'm coming with you . . . don't even think about sticking me on that slow fucking boat to Earth. I'm one of you, like it or not." Aila turned back to face Justin and GG. "You got that?"

"We got that, girl," GG-Guns said, offering her a rare smile.

chapter 50

Justin Trip

Justin tried not to look at Aila. He didn't want to make her feel like her emotions were under a microscope. They sat next to each other behind Babar and Lena, who were manning the helm. Even now, as Babar piloted the Stinger out through *Victory's Flight*'s bay—out into the deep dark space beyond—he could tell she was having second thoughts. But it would have been worse if she'd gotten on that shuttle—she would have regretted not being a part of this. Not seeing things to the very end. He knew this, because he'd come to the same determination himself. Just as Aila was worried about her father, Justin was worried about his mother. He glanced her way and saw that she was fiddling with GG's iPhone. Probably texting her father, telling him she was fine. Would be coming home just as soon as she completed whatever this *thing* was that they were about to do. Justin had relayed that same text to his mother.

Aila said, "You know . . . they're seeing each other. Well, kind of."

He saw she was now looking at him. "Who's seeing each other?"

"My dad . . . your mom . . . they met in the hospital. Don't you think that's—I don't know, off-putting?"

Justin looked at her. Yes, it was off-putting. Downright weird, even. "I guess. I don't really want to think about it." He made a face and she laughed.

Lena abruptly stood up and headed out of the bridge. "I'm going back, going to spend some time with my mother." She paused to look down at Justin. "Come with me. You should meet her." She stared down at him, giving him a now-familiar look—a mix of frustration and disappointment.

"Fine, I'd be happy to meet your mother," he said, standing up and following her out into the passageway.

Lena said, "She's only here because of you, you know."

"Your mother?" he said.

"No, stupid . . . Aila. The way she looks at you. What's that human expression? Puppy dog eyes?"

"Nah, we simply have a lot in common. We're friends. What you're seeing is concern, nothing more than that." He wanted to change the subject, so he asked, "What's it like, seeing your mother after so long?"

She slowed and looked back at him over her shoulder. "We were never close. Not so different from the relationship Markus had with my father. My mother thinks I'm too impetuous. Would have wanted me to follow more in her footsteps . . . certainly not follow in my brother's footsteps to venture off and live with Relian High Priests in the Shan Bahn Mountains on Calunoth."

She stopped outside the Magistra's hatchway. "Be careful what you say. What you commit to. She can be . . . manipulative and cunning."

Justin wanted to say that the apple hadn't fallen far from the tree, but he held his tongue. The hatch slid to one side, Lena walked through, and Justin followed.

Magistra Tammera Pietra sat upon her bunk, her back propped against the bulkhead. She had changed into an ornate silken gown inlaid with reflective threads of gold and silver. The neckline plunged low enough to reveal the cleavage of her breasts. A small furry animal about the size of a ferret lay curled up in her lap. Both looked up as they entered. The ferret look-a-like bared its small pointy teeth and growled.

"Stop that, Mitty!"

Mitty's pointy ears lowered at being reprimanded.

"Mother . . . I'd like to properly introduce you to Justin Trip."

The Magistra was as stunningly beautiful as her daughter. They shared the same eyes—the same long, wheat-colored hair. Both had small, perfectly proportioned human-looking features. But Lena's mother had one trait her daughter did not—a welcoming, warm smile that Justin was fairly certain had melted the hearts of many men in her life. What he hadn't expected to see now were tears welling up in her eyes.

"I apologize. Your likeness to . . . Markus."

Justin felt guilty, wanted to apologize himself. But how does one do that—apologize for looking like another person?

"Come. Sit next to me." She padded the mattress next to her. Justin did as asked while Lena pulled the chair around from the small desk.

Tammera Pietra looked at Justin for a long moment before turning her gaze to her less-than-happy-looking daughter. "I hadn't realized the emotions stirring between you two were so . . . heated, and so complicated."

Justin felt his face go hot.

Lena shot laser beams at her mother through narrowing eyes. "Mom!" She looked away, clearly frustrated. "My mother is an empath. She can't so much read minds. But she can read emotions as easily as one reads words in a book. She knew my father was in love with her, even before *he* did."

"It's a cultivated ability . . . one must work at it with diligence, with practice," the Magistra said.

"Here it comes," Lena said crossing her arms and tilting her head to one side. "Daughter . . . you have this same blessing. An ability that will gain you favor

throughout your life. If you would only—"

"I prefer not to live my life that way, mother. It's cheating. A form of deception. It's not for me, okay?"

Her mother let out a resigned breath. This was undoubtedly

a conversation they had had many times before. The animal on her lap began licking its genitals.

"Fuck, Mitty... can't you ever give it a rest?" Lena said, exasperated.

Justin tried not to laugh, which brought back the Magistra's own smile again. "My daughter is a force in the universe like none other. You will have your hands full with her in years to come, young human. I both envy and have misgivings for what lies ahead for you."

"Mom, enough!" the princess exclaimed. "I don't feel that way about him," she said, then looked at her mother with a stare that could stop a locomotive.

But Justin had gotten the full implications, anyway. The fact that her mother could read her daughter's emotions, better than she could herself, made Lena's denials more than a little desperate sounding. Justin was enjoying this moment. He had thought the princess not so much hated him, as just endured his company. To learn there may be something more... this was too good. He looked at Lena with a superior, *I know the real truth now,* expression.

The princess rolled her eyes. "Thanks, Mom... really appreciate you complicating things. Can we talk about the mission? What this is all about?"

Justin noticed Mitty had a pink little boner going now.

"One of us, either your father or myself, must be sitting back upon the throne by the time the rebellion meets up with the Empire's Crimson fleet. The Prime Minister will see my presence here as little more than a desperate attempt, the

Pietras bargaining for their lives. Having Chancellor Harrage Zeab will get this Stinger past Calunoth's high orbit patrols, not to mention Cristine Castle's castle guard."

"Or they could just as easily shoot us shoot us out of the sky," Lena said.

"That is a possibility. This is no small risk," her mother said.

"And the stakes are beyond high," Lena added. "What makes you think Zeab will ..."

Justin said, "Play ball?"

Both the Magistra and Lena looked at him. Mitty too was now staring up.

She continued, "I've had this vessel's medical bot surgically implant a kind of insurance policy into Zeab's lower spine. A remote signal will inflict enough pain to drive the chancellor down to his knees without causing any real long-term injury. Anytime we need to remind Zeab to keep to the plan, a simple press of a button can remind him."

"And who's responsibility will that be?" Lena asked.

"The one you call GG-Guns ... he and I had a nice discussion prior to lifting off this morning. It seems the human was once a warrior and is not unfamiliar with inflicting pain when necessary. He seemed quite willing to take on this ... duty."

Justin didn't doubt that that was true. GG-Guns did not seem the type of person who would have regrets about that.

"He is in the hold with him now ... getting to know the prisoner. Practice using the remote's button."

At that moment, Justin inclined his head. Had he just heard a high-pitched scream from the hold?

Five minutes later, Lena and Justin were standing outside the hatchway to the hold area. She placed a hand on Justin's chest, stopping him from entering. "Just so you know. No matter what my mother says, I would never get involved with you . . . romantically. The mere thought of it makes me ill." She pushed him hard enough to make him take a step backward before entering the hold.

chapter 51

They found Chancellor Zeab lying on his back on the deck. His cape had been removed, and his damp, frilly shirt was open to the waist. The temperature in the hold was at least twenty to thirty degrees warmer than the rest of the ship. GG-Guns was leaning, looking relaxed against the far bulkhead, and the two of them seemed to be having a conversation. The hatch door slid open behind them and Aila and Babar entered. Minutes earlier, Justin had felt the telltale vibrations emanating up through the deck plates—Babar had engaged the dual antimatter Zyln drives and they were now traveling at top speed.

It was obvious GG had been making use of the small remote he held in his right hand. Still grimacing, Zeab's face was sweaty—his half-lidded eyes depicted an individual who had been in the midst of relentless torture.

Babar strode forward, his face stern. "This is not what I told you to do!" Babar tried but failed to snatch the small device from GG's hand. "I said introduce our guest to the zapper, not torture him to death!"

GG shrugged. "I didn't like the ugly alien's snarky attitude. Didn't think he was fully understanding the importance of our situation. What we wanted him to do."

Babar knelt down next to Zeab and checked his pulse. Aila was glowering at GG-Guns. Justin could tell she too was about to verbally lay into him as well. He placed a hand on her shoulder and leaned in. He whispered into her ear, "I think this is all pre-planned . . . like a good-cop, bad-cop type routine."

She jerked away, still looking horrified. "Even so . . ."

"Hold on. Let's just see what happens. Give it a second."

The princess knelt down next to Babar, "Maybe I should be the one who holds on to the zapper."

Zeab's eyes opened wider as he looked up to see Lena looming over him. Her smile held no warmth. "No! I'll do what you want. Just stop with the shocks . . . my spine . . . I swear, it'll break me in half. AAAAAH!!!"

"You mean like that?" GG-Guns said holding out the zapper with the button depressed.

Aila, fist clenched, reached the far larger GG-Guns in two seconds. She punched him hard in the mouth—surprising him more than hurting him—but he'd fumbled the zapper and it fell to the deck. Aila picked it up and stepped away from GG. Looking down, she showed it to Zeab. "I'll hold on to this for now. But don't think for a second I won't use it."

Babar said, "We'll have your garments cleaned. Let you take a shower. But I assure you, the first time I suspect you're up to something, anything, that zapper goes back into GG-Gun's possession."

Zeab closed his eyes. It was subtle, but he nodded that he would comply.

"We'll arrive at Calunoth tomorrow morning. Do not forget your story . . . that we are here on the behest of the Emperor. The Magistra is to be treated with the care and respect commiserate with her previous esteemed position as Magistra of the realm. Your one job will be to get us into the same room with Prime Minister Yansle."

"And which one of you is the assassin?" Zeab asked with a sneer—looking to each of them.

"Whichever of us gets to him first," Lena said. "Just get us close."

Chancellor Zeab laughed. "Sure . . . somehow, you may actually achieve what you set out to do. But you'll never leave Cristine Castle." He turned his gaze to Justin and then to Aila. "Do these human accomplices of yours know? Know that they are on a suicide mission? That they'll be forfeiting their lives purely for politics, politics on the other side of the galaxy from Earth?"

Justin said, "Three of your warships were there in Earth's high orbit. There's no way you didn't transmit our planet's coordinates back to the Empire. How long will it be before more ships arrive there? So, don't pretend Earth, humanity, doesn't have any skin in the game. It's just a matter of time."

Zeab smiled, "Perhaps. The Empire can always utilize more slave labor for their off-world mining operations. And I do remember that pretty world of yours was rich with mineral deposits."

Aila said, "Here, GG . . . you can have this." She handed the zapper back to him. "You're right, he doesn't fully understand the importance of our situation. What we need him to do."

* * *

They reached Calunoth space within fourteen hours. With the exception of the Magistra, they were all huddled together within the bridge compartment. Justin studied the projected holographic display. As expected, numerous battle groups were patrolling local space. It would be impossible getting anywhere near Calunoth before being apprehended, or more likely, destroyed. While Babar was seated at his usual station at the helm, it was now Chancellor Zeab who sat in the copilot's seat next to him.

Ocile's voice broke the silence, "There is an incoming hail, sir . . . designated, priority Urgent. Shall I open the channel?"

Babar glanced over to Zeab, then said over his shoulder, "Who has the zapper?"

"I do," GG-Guns said, standing at the back of the bridge.

"You know what to say . . . to do?" Babar asked Zeab.

"Just open the channel. I am the least of your worries."

"Go ahead, Ocile . . . open the channel"

"This is Dynasty High Command, Officer Corfu. Identify yourself. You are entering secure space—identify yourself at once!"

Justin recognized Corfu's voice from the last time he'd heard it.

Chancellor Zeab spoke, his pompous, arrogant tone unmistakable. "You will clear this vessel for direct approach. This is Harrage Zeab, Chancellor of Demyan Empire Broudy-Lum StarStation. I come as an emissary of Emperor Chi-Sacrim. You will inform Prime Minister Yansle of our imminent landing at Cristine Castle, and do so at once."

The ensuing silence lasted for several drawn-out minutes before Officer Corfu was back again. "Chancellor Zeab, the prime minster is on the line."

"This is Prime Minister Yansle, um, Chancellor. First of all, welcome to Calunoth. Unfortunately, this is not a good time—I do not see this visit, any kind of a meeting, on the books—"

"Listen to me carefully, Yansle. That is, if you wish to hold onto your position of Prime Minister once the Crimson Fleet arrives at your doorstep here in Dow Dynasty space."

"Yes, well, of course accommodations will be made for you."

"Good. Now, much has changed in the last few days. Emperor Chi-Sacrim assured me you would not be obstinate. That because of your strong prior relationship you will welcome myself, along with the Magistra, the prince and princess . . . for a short visit."

"A visit. The royal family, here at Cristine castle. This is— most unusual . . ."

"Never the less, you will grant us clearance to land. You have wasted enough of my time already."

"You do understand, Chancellor . . . that the royal family is no longer in power. In fact, they are suspected of treason to the realm. Inciting rebel forces out among the fringe territories. Bringing them here . . . most unusual."

"Yes, well, we may be able to subvert any further uprisings. That is why we are here. Now, clear us for landing. That or you can deal with the Emperor himself."

"This is Dynasty High Command, Officer Corfu. You have been cleared for entry into Calunoth space. Accompanying security has been assigned to you."

Justin saw, both out the window and on the Holo-projection, that five FareCat Fighters had positioned themselves around the Stinger.

Babar took manual control of the helm. "Hold on everyone, things will get choppy when we hit the atmosphere."

RP9 hovered into the bridge. Babar said, "Oh, and everyone gets a cuffcom unit. Put it on now. Any questions on how to use it, ask now."

Justin watched as the little bot delivered a curved, thin, rectangular slice of blue-tinted crystal to each of them. He already knew what to do with it—either from Markus's knowledge or from a previous MemPack learning tab, he wasn't sure which. He placed it atop his left wrist. Using the thumb and forefinger of his other hand, he slightly compressed the two ends of the crystal and watched as a semi-transparent, three-inch-wide display band encircled his wrist. It was energy-based, but it looked and felt solid. Tapping the cuffcom's face, he watched as a series of text lines begin to scroll across it. It was a message from Ocile, confirming connection to the ship's communications platform.

The plan was for GG-Guns to play the part of Magistra Pietra's personal security. While Justin would easily pass for the prince, there would be no plausible explanation for Aila to go along with them. Babar ordered her to remain behind on the Stinger, and she wasn't thrilled about it.

Justin had caught a glimpse of Calunoth from out the window during their descent. It was beautiful and, in many ways, similar to Earth. Although, this planetary system had dual Suns, and the color of the sky was a different blue than back home. Now, as they filed out of the bridge and headed down the passageway toward the airlock compartment, Aila, bringing up the rear, tapped him on the shoulder.

"Justin?"

He turned. "What is it?"

"You know, Zeab . . . what he said. About this being a suicide mission?"

Justin waved away the comment. "He was just talking out of his ass to scare us."

"I know. But, just in case he wasn't." She stepped in close and kissed him on the lips. After a moment, he kissed her back—both their eyes remained open. He slipped his arms around her waist and pulled her even closer. He felt her hands come up and cradle his face. When she finally pulled away to say something, he wanted to resist. He wanted to keep on kissing her like that forever.

She smiled briefly, and then became serious again. "I'm afraid, Justin. Afraid you'll be killed. That you'll all be killed. I'm afraid I'll be left here on this shitty little ship all alone. I'll be stuck here on an alien planet where I don't know a soul. Most of all, I'm afraid I should have just gone home when I'd had the chance. Oh God . . . I don't want you to go and leave me here alone."

He looked in her eyes and saw the fear there. He wondered how he could have been so insensitive. Of course, she was scared. Of course, she didn't want to be left alone. She was a young kid of eighteen—they both were—who was out here in the middle of space for just one reason. To be with him.

"Then you should come with us . . ."

"But there's no reason for me—"

"Fuck the reasons. Come with me. By the time we reach the bottom of the ram I'll think of something."

She laughed and took one of his hands in her own. "Thank you . . . but I may have an idea."

chapter 52

The two of them made a quick stop-off in the medical bay. Justin knew the others were waiting outside the ship, probably down at the bottom of the gangway. But Aila's idea was pretty good. Damn good, actually. Ocile had been receptive to it and had come up with a two-part procedure. One part cognitive enhancing, and the other physical alteration.

RP9 was currently busy manufacturing a specialized MemSnap for Aila. It was one the Neural Center had never previously concocted.

"Can you hurry, RP9 . . . they're waiting for us," Justin said, looking at his cuffcom. "Crap, Babar's already sent me four messages."

Ocile's voice emanated from above, "This is a most complicated procedure. Patience, please."

They heard the telltale *pffft* sound as compressed atmosphere was being injected into the MemSnap tab. Justin looked over to Aila, "You still sure you want to do this . . . be a Guinea Pig for this kind of operation?"

She nodded. "I'm sure."

RP9 was done and held the small MemSnap out to Aila in one of its tiny claws. "The tab is ready."

"Just give it to me," she said, taking the tab, snapping it, and holding it under her nose. She sniffed in the suspended blue cloud, which immediately made her cough and gag.

Justin said, "What's happening? Is it poisoning her?"

"This was a much stronger solution than would usually be administered. She should be fine in a minute."

It took two before she was breathing normally again. Aila nodded and smiled. "Okay . . . now the second part."

Justin, looking indecisive at RP9, said, "How's this next part done?

RP9 rose higher and moved around to the back of Aila's head. "Please lift her hair out of the way. Aila, you must remain perfectly still in order for the device to be properly implanted."

The drone-bot was holding something about the size of a grain of rice within one claw. Justin looked to Aila.

She nodded. "Let's just get this over with."

"You sure?"

"Yes!"

He reached behind her and gently lifted her hair away from the back of her neck.

RP9 moved in closer, and a green projected laser target appeared on her skin at the nape.

Psst!

It happened in the blink of an eye. A tiny bead of blood formed where the targeting laser had been only a second before.

"Let me get that for you," Justin said, using a swab provided by RP9 to dab at the injection site. "Does she need a Band-Aid or something?"

But he saw that it had already stopped bleeding.

"The operation is complete. There will be a lag time. Full effects may take several minutes," Ocile said.

Aila stood and blinked her eyes several times in succession.

Justin stood up too. "So, what does it feel like?"

"Um . . . like a bee sting, I guess. It doesn't really hurt. But I know it's there." With that, she brushed past him and was already exiting the medical bay and hurrying aft. He heard her call back, "Thank you Ocile. Thank you RP9. Justin . . . last one out turns off the lights."

He caught up to Aila outside the ship at the top of the gangway. She was staring, more like captivated, by what lay beyond. Previously, Justin hadn't given much thought to what Cristine Castle actually was or looked like. But it wasn't this. This was something out of a storybook—more like the size of a city, it literally glowed a bluish aqua color. There were a number of castle towers and parapets and tall spires, half of which were high enough to pierce the few puffy white clouds above.

"It's magical . . . like Oz."

"We're waiting . . ." Princess Lena said from below.

As spellbinding as the castle was, what greeted them below was almost as impressive. Upon the rolling green hills here outside the castle walls, there were no less than a thousand uniformed soldiers standing in four separate formations.

At the bottom of the gangway stood a greeting party of

about twelve individuals—including more uniformed guards and several formally adorned dignitaries. At its forefront, dressed in a billowy black frock thing, was presumably Prime Minister Yansle. He was short and a tad overweight. Thick gold necklaces hung long from his neck, and each stubby finger was adorned with jeweled rings. Atop his balding pate was a red-feathered headdress affair that looked, at least to Justin, ridiculous. He smiled disingenuously up at them.

Babar, Lena, Magistra Pietra, and GG-Guns, as well as Chancellor Zeab, all looked up to Justin and then Aila with a mixture of expressions—impatience, frustration, and irritation.

Lena said, "Ah, finally . . . here's my brother, Justin and—"

Justin and Aila were already descending the ramp, "This is Aila, our ship's cyborgenic unit."

If everything had gone right, if the Stinger's AI Neural Center had done what it said it could, Aila would have full access to the Neural Dome—just as RP9 would have. The tiny device implanted into her brainstem should already be making bio-thread connections within her cerebellum at the base of her skull. Only now he thought of the one question he'd not asked Ocile. *Was this procedure reversible?* But Aila would have asked. He was sure of that. He reminded himself to find out later.

Justin and Aila joined the procession, which was already moving toward the castle. Lena fell back and whispered, "What's with all the cyborg crap?"

Justin continued to look about, flabbergasted. "You grew up here? Lived here?"

"Yeah, so what. Answer me?"

Aila said, "I am a cyborg. Part organic being and part advanced AI interface. Go ahead ... ask me anything."

Lena rolled her eyes, "You're both idiots. Just don't get us killed playing your stupid games." She hurried forward to catch up with her mother.

Justin leaned closer to Aila, "So it's working?"

"I don't know. I think so. Ask me something. Something that I wouldn't know the answer to."

Justin thought about that as they approached the castle's entrance. There wasn't a moat and a drawbridge, but there were two thirty-foot-tall doors opening before them. "Okay, tell me what's making the castle glow blue like it does?"

"The castle was built about twelve hundred years ago ... materials for the structure are all local. Forged metals, mostly strontium aluminate, doped with europium, which absorbs light energy during the day from Illium and Thrish, Calunoth's dual stars—"

"Okay, okay, I believe you." He looked at her. A crease had formed between her brows. "Just try to look more ... cybergenic like."

"You mean like a robot?"

"Yeah, you look way too human."

"Oh. How's this?" she said making her face go totally expressionless.

"Yeah, that's better."

She said, "Do you want to know what the odds are of us defeating the thousand-plus armed guards here on the castle grounds?"

"No. You can keep that to yourself."

The contingent was led into the castle's main entrance hall, one that Justin equated to some of Earth's most famous cathedrals. Although nothing on Earth could compare to the scope and grandeur of this structure. Sunlight streamed down from windows high overhead. They moved to the center of the hall, where Prime Minister Yansle was speaking to the group, "Again . . . welcome to Cristine Castle. Magistra Pietra, Prince, Princess . . . you honor us with your presence. Chancellor Zeab, good to see you so soon again."

So soon again? Justin repeated to himself. That can't be good.

"Walk with me . . . I trust the Emperor is well?"

Zeab placed a friendly hand upon the Prime Minister's broad back. "The Emperor's splendid . . . jubilant, that our two realms are progressing toward total disarmament. He looks forward to unprecedented new channels of commerce opening up soon.

"Wonderful, just wonderful. Come, a conference chamber has been prepared for our meeting. Please follow Baron Vin Gar, there . . . he will show you the way."

"Won't you be joining us?" Babar asked in a pleasant, but somewhat-baffled tone.

Justin wondered if they should strike now when the Prime Minister was physically within reach. Sure, it would be suicide, but he was fairly certain he could have the squat little man's neck snapped in mere seconds.

"Most definitely, shortly, I promise." With that, the Prime

Minister spun on his heels and flaunted off down an adjacent passageway.

"This way, please stay together . . . easy to get lost in such a vast space," Baron Vin Gar said.

Justin watched him lurch forward as if unaccustomed to his own legs. He was tall and skeletally thin. Somewhat hunched, he reminded Justin of a movie character—a kind of ghoulish, keeper-of-the-crypt-type fellow.

Princess Lena said, "I assure you, Baron, no one knows their way around this castle like I do . . . lest you forget, this was my playground as a child."

The Baron offered back a constipated-looking smile, "I'm sure you're correct, Princess . . . this way, follow me."

They moved into an adjoining passageway which in turn let to another and then another. Soldiers dressed in fancy palace guard uniforms lined both sides of the passageway no more than ten feet apart from one another. Justin had to double his pace to get close enough to Babar to ask a question.

"These guards . . . are any of them the same as when you were in charge?"

Babar's eyes looked left and then right. "I see a few familiar faces. But that doesn't mean they maintain any loyalty to the royal family. Now step back and hold your tongue."

They descended a flight of stairs, walked for several hundred feet, and then descended another flight. Justin could see Lena was shaking her head, getting perturbed about something.

He heard her whisper, "Mother . . . what's going on? There aren't any meeting chambers down on the sublevels."

"*Shhh,* I'm sure there are... perhaps they've made alterations—"

"I'm afraid she's right, Magistra," Babar said. "There are but three possible destinations down here. Ghe electrical and mechanical operations, the storage holds, and..."

"The castle Keep," Lena interjected too loudly.

"Keep, as in dungeon?" Justin said.

No one answered, but Aila shot him an all-knowing AI-infused nod.

Thirty yards ahead, the Keep's broad and tall double doors were constructed of aged timber and had been left wide open for them.

Justin thought he heard a voice. Then he heard it again, *Get yourself locked in that Keep and it's all over. Do something, you imbecile!* Hello to you too, Markus, Justin thought.

Zeab was casually speaking to the Baron up ahead, as if nothing was wrong. The Keep entrance loomed before them. Now, he could just make out the dim contours of hewn rock surfaces. *Yup, that's a dungeon all right.*

Casually, Babar took a glance backward. Took in all of them directly behind him, as well as the ten or twelve palace guards who had fallen in farther back behind. They had reached the Keep's entrance. Magistra Pietra stopped, which in turn stopped the entire procession. "Baron Vin Gar, it seems we have made a wrong turn somewhere along the line. This certainly is not a conference chamber."

The Barron let out a resigned breath. His affable smile was replaced with a far more menacing expression. "Did you really think you could simply waltz in here as if you still owned the place? You stupid, arrogant bitch. I had suggested your spacecraft be annihilated long before landing here, but the Prime Minister has other plans for you."

Chancellor Zeab's smile only widened. "You really are a pathetic lot . . . and your expression, Magistra, is priceless. One that I so hope remains once you are back inside your stasis tube back within the Museum of Calico." He turned his attention to Babar. "Apologies to you, my old friend. The Emperor has requested that just your head, in a bucket, be returned to him."

Chancellor Zeab and the Baron shared a commiserate chuckle.

Babar nudged GG-Guns. "What are you waiting for? Push the button."

GG-Guns took three steps forward and joined Chancellor Zeab and the Baron at their side. A bit overdramatically, he held up the zapper device and handed it to Zeab. "Here you go, boss."

After a stunned silence, Aila was the first to say something. "Once an asshole, always an asshole."

The big gangbanger smiled ruefully, "Hey, I'm a survivor . . . simple as that." He looked as if he wanted to add something else to that. "By the way, killing your cousin . . . that was no accident. He got what he deserved."

Together, the three of them strode off back the way they'd just come. The Baron said, without looking back, "Lock them up. Anyone tries to escape, please feel free to exercise appropriate corporal punishment."

chapter 53

With the royal guard's energy rifles now leveled at their heads, the five of them had their cuffcoms confiscated. Then, not so gently, they were prompted to enter the castle keep.

Aila said under her breath, "If you're thinking of making a move, Justin, those weapons are referred to as Kinex-Pulsars. They fire up to five thermal plasma bolts per second."

Lena said, "Why thank you, Professor who-gives-a-shit . . ."

"Be civil—you're a princess, Lena," her mother scolded.

They were escorted deeper into the keep—as they went farther and farther in, Justin was certain it was getting darker. And there was a distinct smell: sour body odor, urine, feces. This place had been recently occupied. He saw there were sets of chained manacles hanging at waist level from various locations all along the stone walls. Metal buckets, a good many of which were tipped over, lay on the ground.

"Mother, why did we even have this horrific place?" Lena said eyeing her surroundings. We kept people down here? Made them piss and shit in buckets?"

"Of course not ... remember, this castle is over a thousand years old. This area was more of a fun novelty—sometimes we gave tours of the castle keep to visiting dignitaries."

"Yeah, well me squatting over a metal bucket won't be much of a fun novelty."

The guards had apparently decided they'd been sequestered far enough into the keep. With no less than five Kinex-Pulsars leveled on him, Babar was the first to be manhandled in close to a wall and then shackled by his wrists there. A guard, looking infuriated, took hold of Babar's face and shoved his head hard into the rock.

"You always thought you were better than the rest of us. But you were just a lackey to the Pietras ... now you'll get what's coming to you." The guard pulled his hand away from Babar's now-bleeding nose and upper lip.

It took close to ten minutes minutes for all five of them to be secured. The three females were on one wall while Justin and Babar faced them from the other, some ten feet away.

Justin had been watching Babar. He didn't seem particularly upset about their current predicament—not in the least. Considering his job title was Noble-Fist to the aristocracy, and keeping the royal family safe was his primary responsibility, one would have thought he'd be a little more ... *something*— agitated, incensed, enraged? But no. He looked perfectly calm. A little bored, even.

"What do you have up your sleeve Babar?" Justin asked.

"Up my sleeve?"

Aila said, "That is a human colloquialism, clearly not

included within your most recent MemSnap English translation package. I'll make a note to update the Neural Dome—"

"Just stop!" Lena said.

Babar said, "I was wrong."

"What does that mean, you were wrong?" Lena said, skepticism in her voice.

Babar looked at Justin, "You had asked me if any of the royal guards looked familiar. I told you yes, but it didn't mean any of them would be loyal to the royal family. I was wrong about that."

"How so?"

Babar leaned forward and spit something bloody into his manacled hands. He held up a single metal key.

"Brilliant!" Magistra Pietra said, flashing an enthusiastic smile.

"No, what is brilliant is what Aila brings to the party. A key by itself would only go so far, but what she, I suspect, is now capable of . . . we may just be back in business."

Aila beamed.

"Really? She's not just annoying?" Lena asked.

"Talk to me about your connection to Ocile," he said.

"Not so much to Ocile, but to the Neural Dome directly . . ."

"Do you have access to Stinger's subsystems? To RP9?"

"Pretty much. I think I could even flush the upper-level toilet if requested."

"Oh boy, that's handy," Lena said.

"I can give you a status of what's happening back at Opalla and the Crimson fleet, if you would like."

Babar nodded. "Don't tell me they've arrived."

Aila said, "The Magistor and the Rebels' fleet are attempting to make a stand. They're outnumbered, already taking losses."

"And the Corthinian-Muan? Where the hell are they?" Justin asked.

Aila's eyes glazed over, as if she was trying to recall something. She shook her head. "No . . . nothing to report on their fleet."

"If you're going to get us out of here, now's the time to do it, Babar," the Magistra said.

Babar was already using the key to free himself. "Aila . . . please access RP9. At the Northeast tower, close to the ground, there's an old exhaust funnel. It should provide access to the castle's internal ventilation system. The drone-bot should just barely fit within the castle's various interconnecting ducts."

"On it," she said. "Okay . . . RP9 is on the move."

Justin watched Aila. She was enjoying this. For the first time, she was feeling useful. Feeling needed. He wondered how long it would take before she realized having something, *someone*, sharing your consciousness could get old real fast.

"RP9 has reached the exhaust funnel. It has a spring-flap to keep out varmints. I've instructed the bot to just get it open and get inside. Okay . . . we're in, and yes, it's a tight fit. RP9 wants to know where it's going?"

Babar said, "To the one person who has enough influence to help us."

"That would be nobody here in this castle," Lena said, rubbing her now-freed wrists. "I don't think GG-Guns will be coming back to our side anytime soon."

Justin said, "No . . . it's Chancellor Zeab who'll be helping us. Right?"

"Why's that?" Lena said.

Babar looked bemused, "Go ahead . . . tell them, boy."

"Eventually—soon, hopefully—RP9 will show up wherever Chancellor Zeab is located." Justin looked at Aila, "You will send a message to his comm unit, that membrane infused to his forearm. You will command him to free us, immediately."

Lena looked up and made a face. "What . . . he needs to help us or we'll tell his mommy? That we'll be mad at him? He has no impetus to do anything for us."

Justin was now enjoying this too. "Aila . . . can you tell me the exact frequency used by the zapper? That same zapper used to send agonizing jolts of electricity into the chancellor's spine?"

"It's actually not so different than a TV remote back on Earth that uses infrared radiation. We're talking 512 gHz, precisely."

Babar asked, "And RP9 is capable of initiating such a frequency upon demand?"

"That's a big 10-4," Aila said.

"God, you're strange," Lena said, but she was smiling just the same.

"I only wish I could be there to witness it," Magistra Peitra added.

Aila began pacing the Keep, "I can do the next best thing and give you a play-by-play report."

They waited for her to speak again. She looked to be concentrating, her bottom lip captured between her upper and lower incisors—*she really is beautiful,* Justin thought. "RP9 made a couple of wrong turns and had to back its way out. The three of them are together in the royal dining room; Chancellor Zeab and the Prime Minister are having lunch. Oh boy, GG-Guns is lying face-up on the carpet. He's been shot. There's blackened scorch marks on the far-right side of his chest."

"Shot in the heart," Lena said.

Aila said, "Human hearts are situated in the middle. Your Parian genetics you're your hearts situated at the far right within their chest cavities."

Lena said, "This is getting really old with her. Just tell us where RP9 is now."

"Above them, behind the vent. I'm instructing RP9 to send the message now ... that he is to free us, immediately. Zeab's checking his forearm. He just made a scoff sound. He's looking around the room."

"Zap him!" Lean said.

"Okay, I will. RP9 is generating a 512 gHz signal." Aila's hand went to her mouth. "Oh my God!"

"What? What happened?"

"Zeab just flew out of his chair ... howled like something's been shoved up his ass."

Babar said, "We still need him to be useful ... restrain from injuring him unnecessarily."

"The Prime Minister's now attending to him on the floor. Leaning over him. He's telling Zeab he's going to get help, to get a doctor." Aila took a breath and shook her head. "Okay ... Zeab is now alone in the room. He's trying to sit up."

Justin said, "Send another message to his forearm. Tell him he has five minutes to get to the Keep and free us. That or he'll be getting another jolt."

She nodded. "He most definitely has gotten the message. He's getting to his feet. He's a bit wobbly." She stopped and looked at the others. "Whoa! Um, GG-Guns is still alive, guys."

"Who cares. Just leave him there," Lena said.

Aila and Justin locked eyes. She said, "I have more reason to hate him than anyone here. To want him dead."

"But you don't have it in you to do that?" Justin asked. "To leave him behind?"

"Do you?" She snapped back.

He thought about it. "I'd like to see him suffer. Some serious payback is due here, and I'm not willing to just forgive and forget what he's done."

"So, we leave him here?" she asked.

"Shit! No . . . I guess not. I can't believe I'm saying this . . . Okay, tell Zeab he has to bring him along. Help him as much as he can."

"Absolutely not!" Lean barked. "He left us to die here!"

Aila ignored the princess. "They're both in pretty bad shape, staggering out the door now. RP9 will have to find another vent along the passageway for any further visuals."

"But they're coming this way?" Lena asked.

"RP9 is tracking his cuffcom unit . . . seems he is."

Justin glanced over to Babar, "So, how do we deal with the Royal Guard outside in the passageway?"

chapter 54

Babar was already heading back the way they'd been led in earlier. Justin and the others followed behind. Babar held up a hand. "Okay . . . the Keep doors are indeed closed and are undoubtedly locked. Let's just hope Zeab follows through." He looked to the Magistra. "Dow Dynasty governance . . . I believe you will need to physically be seated on the throne, once the Prime Minister has been . . . properly dealt with."

"I am well aware of Dom-Dynasty's established constitutional law. That is, unless it's been changed since our untimely eviction."

All eyes went to Aila.

"Neural Dome is accessing the Cristine Castle's Prime . . . the central AI here."

Lena rolled her eyes.

"Actually, it looks like the constitution is the same as it was when you all left on holiday years ago, when you were abducted. Prime Minister Yansle has been operating, governing, via an addended amendment," Aila said. Her eyes lost focus again as more information became available. She smiled at Magistra Pietra, "Yes, I see where Babar is going with this ... once you are physically situated on the throne, things automatically revert back to where a Magistra and Magistor have full imperious authority."

Babar said, "Getting her back on the throne is certainly a good first step, but it will do little if that Crimson fleet isn't dealt with too."

"One step at a time, Babar," the Magistra said. "I have faith in my husband ... he won't let us down."

Justin said, "So, where is this throne you're talking about?"

"It's thrones, plural. Me and Markus have one too," Lena said.

Magistra Pietra was looking more apprehensive now, "The thrones are there in the great hall ... where we entered the castle. Up on a raised dais at the far end."

"Hold on, I can see them entering the passageway!" Aila said. "Chancellor Zeab and GG-Guns ... they look like crap. Stumbling around, Zeab is having a hard time dragging GG's bulk. Zeab is telling them GG is to be tossed into the Keep the with other prisoners."

"Clever," Babar said. "Now let's just hope the chancellor doesn't try anything."

Aila made a face. "And chance another zapper jolt up his ass? I don't think so. Hold on ... something's happening—" She was cut off by the sound of the Keep door's lock being turned.

Babar said, "Okay, we'll have to split up once we reach the great hall."

Aila tried to continue with what she was saying, "In the hall—"

Lean talked over her, "Don't you mean if we reach the great hall, Babar? There's the Royal Guardsmen in the passageway. And let's not forget about the thousand-plus Castle soldiers we saw out front."

Frustrated, Aila said, "That's what I'm trying to tell—"

Now Babar too was speaking over her, "That guard . . . the one who slipped me the key. That was Royal Guardsman Sergeant Mintz . . ."

The Keep door was starting to open.

"He was a friend and, I'm now convinced, a loyalist to the magistrate."

Lena made an impatient twirling hand gesture, "Hurry, spit it out!"

"If my hunch is correct, we'll have some help out there. Lena, stay with your mother. Do whatever you have to do to reach the far end of the great hall . . . get to the thrones."

"What about us?" Justin said.

"I'll need you and Aila with me."

The doors swung all the way open to reveal Chancellor Zeab and two Royal Guards propping up GG-Guns between them. Babar rushed past them to peer down the passageway. Justin had no idea what was waiting for them out there, but heard multiple footsteps approaching. Royal Guardsman Sergeant

Mintz came into view, and he and Babar embraced each other, giving hearty pats on the back.

Lena and the Magistra looked confused.

"This is what I was trying to tell you," Aila said. "There was a skirmish out in the hallway. Guardsman fighting guardsman."

"Well, speak up next time!" Lena said.

Mintz said, "Ah, it is so good to see you again, Loham Babar—Noble-Fist to the aristocracy. Mintz looked to the Magistra, lowered down to one knee, and bowed his head. "Please forgive me, Magistra Pietra . . . we thought you all dead."

She placed a hand on his head. "Rise, Sergeant . . . time is short. Tell us the situation. Who is with us? And where is the Prime Minister?"

"I can tell you exactly where he is," Aila offered.

Sergeant Mintz eyed Aila curiously, then said, "We are but a few . . . perhaps two hundred I know to be fellow loyalists." He gestured to his own cuffcom unit. "I have been in contact with many. They wait your instructions."

Justin, while listening to the sergeant, took a look out into the passageway. There were seven armed royal guards standing there, waiting. No less than twenty others were splayed out on the floor running the length of the passageway.

GG-Guns groaned, holding a hand over his injured chest wounds. "I need a doctor." He looked at the chancellor. "Why did you shoot me?"

"You told us what we needed to know . . . good information. But you've already proven you can't be trusted, human."

Justin began patting the chancellor down and found he had

a plasma pistol hidden within an inside pocket. He confiscated it. "Please tell me he didn't have this before."

Babar shook his head, "No, must have come from the Prime Minister. Sergeant, please have one of your men take the good Chancellor Zeab here to the farthest, deepest section of the Keep and lock him in irons." Babar turned his gaze to GG-Guns. "Justin, he's your . . . friend, whatever. What do you want to do with him?"

Lena said, "I'd just shoot him."

Justin stepped in front of the injured, hunched-over gang-banger. He stared into GG-Gun's eyes. "How many times are you going to betray the same people trying to help you?"

"Hey, I didn't ask to be brought out here . . . to some random corner of the fucking galaxy. Just trying to survive, man. That's all. It's nothing personal."

"But it *is* personal . . . so I now have a choice to make. Put you back there deep in the Keep, next to your newfound friend, Zeab, or trust you and bring you along with us. Your chances of survival either way aren't good. So, what's it going to be?"

"Take me with you. Don't leave me here."

"Give me one good reason why I should?"

GG shrugged. "I can't. But I won't forget it . . . I'll spend the rest of my life making it up to you. Trust me this one more time, man."

Reluctantly, Justin said, "Fine. Don't make me regret this."

Babar said, "We have a lot to do and not much time to do it in. Sergeant Mintz, you will leave half your men here with me. With the others, you are to give safe passage to the

Magistra and the Princess. Get them to the Great Hall. There, protect them with your lives."

"On my honor, I will not let you down." Mintz began barking off orders to his men.

Justin watched as the Magistra and Lena were encircled and quickly ushered toward the exit. Prior to her disappearing from view, Lena shot Justin a curious look, one that exhibited more raw emotion than he thought she was capable of. Then again, he may have misinterpreted what he'd seen.

Babar was speaking again. "Justin . . . you and Aila have to find the Prime Minister. Take the rest of the sergeants' men. But he must be dealt with. He cannot be left alive. If you can't do what needs to be done—"

"Oh, trust me," GG-Guns said, grimacing and standing taller, "I'll ensure that alien motherfucker is put down."

"What about you . . . what are you going to do?"

"Sergeant Mintz here and I need to deal with the thousand-plus security forces outside the castle. Have no misconceptions—what we are attempting here is a hostile coup . . . and not everyone will be onboard. Things may get ugly real fast."

chapter 55

Magistor Gunther Pietra

Battle Cruiser, Victory's Flight— Fringe Territory—Vicinity of Exoplanet Opalla

Captain Elik entered into his own ready room directly off of *Victory's Flight*'s bridge. He spotted the Magistor and picked up his pace. A blood-stained bandage was wrapped around the top of the Captain's head, and he was walking with a definitive limp. "My lord . . . latest damage reports are in; we have breaches on Decks 5, 9, and 12. Aft shields are completely down, while mid and forward shields are at 15 and 20 percent, respectively. We cannot take another direct hit; we must fall back . . . let our response teams attempt necessary repairs."

The Magistor stood at the ready room's forward observation

window. He flinched as three consecutive explosions tore apart a nearby Rebel destroyer—the *Glory II*. He had watched the ensuing battle from this same spot for close to three hours now. Watched as the Empire's Crimson Fleet of newer and technologically more advanced warships had first skulked into view like a menacing dark fog. This fleet of three hundred spectacular warships, their battle plating a lifeless dark gray, was named for the glowing dark crimson band that encircled the mid-ship perimeter of each vessel.

"And what message would that convey to our enemy ... more importantly, to our own Rebel forces?" The Magistor did not wait for the captain's reply. "We have but one obligation here, good Captain ... not to win, not to prevail, but simply to curtail the Empire's further advance into Dow Dynasty space."

"May I suggest, at the very least, you leave this ready room?" He gestured to the splintering, zigzagging cracks spanning the width of the observation window mere feet in front of the Magistor.

A fiery ball—this time another battle cruiser, toppled end over end—streaked across the space battlefield beyond. Sure, none of their ragtag warships had a full crew compliment, but even so, the Magistor was certain another hundred loyalists at least had just offered up their ultimate sacrifice to their cause—to him.

Magistor Pietra turned to look at the battle-worn officer. "I will remain here, Captain. Please ... return to the bridge. It won't be long now ... before our own lives will be lost to this dark nemesis. As intelligent a warrior as you are, you certainly must have anticipated this same outcome . . . as I have."

Captain Elik considered his lord's fateful words. "I am not naïve, of course . . . there was little hope the Corthinian-Muan would, miraculously, make it here in time—to our aid, to stand with us against the Empire. But hope I did." The captain started to turn away, then faced the Magistor once more. He glanced to the cuffcom on the Magistor's wrist. "Your wife . . . the prince and princess. Any word? Has the Magistra retaken the throne?"

About to answer, he hesitated, considering the implications. Whatever words he spoke next would be repeated across this Rebel fleet. Soon, those same words would be transmitted to nearby territories, and then would spread out to the farthest reaches of Dow Dynasty space. The Magistor had no clue what was happening many light years away within Cristine Castle. Would they be words of hope and validation of what was happening here today, or words of defeat and catastrophe? "Oh yes, Captain . . . all is well on our home world," he lied. "As we speak, my bride, my wife, has retaken her rightful place upon her throne. Cristine Castle is once again the beating heart of the realm. So, go now, relay this information. Let it spread across the far reaches of Dynasty space. Our many star systems must ready their defenses, be it lone starships, or numbered warships and fleets of their own . . . this is the time we must unite. This is the time to rally behind their Magistra back home. Go, tell them a terrible war is coming. A war unlike any other we have faced before."

Magistor Pietra brought his attention to the ensuing battle beyond. More than half the Rebel fleet had been destroyed, while not one of the Crimson fleet's warships had been lost. *Please don't let this all have been in vein,* he thought.

He watched as two seemingly unrelated things occurred at the same time. First, he caught sight of a burst of flames— the exhaust thruster spewing out of an incoming Empire smart-missile. *Victory's Flight* was its intended target. He had no doubt about that. Next, he saw something far more impactful. A lone warship had suddenly hyper-jumped into local space. One moment, nothing—the next it was right there. So white, so pristine was this craft, it seemed to actually be glowing against the contrasting blackness of space. A second ship, then a third, and then too many to count were jumping into the fray of battle. Immediately, cannon fire erupted from every one of the beautiful Corthinian-Muan warship's turrets. A nearby Empire Destroyer suddenly erupted into an enormous ball of fire—which quickly dissipated within the oxygen-starved vacuum of space. Within the span of five seconds, three more Empire warships blew apart, atomized by the destructive power of their Corthinian-Muan counterparts. Only then did the Magistor bring his attention back to the rapidly approaching, locked-on Empire smart-missile.

chapter 56

Justin Trip

Having ascended both of the sublevel stairways, Justin, Aila, and the lagging-behind GG-Guns hurried along the hallway. A number of lifeless royal guards were sprawled on the floor. Up ahead, Justin saw the guard-encircled contingent that included the Magistra and Princess Lena. They were entering the Great Hall, where they suddenly veered right—where they'd be headed toward the royal thrones.

Justin felt his wrist vibrate and saw that Babar was contacting him via his cuffcom.

"Babar?" Justin said. "Where are you?"

"Bringing order to the realm . . . now, listen to me carefully. The baron is dead. I killed him myself. But the Prime Minister—he's about to board his personal spacecraft. Go after him. Take the Stinger."

Justin could hear weapons fire, distant soldiers yelling—the sounds of battle.

"Me? Wait . . . why . . ."

"Just listen to me! Loyalties are still in flux here. I've got my hands full fighting those still siding with Prime Minister Yansle. There's much resistance. I suspect that will change once he leaves to save his own tail. But I cannot leave the Magistra and Princess's side. Not this time. But Yansle cannot be allowed to escape into Empire space . . . this must end here, today!"

Justin heard more sounds of battle and Babar grunting, clearly in the midst of some kind of hand-to-hand fighting.

Justin said, "Alright . . . we'll get the Prime Minister. Good luck here." He cut the connection as they now entered the Great Hall themselves.

"What are we doing?" Aila asked.

Justin saw that GG had lagged even farther behind, had stopped and was now leaning against a wall, breathing hard. He considered simply leaving the guy here. He deserved nothing more.

Off in the distance, at the other side of the Great Hall, he saw another skirmish had broken out. He guessed there were at least fifty combatants going at it—as the Magistra and Princess were fighting their way toward the raised dais. Stray plasma fire streaked across the room. He saw Lena fighting two opponents, then three, while her mother, holding a short sword, was embroiled in her own violent confrontation. He wanted to go to them, help to even the odds. His eyes lingered on Lena.

"We have to go," Aila said. She was standing close, her

hand upon his forearm. Her eyes conveyed her own inner conflict and pain. He knew then that, as crazy as it was, he had feelings for both Aila and Lena—perhaps equally. *How was that even possible?*

"Head off to the Stinger. We'll be right behind you!" Justin said, hurrying back in the direction of GG-Guns. But she ignored his demand, and remained at his side.

"No, we're staying together!" she said.

They reached GG and got him positioned between them—supporting his not-insignificant weight. They made it to the castle's entrance, crashing through the doors—even GG-Guns was now running.

Justin had not expected the utter mayhem taking place outside. Armies in the midst of fighting themselves—how they knew who was loyal to the royal family instead of the Prime Minister, he had no clue. What he did know was that the carnage was breathtaking.

"There!" Aila shouted above the sounds of battle. She pointed off toward an alternate, farther-off series of castle outbuildings, where a number of adjacent landing pads were situated. Easily twice the size of the Stinger was a sleek-looking, bright red spacecraft. Its thrusters suddenly engaged as it proceeded to lift off. Six other Stingers emerged from around the outbuildings, joining into a formation with the Prime Minister's vessel.

He saw that Babar's old and battered-looking Stinger was right where they'd left it. "Move it ,GG!" Justin yelled over his shoulder, sprinting toward the little ship. Aila was right behind him. "Can you get the drives spinning up?"

"Already on it," Alai said.

The aft gangway was in the process of descending, and sure enough, both of the winged-drives were revving up. He stopped when he reached the top of the ramp and looked back. The battle raged on beyond. Justin looked for Babar, who was out there somewhere, leading those combatants still loyal to the Magistor and Magistra.

Aila reached the ramp, hurried up, and flew past him into the aft airlock. GG-Guns, huffing and puffing, had reached the gangway, but there was no way he'd make it any farther on his own. Justin met him halfway down and managed to get him into the ship. "Get yourself into the medical bay . . . you're useless to us injured."

By the time Justin was seated at the helm controls, Aila was already seated in the copilot's seat. He saw she was enjoying this, not even trying to hide her smile. Taking the controls in his hands, he engaged the gun ship's lift thrusters. The projected 3D model showed the Prime Minister's battle group had already reached Calunoth's upper atmosphere.

"We can't let them jump to lightspeed," Aila said.

"How soon before they'll reach open space?" he asked, fully throttling the Stinger forward and upward.

"Two minutes, thirty seconds . . . roughly."

"Anything you, with your Neural Dome connection, can do to slow them down?"

"Maybe . . . we're attempting to communicate to Yansle's

StarBreaker. That's that red ship of his. Right now we're back-dooring into its AI, indicating to it that there is a catastrophic antimatter containment breech. That going to Z-Speed would blow up the ship."

"Can't you just do that? Blow up the ship?"

"No ... the most we can do is trip a few onboard sensors. Generate a few false readings. That sort of thing. Have the ship's AI second guessing itself. It looks like the pilot's slowing, heeding the warnings."

Justin saw that the battle group had just reached open space.

"Uh oh ... I think the StarBreaker's AI might be smelling a rat. The prime minister is screaming for the pilot to engage the Zyln drive," Aila said.

"So, they know we're pursuing them?"

"Of course they do. But we're now triggering all kinds of additional warning lights on the StarBreaker's helm console to flash on and off. An alarm klaxon is blaring." She laughed. "Prime Minister Yansle is practically pissing his pants."

Justin observed how Aila was using the possessive *we*, as she referred to herself along with the Stinger's Neural Dome.

He could also see that they too had now reached open space.

"Crap, the StarBreaker's AI is shutting down our spoofed alarms and warning," Aila said.

"Yeah ... well, it slowed them down. Heads up, there they are." Up ahead, Justin saw the tight formation of seven spacecraft.

"You do realize we're outnumbered, six Stingers to one, not to mention whatever weaponry the Prime Minister has on that StarBreaker of his?"

Justin felt Markus's consciousness making itself known. Justin almost stepped aside to let the warrior within again take full control of his psyche. *No . . . not this time, Markus. You want to be a part of this, be a part of me? We need to do this together.*

You'll just get in the way . . . slow me down . . .

So be it, then. We do this together, or I attempt this on my own.

Justin felt the rise of Markus's brooding anger—his righteous indignation.

"Their weapons systems are online. Their shields are up," Aila said, eyeing the 3D battle model. She looked at Justin. "What are you doing? What's wrong with you?"

Justin shook his head, snapping out of his momentary distraction. The battle group ahead had repositioned, taking up a more defensive formation around the Prime Minister's sleek red vessel. A ship that at any second, he knew, could and would just jump away.

He ignored her, waiting for some indication of what Markus would do. Then he heard the voice within concede.

Fine . . . but you're making a mistake . . .

"Incoming!" Aila yelled.

Justin, seeing what she was referring to, was already maneuvering the Stinger. Plasma bolts connected with their starboard side, heating up their shields. Aila, returning fire, was simultaneously manning the plasma cannons as well as the rail guns. Space beyond was ablaze with weapons fire.

"All we care about is keeping that StarBreaker from jumping!" Justin said, piloting the gun ship, knowing he was still in full control—Markus was staying back. Taking evasive action, he dove the ship, made a sharp left turn, and just barely missed two of the enemy gunships. He heard the sound of a weapons lock confirmation tone, as Aila sent several hundred rail gun projectiles into one, and then another gunship. Both blew up within two seconds of each other.

"Got them!" she yelled. Her momentary excitement was dashed. "Yansle's readying to jump!"

"Concentrate all fire on that StarBreaker!" he yelled back.

"Get closer, then . . . you're like a million miles away!"

"A little busy avoiding us getting blown up, if you hadn't noticed," he snapped back. He dove and maneuvered the Stinger to avoid more incoming plasma fire. He realized the StarBreaker was now off to their left, and two enemy gunships were closing in on their tail. He'd deal with them first. There was an unmistakable sound coming from behind as their aft shields started taking the brunt of combined weapons fire.

"Aft shield down to 30 percent," Aila said.

"Forget them . . . target Prime Minister Yansle. I'm swinging us around to deal with our friends behind us!" Justin piloted the Stinger through a myriad of complex maneuvers in order to change places with their pursuers. By the time the StarBreaker, along with its two flanking gunships, came into view up ahead, Aila had all of the Stinger's weapons, six 360-degree pivoting plasma cannons and two of the big Pounders directing fire at multiple targets: the four remaining gunships as well as the prime minister's StarBreaker.

"Keep it up, Aila!" he encouraged her.

Additional weapons fire coming from the StarBreaker in front of them had their forward shields now glowing amber and then bright red. Two gunships suddenly fell back and nestled in close behind them on their port and starboard sides. Between the onslaught of weapons fire from in front, and now from behind, Justin knew they were in trouble. Trapped, they had mere moments before they'd be blown to space dust. Reluctantly, Justin inwardly said, *Okay, Markus... I think I need your help.*

"Justin!" Aila yelled.

"On it!" he yelled back, even as he felt himself withdrawing deeper inward, as Markus was becoming more of a presence sitting there at the helm. Justin was tempted to fight, to try to regain full ownership of his psyche, but realized Markus had kept to his word—he was not jockeying for dominance here. Markus gunned the dual Zyln Drive engines while banking the Stinger starboard in a sideways loop and then up and over into a barrel roll. Both Aila and Justin audibly gasped as the G-Forces drove them hard back into their seats. The space battle raged on, and surprisingly, Justin and Markus began to work well together. It was as if they were taking turns piloting the craft at various intervals. Jointly, they knew they were, and always would be, two separate beings. And perhaps for the first time, Justin didn't feel threatened by this inner co-pilot consciousness. This was *Justin's* physical body, and nothing was going to change that. Markus suddenly took the initiative and jammed the controls all the way to the right, missing the three vessels by little more than a breath. *Watch and learn, human . . . school is in session!* Markus had positioned the Stinger for Aila to take the shot, and she didn't hesitate. One of the StarBreaker's flanking gunships exploded in front of them.

Justin smiled, mentally giving Markus his just due—the prince's piloting skills were beyond remarkable. One of the two remaining gunships, now trailing behind, was making serious trouble as it engaged its powerful railguns. Markus was doing all he could to evade the onslaught of explosive projectiles.

"Our shields are pretty much toast!" Aila said.

Justin watched on the projected 3D model as Aila concentrated her own weapons fire on the StarBreaker's flanking gunship. What happened next took them all by surprise. The gunship's port-side Zyln Drive exploded. Suddenly, unable to maintain steady forward velocity, the doomed gunship flipped up and over, right on top of Prime Minister Yansle's StarBreaker. With an impact of that magnitude, Justin expected there to be a resulting explosion, but neither ship erupted into a ball of flame. Wedged together, the two ships continued to break apart as large sections—wings, pieces of hull, a body—were being left behind in their tumbling, end-over-end wake.

"There goes the one remaining gunship. It's escaping," Aila said, gesturing out the side window. A bright white flash confirmed the gunship had jumped to Zyln. "God, that was close! Don't think we couldn't have lasted too much longer. All our shields went offline right before that last one jumped away. We were sitting ducks." She let out a breath, looking over to Justin. "That was some pretty wicked flying. Should we be thanking Markus for that?"

"Not completely," he said defensively. "But yeah, a good part of it was Markus." Without being asked, Markus's consciousness settle back deep into the depth of his psyche.

Aila let her head fall all the way back to the headrest. Staring upward, she said, "Just the same . . . that was way, way too close."

"Agreed," Justin said, still feeling the last of Markus's presence fading away. "Hey, is Ocile still tracking Prime Minister Yansle's busted-up StarBreaker? No one's still alive on either of those ships, right?"

Aila's eyes momentarily lost focus. She shook her head. "No life signs. Prime Minister Yansle is dead."

"Good!" came a deep voice from behind.

Both Justin and Aila turned to see GG-Guns, now wearing a fresh uniform, enter the bridge. No longer stooped and racked with pain, he smiled and took a seat behind them.

"You look better," Justin said.

"Uh, yeah . . . thanks to you two. Still can't believe you rescued me."

"Neither can I," Aila said, not looking particularly happy with his presence there.

chapter 57

Justin Trip

"Yeah, GG, I'm sorry, but that's it," he said. "You've used up any good will I have left in me. And I'm sure Aila feels the same way."

She nodded. "It's well past that for me."

GG-Guns looked truly sorrowful. "Nobody's never done nothin' like that for me before. Saving me like that... especially after I turned traitorous and all. I learned a long time ago, I needed to watch out for number one, cause no one else would. So, I guess I was wrong about that. Look... I promise, going forward I'll always have your backs, no matter what. I know words are cheap, so you'll just have to see for yourselves. All I can say right now is, again, thank you."

Aila rolled her eyes. "Come on, GG... Can you honestly tell us that if Chancellor Zeab wasn't locked away in that castle keep, you'd be acting so contrite? You would have flown off with him and left us to wither and die in that dungeon."

Before GG-Guns could answer, the projected 3D display flickered and came to life. Babar's staticky image wavered and then became more steady. "Tell me the status of Prime Minister Yansle."

"Good to see you, too, Babar. And yes, we're fine . . . thanks for asking," Justin said.

"I can already see you're fine. Status?"

"Yansel's dead. Though one of the gunships escaped. Jumped to lightspeed."

Babar mulled that over. He looked battle-worn. He wiped at a trickle of blood at his hairline.

Aila asked, "And you, Babar . . . have you retaken Cristine Castle?"

"Yes. Well, for the most part. Many lives lost on both sides. But, yes, we have won the day."

GG-Guns said, "You don't look like someone who's won the day."

Babar looked tired and older than he had even hours earlier. "I have recently learned . . . news of the space battle above Opalla." Babar looked away, appearing lost in thought.

Justin said, "With the Empire's forces . . . that Crimson Fleet." Expecting the worst, he asked, "The Corthinian-Muan Fleet—they didn't arrive?"

Babar attempted a smile. "No, they arrived in time. It was a force that not even the Empire's Crimson Fleet could stand up to. In the end, between the Corthinian-Muan and our Rebel forces, the Crimson fleet was decimated."

It only occurred to Justin now what must have happened. He exchanged a quick look with Aila, who had evidently come to the same conclusion. "And Magistor Pietra?" he asked softly.

Grief momentarily took hold of Babar. "I was informed by delayed lightwave communications that yes, my Lord, Magistor Gunther Pietra's Battle Cruiser, *Victory's Flight,* was struck by an Empire smart missile late last night. He is gone . . ."

The three of them within the bridge were speechless. Justin's thoughts went to Lena and her mother. "Have you told—"

"Yes, Justin, I have," he said curtly. "Both are devastated . . . as I am. We will need time to grieve in our own ways." He let out a tired breath. "Also, I have just learned, the Empire has officially declared war upon both the Dow Dynasty as well as the Corthinian-Muan." He squeezed his eyes closed, again fighting his emotions. "Even beyond the terrible anguish the Magistra and princess are burdened with, they now must prepare for war. Dark days are coming to this realm . . . very dark days."

Silence filled the confined space until Justin asked, "What do you wish us to do now?"

Babar looked back at them—contemplating, then coming to a decision. One corner of his mouth turned up. "Maybe some good news in all of this. Justin . . . The royal family, the people of Calunoth, and all of the Dow Dynasty, owe the two of you a great debt . . . *I* owe you a great debt."

"We did what anyone—"

"Hold on. . . . I'm not finished, Justin. As a result of my actions, using Earth as a refuge, albeit in a time of great necessity, I did your people a great disservice. I made humanity known to the Empire. The Empire does not look kindly upon those worlds that choose sides against them—"

"*Worlds* that choose sides? The world doesn't have any idea what we've been doing. It was just us," Aila interjected.

"Aila, that will make little difference to Emperor Chi-Sacrim. And thus, the repercussions may be swift and definitive."

GG-Guns spoke up, "Earth will be destroyed? They can do that, destroy a whole planet? Like a Death Star-type thing?"

Babar smiled. "More like a heavy cruiser battle group. But that's not going to happen.

"Why not?" Aila asked.

"Because, Magistra Pietra has inducted Earth and the surrounding frontier space in that quadrant to be included within the borders of the Dow Dynasty. With that comes the protections from neighboring members and Dynasty security forces, as well as the Royal Fleet itself. Of course, with war imminent . . . the latter may be engaged in other operations for some time. Nevertheless, Earth will have our protection."

"Thank you, Babar, and thank Magistra Pietra, too," Justin said feeling overwhelmed by it all and not entirely able to get GG's Death Star reference out of his head.

"You still haven't answered Justin's question. What can we, the three of us, do to help you?"

GG-Guns interjected, "Oh, and I guess we'll need to get a ride home too . . ."

Confused, Babar said, "Why would you need a ride home?"

"Because Earth is like a hundred light years away from here," GG said with a shrug.

Babar raised a hand, "I have much to do . . . like securing Cristine Castle and providing the Magistra and Princess necessary security, as things here are still dangerous for them. So just let me finish. First—Justin, Aila . . . the two of you are to be knighted by the Magistra herself. You will be realm subjects of high favor. That will happen just as soon as the paperwork is in place and we can schedule the occasion here at Cristine Castle."

Both Aila and Justin were speechless.

"Secondly, your world's governments must agree to the terms of Earth's inclusion into the realm. Although, they'd be insane not to accept."

"So, wait . . . I'm not going to be a realm subject of high favor? Um, knighted?" GG asked, looking wounded.

"Come on, GG. You've proven yourself to be untrustworthy when it suits your best interest. How about we see how things play out over the next few months?"

Babar turned his attention back to Justin and Aila. "Justin, Aila, you asked if you can help. The answer is yes. Your first assignment will be to deliver Dow Dynasty Attaché, Minister of Realm Affairs P.P. Glick, to Earth. Upon arrival, over the course of several weeks, he will meet with your various world leaders to work out the details of becoming a space-faring intergalactic member of the Dow Dynasty. Earth will greatly benefit from trade, and of course, new technology beyond anything humans would have achieved on their own for many hundreds of years. All that will be asked of your leaders in return is a moratorium on all planetary wars."

Justin and Aila exchanged a steely look. *We humans really*

like our wars, Justin thought. But then again, just maybe, this opportunity would be the catalyst to changing things.

Both Aila and Justin nodded enthusiastically. Justin said, "I'd be honored to be a part of that, Babar."

"Me too," Alia added.

"One more thing. Things here at Cristine Castle, obviously, are in turmoil...dangerous, for any of the royal family. Along with Minister Glick, you'll be taking another Dynasty representative along with you to Earth."

"Sure, anyone," Justin said but saw Aila was looking less excited about this part.

"Magistor Pietra wants Princess Lena as far away from Cristin Castle and local Dynasty space as possible. Take her with you...keep her safe, and I will be forever grateful."

Justin heard Aila sarcastically say, "Just terrific," under her breath.

"Oh, and the Princess has made one request of her own... that you two, Justin and Aila, can take full ownership of that Stinger craft, if you are so inclined."

The two looked at each other and didn't even try to hide their excitement.

"Shit, man...so they get knighted and a starship? Really?"

Babar looked to GG-Guns with a bit more sympathy. "GG, even from here, I'll be keeping an eye on you. Prove to me you can be a loyal subject to the Realm...then we'll talk."

The End

Thank you for reading Gun Ship. If you enjoyed this book, PLEASE leave a review on Amazon.com—it really helps!

To be notified the moment all future books are released, please join my mailing list. I hate spam and will never, ever share your information. Jump to this link to sign up:

http://eepurl.com/bs7M9r

Acknowledgments

First and foremost, I am grateful to the fans of my writing and their ongoing support for all my books. I'd like to thank my wife, Kim—she's my rock and is a crucial, loving component of my publishing business. I'd like to thank my mother, Lura Genz, for her tireless work as my first-phase creative editor and a staunch cheerleader of my writing. Others who provided fantastic support include Lura and James Fischer and Stuart Church.

Made in the USA
Coppell, TX
07 December 2020

43159765R00227